Praise for Zoje Stage's

WONDERLAND

"If art imitates life, horror fiction is a great mimic, predicting and exploring the frightening and surreal realities of the contemporary world. Exhibit A: Zoje Stage's mind-bending, trippy second novel, *Wonderland*...The question of responsibility for the nightmare lingers as does the line between reality and imagination."

—Danielle Trussoni, *New York Times Book Review*

"A beautifully choreographed and astonishing second novel from the author of the much-celebrated *Baby Teeth*...The horror genre has found an eloquent and unflinching new author."

—*Booklist* (starred review)

"Oh, fright fans rejoice. That sure hand you're looking for? That relentless climb, that crescendo of cold sweat? It's all here. Deep in the woods, under a lot of snow, steeped in mad, unfamiliar nature. Zoje Stage is in total control of your nightmare. For those who live to be scared, *Wonderland* is the book you'll be glad you cracked open at home, alone, at night."

—Josh Malerman, author of *Bird Box* and *Malorie*

"Proving that the scares in her debut *Baby Teeth* were no accident, Stage returns with her second novel, this time ratcheting up the supernatural element...Reminiscent of the severe disorientation and trauma in Mark Z. Danielewski's *House of Leaves* and the nature-seeking-revenge theme of Stephen Graham Jones's *The Only Good Indians*."

—*Library Journal* (starred review)

"Thought-provoking, strange, and eerie, a Grimm's-style allegory for what it means to be a mother/parent as the world burns."

—Paul Tremblay, author of *Survivor Song*

"Stage perfectly captures the fears and frictions that accompany household moves and career changes; indeed, her keen portrayal of domestic upset is what grounds the story and imparts verisimilitude."

—*Kirkus Reviews*

"*Wonderland* shows the terror lurking below the surface of domestic bliss, when we realize our familiar and cozy world may not be as it seems. Zoje Stage is one of the few writers who can make the supernatural feel totally, dangerously real."

—Alma Katsu, author of *The Deep* and *The Hunger*

"A provocative, philosophical page-turner."

—Bill O'Driscoll, *Pittsburgh Post-Gazette*

"Sublimely suspenseful...Stage is a literary horror writer on the rise. Her refined prose and knack for emphasizing small but disquieting details make *Wonderland* a standout summer suspense selection."

—Julie Hale, *BookPage*

"A novel that's sure to leave you sleeping with the lights on."

—Sabienna Bowman, *PopSugar*

"Stage's foreboding sophomore novel combines the bone-chilling paranoia of *The Shining* with the uncanny suspense of

Suspiria. Just as deliciously unsettling as her unforgettable debut, *Wonderland* is a must-read for horror and thriller fans."

—Layne Fargo, author of *Temper*

"*Wonderland* is part ghost story, part family drama, part psychological thriller. And, beyond that, it is beautifully written. I was captivated through the entire story."

—T. Greenwood, author of *Keeping Lucy* and *Rust & Stardust*

"As in *Baby Teeth*, Stage employs her background as a playwright and filmmaker in the new novel…Stage also has a trait that is crucial to success in the thriller/mystery genre: She's completely ruthless."

—Rege Behe, *Pittsburgh City Paper*

"Stage plucks the strings of a mother's worst fears like none other through this wondrous adventure as it unravels into claustrophobic terror. Hauntingly beautiful and scary as hell, *Wonderland* takes you deep into the woods of one woman's mind and her harrowing struggle to save her children."

—D. M. Pulley, author of *The Dead Key* and *No One's Home*

"Masterfully depicts an unknown force that embodies the oppressive tension that can come with being trapped with one's family, cut off from the rest of society. Its release in the context of worldwide quarantine and stay-at-home orders during the Covid-19 pandemic is eerily timely, but Orla has much worse demons to face than the ones inside the mind. This story of domestic challenges and mounting horror will please fans of Shirley Jackson."

—*Shelf Awareness*

"*Wonderland* is a mesmerizing journey into the darkest realms of the supernatural; a family, escaping the perils of city life, discovers that the splendors of nature can mask a hidden face of savage, unnameable terror."

—Kathleen Kent, author of *The Burn*

"Stage knows how to set a scene, ramp up the suspense, and make you feel so trapped in it that the horror becomes palpable."

—Rebecca Munro, *BookReporter*

"Five words: Don't go into the woods. Thanks to this book, now I'm afraid of trees, psychotic children, magic, ghost stories, families, polar bears, shotguns, and my own shadow."

—Rea Frey, author of *Not Her Daughter* and *Until I Find You*

"A maybe-I'm-crazy-or-maybe-there-really-is-something-there intense, suspenseful plot...You too will be aching to talk to somebody about the ending!"

—*BuzzFeed*

"What a stunning sophomore book! Stage masterfully takes the reader through this chilling tale, hitting you hard in the gut as the dread and tension rise ever higher. I was nauseous, fearful, and loved every minute of it."

—Erin A. Craig, author of *House of Salt and Sorrows*

WONDERLAND

BY ZOJE STAGE

Getaway
Wonderland
Baby Teeth

WONDERLAND

ZOJE STAGE

MULHOLLAND BOOKS

Little, Brown and Company

New York Boston London

Copyright © 2020 by Zoje Stage
Reading group guide copyright © 2021 by Zoje Stage and Mulholland Books

Hachette Book Group supports the right to free expression and the value of copyright. The purpose of copyright is to encourage writers and artists to produce the creative works that enrich our culture.

The scanning, uploading, and distribution of this book without permission is a theft of the author's intellectual property. If you would like permission to use material from the book (other than for review purposes), please contact permissions@hbgusa.com. Thank you for your support of the author's rights.

Mulholland Books / Little, Brown and Company
Hachette Book Group
1290 Avenue of the Americas, New York, NY 10104
mulhollandbooks.com

Originally published in hardcover by Mulholland Books, July 2020
First Mulholland trade paperback edition, July 2021

Mulholland Books is an imprint of Little, Brown and Company, a division of Hachette Book Group, Inc. The Mulholland Books name and logo are trademarks of Hachette Book Group, Inc.

The publisher is not responsible for websites (or their content) that are not owned by the publisher.

The Hachette Speakers Bureau provides a wide range of authors for speaking events. To find out more, go to hachettespeakersbureau.com or call (866) 376-6591.

ISBN 978-0-316-45849-8 (hc) / 978-0-316-45852-8 (pb)
LCCN 2019947256

Printing 1, 2021

LSC-C

Printed in the United States of America

For the cherished women who keep me sane—
Deb, Lisa, and Paula

And for the superhero moms
who carry the world

WONDERLAND

There were no words; words no longer existed. Time and consciousness were fluid. Abstract. But there was an awareness. And with it, an urgency. Death.

Death.

Death like a drumbeat, calling from the past. It had a familiar scent. Death.

As if she had encountered it before.

1

Orla tried not to think of it as an amputation, but that's how it felt. When they left the New York City apartment behind, that was a leg. She'd hobbled northward weeks ago and now, waving goodbye to her husband's Plattsburgh family, that was an arm. She buckled her seat belt with her remaining hand, gazed down at her remaining foot, boot-clad and muddy. This body would never dance again. No more exhilarating reveals as the curtain rose on the stage. No more applause. No more making her sinewy limbs as fluid as a piece of music. Only bare-bones living. And endless woods.

Shaw had been such a good partner in the first couple of weeks after her retirement. He'd focused daily on the positives: her perpetually strained muscles could finally heal; she'd suffer no more blackened toenails; she wouldn't have to spend hours a day in the company of sweaty, smelly people. In the spirit of the new life they were planning, she'd acknowledged the truthfulness of his optimism. But she didn't have a clear memory of having made such complaints, at least not frequently, and not with the intention of wishing her life had been different. Sometimes the writer's pencils wore down, and sometimes the painter's brushes became stiff. These were casual obstacles of the trade, as were her aches, not reasons to abandon one's art.

Yet she knew, in her marrow. Forty-one was old for a ballet dancer and everything required more effort than it once had; the time had come. And she'd agreed—the end of her time would mark the beginning of Shaw's. It was his turn to pursue his artistic dreams.

Some days she felt nothing but the excitement of such a big change, a true adventure. But other days…moving deep into the Adirondacks was a bit more extreme than what she'd once envisioned, when "leaving the city" meant moving to a place like Pittsburgh, where she'd grown up. A smaller city, it was the best of all worlds: diverse, cultural, affordable. They could have a nice family home there, sprawling by Manhattan standards, and the children could have their Lola and Lolo. Her parents would have been so happy to have them so close. But, as a couple, they also embraced the philosophy of seizing the day. And exploring. And the possibility of making discoveries about yourself in unexpected places.

"Carpe diem," she murmured.

Her moment of acceptance shattered, flash-frozen, and she caught her breath. There, on the side of the road. A pair of legs. A bloated body.

The car drew closer and it was real enough—not an illusion—but the back half of a deer, not a human. She saw the rest as they passed, the front legs crossed in prayer, blood staining the snow around its skull. The road dissolved behind them, obliterated by the sideways sleet. It hadn't felt like this before, when she knew they'd be returning to Walker, Julie, and the boys at the end of the day. The trees got denser and swallowed the light. There was no going back.

Shaw whirled his attention from the road to her. "Did you just say 'Carpe diem'?"

Orla shifted her back to the hostile world just beyond the glass. His grin reminded her to resume breathing. There were flecks of bluish paint in his hair; it had become a common sight during the past year, when he finally understood the quivering arrow of his internal compass. He'd started with small canvases and acrylic paint, but over the months the canvases grew, and their apartment took on the aroma of linseed oil and turpentine when he switched to oils. He wasn't the tidiest of painters and some part of his skin or clothing—or hair—provided a preview of his day's work. Though what was in his hair now was surely from their daughter's newly rehabbed bedroom.

"Did I?" she asked. "I guess I did—that's what we're doing, isn't it?"

"Exactly. We're carpe-dieming to the fullest!"

She snorted; sometimes his enthusiasm was contagious. Hoping to catch a glint of a smile on her daughter's face, she turned toward the back seat. Behind her, Eleanor Queen sat gazing out the window, eyes on the sky. Orla prayed she hadn't seen the dead deer. She wanted the wilderness—which was still what she called the Adirondacks—to be good for her contemplative child. Eleanor Queen—just El or Eleanor to some, but never to her mother—hadn't seemed stalwart enough, aggressive enough, to survive into adulthood in the city. At nine, she was still afraid of the dark, one of many fears that Orla and Shaw accepted in a resigned way; they couldn't, as imaginative people themselves, promise-promise-promise that nothing frightening lurked in the dark. And they respected that their daughter had pragmatic fears: bustling stairs that descended into the subways, sirens that screamed of danger, sidewalks with their crush of hurrying pedestrians.

Beside her daughter, four-year-old Tycho sat in his car seat bouncing a fuzzy, long-limbed moose on his knee. He sang under his breath with his own melody and lyrics: *"Driving down the road...going to our home...driving in the car...going very far..."*

As much as she'd tried to fully embrace the move—for her children's sake, and because Shaw wanted it so very badly—a fear shadowed her that her urban family wasn't suited to the wilds of nowhere. It followed her as they rode in the car, a black specter with an inky, human shape that she could almost see at the edge of her vision.

She turned back to Shaw, ready to request his reassurance (for the hundredth time) that they'd thought through every contingency and were truly ready for their new lives. But looking at him, she didn't need to ask. So content and eager, his hands at ten and two, he drove their new-old four-wheel-drive SUV like it was what he'd been waiting for, and he was finally where he belonged. And maybe he was. She saw him with new clarity. The scraggly beard, the dirt under his nails, the way his bulky coat looked twenty years old in spite of being a recent purchase. The Adirondacks was his territory; Plattsburgh, where they'd spent the past three weeks with his brother, his hometown. When she'd Googled *cities near Plattsburgh,* she'd gotten a list of honest-to-God *hamlets;* the nearest actual city, by her standards—Montreal—wasn't even in the same country. Maybe Shaw had never really been a city boy, but his creative impulses had driven him there.

Had Orla's divinity kept him there? Sometimes she saw herself through his eyes—his shimmering awe of her talent, her drive.

Maybe, when they first became lovers, he'd thought a bit of her golden dust would rub off on him. He didn't complain when it hadn't and never suggested giving up on his own dreams. She respected him for that, and they stuck to their city lifestyle even when their friends moved onward, seeking a different life or more space in Brooklyn or Astoria. And then came

Eleanor Queen. And Tycho. She'd made two post-maternity comebacks—rare for her profession—but the Empire City Contemporary Ballet wasn't as elite or competitive as the city's more renowned companies. And she had worked for it—to get in, to stay in, to come back—beyond even what her abilities and body might have predicted for her future. So they became the classic Manhattan family, squashed in a six-hundred-square-foot one-bedroom apartment, making it work against the odds.

Shaw slipped a CD into the dashboard player. Acoustic music, surprisingly melancholy. He never asked anyone else what they'd like to listen to. Orla might have been the primary breadwinner, supporting her family with her formidable albeit not quite star-worthy talents, but it was Shaw who set their family's beatnik tone. Orla's father called him, privately, a dabbler. She didn't think that was entirely fair, since Shaw took on most of what should have been shared household duties. But it was undeniable that Shaw's true calling was hard to pin down. He'd played guitar at several Village open-mics. Read his poetry at others. He wrote a screenplay, and took photographs, and whacked away at pieces of wood that never quite became the sculptures he envisioned. But that had changed during the past year when he'd settled on a medium and the daily discipline needed to pursue it.

After becoming mesmerized by a particular exhibition while gallery-hopping in Chelsea (a favorite, free activity) and revisiting the exhibit numerous times, Shaw claimed an unfamiliar certainty: He knew what he needed to do. He channeled his energy into painting somewhat surreal versions of things he'd photographed. Cityscapes had attracted him at first, a blend of gritty realism with a touch of unexpected whimsy. Sophisticated and polished, they made his previous efforts look like doodles. But his real desire was to turn his eye on the natural world. Had it just been a matter of his needing more space—which he certainly did if he wanted to continue painting anything larger than the lid of a shoebox—Orla might not have been convinced to make such a rural move. But he needed nature now the way she'd once needed a metropolis with the heart of a diva.

They'd visited the land for the first time six months ago; his brother, Walker, had alerted them to it soon after they started talking about what they *might* do and where they *might* do it. Neither of them had particularly liked it; the old wooden farmhouse was a mess and more cramped than Orla had desired. They hadn't even bothered to show it to the kids then, not considering it a real contender, though they'd poked around the nearby, undeniably quaint town of Saranac Lake Village. The only thing Shaw had really sparked to was the tree: a giant evergreen fifty yards behind the nothing of a house, its massive trunk rocketing upward from the middle of the earth, surrounded by smaller trees, like attendants in waiting.

While the real estate agent made phone calls in his car, Orla and Shaw had strolled back to the tree, Shaw attuned to its siren call, a glow on his face.

"I saw a tree like this once, a bit north of here, when I was camping with my dad. Was just a kid, maybe nine—Bean's age. I told my dad I could *feel* it. I felt *something*. Maybe it was the first time I realized, or thought about, how there were things in the natural world that outlived us, that saw history and maybe recorded time in their own way. My brother just teased me— par for the course back then. But my dad said something really weird—so weird that I always remembered it, and Walker shut up, no witty comebacks."

"What did he say?" Orla slipped her hand into his. Shaw's father had died of pancreatic cancer years ago, and she often wished she'd gotten to know him better.

"That sometimes when you're out in the world—he meant

the mountains, the forests; he'd always lived here—you recognize the other parts of your soul." Shaw looked at her then, still pondering those words. "I had no idea what he meant, but after that, every time I went into the woods I was looking…for something."

"For parts of yourself."

"Maybe."

"Your dad taught you…to see how we're part of something bigger. I like that."

"How we're connected." He'd held her face in his hands and kissed her. Orla got light-headed, giggly, like they'd gone back in time and were newly in love.

Just as they'd reached for the tree, fascinated by the ancient bark, the real estate agent's voice cut through the air. They hurried back.

Orla thought that had been the end of it, an interesting possibility and a pleasant visit. But after they got home, Shaw began reporting a recurring dream: Orla and the kids living on that land. Blossoming. And visions of himself in the room off the living room, conjuring his masterpieces. They resumed talking about it. The surrounding trees had been so beautiful in the spring, a tapestry of bursting green, with that special tree off in the distance.

"It's like it's our guardian," Shaw had said. "I see it, towering, in my dreams."

And his work improved and evolved, incorporating more and more wild greenery even though they hadn't yet left the city. As his process and his vision solidified, he became more convinced.

"It's calling to me. I think it's my muse." The ancient tree began to invade his work, peeking over the tops of buildings.

Orla had never been called by nature, but she believed him. It was a new thrill—for both of them—to see him find himself by losing himself in the creation of his paintings. Orla liked how the land reminded Shaw of his father and the philosophical lessons of his youth. When they checked back in with the real estate agent three months later, the price had dropped. The house had been empty for a while; out-of-state relatives were anxious to sell. They put in a lowball offer, and when it was accepted, a trajectory was set in motion.

2

"Are all the windows in now, Papa?" Eleanor Queen asked from the back seat, sounding as concerned as usual.

"Double-paned. Keep the wind out." Shaw grinned at his daughter in the rearview mirror. He'd become more animated in recent months—noticeable when they'd first committed to the move, but it had increased over the previous three weeks as he grew eager to settle into his new studio. Sometimes his enthusiasm manifested in him pacing or speaking too quickly or tapping his fingers or foot. Gradually her mellow husband was becoming more manic; Orla wasn't sure she liked it.

Though the kids hadn't seen the house before they'd left the city, they'd monitored the renovations via day-trips while they all stayed at Walker's. It had been fun bunking up with the other Bennett gang. Shaw had an effortless camaraderie with his brother, and his sister-in-law, Julie, was so nice. Orla (a Bennett by marriage, even if she'd kept her last name, Moreau) had enjoyed their buoyant conversations and domesticity. The boys, too, had been surprisingly accommodating. Twelve-year-old Derek hadn't minded giving up his room for Shaw and Orla, and fourteen-year-old Jamie had welcomed all the younger kids into his. Eleanor Queen and Tycho giggled at night as they shared a single inflatable mattress, head to toe and toe to head. Even though the children were cousins, Orla had considered it remarkable that the boys had been so quick to entertain a nine-year-old and a four-year-old for days on end. Good kids. They'd shuttled back and forth in various configurations of adults and offspring to get the new-old house ready.

Her daughter's voice brought her back to the present. "And we won't be cold?" Eleanor Queen asked, her voice full of worry.

The road was wet and black. The trees bare and black. Streaks of icy snow shot in horizontal bullets past the windows.

"Brand-new furnace," Shaw said with a grin. "*Thousands* of dollars!"

"That'll keep everything cozy-warm," Orla said, turning to soothe her daughter. "And we got the chimney cleaned for the wood-burning stove, so that's all ready too. I can already see you snuggled up in front of it, reading a book."

Eleanor Queen started to smile. But then the pelting snow, a full-on blizzard now, caught her attention again and her little brow furrowed.

Shaw was as proud of the damn furnace as another man might be of a fancy Italian motorcycle. "This is the heart of the house," he'd said as they stood in the basement watching its installation. "The heart of our new home."

But for Orla, the cost of everything was becoming a concern. The house and property. The SUV. The furnace and windows. The new generator, in case the electricity went out—even their water, brought up by a pump linked to a deep well, depended on electricity. And the day-to-day things they needed to keep everything and everyone up and running, alive and healthy. They'd paid cash for as much as they could, but she kept a watchful eye on their reserves.

The Chelsea co-op, which they'd owned for twenty-two years, had sold quickly and earned them a nice profit, and she'd offered to pay her father back for the down payment, as promised. He'd declined it. "Keep it to help with the kids' education, in case I'm not around."

Everything about his words bothered her—that he didn't foresee being alive when her kids were ready for college, and that he understood the more immediate problem: their savings simply weren't going to last that long and they needed it for mortgage, food, utilities, car payments, incidentals.

Maybe Shaw expected her to get a job if things got iffy. It was his turn to be creative, her turn to manage the household. He'd supplemented their income with various jobs over the years—waiter, bartender, tax preparer, temp. Maybe such options would have been available to her if they were living in Plattsburgh, about an hour northeast of their homestead. But their place in the woods—a forested piece of land with a view of no one and nothing man-made, up a dirt-and-gravel road on a gently sloping hill—was beyond any clearly defined boundaries. After living in walkable, public-transportation-friendly New York since she was seventeen, Orla was just now learning how to drive, but she wasn't yet comfortable behind the wheel. Even in good weather, it was too far to walk anywhere. And in bad weather…

She gazed out the window. The extended region had the dubious honor of having the coldest winter temperatures in the continental United States. Not to mention occasional snowfalls by the foot.

Julie had sent them on their way with a big bag full of extra and outgrown winter gear—snow pants, boots, mittens, even a couple pair of snowshoes—and some tomatoes and green beans she'd canned over the summer. Was the summer season actually long enough to grow vegetables? Were those skills Orla would have to learn to help stretch their funds—growing, canning, preserving?

She'd tried to fill her children with a sense of adventure, especially during the weeks when they'd been without a habitable home of their own. Tycho either didn't notice or didn't care that his life was in flux. As long as someone he knew was within his field of vision, he was happy. But it bothered Orla that Eleanor Queen still had such basic and essential concerns. She'd been to the house several times, had witnessed the progression of improvements. So why didn't she think it was ready? Where did she think her parents were taking her?

Eleanor Queen had watched the workers remove the old windows from the farmhouse. When the reflective glass of the big living-room window was gone, leaving a shockingly dark hole, the girl had clutched Orla's hand. "Are we going to die?"

"Of course not!" Orla had said with a laugh, giving her a squeeze. But for a second there had been only the squish of puffy jacket, and Orla's blood throbbed with the panic that her daughter had abruptly evaporated. Then she felt Eleanor Queen's little bones, and the sensation passed.

"Are you excited to have your very own rooms?" Orla said now in a cheery voice, pushing the uncomfortable memory away. Shaw slowed down as visibility diminished.

"Yay!" Tycho said, though he was probably the one who cared the least. Which was fortunate, considering his sliver of a room seemed to have been an afterthought, little more than a closet with a window, created by the addition of a wall that severed the largest of the upstairs bedrooms. But it was still more personal space than he—or any of them—had had. After Eleanor Queen was born, they turned the one bedroom into a nursery and bought themselves a new sleeper-sofa for the living room. A few years later came the bunk beds. The four of them were very accustomed to compact living.

"And Papa has his very first studio, where he can create his masterpieces!" Orla said. She grinned as Tycho's face lit up, always delighted for everyone. She was still smiling when she turned to Shaw. He looked funny when he was happy, the progression of half-moon lines around his eyes and his teeth on full display, angled this way and that, his upper teeth sitting directly on his lower ones. A crazy grimace. But she was glad for his happiness.

"My own stu-di-o," he sang, tapping a rhythm on the steering wheel in contra time to the music on the CD. *"Where I'll do my painting-o."* Tycho wasn't the only one in the family who liked to croon little ditties.

The studio, as it had been in his dream, was the spacious bedroom directly off the living room. For the first time in fifteen years, Shaw would have his own workspace, with a door. Orla was a bit envious, but reminded herself that if he was in the studio, she could go to their bedroom upstairs—and shut the door. It would be new for all of them: the many rooms, the many doors.

Tycho's eyes fluttered with sleep; the moose in his hand was splayed across his lap, already down for the count. Ever aware of her own body, she too felt a heaviness, a desire to hibernate. Yesterday's Thanksgiving feast still trudged through her system. And her legs (still two, in spite of the lingering sensation of their having been severed, cleaved) ached and she longed to jump from the car, grab her heel, and extend her leg up to her ear.

They'd always said Plattsburgh wasn't so far from where they'd be and that they'd go there often for shopping and family visits. But as they drove down Route 3, the world seemed to elongate behind them, stretching beyond recognition, obliterating the landmarks that would guide them back. Orla struggled to accept that they were still in New York—State, not City—but how could it be so different? It had been easier to agree to this when it hadn't seemed so utterly foreign. *North of the city* hadn't sounded so bad, with the word *city* dangling on, unwilling to let go, and New York still their resident state. But the city was gone. Her life was gone. And the landscape— unrecognizable.

She turned up the music, hoping to blot out the wind screaming beyond her window. *You owe him this,* it said. *You promised.* Shaw peeked at her, elated, and she let him assume the best, that she was as happy as he was. But even the dulcet tones of the strummed guitar wouldn't let her off. *Owe.* In the vibrating strings. Her husband would never say it, but it existed in the silent space between them. *My turn. We agreed.* And even softer, beneath that, a voice she'd struggled to suppress. *Your part is finished.* The curtain had fallen and wouldn't rise again. And she was afraid of the dark.

3

The snow had laid down a thick carpet by the time they snaked their way up the driveway. The kids were wide awake, faces pressed to the windows. They'd all been in the house before, of course, but none of them had spent a night there or seen it under such wintry conditions. Shaw turned off the music, and the fog they breathed, the recycled mishmash from all of their lungs, hummed with expectation.

"So pretty!" Tycho said when the farmhouse came into view.

Bless his heart. It must have been the snow, like frosting on the tree limbs with smears of white on the roof. Blue-gray paint, so old it looked mostly washed away, and the windows were trimmed in what might once have been a festive red, now rusty scabs. They'd need to have the exterior painted if they were to keep the wood protected, but next year; they'd already spent so much. It looked fragile to Orla, nothing like the massive steel buildings, the stone and brick and solid permanence of her past life. A gust of wind could blow it down. Two stories of decomposable wood, pitched roof, a porch made of matchsticks, and windows of watchful eyes and open mouths.

"All right, everybody ready?" Shaw pulled into the detached, three-walled garage, its flimsy boards even more weathered than the house's, its roof equally as steep to prevent it from accumulating too much snow. Along the outside of the near wall, a bank of firewood, half covered by a blue tarp, sat ready for use. And around the back wall, out of view, was their generator. They'd had the electrician reroute the critical circuits in such a way that if they lost power, the generator would automatically kick on and take over.

The kids unbuckled and hopped out, their tongues ready to catch the snowflakes.

"Wish we could've left some windows open," Orla said. Painting the bedrooms had been the last of their home improvements before their furniture was delivered from storage, and she worried about the fumes. She worried about other things too, more nebulous and harder to express.

Shaw grabbed luggage and groceries out of the back of the SUV. "It should be okay, been a few days."

Eleanor Queen and Tycho spun in circles, enjoying the snow. In a flash of memory, Orla saw herself and her brother, Otto. It happened at rare moments, a ghost image from her past— a flickering film that quickly dissolved—when she saw her children playing together. "Ready to come in and check out your finished rooms? We can get all your stuff unpacked."

Tycho, incapable of moving in a restrained fashion, ran toward the porch, arms flailing. The porch's railing dipped slightly in the center where the ground beneath it had settled unevenly. Shaw, bags under each arm, opened the front door with his son hopping at his heels, both a-chatter with shared eagerness. The house swallowed their sounds as they entered.

Abandoned by her playmate, Eleanor Queen lingered in the yard. She looked up at the sky. The woods. Her dark eyes alert and watchful.

"Eleanor Queen?"

Still the little girl assessed her surroundings, with more wariness than she'd shown on previous visits to the house. Orla felt a chill as she watched her. What was she concentrating on with such rapt attention? The girl squinted, cocked her head, like someone trying to make sense of a distant sound. To make sense of something that Orla couldn't hear, or see.

"Love? What's wrong?"

"What kind of tree did Papa say that was?" Her mittened hand pointed to the giant that reared up fifty yards behind their house. Its immense boughs frowned down on the munchkin trees that surrounded it. Maybe it was the slate sky, or the other trees without their leaves, but the great pine looked even older than it had in the spring, like an old person drained of color.

Orla tried to recall what the real estate agent had said when he'd shown them the property. He'd boasted of the tree being over five hundred years old, she remembered that. "Eastern white pine, I think? We'll ask Papa again. It's so big because it's *five hundred* years old."

Eleanor Queen continued to gaze at it with an intensity that Orla found disconcerting. She didn't see admiration for the ancient tree on her daughter's face, or curiosity. But something more troubling.

Trepidation.

"Well, come on, we can get your snow pants and gear if you want to play outside." Orla really didn't think that's what her daughter wanted in that moment, but it's what Orla had hoped for her when they'd talked about the North Country, that she would like the tranquillity, the slow pace of the wilderness. Eleanor Queen wouldn't have to worry about getting run over by a taxi or crushed against a pole in a crowded subway car. Perhaps she just wasn't used to how quiet it was, how different. How the wind, in a silent place, made everything speak.

Eleanor Queen abruptly turned and charged toward the house.

Orla didn't want to think it was fear she saw on her daughter's face. But she hesitated in the yard as Eleanor Queen scrambled inside. What had spooked her? Was something out there? She scanned the terrain at the back of their property. The air carried the cozy fragrance of wood smoke—had Shaw lit the stove already? Or was that a plume rising above the trees? Impossible; there were no homes, not even distant ones, visible behind them.

Movement caught her eye and she refocused on the giant pine in time to see a cascade of snow drop from its ragged limbs. The wind had settled and she didn't think it the source of the snow's collapse. Could a tree shiver? Shake off the cold and wet like a dog? She heard a sound she couldn't identify…a soft *pfloof*. Again, and again.

Her mouth dropped open. Something was moving toward her, something quiet but immense. Her gut said, *Run!* The nerves in her spine jangled a warning, but she couldn't turn away.

One by one, the trees shook off their snow. That was the sound: inches of accumulation on hundreds of branches falling in a swoop onto the white, cushioned ground. But it wasn't all of the trees; that's what was wrong, that's what chilled her blood and kept her agog. It was a path of trees, starting with the goliath and moving forward. Orla wanted to think, *Chain reaction,* but her mind flung aside such logic.

It was coming.

When the snow tumbled from the final tree at the edge of their back clearing, a great gust of wind swept toward her. Finally Orla came back to life and lunged for the porch. She stumbled inside and locked the door behind her.

As she pressed her back against the door, confused by her narrow escape, her eyes met her daughter's and her blood froze all over again. A cloud of snow battered against the windows. And then all was still once more. But Eleanor Queen huddled in the corner behind the cold stove, wide-eyed. Upstairs, Shaw and Tycho carried on as if all were normal, chatting, making the floorboards creak as they moved stuff around.

Orla hadn't meant to make it worse, but her daughter looked terrified. What had even happened? She'd never been in a forest after a blizzard. She felt silly now, a lame barricade between Mother Nature and common sense. She stepped away from the door, shrugging it off.

"It was just the wind after the storm," she said. "Like the way earthquakes have aftershocks."

"You kept it out."

"Of course—" But before she could say anything else, Eleanor Queen darted out from behind the squat black stove and raced up the stairs, calling for her papa.

Orla had half a mind to do the same, run up and call for Shaw. Ask for a hug. She heard him, cooing away their daughter's fright.

"'Tsokay, Ele-Queen." Tycho, mimicking his father.

That made her smile. Overreacting wasn't going to help. Orla listened at the front door; it was quiet. She cracked it open and peered out.

Nothing moved. Crystals glittered on the snow. It was pretty, but she didn't fully trust it. Walls felt more reliable, and more familiar. In her mind, *home* was the place within the boundary of the walls, not what lay beyond it. She left the door wide open, to facilitate a hasty retreat, and returned to the car to fetch the rest of their things.

4

It was a crappy bathroom by most people's standards, nothing anyone would swoon over on *House Hunters,* but longtime New Yorkers had a different appreciation for *space*. They had friends who had to squeeze into a tiny corner shower, barely big enough to hold an adult, set beside a toilet where, still sitting, you could lean forward and wash your hands in the sink. Now they had space—a precious commodity—though the black-and-white vinyl floor would have to be ripped up someday. But it was serviceable for now. The white pedestal sink was charmingly old-fashioned, and the throne, as Shaw liked to call it, faced the frosted window. Orla had already put a little bookcase beneath the window and filled it with their folded towels and extra toilet paper, but maybe she needed to add an actual book or two. Perhaps the leisurely pace of their new life might involve more alone time in the therapeutic comfort of the bath.

She slipped out of her sweatpants and thermal shirt, swept them into a pile with pointed toes, and stepped into the claw-foot tub. It was deeper than their old tub, and she inhaled the steam rising from the hot water. With her calves propped on the opposite rim, she gazed at her knees, her feet. They splayed out in opposite directions, a sign of her effortless turnout. There were hard knobs on the tops of her toes from decades of pointe work. Her black hair draped over the edge of the white porcelain, and she felt the warm air coming up from the vent stirring it. The furnace in the basement was doing its job, sending heat out through its veins.

This was what she needed. After nearly three months of turmoil, of deconstructing the status quo, finally she could relax. Her limbs melted into the water, though her thoughts weren't as easy to soothe.

Her body, when it was moving, stretching, spinning, leaping, was a wonder that made her grateful. A machine of muscle and flesh. But lying back, naked, unmoving, all she saw were bones and the flat angles of her stomach. She looked more like a stick insect than a woman.

Friends called her exotic, but Orla had never figured out why her strangeness was so appealing to people. She gave the impression of towering over her husband when in fact she was only an inch taller than Shaw. But everything about her was long, exaggerated. Even her facial features. A couple of her less politically correct friends enjoyed asking new acquaintances to guess her ethnicity. They'd say Greek, Persian, Italian, Israeli, Peruvian, Syrian. When they gave up, she told them she was just another Generican—a generic American. But that never satisfied their curiosity. So she'd tell them about her Venezuelan/Irish mother, and her Filipino/French/American father. Then they'd ask, "How many languages do you speak?" only to be disappointed by her answer. Being a Generican who spoke only English didn't fit with people's idea of who they thought she should be.

She carried these dichotomies with her, the half-admirable/half-disappointing realities of her life. Not quite a woman of the world. Not quite a star in her field. Not quite beautiful in any traditional sense. Other women expressed envy for her slenderness, but Orla longed for a little flesh, some softness to her breasts. She'd never loved her body more than when she was pregnant, and when everyone marveled at how quickly she returned to her pre-pregnancy physique, Orla missed the roundness, the goddess she had briefly been.

Shaw's physical attraction to her had always been strong, but that was only one element of her intrigue; by example, she kept him motivated to keep forging ahead with his difficult, and sometimes elusive, creative goals. He'd enjoyed being a stay-at-home dad, but since he'd found oil painting—and his subject matter—his focus had realigned. At thirty-eight, he considered himself in his prime. He'd lived enough to have real experiences to draw on, and he'd explored everything; at last, his talents and interests were clear.

She wasn't accustomed to that feeling yet, that he had important work to do and hers was finished. Even if they'd stayed in a city, it might have been hard for her to figure out what to do next. But *here*? It was never that she didn't want to encourage him, or take a step back to give him his moment to shine. But his plan meant embarking on an entirely new life. Some of her lumpy misgivings had been selfish; what would *she* do out there in the wilderness?

Under the bathwater, her hands made fists around invisible stones, rubbing, rubbing. She'd caught herself doing it, worrying those invisible stones, many times over the preceding weeks. Every day she'd spent at Walker and Julie's, the thought surfaced: *We don't belong here.* Shaw might once have been Mr. Outdoorsy, but for going on two decades, his "survival" had required trendy coffee and a choice of Vietnamese restaurants. He liked gallery openings and the IFC Center. He experimented with his facial hair and wore garish colors with spectacular aplomb. Once upon a time he'd left Plattsburgh precisely because he was too weird for his flannel-and-jeans-wearing family. Walker, all grown up, didn't tease him anymore and embraced his return to the North Country. But in the face of such isolation, Orla understood this new way of life was something they couldn't play at. Shaw had accepted Walker's gift of two of their father's long guns—a thirty-ought-six rifle with a telescopic sight and a double-barreled shotgun—and planned to hunt. He swore he still remembered how to dress a deer, something he'd done his entire childhood, but Orla only knew him as a man with hands reddened by paint, not blood.

There would be real-world consequences if they ran low on food—no running down to the corner bodega, no ordering in from whatever restaurant they craved. And what if one of the children got seriously hurt? How long would they have to wait, or drive, for help? They'd prepared well, but that didn't quell the anxiety.

It didn't feel right.

It didn't feel right, and she couldn't explain it to Shaw, this hunch. (This woman's intuition?) He would say she just wasn't used to it. And he would be right. He would remind her of her early days in New York City, a teenager taking classes, auditioning, overwhelmed on a daily basis. But she'd found her place, made her home. That's what he expected of her here and she didn't want to let him down, so she kept the unnamable misgivings to herself.

She lurched to her feet, letting the cooling bathwater cascade down her body. She'd committed to Shaw and her family. Her children needed her strength—her flexibility—and she needed to demonstrate the fine art of being adaptable. With more resolve than she'd felt all day, Orla grabbed a towel and quickly dried off.

*　　*　　*

Her sleep sweats were comfy and warm. The pants left her ankles exposed, but the sleeves hung over her hands, the result of her constantly pulling the fabric over them and balling it into her fists. The design on the front commemorated the Empire City Contemporary Ballet's thirty-fifth anniversary, the letters crumbled and faded, worn from age and washing. When she emerged from the bedroom, Shaw was quietly closing Eleanor Queen's door, having just said his good-nights.

"I'll be in my studio," he whispered and threw Orla a kiss. "Roomy!" He opened his arms, gleeful, and the word echoed in the stairwell as he went down.

She headed to Tycho's room, to the right of hers and Shaw's and farthest from the stairs. The mothball scent from its most recent life as a closet lingered, but the bunk bed just fit, leaving two feet of walk space beside it and enough room to open the door. Orla went in cautiously, and, sure enough, he lay snuggled on the bottom bunk, fast asleep, his stuffed moose clutched in his hand.

She stood by the window for a moment looking out toward the garage and beyond, taking in the eerie glow of the moon curtained by clouds, and the slow descent of fat flakes of snow. Though Shaw and the real estate agent had told her which direction each side of the house faced, she couldn't remember. She hadn't shaken old habits—to her, "north" meant Harlem, the Bronx; "south" meant Tribeca, Battery Park. Maybe the sun would steal into Tycho's room in the morning, pry open his eyes with molten fingers. Maybe it wouldn't bother him; he possessed the young child's gift of sleeping deeply in odd positions and strange circumstances. Still, they needed to get blinds or curtains for all the windows. She was planning on doing a lot of online shopping come Monday afternoon, after their satellite internet and phone were installed. It would be a relief to be reconnected to civilization, with constant access to the outside world and streaming entertainment.

The internet phone was really just a backup, another safety precaution, as the satellite should provide a more reliable connection than the spotty service they got with their cell phones. Once they were online again, Eleanor Queen could get back to "school"—they were online-homeschooling her for the full year while they explored their options in Saranac Lake Village. Changing schools would be hard enough for her without her jumping in somewhere midyear. They'd decided to ease their sensitive daughter through the changes as softly as they could.

Orla suppressed a laugh when she turned around and saw that her son had "helped" unpack by tossing every single one of his stuffed animals and miscellaneous toys onto the top bunk, where his sister used to sleep. In the coming days she'd dig out his colorful milk crates and help him get organized. Or…his toys were off the floor, and there was barely room to store his clothes. If Tycho liked it that way, maybe she'd let him leave his mound as it was. She knelt beside him and kissed his cheek, tucked the striped comforter over his exposed arm so he wouldn't get cold. The house was warm, but they'd lower the thermostat for the night. "Good night, sweet boy."

She left his door cracked so the hallway light could guide him to the bathroom if he woke in the night. Though likely he'd call for one of them; he was easily frightened upon awakening in an unfamiliar place. Orla passed the master bedroom— big enough for a queen-size bed and their dresser—and the bathroom and rapped softly on Eleanor Queen's door before opening it.

The window in her daughter's room faced the other side of the property and gave her a view of a narrow strip of yard and a wall of trees. Her new bed, dressed up with all her new flowery bedding, was set up in the corner. Beside it was a little white table onto which she'd clipped her lamp with its rainbow-y holograms dotted around the pink and purple shade. It had been clipped to her headboard when she'd slept on the bunk above Tycho.

Eleanor Queen sat with her pillow at her back rereading one of her favorite books. At her cousins', she'd read from their shelves, adventure and science books meant for slightly older readers. Orla's left fist gripped her worry stone, muscles clenching around nothing but her own anxiety. How would they fare without a neighborhood library? Eleanor Queen was an avid reader, but it didn't bode well that she still preferred her old books to the e-reader her grandparents had gotten her for her birthday. She, Shaw, and Eleanor Queen had spent hours loading books onto it so she wouldn't run out of reading material before they got fully situated.

Orla sat on the bed beside her. "You don't like your e-reader?"

The girl shrugged. "That's for when I run out of paper books. Don't worry—"

"I'm not worried."

"Yes you are." As Eleanor Queen reached out and took her mother's fist, Orla realized what she'd been doing and relaxed her hand. "There's nothing like being in bed with a big book on your lap."

Orla laughed. "Spoken like a fifty-year-old librarian." She kissed her daughter's forehead and swept the hair away from her face. Her daughter looked like her, the same coloring, though her limbs and features weren't as exaggerated. Tycho, with his unruly hair and wan complexion, looked like Shaw. They talked about it in private moments, how they each had a child who favored them. The physical resemblances felt important, like a reminder that the children might have inherited other qualities of theirs too. Part of their parenting strategy was to remember how they'd felt as children, what they'd wanted, how they'd wished to be treated.

"Lots of big changes," Orla said. "Does it feel weird not to climb a ladder to get into bed?"

Eleanor Queen grinned with her lips tight over her bulging front teeth. "I like the walls."

"The color?"

She nodded, as if embarrassed by being so pleased. They'd painted all four walls a bright turquoise. In the room she'd shared with Tycho, they'd had to compromise: two pale green walls for him; two lilac-colored walls for her. But she didn't like purple as much anymore.

"Are you getting used to being away from the city?"

Eleanor Queen shrugged. "Some of it's nice. But it feels weird."

"Weird how?" Weird-bad? Weird-scary?

"Weird like there's nowhere to go."

Orla laughed. "Yes, my love, you and I both are going to need some time to adjust to that. But we will. And we'll find magical things—nature is full of wonders; that's what Papa says. I don't know about you, but I'm looking forward to finding amazing things."

"Me too. But maybe they won't really be magical—like, not real magic. They'll be real things. Different things than what's in the city."

"Yes, I think you're absolutely right." She rubbed her nose against her daughter's, making Eleanor Queen giggle. "My wise girl. I love you."

"I love you too."

"Good night."

"G' night."

Orla started to close the door, then stopped. "Want me to leave it cracked?"

"No, that's okay..." The girl's voice wavered with uncertainty, though Orla saw her determination to overcome her fear.

"I'm sorry your night-light wasn't in the box, but we'll find it. Why don't I just leave it cracked for tonight?"

"Okay." Eleanor Queen grinned with relief and dug her nose back into her book.

Orla blew her a kiss, and left the door ajar on her way out. She didn't have to tell Eleanor Queen when to shut off her light; her daughter would do it when she was tired, and Orla trusted her judgment. Her daughter seemed content enough, the missing night-light notwithstanding, but Orla couldn't so easily shake off what she'd seen earlier in her face, before Orla got spooked by the wind. What lurked in a forest? Ravenous animals? Escaped convicts? They had no immediate neighbors, so in theory, no one should be close enough to see them, spy on them. But her city self (her biased-by-stupid-movies self) thought some number of people who chose to live in the boonies were bordering on mutants. Inbreeding cannibals and the like.

Little fingernails tickled her spine as she freaked herself out with her thoughts; she wished she'd already bought coverings for the windows. What if something—someone—was out there right now? Watching her move from room to room?

She started down the spiraling wooden steps but stopped after three and paused on the triangular landing. The window there looked out toward the back of the property, but the lower view was blocked by the first-floor kitchen's gently slanted roof—an extension that had been added in the 1960s. The snow had stopped falling for now, and the moon, free of clouds, lit up the white ground and highlighted the trees' talons as branches swayed in a silent wind. And the giant was out there—the solitary eastern white pine (Shaw had confirmed it)—its height almost freakish. What if it had grown so big by gobbling up smaller trees? Hadn't she once read Tycho such a story? What if it changed form under the cloak of darkness and tiptoed around the land at night, crushing rabbits and mice under its feet?

An owl called and her body responded, muscles tightening with bitterness; she didn't understand these creatures. Honking cars made sense. Neighbors screaming in Chinese made sense. She'd never thought she'd miss such mundane, once annoying sounds.

She'd been surprised when Shaw so readily accepted the guns from Walker. But after a short argument, whispered in Julie's tidy mudroom, they'd agreed Shaw would purchase a gun locker. It was terrifying to think of the children having access to such deadly weapons. But maybe he'd understood something she hadn't: the need for them.

As she hurried down the rest of the stairs, she called out to him, "Babe? Do you know where the guns are?"

5

Orla glanced around the living room, with its recently painted gray walls and white trim, on her way to Shaw's studio. They'd thought the paint would mask or absorb the aroma of wood smoke. They hadn't used the wood-burning stove yet—squat and animalistic, its territory a corner of the room upon a bed of bricks. But the decades of its use lingered in the hardwood floors, the ceilings. Their sleeper-sofa and ugly-but-comfy plaid chair, end tables, lamps, and bookcase were in place, along with the currently lifeless smart TV. But a large percentage of their unopened boxes were stacked against the interior wall, filled with books, framed pictures, knickknacks, random clothing, and most of the kitchen stuff. Her eyes appraised it all, seeking among the boxes one long enough to hold the guns.

Shaw's door was wide open and she found him at the front-facing window, gazing outward. Though Eleanor Queen might physically resemble her mother, in other ways—her sensitivity—she was very much her father's daughter. The look on Shaw's face was like Eleanor Queen's that afternoon, trying to decode their new surroundings.

"Did you hear me?" she asked softly, hesitant to startle him from his trance.

"Yes, no…" He blinked and turned to her.

"The guns." Orla couldn't quite decide if she was being paranoid. But a practical part of her knew the search had a valid purpose. "We don't have the locker yet."

"No, no, don't worry. They're in here." Shaw nodded toward the studio closet and reached out to take her hand. "I figured the kids wouldn't be in here anyway, so they're up on the shelf for now. I can get one in Plattsburgh in a few days, or order one next week."

Orla nodded, not relieved. She couldn't really imagine either of her children dragging over a step stool to root around for a weapon in their father's personal space. But how many families had made similar assumptions and been proved wrong? Another part of her didn't want the guns hidden at all but stashed on hooks above the front door—wasn't that how they did it in Westerns? So the hero could grab one when the bad guys rode up?

"Hey, what's wrong?" Shaw placed a hand on one of her cheeks and kissed the other, his body pressed like a shadow against hers.

"I don't feel…completely safe," she admitted.

"What do you think's gonna happen?" He asked the question with gentle concern.

She shrugged. "Bears?"

They stepped back, arms around each other's waist, and stood facing his studio. Orla's eyes wandered around, taking in the progress of his unpacking. Maybe it was all the extra space, but the new place was already having one positive effect on him: everything was so tidy and well organized. His guitars, an acoustic and a hollow-body electric, sentenced to a life of confinement in their apartment, now stood on display in one corner beside his small amp. He'd set his easel next to the front-facing window and a blank canvas stood at the ready. His paintings were leaning behind the door, their images toward the wall. His petite, once-cluttered desk sat by the smaller window, and set atop it were his laptop and a half-empty box marked PAINTING STUFF. On the floor, still sealed, was a box labeled PHOTOS 'N' STUFF and two liquor boxes that she knew held his CDs.

Back in their old apartment, his "stuff" had been crammed into every available space in the living room, which, true to its name, was where they'd done all their living—eating, watching, reading, creating, playing, sleeping. Here, his things didn't need to be stashed on top of bookcases or stacked in a corner like a Jenga game. Orla gasped, seeing something for the first time: No wonder he'd struggled to stick with things; their home had been the opposite of inspiring. It had been a mess.

"This is great," she said. A tiny bit jealous, she wanted to put a portable barre on her online-shopping list. Maybe they could set it up in the living room and she'd have a place to do pliés, ronds de jambe, développés. While he developed his craft, she didn't want to lose her finely tuned body. "I can see it. The light will be great during the day…this is the room—the space—you've needed."

"It is." He grinned, then grew serious again as he looked at her. "Are you really worried about bears?"

"Maybe. I saw that list. On Julie and Walker's fridge. All the animals and their hunting seasons. Bears. Bobcats. Coyotes."

"Well, I've got my license; I can shoot them if they get too close. And there are lots of harmless animals too. Deer. Geese. *Frogs*." He gave her a little squeeze. A grin. Another peck on the cheek. But his efforts to relieve her worries didn't work. Orla's gaze remained fixed on the front window, on the dark mysteries lurking beyond the thin membrane. What had he sensed out there? The same thing their daughter had? "You're really worried," he said.

He stepped into her line of sight, and she returned to the present, the room.

"I just don't…this is all foreign to me. Am I going to walk out the door and find a bear in the yard? Are people going to be hunting on our property? Is it safe for the kids to play outside?"

"Whoa, whoa, hold up. *This* is the place where it's safe. This is where no one gets mugged. Pedestrians don't get run over by asshole drivers. Construction cranes don't fall over and crush people; buildings don't collapse. And Homeland Security isn't crawling everywhere with armed guards. I know you're not used to it, but this—this isn't what's frightening about the world. Okay?" He was so lovingly sincere.

"I know. I mean, a part of me knows." She wrapped her arms around his neck.

He swayed with her, the two of them moving from foot to foot as they often did when they embraced.

"It's a big change," he said, his lips tingling against her ear. "But I wouldn't have suggested this if I didn't think you, the kids, would thrive here. Bean might come out of her shell a little. And Tycho—I loved having this as my backyard when I was growing up. And you." He pulled away a little to look her in the eye. "It wasn't just a selfish suggestion on my part—"

"I didn't think that."

"Not even a teeny-tiny—"

"Okay, well, there were moments, but not in a bad way, truly—"

"I know." His smile reminded her that sometimes he could read her mind. "I was hoping…I thought it might be hard for you to be in the city, which has always been about ballet—why you went there, why you stayed. I thought it might be harder to be retired and still there. Everything would be a reminder. I didn't want you to feel…a loss. This is a completely new chapter. You can be a new person; no one's going to ask you every time they see you if you miss it."

She hugged him tight. He'd always had the capacity to astonish her. "Thank you. I guess, with the flurry of preparations, I haven't really figured out what I'm going to do. Next." She leaned back a little, fingered his paint-streaked hair. "I mean, be with the kids more. Help Eleanor Queen with her schooling this year. Maybe, if you strike it big, I can be your personal assistant."

"I like that!" His fiddly hands tapped a rhythm on her hips as he bellowed an impromptu aria: *"My canvases you'll stretch, and my brushes you will fetch—"*

"I was thinking more of scheduling your interviews and answering your fan mail."

"Now you're talking." He gave her a loud smack of a kiss on the lips.

Orla released him, watching as he went to his desk, scooped more tubes of paint from the box, seemingly without a worry in the world.

"But just in case," she said, downplaying how important it felt, "could you teach me how to shoot?"

Up early the next morning, bothered by the downstairs mess, Orla stacked glassware and mugs in an upper cabinet, enjoying the challenge of making little or no noise. She smiled as she put away her favorite mug. Covered with crooked hearts, Eleanor Queen had painted it as a six-year-old for a Mother's Day gift. It was extra-special for the memories it evoked: Shaw arranging furtive trips to the Paint-a-Pottery shop in the days when he took baby Tycho everywhere in a kangaroo carrier. Some of her "memories" were things described to her by Shaw, moments she'd missed when the children were little. Now she wouldn't miss any more of those moments.

The kitchen, though fully functional and with lots of counter space, had no appliances younger than thirty years old. But the linoleum floor had recently been replaced with tile, and the rustic cabinets were hickory with antique door pulls that she rather liked. The real estate agent had told her the original kitchen had been half the size and with a much lower ceiling, as if the fact that it had been worse fifty years ago made its current state a selling point. Once they got a proper table and matching chairs, it would be a homey place to prepare and eat their meals. Though first they needed to get something to stop the draft that was leaking in under the back door. The cold air swirled around her ankles, made her feel like something mischievous was grinning as it tickled her.

Upstairs, a door squeaked open, the sound followed by a shriek. "Papa! Mama! We got ten feet of snow!"

Orla chuckled. Another door squealed on its hinges— probably Tycho expecting to find her in bed beside Shaw. She imagined Shaw with the pillow folded over his ear, his preferred position for sleeping.

"Ten feet, Papa! Ten feet!"

She heard a rumbly, deep voice but couldn't decipher Shaw's reply. A moment later, Tycho came galloping down the stairs. "Mama!"

"In here, love."

He raced into the kitchen. "We got ten feet of snow!"

Orla scooped her little boy into her arms. She carried him on her hip and went to look out the living room's front window, where she could get a better sense of the accumulation. Snow covered the first two of the four steps leading up to the porch.

"I think maybe…ten *inches*? Twelve? Maybe a little deeper where it drifted?" she said.

Shaw lurched down the stairs in sleepy thuds, pulling on his raggedy tartan bathrobe. "Please, tell me we didn't get ten feet—that wasn't in the forecast."

"Inches, not feet," Orla assured him.

Eleanor Queen came down next, nimble as a sprite. She sprang on her toes toward the window, rested her fingertips on the glass.

"Wow," she whispered.

"Beautiful, huh?" Shaw asked, untangling the sleep nests from his daughter's hair.

The previous day's clouds of doom, depleted of their heavy burden, had dissipated. Orla couldn't explain it, but the house felt more solid in the sunshine with a blue sky above. The snow, now that it wasn't whipping through the air, looked less menacing. It struck her that the place was welcoming them, laying out its blanket of white wonder, enfolding them in its charm.

"What do you say I make us a nice hearty breakfast," she said, "then we go play in the snow!"

Both of the children cheered. Shaw gave his toothy grin.

The children had played in snow before, of course, in the trampled communal spaces of the city's parks. But never in their own yard. They'd never been able to build something that would last unmolested until they went to play again.

"We can make a snowman," Tycho said.

"A snow *woman*," said Eleanor Queen.

"A snow *dragon*!" Shaw roared. Tycho hopped down from Orla's arms so he could join his sister as their father chased them around the room, roaring.

Orla caught that flicker again of a moment from the past. The family home. Her father making her little brother laugh. Though none of them ever chased delicate Otto, lest he stumble and break.

6

Long underwear. Sweaters. Thin socks beneath thick socks. Tycho hopped on one foot and then the other as Orla helped him into his snow pants; Eleanor Queen shimmied into hers on her own. Orla was grateful she'd taken Julie's advice and invested in a pair of proper—tall and warm—snow boots for herself. Tycho tried fastening his boots, then gave up and plopped onto the floor in front of the door to let Orla do it. Next came the coats, scarves, hats, mittens. Orla didn't bundle up quite as well—she wasn't planning on being fully immersed in the snow—and when they were all ready, she opened the front door and the kids went out, bounding off the porch.

"Shaw? We're heading out."

"Okay. I'll be out in a minute."

She didn't know what he was doing in his studio—she'd expected him to join them on their first adventure in the snow—but she couldn't keep the kids waiting after they were all suited up.

As soon as Orla stepped off the porch, she lifted a hand to her eyes to shield them from the blinding brightness of the sunlight on the white expanse. The kids, giggling with the pure joy of creatures at play, were already scooping the snow into mounds. They'd get up and stumble a few steps, then fall into the cushioning white, their hands touching every unblemished surface as if they couldn't claim it quickly enough.

Orla strolled a few paces away from the house, enjoying the crunch beneath her boots. It warmed her heart to see Eleanor Queen so carefree, so lost in the moment that her active mind finally gave her a few seconds of peace.

"Is Papa gonna help us make the snow dragon?" she asked.

"I think so." Orla looked back toward the house. Shaw was just inside, pulling on his coat.

"What's that?" Tycho shrieked, excited. He pointed at something several feet away. Orla tramped over to take a look.

"Huh. Isn't that interesting?" Her son had spotted what looked like a rolled bundle of snow, like a Swiss roll, or the giant bales of hay she'd seen on rare drives in the country, although this was less than a foot across. "Eleanor Queen? Come look!" When her daughter was at her side, she pointed at the flat patch of snow behind the rolled-up part. "See? It's like the wind blew it into that shape."

"That's so cool."

"Is it gonna keep getting bigger bigger and bigger?" Tycho asked, holding his hands as far apart as they could go.

"I don't know." Orla took out her phone and snapped a picture of it. The kids, already losing interest, ran back to play. Orla dug around on Google, trying to figure out what search terms to put in. The signal was decent for once, maybe because of the cloudless day—or maybe this was the one spot in the yard where the mountains weren't in the way. "I found it!" They ignored her, but Orla read through the listings, fascinated.

Shaw came out of the house carrying a pair of snowshoes and a map, a day pack slung over one shoulder. Wisely, he'd thought to put on sunglasses.

"Hey look!" Orla called. "We have a snow roller in our yard! That's what they're called…" She consulted her phone. "Also snow bales or wind snowballs. They're a meteorological phenomenon. And yes, Tycho, they can get really big. Or many can form in the same place under the right conditions…"

No one was really paying attention to her. Tycho, catching sight of his father's snowshoes, slogged over to the porch where he was putting them on. "Can I try?" he said, reaching out.

"Not this time, Tigger. These are too big for you."

Orla kept her phone out as she waded back to the house. She'd always thought snowshoes were wooden and webbed, but the ones Shaw was fastening on were high-tech steel frames with strategically placed crampons. Julie had sent along some less expensive and smaller ones for the kids, hand-me-downs from Jamie and Derek. But evidently Shaw was planning a solo outing.

"No one cares about the phenomenon in our yard? Where are you going?" she asked. Behind her, she heard the *whisk-whisk* of Eleanor Queen's snow pants as she strode over to join the rest of her family.

Shaw waved the topographical map. "Thought I'd survey the property—it's all marked. And take some pictures. I'm psyched to start on my nature work. Mostly, I just wanted to walk around. Looking for inspiration, and the trees might tell me something." He winked at Tycho.

"Do trees talk?" he asked his papa.

Orla caught the turn of Eleanor Queen's head as she looked up toward the towering pine.

"Oh yes," said Shaw. "But you have to listen very hard. See all these…" He gestured around them and both kids watched his hand sweep over the audience of attentive trees. "They speak their own language. They whisper it in their branches and send messages through their roots—they touch underground, rippling currents filled with all the news and gossip. Sometimes, when it's very windy, they have a lot to talk about and you can hear them chatter and argue. But when the air is still, you have to concentrate."

"What do they talk about?" Tycho asked.

"Oh, the things they've seen from way high up, and way down low. The animals and bugs who come to visit, the birds who build nests in their branches. In the city, we have the bustle of life in big apartment buildings. Here, we have the forest, busy in a different way."

"Wow," said Tycho, wide-eyed and enchanted.

Orla saw the effort Eleanor Queen was making to hear them, the community of trees, her utter faith that they were communicating with one another, or her, just beyond her range of comprehension.

"Papa doesn't mean it literally," Orla said to her daughter, tugging the left side of her hat back over her ear, trying to distract her.

"Oh, I do! I've learned amazing things from trees—why do you think I wanted to come here?" He winked again and Tycho knew his cue to join his father in a giggle. But Orla could've shoved snow down Shaw's shirt. Couldn't he see how impressionable his daughter was? Even if, at nine, she was better able to tell reality from fantasy than her brother, what did she know about the wilderness? It was dangerous to anthropomorphize things for the amusement of a sensitive child.

"Papa's right," said Eleanor Queen, her attention still on the trees. "I can *almost* hear them…"

Shaw grinned, but Orla gave him a see-what-you've-done glare—which seemed to prompt him to head off on his adventure. "Okay, my tribe, I will see you upon my return!"

Their property was officially just over six acres, but it was surrounded by heavily forested hills that looked endless. Only the flatter area immediately around the house had been cleared. Orla didn't want to express her disappointment at his departure, not so soon after their awkward conversation the night before about not feeling safe. He'd seemed to take her concern seriously, but not so seriously that he considered her—them— in any real danger. Which was good, on the one hand, but he hadn't even said anything over their oatmeal and bacon about going out on his own. She couldn't decide if she was angry that he wasn't sticking around to help the kids with their snow creature, or afraid of being left at the house alone for the first time. In the middle of nowhere. She wished they'd gotten the internet hooked up *before* they'd moved in. The rest of the world felt so far out of reach.

"Does your cell work out there?" She trailed behind him as he tramped toward the tree line behind their house, the snow-shoes keeping him aloft. The signal on her own phone dropped to almost nothing as they neared the woods.

"Don't know. I didn't bring it."

"What if something happens?"

"Like what?"

"I don't know…like you slide off a cliff and break your leg." Things like that always happened in movies with mountains and snow.

He stopped before entering the forest. "I won't go that far. And there are no cliffs out here. Don't worry. Back soon!" She offered him her phone, but he waved it off. It was all so easy for him. Maybe it had taken those years in the city to make him realize this was where he belonged. He seemed to need no adjustment period and hadn't once expressed a longing for the coffee places and delis that had so recently been a fixture of his routine. But she already longed for a twenty-four-hour diner with a menu as long as *Moby-Dick* and Spanish-speaking waiters who—such a cliché—knew what she liked to order.

"Papa?" Eleanor Queen ran over, the gloom of apprehension returning to her face. "What about the snow dragon?"

"Don't worry, Bean, your mom can get you started. And I'll help when I get back. Or—it's not like the city—we can work on it a bit every day. This is all ours." He spread out his arms. "The cold is staying. This snow's not going anywhere."

Shaw was good at making Eleanor Queen smile. Orla would always love him for that. Even if he did occasionally get side-tracked by his own impetuous ideas.

He tromped off into the trees, promising to report back on anything interesting he found or heard. The trunks looked so stark against the snow, like a thousand otherworldly doorways. A wind flittered in the branches, and Orla hoped the trees weren't gossiping about her and her silly, urban, unprepared ways. At least Shaw looked like he knew what he was doing. Orla marched back to the children and, despite her original intentions, got on her knees and helped them build up their mounds of snow. "This can be the dragon's back," she said.

"And it has to have a very long tail," said Eleanor Queen.

"And breathe fire!" said Tycho.

"No fire; the snow will melt."

"Oh yeah." Tycho never minded when his sister corrected him; he just laughed, realizing his goofy mistake.

They chattered about all the things their dragon would need—scales and teeth and ridges and wings. Orla pushed her hat up on her forehead, squinting, refreshed by the presence of the sun. On the branch of a nearby tree she spotted a cardinal, postcard-perfect, its red a merry greeting in the snowy landscape.

At some point they started using the dragon's spine as a wall and Tycho claimed one side of it and Eleanor Queen the other. They tossed loosely formed snowballs at each other. Orla excused herself then; her pants were wet, and even the children had lost interest in their sculptural task.

"I'll just be right in the living room, okay? Unpacking the books." They shouted okay without bothering to look at her. Orla slipped off her glove and snapped a quick picture to text to her parents, show them how well the kids were doing. When she reached the door, she stopped; she'd never just left them outside before. For the first time she appreciated the safety, the impossibility that anyone could drive up and snatch one of her children while she had her back turned. She didn't have to worry about them falling and encountering concrete or broken glass. And no aggressive kids were going to push them away as they played.

She let herself in and took off her boots, brushed the snow off her jeans. They stuck to her legs, cold, and all she wanted were her soft, warm pajama bottoms. She threw off her coat and flung it onto a box, then hurried upstairs to change.

In her room, she stood in front of the window, peering down at the kids as she stripped out of her pants. They were fine. Not going anywhere. Twenty feet from the front door. She told herself to relax. It was new, the children playing alone and out of her presence. But that's how she'd played when she was growing up. Roaming the neighborhood with gaggles of kids, staying for hours in someone else's backyard. She'd loved being independent, trusted by her parents to return at their designated time. She knew she could count on Eleanor Queen to stay within view of the house and not let her little brother wander off. It was part of growing up, being entrusted with incremental responsibilities. So Orla assured herself. Still, she quickly slipped into her pajama pants and slippers and headed back downstairs.

They were planning to get a bigger table, but for now they were still using the folding card table they'd had in the apartment. Orla pushed the remaining kitchen boxes past the threshold, then hoisted one onto the table and another onto the counter. The living room was more manageable then, with more space to maneuver in and fewer boxes to focus on. She poked her head into Shaw's studio before settling down with the boxes of books. He'd been up late, and the room looked completely finished.

It was all coming together.

She caught herself feeling more optimistic than she had in months. The craziness and stress of being perpetually between places was finally all behind them. It was time to unwind. Get settled. Embrace their fresh start—and the magic Shaw wanted them all to experience.

Orla bent over and pressed her forehead into her knees as she held her wrists loosely behind her heels. It felt so good, the stretch along the backs of her legs. She could've stayed there forever—or at least another five minutes. But then her children started screaming. Spears of high-pitched terror. She bolted upright.

7

Orla clambered for the front door, not bothering with her boots or coat. Outside…

White.

Nothing but white.

Blue sky and sunshine gone. The force of the wind made her stumble as she headed down the nearly invisible porch stairs.

"Tycho! Eleanor Queen!"

"Mama! Mama!" The children were yelling, but she couldn't see them.

The wind tore at her flimsy clothing and she clutched her arms against her chest. She slipped down the last two steps, falling onto her knees as one bare hand sank into the snow. The children were out there, and not far, by the sound of their voices, but the whipping snow obliterated her field of vision; she struggled to even keep her eyes open.

"Tycho! Eleanor Queen!" she screamed. "Keep shouting so I can find you!"

"Mama!"

Orla staggered toward their voices, her skin prickling with goose bumps and her heart knocking against the thin bones in her chest. She stretched a hand out in front of her and groped blindly, expecting to grasp the downy padding of one of the children's coats. They sounded so close. Except when the wind seemed to carry their voices away. Once, Orla twisted her head and looked up toward the sky, convinced she'd heard her daughter being sucked away into the atmosphere. "Eleanor Queen!"

"Here, Mama! We're here!"

Orla tripped over something. The dragon. Finally, she saw color in the whiteout. She grabbed for it. The red of Eleanor Queen's snow pants. She tugged at the red with one hand and grabbed at her son's blue coat with the other. The children scrambled for her, pressing their faces against her collarbones. She held them with all her strength, grateful to have them in her arms—and grateful for the warmth they provided. They couldn't stay out there much longer—Orla would be the first of them to freeze to death. She made herself stand, even though her cold muscles resisted such exertion, and dragged the children up to their feet.

The wind pushed, pulled, as the snow slammed in her face— where was the house? She took her best guess, lifted the kids, one in each arm, and plunged forward.

After a few steps…

Everything went still. The roaring wind died so suddenly that at first Orla thought she'd gone deaf. Then she realized there simply wasn't anything to hear. As the snow settled, falling gently back into place, the clarity of their surroundings emerged. The house. The garage. The trees. The blue sky— free of clouds. The sun, undiminished.

Orla took a moment to catch her breath. She let the children slip off her body and onto their feet. All three gazed around them, stunned by the ferocity of the weather, and shocked by its sudden departure. It was only when Eleanor Queen began whimpering that Orla regained her urgency. She clutched them to her sides and half dragged them back toward the house. Tycho struggled through the deep snow, so Orla hoisted him up and carried him like a baby in her arms.

Eleanor Queen dashed across the porch and held the door open for her mother. Once they were all past the threshold, they collapsed—Orla and Eleanor Queen in tears.

"What happened, Mama?" Tycho asked, his face pink and amazed.

"Blizzard—snow squall." Her hands were frozen almost stiff. And her slippers were soaked all the way through; her toes sizzled with pain. Her exposed skin felt like it had been whipped. With clumsy hands, she helped Tycho out of his boots and gear.

"It came out of nowhere." Eleanor Queen's eyes were wide and hopeless.

"Come on, everyone out of your wet things and we'll get warmed up." Though in truth, only Orla was chilled to the bone. "Mama can't stop shaking."

She didn't want her children to know her terror; better to pass it off as cold. Whatever had happened…what *had* happened? A freak weather burst? She'd seen bouts of wind like that tear through the five boroughs like a formless tornado, leaving strewn garbage and shattered tree limbs in their wake. In all their preparations, Shaw hadn't mentioned anything about dangerous snow squalls or the weather being so volatile and unpredictable. The flush of anger that he'd kept things from her brought warmth to her freezing limbs.

Eleanor Queen didn't want a bath, but she helped run one for Tycho as Orla toweled off in her bedroom. Orla put on two layers of sweatpants and shirts, two pairs of socks. Before joining the kids in the bathroom, she ran downstairs and turned the thermostat up to seventy-two. Her bones ached from exposure and she wouldn't have minded a few minutes submerged in the warm water, but the kids needed her.

As Tycho splashed in the bubbles, playing with a toy airplane, Orla sat on the closed toilet, with Eleanor Queen— cocooned in pajamas and a fleece blanket—on her lap. Tycho seemed undamaged by whatever had happened outside. He was back to humming one of his little tunes as his airplane made repeated crash-landings in the water. But Eleanor Queen trembled inside her cocoon in spite of Orla's strong arms around her.

"It was just a bit of bad weather. Winter can be mischievous like that." Orla didn't fully believe her own words, but she cooed them into her daughter's ear, hoping to ease her fear.

Eleanor Queen shook her head.

"No?" Orla asked.

Eleanor Queen shook her head again. "It wasn't regular weather."

"No, I'd say you're right about that. It was very sudden and intense, but still—it's just snow and wind. And it didn't last. It scared you, but you're okay. You weren't going to get lost or—"

"It wanted to eat us."

"Shhh." Orla rocked her. "It didn't want to eat you any more than the sun wants to kiss you or the rain wants to wash your hair."

From the tub, Tycho giggled.

"It did, Mama—I felt it." Eleanor Queen nestled even deeper against Orla's body.

She'd never felt such a strong urge to dismiss her child's feelings, but if she accepted Eleanor Queen's bizarre explanation—so different from the very real and immediate things that usually frightened her—then Orla wouldn't know how to reassure her. "You felt scared because it was hard to see with all the snow, and hard to breathe with all that wind. It's okay to be scared—everybody gets scared. But it's over, and you're safe."

Orla wished Shaw were home. He'd put their daughter at ease. Maybe he'd even put Orla at ease. She felt something too, a layer of fear she couldn't explain. Shaw would set her straight just as she was trying to do with Eleanor Queen.

A lingering spindle of ice twirled along her spine. What if Shaw had been caught in it too? Maybe there wasn't a cliff he could tumble over, but that didn't mean he couldn't get hurt and need help. And she wouldn't know how to find him. *Come home. Come home.*

"Okay my little loves." She set Eleanor Queen on her feet and stood. "Before our little Tigger gets all wrinkly like a raisin."

As she held open a fluffy towel, Tycho shot up out of the water. "I don't like raisins. Can we have hot cocolate?"

"Hot chocolate—does that sound good?" she asked Eleanor Queen, still hoping to find a way to comfort her.

The girl nodded, the blanket up to her ears and clutched beneath her chin.

Orla quickly dried off her son. "Then it's a plan." At least it gave her a direction, a distraction. And the assurance that in this, at least, she could give her children what they wanted.

She kept the kids busy with small tasks. They took turns feeding crumpled newspapers and twigs into the wood-burning stove. Orla lit it, and they all watched, mesmerized, as the flames spread and grew stronger. Then she settled a dry log atop the blaze and shut the stove door, all the while babbling about how warm it would be, how cozy, how soothing on a cold winter day. The devil on her shoulder dissected her words, ready to pick a fight: It was barely winter yet, still November, how bad were things going to get? But she'd save those arguments for Shaw. She let the children fold up the card table's legs, and the three of them made a production of carrying it into the living room—though Orla could have done it one-handed in a matter of seconds.

Eleanor Queen went on a search through the cabinets to find the newly unpacked mugs. Tycho tipped a packet of hot "cocolate" into each of them, spilling a halo of fine brown powder around the base of every one. Orla poured the hot water but let Eleanor Queen do all the stirring when she insisted she could do it without splashing even a single drop over the brim. And she was true to her word.

They hung out in the toasty living room for hours, playing Yahtzee, Uno, Chinese checkers. Orla heated up some canned soup for lunch—the freezer wasn't yet stocked with homemade staples—and pretended she wasn't worried that Papa hadn't come home yet.

The day remained sunny and clear, though neither of the children asked to go back outside to play. Tycho ended up taking a nap on the couch. Eleanor Queen slunk off to her room, her books. Orla started washing up the dishes, but stopped when she realized that each member of the family was in a different place—three different rooms inside, and somewhere outside.

A new fear struck her.

Would they grow apart? Would they instinctively seek their own solitude and forget how it had been when they were always on top of each other? It was something they'd sometimes complained about, but now Orla could see the disadvantages of having more space—the slow stretching of their connections to one another. For years, *making it work* had been a daily exercise in compromise, new dances with new choreography— sometimes a waltz as she swept around the obstacles, the people, on her way across the room; sometimes a polka with an impromptu do-si-do to avoid a collision. Would they stop trying to read one another's moves, moods, now that being in close proximity wasn't a necessity? Instead, would they walk away and succumb to the silence and separation that seemed to reside like a feral entity in most family homes?

She wouldn't allow it.

Orla abandoned the kitchen duties and returned to the living room. The boxes were already open so she started with the children's books, and it took little additional effort to slide them noiselessly onto their shelves. Sometimes she glanced at Tycho as he slept, floppy like the baby he still was. What a sweet boy he was going to be. She could imagine him in school someday with equally sweet and curious friends. They'd talk about going to Mars in all seriousness, their future as astronauts never in doubt. He knew there was a real-life Tycho who'd been an astronomer, although her son was actually named after his papa's best friend Lawrence's parrot. The parrot-Tycho liked to count down from ten and squawk, "Blast off!" For a brief period, she and Shaw had silently cursed his astronomer-parrot namesake as toddler Tycho—well acquainted with the parrot—screamed "Blast off!" in answer to every question.

The memory always made her smile; while other two-year-olds said "No" to everything, her little boy was ready to shoot for the moon. He'd be a remarkable man someday. She'd do everything possible to make sure he retained his kindness, his easy comfort with loving and being loved.

Just as she was about to project Eleanor Queen into the future—a girl who, even by name alone, would never settle for princess status—something clattered at the back door. Her pulse quickened and she sprang to her feet, ready to gather in her children, or fight. The first irrational image that came to her mind was of a fox—or foxes—with nimble hands and small tools, seeking to break in and rob the place. *You've been reading too many picture books.* Her second thought was a black bear, ready to shove its paw through the kitchen window in search of leftovers.

A *thump*.

A *whack-whack*.

She eased toward the sound, wondering which kitchen utensil could be used as a weapon. What was even available? A bamboo mixing spoon? A saucepan?

Should she get one of the guns?

Shaw stumbled in, bringing with him a spray of snow and a burst of cold.

Her panic deflated, but not before the worst thought ever assaulted her relief: *This is how families are shattered by fatal mistakes.* If she'd gotten the gun; if, in her fear, she'd seen a blur and not her husband...she'd never have been able to forgive herself.

He panted and propped the snowshoes against the wall, where slush dribbled off them. Orla crossed her arms over her chest, full-on angry. Despite the imagined catastrophe, she was certain that whatever had delayed him for so many hours was his own fault. She had the luxury of such condemning thoughts after seeing that he was, beyond his exhaustion, all right.

"Where have you been?"

He collapsed on the one kitchen chair that wasn't in the living room with the folding table. After unzipping his coat, he just sat there, depleted of energy, his body slumped.

"Get me some water?"

Orla filled a glass and handed it to him. Her outrage withered. Whatever he'd endured—though it hadn't resulted in broken bones—hadn't been easy. Or fun. He gulped down the water.

"More?" she asked.

He shook his head and handed back the glass. With effort, he hoisted one ankle up to his knee and started untying his boot.

"What happened?" Something wasn't right. And of all of them, Shaw was the one who'd greeted the wild North Country with zeal. Now he looked defeated. "Did you get lost?"

He uttered a bark, half laugh, half cry. "I didn't think I was gonna find my way back."

"Baby." Orla went to him and he wrapped his arms around her waist. And wept. His tears made something crackle within her; simultaneously, the basement furnace's internal fire bloomed to life. Was it uneasy too? Afraid? She'd never deny her husband his manly right to cry, but what had so shaken him? She wanted to ask him if they were safe but instead held him until he quieted, then got on her knees and undid his other boot. Lifted off his hat. Eased him out of his day pack. She left the boots on the doormat, so it would soak up the melting snow, and moved the snowshoes onto it too, leaning them against the closed door.

"Do you want something warm? Coffee? Tea?"

"I'm too hot," he said, slipping out of his coat, tugging at the neck of his sweater.

She pulled it off over his head; the T-shirt he wore beneath it was soaked through with sweat.

"Papa?"

Eleanor Queen stood in the threshold between the two rooms, watching. Cautious. Orla wondered how long she'd been there. Had she heard that he'd been lost? Had she seen him cry? Shaw's state was unlike him; neither of them tended toward the overwrought. And for the first time she realized she had nothing to picture when her husband was out there, alone. In the city, she knew all of his favorite places, could imagine him in his element when they weren't physically together. But here…

She shuddered, glad she hadn't thought of it sooner, the nothingness, the vacuum he'd disappeared into the moment he left the yard.

"I'm okay, Bean." He used his nothing-to-worry-about father voice and held out his hand to her.

Orla smoothed back his sweaty hair, ashamed she hadn't run

to greet him, to comfort him, the moment he'd come through the door. She stood there with an arm around his shoulder, smiling at Eleanor Queen so she wouldn't be so hesitant.

"Papa's fine. Had a long day in the woods."

Eleanor Queen kept her eyes on her father. She approached with the same vigilance she usually reserved for dogs; she didn't trust them even when they were sitting quietly, always afraid they would start barking or jumping. When she was within reach, Shaw reeled her in and gave her a kiss on the head. But she wouldn't let him keep her in his embrace. "Did it try to eat you?" she asked, pulling back.

"Did what try to...what?"

"We had a little adventure of our own," Orla said. "A little blizzard. Out of nowhere. But everybody's fine now."

A perplexed look lingered on Shaw's face. "It snowed here?"

"Briefly."

"It didn't snow where you were?" Eleanor Queen asked.

"No...no." He tried to laugh it off. "Man, I knew we'd get some crazy weather here, but it's not like it was when I was a kid."

With one hand, Orla massaged the tight muscle between Shaw's shoulder and neck. He looked up at her, giving her a conspiratorial raise of his eyebrows. It was a gesture they both understood and had used before, a silent request to postpone further discussion until they were alone, when neither of the children might overhear.

The house was so warm—too warm—but Orla shivered. She willed time to slow down, afraid of what Shaw would tell her after the kids were asleep. His words might confirm a scenario she wasn't sure she could gracefully handle—that maybe he didn't know how to live here either.

8

Supper was a moody affair, the family's usual chatter replaced by exaggerated slurps and chewing noises—or so it seemed to Orla. Eleanor Queen stared at her plate, poking fork holes in her noodles. Tycho let out an exuberant—annoying—*Aaaahh!* every time he gulped his milk. Shaw's fork clanged against his plate so much—what was he even cutting?—that Orla started to believe he was intentionally trying to get on her last nerve.

"What movie do you guys want to watch tonight?" Orla asked, hoping to break the weird tension.

"I'm probably going to skip the movie." All eyes turned at Shaw's uncharacteristic announcement. He must have seen the question on their faces. "I've got work to—"

"You love movies."

Orla wanted to kiss her daughter for sounding so accusatory; those were exactly the words and tone Orla might have used, especially if she'd wanted to pick a fight.

"Yes, my little Bean, it's undeniable. But I have an idea brewing, and it's time for me to start sketching."

"Did the trees tell you something?" Eleanor Queen asked, a hint of haunted awe in her voice.

Orla gave Shaw a withering glare. He knew better than to make light of it this time.

"No—nothing I could understand, anyway. I had to think up some stuff all on my own."

"Oh." She returned to piercing her noodles, disappointment evident in her heavily drooped head.

"Okay." Orla stood, quickly gathered up plates. "This weirdness has to end. You"—to Shaw—"get to your studio and do your thing. We"—to the kids—"are going to pick out the best movie ever."

Tycho skipped out of the room. Shaw and Orla exchanged glowers but waited until Eleanor Queen slipped away before speaking again.

"You are not helping," Orla whispered as they rinsed off the plates.

"What do you want me to do?"

"Act like you care that this isn't easy for the rest of us."

"You mean for you."

"Does Eleanor Queen seem especially happy?" she spat at him as softly as she could.

"It's our first full day, it takes time—"

"And you didn't have the best day either, hate to bring it up. So running off to your room to hide—"

"To *hide*? I came here to work!"

"What about the rest of us?"

He sidled up so close to her his spittle stung like venom against her cheek. "Don't think I haven't always known that you wanted me to *do* something, succeed at something. Well, I'm getting on track, my work is better than ever. I never got in your way—I supported your decisions, even when you changed your mind."

She knew he was referring to her abrupt change of plans after Tycho was born. Shaw thought she'd given the ECCB her notice, but she hadn't yet, in case…she still felt strong then; she wasn't ready. They'd been arguing about it for days—Shaw insistent for the first time that it was *his turn*—when Orla had blurted out the unforgivable.

"Are you going to bring in a regular paycheck? While you pursue your dreams? Because that's what I do—make a salary we can count on. It seems to me you have it easier if I keep working, because then we don't need to rely on you for most of our money."

She might as well have stabbed him in the gut with his abandoned knitting needles. She'd apologized immediately. But it didn't matter how many times she said she didn't mean it, because the truth of it, the tools of his "trade," lay scattered around the perimeter of their apartment. Orla had insisted that she believed in his talent, though he hadn't, at that time, found his calling. But Shaw came back with the most self-damning rebuke of all.

"I'd never have been able to stay in New York without you. And your co-op."

It was a pitiful admission and she'd struggled to decide if it was brave of him to confess it or a sign of something more pathetic that might unravel their future. Things had been tense during the final few weeks of her maternity leave. But once she was out of the house again, back to the routine they'd made work for many years, everything settled down. They hadn't had another serious argument since then. But neither had they ever experienced a scenario where they would both be home together indefinitely.

Their first full day in their new home had not gone well. And if this was how he was going to behave in the North Country, the move was going to be a mistake beyond what she'd imagined. They—she—had anticipated needing an adjustment period; they were well aware that everything about their lives in upstate

New York would be different than it had been downstate. But what if they'd failed to factor in an inability to constantly be in each other's company? And what if Shaw's grumpiness—or even the fear he'd experienced on his misadventure—was a sign that he was having second thoughts? *He* wasn't allowed to have second thoughts. Especially after one day. They had all uprooted their lives for *him* in support of a landscape he desired to put on canvas, in support of his one hundred and thirty square feet of personal space.

Orla considered blaming the house. Its previous owner had lived here for decades, and died here—perhaps in Shaw's studio. They'd found an enameled chamber pot in the room's closet when they cleaned it out; maybe in his final years, the old man had been too rickety to climb the stairs to the only bathroom. Was there a filament of him still here, slithering between them, making silent, grouchy demands?

More likely, it was the many rooms, the many doors. Were they growing apart already? Or did they need more rooms, more doors, to maintain the boundaries of their own identities? As much as she wanted to blame something, Orla recognized it was the people within the rooms that mattered, and how they handled their emotions.

As the movie faded to black, Eleanor Queen clapped at the triumphant conclusion and Tycho jumped up and down. Shaw popped his head out of his studio and asked if Orla needed help getting the kids ready for bed. She said no but went upstairs feeling buoyed by his offer. He had sounded more like himself; hopefully their day of minor struggles wouldn't wreck their equilibrium for long. When she came back downstairs, Shaw was waiting at the bottom holding two glasses of American Honey. For the first time all evening she grinned, and accepted the whiskey.

"I'm sorry—" they both blurted.

She followed him to the couch and scrunched into her pre-ferred corner. Shaw set the whiskey bottle on the floor between them and curled in beside her.

"I'm sorry," he said. "I didn't plan on the day being so stressful, and I'm not handling it well."

"I'm sorry too."

They clinked their glasses together, optimistic winners of a consolation prize.

"To trailblazers," he said.

"I don't know if I'm exactly blazing a trail; maybe singeing it a bit."

He snorted. "Well, tomorrow's another day. And I won't be so…I'll stick around, I promise."

They sipped in silence for a moment, gathering their thoughts. It felt good to be beside him, just the two of them, no one else around; it had been a while.

"You found a good idea?" she asked. It was important to her that he knew of—that he felt—her faith in him. "I guess I shouldn't have reacted that way—it's been weeks since you could work."

A dreamy look came to his face. "I can't really explain it. The imagery I see…the *certainty* I feel. It's even stronger now. Like the muse is saying, 'This! Look at this!'" He shook his head in wonder. "I printed up a few of my photos just for shape, depth. And started sketching, painted the first background layer."

"I'm glad, Shaw. I really am." Their fingers met, entwined. "Can we talk now? About today? The kids were so scared."

"I don't really understand—what happened?"

"I don't know. They were playing. I came in to do some work in the living room. Next thing I know, they're screaming. There was a total whiteout—"

"Oh my God."

"I couldn't see a thing. I found them and started helping them inside and then...back to clear, sunny skies. Like nothing ever happened."

"That's really odd." His face spoke more than his words, and she wondered if he was thinking of his own frightening experience.

"Tycho was more or less unfazed afterward. But Bean...I just...I so hoped this would be something she's not afraid of, and I don't want her to be afraid. Especially on the first day."

Frustrated, Shaw shook his head, reminding Orla of the rocking of an Etch A Sketch, erasing an image. "I know. I'm sorry. I should've stayed—I know...I kept thinking, when I was out there and couldn't get back, that it was my punishment. I was thinking the whole time that I shouldn't have left, you're all new to this place, and it was my...I convinced myself—I was sure the forest was punishing me. For bad decisions."

Orla didn't like how he was anthropomorphizing the wilderness again. She didn't think Mother Nature interacted with individuals any more than she believed Jesus did. And it reminded her too much of Eleanor Queen's unsettling description—like a bad dream come to life, of something wanting to eat her.

She inched closer to him and squeezed his hand. "I still don't understand why you couldn't get back?"

Shaw downed the rest of his drink—fortifying himself?—before he continued. "I had the map. I had the compass. I know how dense the trees can be around here. Growing up, several times a year, we'd hear stories of tourists who wandered off the trails and the search and rescue teams were mobilized. It should have been easy, so easy, to see where I'd been—leaving tracks all over the place in the snow.

"I hadn't even gone that far...fifty, sixty yards out to the big pine—we'll have to take the kids to check that out, must be five feet across its base. I didn't think eastern whites could even get that big. So, anyway, then I went just beyond it up to the northern edge of the property, and I hung a right, following the boundary markings on the map. It was beautiful, the trees powdered with snow, the blue of the sky. Everything pristine. Quiet, muffled, the way snow does."

His head made a metronome of *no*s as he tried to puzzle it out. "I got the camera. Started taking pictures. Then I caught this…wood smell. Something burning. And I knew there shouldn't be any homes out that way, but I started following this smoky smell. And I came to, like, this ruin. A chimney. An old stone—"

"Was there something burning there? When we first got here—"

"No, not at all. It was probably just carried in from another direction. So I took a few more pictures and then wanted to continue on, follow the perimeter of the property, come back home. But…I couldn't see my footprints. They should have been everywhere, I was just traipsing around. I thought…maybe there was some wind, and it covered the tracks. But…I would have felt that much wind. It would have taken time to bury all those…"

An electrified needle pricked Orla's scalp, raising the hairs across her skull. It sizzled down her arms and she hunched her shoulders up, her body contracting, reacting to the presence of wrongness.

"Something's wrong out there." She blurted the words out before she could even think. Instinct.

He shrugged. "I'm just…maybe I'm more out of practice than I thought."

Orla suspected Shaw wanted to reassure her—that's what one did in response to someone's crazy supposition, especially since she sounded like a tepid, poorly written character in a horror movie. Perhaps she was overreacting to everything, out of her element and spooked by her own imagination.

"And it was so weird because I should have been able to use the big pine as a marker, the way you used to be able to use the Twin Towers to get oriented, north and south. But…I couldn't see it…so I checked my compass, but it was frozen."

"Was it working before you left?" An alcohol-inspired paranoia was setting in, or something even more ridiculous. Maybe there was a spaceship buried on the land, or some old meteor that messed with magnetics and weather, and…all she knew about surviving in the wilderness came from movies she'd seen with Shaw. And if those had been rather horrifying movies— or cheesy black-and-white science fiction flicks— that was Shaw's fault for having such twisted cinematic tastes. And he wasn't helping. Maybe he was embarrassed, afraid they were in over their heads. He'd never been the leader before, and now he couldn't even navigate around his own yard.

"I didn't check it before I left, I just assumed…"

"You have to be more careful." She took a gulp of the sweet whiskey, hoping to swallow down the lumpy pill of her anger.

"I know, I'm just…it's been a while."

So maybe the compass had never worked. And maybe the wind really had covered Shaw's footprints. And maybe they were both feeling the pressure because they didn't have the internet, and everything familiar was far away, and everyone trusted that they knew what they were doing, and no one had said, *Are you really sure about this?* To the contrary, all their friends—even Orla's parents—thought the move was enviable, an accomplishment. Slowing down. Simplifying. Everyone talked of how great it would be to see natural wonders right outside their window. Because Shaw was *from there*. He *knew what he was doing*.

"I panicked, I guess. Walking in circles like a stupid...maybe I was just afraid of myself, of what I'd done to our family. And what if the kids don't like it, and what if you don't like it. And there I was, like an asshole, walking in circles—"

"Stop, babe. Please don't talk about yourself that way. You were scared, and just like I said to Eleanor Queen, you're allowed to feel scared. It can't be like when you were a kid— you're not a kid, and we have responsibilities, but they're *our* responsibilities. You're not—"

She froze when Shaw lurched off the sofa. At first she thought he was upset about something or trying to avoid their conversation. But then it registered: the look on his face. Alert. Afraid. Searching. Had one of the children cried out in their sleep? But she didn't hear anything—from upstairs, or anywhere else. Her arms goose-pimpled again. "What is it?"

By his posture, his focus, the cock of his head—*just like Eleanor Queen*—he was searching for a sound. A sound she still couldn't hear.

"Shaw?"

He stepped toward the front door, then abruptly turned and strode a few paces toward the kitchen. Just as suddenly as it came on, his intense look dissipated and his shoulders relaxed. Rattled, he finger-combed his hair and dropped back onto the sofa.

"What was it?" Something crawled inside her skin.

"I don't know. I thought I heard...I heard something. Never mind." He sat forward, plucking up the American Honey bottle.

Orla thrust her glass next to his and he splashed the golden alcohol into both. Her heart drummed a warning as she gulped it down. But Shaw settled back in, ready to pick up where they'd left off. The lines around his eyes appeared more pronounced than they'd been only moments before. He needed a good night's sleep.

"Why don't we—" She wanted to lead him to bed, but he thrummed with an energy that defied how exhausted he looked. Fingers tap-tapping a message against his glass, reminding her of Morse code.

"I want you to know," he said, "I did more in-depth research about this area, since we hadn't been seriously thinking of this as our destination when we first visited St. Armand and North Elba and Harrietstown. And it's not just for the tourists—there are lots of creative folks in the village year-round, and there's at least one place, a community arts center, where I might be able to do some teaching. I e-mailed them a while back, just to know our options. I could teach drawing or painting or digital photography—or guitar. I'm not gonna let us run out of money."

"I appreciate that, but that's not what I want for you. I've seen the progress you're making—in the past year, and even more in the past few months. I want you to have this time—this is your time. We have resources to live on—"

"But just in case. And our savings won't last forever. So that's a possibility. You might even be able to teach ballet there."

Orla sat up a little straighter, as if the very thought of doing something dance-related required better posture. Her body felt lighter than it had in weeks. "I'd like that. That would be an awesome part-time gig." She hadn't considered teaching ballet a viable possibility, not in the wilderness. When she'd done her own supplemental research, she hadn't been able to get past the emptiness, the limitations. Everything was farther away than she was used to, but that didn't mean civilization didn't exist—people, and the various gathering places that drew them. The future suddenly seemed less foreign, less abstract. Promising, even.

"If we can fortify what we have with part-time stuff, it's still creative—"

"I want you to be able to do your own work," she said. But it was reassuring.

"I will—I am. This new one…" He nearly vibrated with excitement. "I swear, I wasn't trying to freak out the kids, but this place…between my dreams and what's really here, what I see…come look!" He abruptly snatched her glass, put it with his on the floor, and grabbed her hand.

At last she could giggle as he led her into his studio. How many times had he asked her to listen to his new poem or song or look at the new thing he'd made? This was familiar. This was a piece of home that would never change.

He'd taped the photographs, printed on cheap copy paper, on the wall beside his easel. The canvas depicted a rough sketch of trees with broad strokes of sky peeking through.

"So I know you can't really tell a lot yet, but the limbs— they're going to be fused together, from one tree to another, like it's one organism. And there are going to be these details in the bark, almost like human anatomy, giving a sense of a nervous system, musculature—but subtle, so you have to look close. And then belowground…this part is all my imagination, because obviously I can't see it, but the roots are going to look like…I haven't completely decided. Maybe human arms and hands—"

"Oh God, that's creepy."

"No no, I don't mean for it to be creepy. I want to convey how there's this…intelligence belowground. A community. Among the roots. And how other things interact with it. So I thought if I depicted the roots with human hands…you know, there might be a rabbits' nest, and one of the rabbits is sleeping in the palm of a hand. Like that."

"Ohh...ah." The revelation came out as two syllables. "Like, nurturing."

"Exactly. Trees work together. And they also provide a lot to the surrounding habitat. I wanted to get across this idea of...interconnectedness. Symbiosis."

Orla spotted one of the other printed pictures and moved closer to get a better look. "Is this the chimney you found?"

"Isn't it cool?" Somehow he managed to sound even more excited than he had when describing his work. "I'm guessing it's got to be really old. Our very own ruin! The one reward for getting lost."

She scrutinized the stack of rocks, but couldn't figure out why Shaw should be so enamored of it. "So was there a house there?"

"Maybe. Some sort of structure stood there, a hundred years ago. Might get a better sense of it in the spring, when we can see the land better."

"Interesting." A hundred years ago the surrounding area would have been even more remote, yet someone had chosen— from so much available land—to build a home not far from theirs. Had this person known something about this place that made it special? Or perhaps they were simply more attuned to a beauty that Orla didn't yet appreciate.

She continued to ponder the rather comforting idea of a by-gone neighbor as she turned her attention back to the sketched lines and washes of color on Shaw's canvas. He had such a vision for it, and that alone amazed her. "Your clarity. Sense of purpose." Shaw beamed. "Who are you and what have you done with my husband?"

They shared a laugh and she wrapped her arms around him.

He kept his eyes on his unfinished painting. "I know people

thought, for the longest time, that I'd wasted so much time, money, on all those random classes, books, supplies…but I'm ready now, and it's all coming together."

"I'm immensely proud of you—I want you to know that. So many people quit, give up. But you knew you had something in you, something to say, a vision, and you kept working until it came into focus."

"I've needed all the things I've done to get to this point."

"I know."

He turned to her, hands on her waist, a crazy-pleased grin on his face. "I love you so much, Orlie."

"I love you too—and I promise I'm going to embrace all of this newness. I want this too—for you, for all of us."

His battery finally faltered and she kissed his drooping head before guiding him back to the living room, the sofa. A smile lingered on his face as he lay down, put his cheek on her lap. She fingered his hair and they stayed like that for a while, appreciating the silence. The noise of the city had been so ever present she'd barely noticed it. But here—this was what quiet sounded like. The soft *whoosh* of the furnace coming on. The occasional hum of the refrigerator. They grinned in unison, reacting to a light thud above their heads, certain of its origin: one of Tycho's toys dropping from his hand to the floor as he slept. They always found toys beside his bed in the morning.

I could get used to this.

She didn't say it aloud because another thought accompanied it. He did believe, on some level, that the trees communicated—which didn't mean he thought they whispered ideas to him. Maybe he only meant that they spoke to one another. He'd never talked about nature like that before, but she understood how the artistic process required people to *open* themselves. To see and listen. To draw new conclusions about the world. It made her wonder…

Her husband, like her daughter, was highly sensitive, and she didn't doubt his ability to tap into things that didn't register for other people. Especially while he was in this state of creative blossoming. Could a place *really* call to someone, like some sort of invitation?

Instead of spooking her, the thought made her smile. It would mean they were wanted. And that was encouraging; she might not always feel like the bungling stranger. She would find her way, and someday feel a true sense of belonging.

9

True to his word to make up for the previous day, Shaw headed out in the radiant morning sun to work on the snow dragon, but only Tycho tagged along to assist him. Eleanor Queen considered it; she looked outside, scanned the terrain, then shook her head without saying a word. She helped Orla unpack everyone's clothes. The boys came in an hour later, the cold rising from their coats, dusted with white, their faces rosy and victorious. After a simple lunch, Shaw retreated to his studio, and Tycho took a nap. When Orla came down from organizing Eleanor Queen's closet, she didn't find the girl on the couch where she'd left her, though her book was there, open and facedown on the cushion.

"Bean?"

She caught an unnatural splash of color from beyond the front window: Eleanor Queen in her coat and hat, nose to nose with the snow dragon. Orla smiled, glad her daughter felt comfortable enough to go back outside alone. Shaw had raised the wall that formed the dragon's spine, with curved mounds on either side for its body. The spine gradually sloped downward to form a long, undulating tail. They'd built up a stack of snow for its front legs and neck and made a blocky head for it. When Orla saw it after Tycho and Shaw came in, it had been only a rudimentary shape, though recognizable as the dragon they intended. But now, after Orla had opened the front door, stepped onto the porch...

The dragon was detailed with swirls and scales, the snow carvings of an expert sculptor. Shaw could have produced such work, but there hadn't been time, and she was sure it hadn't looked like this earlier, with a finely shaped head, large, protruding eyes, and an open mouth that...moved. Eleanor Queen gazed at it, its face at her eye level, and though Orla couldn't hear it speaking, she could see her daughter nodding in reply. The dragon's mouth curled into a grin—and then, seemingly aware of the trespassing observer, it turned its head toward Orla.

She raced off the porch, panicked. "Eleanor Queen!" Her daughter was too close to it. The dragon was surely only pretending to be friendly—at any moment it would open its mouth and swallow her child.

Eleanor Queen turned a little toward her mother's voice, unalarmed.

When Orla looked again, the dragon was a primitive pile of snow pushed together by the mittened hands of a father and son. She stumbled, stopped. Reality wriggled, but she tried to proceed as if things were normal. "What are you doing out here?"

Eleanor Queen shrugged. "Nothing. Just saying hello."

Maybe it was the snow, white everywhere she looked, but Orla felt dizzy. Everything spun and for a second she thought she was inside a child's snow globe, being shaken. She wobbled, then steadied herself. "I thought it moved."

"Mama?" Eleanor Queen hurried over, tramping along the flattened area where her father and brother had collected their snow. Her brow furrowed as she gazed up at her mother. "You okay?"

"Let's go inside." Orla let her daughter go ahead of her and looked back one more time at the snow dragon. A lumpy nothing. She blinked hard. Had she imagined it?

When she came in and took off her wet shoes, Eleanor Queen was already back on the couch, reading.

"Are you having more fun now? Playing outside?"

"Yup. Sometimes. It's better when everyone's being friendly." She kept her eyes on her book.

Everyone? Who else could've been out there besides family?

"I'm glad." Cold air blew against her back and Orla realized she'd neglected to shut the door. But after she closed it, she still felt shivery and hugged her arms tight against her body. Children had playful imaginations. That didn't bother her. But what had Orla seen? Had the movement been due to a trick of the eye? The wind? Could sun glare on snow create a mirage?

Whatever it was, it left her feeling unwell. "I'm gonna go upstairs and lie down for a minute."

"Okay, Mama."

Orla spent the rest of a lazy Sunday afternoon in bed, hoping she wasn't coming down with the flu.

On Monday she felt like herself again, and soon after exchanging a few texts with Julie, she heard a van rumble up the drive. It was installation day for their satellite dish. A flurry of excitement ensued when the doorbell rang: Tycho shouted, "Someone's here!"; Shaw whipped open his studio door; Eleanor Queen galloped down from her room. It had been four days since they'd seen anyone but one another, and they all clustered in the open doorway, grinning at the satellite guy as he stood on the porch. Occasionally, during the ballet's off-season, they might have spent an entire day at home as a family, especially if it was raining and they needed a break from running around. But nothing about their previous lifestyle had tended toward reclusiveness.

The satellite guy—who Orla, after decades of living in one of the world's most diverse cities, could only think of as a commercial-perfect white dude; he even had a camera-ready, but also genuine, smile—slipped inside partway through his work to check on their signal. When it needed a bit more tweaking, Orla donned her coat and boots and followed him back out.

The snow dragon looked to have solidified overnight, its arched spine trimmed with ice. But it was otherwise ordinary and nonthreatening, and she brushed off the previous day's woozy delusion as the symptom of a twenty-four-hour bug. She watched as the satellite guy climbed up the ladder to fine-tune the dish's angle, unperturbed by the cold, the snow, the height, or the roof's steep pitch. As Orla moseyed away from the house, he whistled a cloudy tune from his perch on the ladder. Orla respected the perfect balance he'd acquired after years of working on a step only a few inches deep. No wobble or hesitation. He probably had a strong core. She spotted movement on the ground ahead of her, a fluttering in the snow. Curious, she moved closer.

Then closer still when she couldn't quite decipher what she was seeing. Even right on top of it, she bent over, squinting against the dazzling white. More movement. Like something digging itself out. She thought of baby turtles, newly hatched, using their flippers to free themselves from the sand.

Was that a wing? A bird, trying to surface through the snow?

No. An ear. Pointy and alabaster. And then she saw a snout and a pair of amber eyes.

Startled, she realized it was a fox and took a half step back. But it wasn't one of the safecracking foxes from her imagination, burglars with miniature tools. This one wouldn't be robbing anyone. It couldn't even stand or walk. It had a bulbous tumor growing out of its back that seemed to be causing it pain. And the look on its face begged for mercy. Orla thought she heard a little mewl. She looked up toward the satellite guy to see if he heard it too, but he kept his eyes on his work, absorbed.

As Orla leaned in again, the fox's tumor moved—a head lifted, and a pair of long, floppy ears, as furry and alabaster as the fox, broke through the snow. Not another fox, but…a hare?

She couldn't make sense of it. Were the two animals stuck on something, caught in a trap buried under the snow? Tentatively, she swept at the snow with her foot, wanting to see what lay hidden beneath. But the more she looked…it wasn't possible, but they appeared to be fused together.

Orla brought a hand to her cheek. Did she have a fever? Was it longer than a twenty-four-hour bug? She thought of summoning Shaw, but he was working, and what if she was hallucinating? She didn't want him to worry or insist she see a doctor; they hadn't even found a new family doctor yet, though they had a list of physicians in the area. And if it really was an animal—or animals, somehow trapped together in the snow— why should she make it his problem? In the city, she'd never needed him to squash the spiders or crawly things she found in the apartment. She'd released the more gentle-looking bugs out the bathroom window and balled up the others in a wad of tissue.

The two-headed thing at her feet looked so…wrong. She considered asking the satellite guy to come see it; maybe this was a mystery better understood by the locals.

The thing—things?—grew restless, writhing as if they wanted to run off in different directions. The fox had a pair of forelegs, but did the rabbit? Were there other legs still hidden in the snow? It/they squealed, thrashing harder, trying to escape each other. The fox barked, growing more desperate. It managed to inch forward, dragging the hare behind it.

Oh God, this just wasn't right. These mangled creatures were suffering, but the pity she felt paled in comparison to the revulsion.

She lifted her boot. The thought of delicate skulls crunching unnerved her. But she had to do something. Put them out of their misery. *Make it go away.* Finally, she brought her boot down, a decisive stomp. Nothing cracked; no blood oozed from beneath her foot.

"Mrs. Bennett?"

Had he seen it? And seen what she had done? Orla turned, and the satellite guy was looking at her. She didn't bother to correct his assumption about her name; sometimes she liked her double identity. The domestic Mrs. Bennett; the professional Ms. Morcau.

"Want to see if the signal's stronger?" he called. "I unplugged the router, so just plug it back in and give it a sec, then turn on Netflix or something."

So he hadn't seen her euthanize a pair of anguished mutants.

"Okay." She looked back at the spot in the snow, fearful of seeing a smattering of tiny bones, or a smear or a twitching, as when a very resilient cockroach wouldn't quite die. There was nothing. The surface of the snow was displaced from where she kicked it around. But there were no signs of any other disturbance.

On Tuesday, with access to her internet curriculum, Eleanor Queen resumed her schoolwork, head bowed over Orla's laptop as she watched tutorials at the kitchen table. Their days settled into a routine: Shaw worked in his studio, door closed; Orla snuck in minutes on her laptop to order window coverings, miscellaneous minutiae, and a basic gun locker, and she played with Tycho—outside or in the living room—between other tasks; Eleanor Queen diligently worked through math and reading and world cultures assignments. Afterward she'd join her mother and brother in whatever they were doing—cooking, playing, folding laundry.

On Friday afternoon, Eleanor Queen's schoolwork finished, the three of them sprawled on the living-room floor and made artistic masterpieces.

"Mama?" Eleanor Queen asked, concentrating on painting a tree. Shaw had found the remnants of a roll of brown packing paper in his supplies and given it to the kids to use. Orla had suggested they make a long, collaborative piece to hang above the sofa between two of Shaw's cityscape paintings.

"Yes, love?"

"Could I keep doing school at home? Even next year?"

Orla looked up from her doodle. She was glad Eleanor Queen liked working independently, but she had hoped her daughter would find friends here, at school. Ones who stuck and didn't overpower her or shove her aside. It had been an important part of Orla's motivation for moving, her expectation that the North Country children would be less demanding, less competitive than the kids at her daughter's city school, less like a jar of frantic bugs desperate to scrabble out into adulthood.

"You like working at home better?" Orla asked.

"Yeah. It's easier to focus, and not as much is going on. And after I watch the tutorials I can do as much as I want."

Orla frowned. She couldn't argue with her daughter's reasoning, that she liked working in solitude and at her own pace. "You know we wanted to get Tycho enrolled in kindergarten for next year—"

"Am I going to school? Yippie!" As he jumped up, his paintbrush released purple droplets onto the scene he was painting. "Oops. Mama, I messed up my zoo."

Oh. Now Orla understood his splotches of color were a menagerie of animals. His face started to crumple and she felt his sorrow, his disappointment, at spoiling his masterpiece.

"It's okay, no damage done—these can be the ladybugs and bumblebees."

"And moth-quitoes! And lighting bugs!" He dropped back down to his knees, his face awash in excitement, and dabbed more pinpoints of color around his animals.

Orla turned back to Eleanor Queen. "So we were going to enroll you too. The schools here are much smaller. Maybe you'd like that better?"

"I don't know. Can I keep doing it this way if I want?"

"Why don't we both keep an open mind and decide after we see the school. And then we can talk about it again. Okay?"

"Okay."

Orla admired the skill and discipline Eleanor Queen displayed in her work. Her tree was very detailed, reminiscent of the pine behind their house that reached for the sky. Its textured bark looked almost like a map, or a maze of rivers. Though it was beautifully rendered, Orla couldn't quite like it. She was tempted to ask her daughter if she'd been influenced by her papa's work, especially the first forest painting he'd completed, which he called *Connected*. Something about her daughter's depiction made it seem more human than tree, but where Shaw had captured a sense of community, of sheltering, Eleanor Queen's tree looked...wicked. Maybe it was the confident, almost haughty stance, the branches too much like knobby arms. If the drawing came to life, it would point its finger at her and boss her around.

No, it would do worse than that.

She touched a hand to her cheek as if she could already feel the mark, the backhanded slap of a branch.

Neither Shaw nor the children had grumbled about aches or

pains or congestion. (Or alarming visions.) But Orla couldn't shake a feeling of...*off*. Something was off. Was this what cabin fever looked like? Could it start so soon?

Once—years before the children were born—she'd set a bag of potatoes in the apartment closet because she thought the darkness would be good for them. Months later, a stench settled in. She thought a rat or squirrel had died under the floor, but eventually Shaw sniffed out the source: the potatoes, long forgotten in the closet, had blackened and liquefied.

Why did being in this house remind her of that? Of something rotten she couldn't quite pinpoint?

No one else was complaining. Although Orla hadn't exactly been forthcoming with her own sensations and delirium. If she couldn't chalk things up to something obvious or shared, she'd keep working on putting them out of mind. Lock up the strangeness in a little mental box so she wouldn't risk infecting her entire family.

10

Saturday began and ended with rainbows of color. Orla first saw them in the morning, reflected on the wall as she sat on the toilet. As the sun beamed through the frosted window, the pattern bedazzled a small section of wall with dots of color. She gazed at it, tempted to call Shaw or the kids in to see it. Specks of refracted light, tiny as pieces of glitter.

That night, after supper, Shaw stayed in the kitchen to wash the dishes, and Orla headed upstairs to hang the last of the bedroom mini-blinds. She'd hang the simple curtains another day—an attractive accessory rather than a necessity. Shaw didn't even think they needed the blinds, with the dark nights and no streetlamps. But Orla anticipated the longer days—months away—when the sun would creep in to set their eyes afire before they were ready to awaken. And she still didn't like the possibility of anyone looking in on them. Even if, in theory, there was no one out there.

She'd done the children's rooms earlier in the day, with Tycho, her helpful assistant, who kept dropping the screws onto the floor. Alone, it would take her a fraction of the time to finish the last upstairs window in her and Shaw's bedroom. Afterward she'd see if she could drag the kids away from the TV, their addiction so easily renewed.

The step stool squealed along the wood floor as she kicked it into place in front of the master bedroom's big window. On the middle step, drill in hand, she was just about to start when something outside flashed across her field of vision. She gasped and had to clutch the window frame to keep from losing her balance as she almost stepped backward into empty air. Hopping off the stool, she tossed the drill onto the bed and ran out of the room.

"Shaw? Eleanor Queen? Tycho? Get your boots on!" she called as she sprinted down the stairs.

The kids had that vacant, gaping TV-glazed look on their faces as they watched Orla pass in front of them and hurry toward their new boot tray and their coats hung neatly on hooks. "Come on! Everybody! Boots, coats!"

"Are we having a fire drill?" Eleanor Queen asked.

"You'll see, come on."

The kids jumped up and joined her, stuffing their feet into their boots.

"Shaw?"

He peered around the kitchen doorway. "What's up?"

"Come on! Outside, you have to see this."

"There in a sec." He wiped his hands on a dish towel.

Orla zipped up Tycho's jacket and plopped a hat onto her own head. When the kids were sufficiently bundled up, she opened the front door and ushered them out. She led them to the edge of the porch and watched their faces light up as they looked skyward.

"Wow!" Eleanor Queen sounded awed, and her eyes went as round as the previous week's moon.

"Isn't it amazing?" Orla could barely contain her exhilaration. She'd always wanted to see the aurora borealis—and here it was, in her front yard. Ribbons of green and teal, pockets of purple and pink. The colors undulated like a dance.

"What is it, Mama?" Tycho asked.

"The aurora borealis—the northern lights. Isn't it beautiful?"

She saw the greenish glow twinkle in his eyes, but Tycho looked more perplexed than impressed. Eleanor Queen, on the other hand...

"It's...wow. All my favorite colors!" She reached up as if she could touch it, and the dancing colors seemed to respond, contracting toward the invisible tip of her finger. Orla gasped at the illusion before howling with delight, and even baffled Tycho giggled, pointing at the sky to try the trick himself.

"What are you guys oohing and aahing about out here?" Shaw shrugged on his coat as he stepped onto the porch.

"Look! You didn't tell me about this!" Orla grinned at the heavens above them.

Shaw came to her side, interlaced his warm fingers with her cold ones. He looked upward. The lights performed their cosmic tricks, wavering and rippling. But his face didn't erupt in wonder or awe. Orla was about to mutter something about the boys in the family and their lack of appreciation for something that people traveled far and wide to cross off their bucket lists.

Instead she said, "You don't think it's beautiful?"

"Of course. But...what's it doing here?"

"What do you mean?"

"We're too far south—we don't get the northern lights here. I mean, a glimmer, maybe, under just the right circumstances, but not like *this*. You have to be near a magnetic pole, like in the Arctic—Alaska, Scandinavia—to see it like this. And it would have been in the forecast."

He sounded almost angry. Orla's good feelings started slipping away, dripping down her arms, pooling in the snow beneath her fingertips. It was only a week since the whiteout; she hadn't forgotten the terror in her children's screams and Shaw circling their property like a ghost, unable to find his way home. And since then, even if not every day, there were the other things that maybe weren't possible that she'd shut away in her mind.

"You can also see it at the South Pole," Eleanor Queen said. "But then it's called the southern lights."

"That's right. Aurora australis," said Shaw. "But still. We're even farther from the Antarctic."

Orla wanted to punch his arm, get him to snap out of his weird mood. He watched the sky in a wary way, like a hiker waiting for a poisonous snake to wriggle off his path. But the defiant lights gamboled on.

"Did you read about the aurora australis for school?" Orla asked Eleanor Queen, impressed by her knowledge.

"No, it was in one of Derek's books."

Eleanor Queen had never shown much interest in weather or astronomy in the city; Orla felt renewed gratitude her children had gotten to spend time with their cousins; maybe it had helped them transition more than she'd realized.

"That's a good idea," Shaw said, coming back to life, his response a puzzling non sequitur. He reached into his pocket for his cell phone.

"What are you doing?" Orla asked.

"Calling Walker. See if they see it too."

He needed a rational explanation, and she couldn't blame him. They hadn't talked again about his scare the previous Saturday, but neither of them had felt comfortable enough since then to go exploring with the kids. Orla had been impressed with his discipline all week, the hours he spent locked in his studio, the multiple paintings in various stages of completion. He'd ordered a second easel, which would be delivered on Monday; for now, his assembly line of canvases were propped up around the perimeter of the room. But maybe his series hadn't, after all, been his only motivation for staying in. Maybe he was afraid to go outside. It was clear he didn't appreciate the light show and, perhaps, feared it on some level. She was glad when the kids leapt into the yard, giggling and tossing up handfuls of snow; they wouldn't overhear Shaw's conversation with his brother, his concern and doubt.

"Hey, it's me," he said into the phone. "Nothing, just standing outside, looking at the sky. What are you guys up to? ... Hey, so I won't keep you, I just wanted to see—do you have unusual lights? Colors in the sky?"

There was a longer pause, and Orla imagined Walker getting up from whatever he was doing and going to the nearest window to pull back the curtain and peer out.

"You sure? ... No, I was just wondering—reminded us of the northern lights, and it wasn't in the forecast, that's all...okay, yeah. And one of these days we'll get a proper table and have you guys over...okay, talk soon."

He put the phone back in his pocket. "Nope. Not there."

"Well, maybe it's regional." She didn't want him ruining something so beautiful. She didn't care if the lights weren't supposed to be there—she'd always wanted to see them. They were a blessing.

"The sky isn't regional." He still sounded resentful.

"Maybe it's global warming, or—"

"There's nothing global about this."

They stood shoulder to shoulder for a time, but Shaw wouldn't relax and enjoy the cosmic display.

"It's nothing, Shaw. Don't get so worked up about it."

"I want to know how this is possible. And last week. And—"

"So what do you think it is? An apparition?"

"What?"

She didn't want to ruin the moment. She wanted to believe

what Shaw had promised though perhaps hadn't meant so literally—that they'd find magic in their natural surroundings. But the odd instances were starting to pile up.

"This isn't the first thing I've seen," she said, her voice low. In the yard, the children slapped clumps of snow onto the dragon, adding ridges to its spine.

"What are you saying?" He turned to her, his eyes wary and hyperalert.

Orla wanted to take it back, blabber about miracles instead, but they'd never make it here if they didn't communicate with each other, and she'd already withheld enough.

"I saw some things, that's all. Things I couldn't explain. Nothing harmful—not like that day with the whiteout. I'm just trying to figure it out. Would it be better for these lights to be here? Just here, where no one else can see? Or better for them not to really be here but we're seeing them anyway?"

Was a collective family hallucination better than a personal one?

Tension registered in Shaw's face as he considered her words. A muscle in his jaw clicked and he nodded.

"No. You might be right."

But instead of clarifying what he was agreeing with or what it meant, he summoned the children in an urgent voice, as if a threat were at hand: "Bean, Tigger, let's go back in. Let's get ready for bed."

They loped through the snow and onto the porch, where Shaw helped them brush off their pants legs.

Maybe there were wonders that none of them understood. Mother Nature could have tricks up her sleeve that newbies like them didn't know about. The snow rollers, she remembered, were a natural phenomenon. But Shaw wasn't waiting around to debate it. He ushered the kids inside and followed them in, leaving Orla alone with her thoughts, pieces from disparate puzzles that wouldn't lock together.

Natural. Phenomenon. Natural. Phenomenon.

She rolled the words around in her mouth until they felt like a secret language.

This new world was strange—but wasn't this what they'd wanted? To get out of their city bubble and have new experiences? She wanted (was desperate) to have faith in all the things that left her uncertain, to believe that the move (their home) was a *good* decision—even if that meant examining paradoxes and acknowledging anomalies that hadn't been relevant in her urban life.

"There *could* be miracles," she said to herself. And after a lifetime of vivid dreams that always left her questioning the foundations of consciousness, she couldn't rule out the possibility of a higher power—one not beholden to explain its every move to her. Mother Nature, Gaia...these feminine, terrestrial (celestial?) energies seemed more plausible to her than the masculine godheads that propped up organized religion. In this new place, she needed to embrace new possibilities, even if just to discover the natural world that she hadn't previously given much thought to.

Orla was willing to accept the possibility of mysteries— especially if they manifested in such beauty. The sky danced. She'd wanted her family to marvel at it, to revel in it, but maybe this dance, this moment, was just for her. She'd never been a religious person, but she felt, all around her, something omnipotent that she couldn't explain. *This is what draws people to nature.* She felt it in her bones, the stardust of her cells acknowledging the stardust of her ancestors. And who was she but a speck among the vastness of the universe? It was important to be reverent, to be grateful—not just scared—as she bore witness to a holy power.

This is why we came. It was starting to make more sense, how Shaw had been called to return.

What an amazing place. A place not to be underestimated. A place that redefined *impossible;* maybe her imagination was more limited than she'd ever considered.

When the chill started to seep into her toes, she turned and let herself back into the house. She kept telling herself, *It's a good thing, it's a good thing, it's a good thing.* And hoped she wasn't just rationalizing, just talking herself into it (just ignoring her intuition).

When Shaw didn't come up to bed, Orla crept down to his studio. With the furnace set low for the night, the floorboards were cold against her bare feet. She'd been thinking about their situation for hours. It made her feel resourceful, and she wanted his approval for finding both a rational explanation and a solution for something beyond her everyday experience.

She tapped lightly on his door before opening it. He didn't acknowledge her as she stood in the doorway; he stayed poised in front of his easel, making quick strokes with a thin brush. From this angle he looked...different. Burly. He needed a shave. There was something almost werewolf-like about him, as if he were becoming as unruly as the land. She had the impression, from the gargoyle-intense expression on his face, that he wasn't painting but performing a dissection.

Curious to see how his work was developing, she crept closer. It was another tree, rendered in dark colors. It had a morbid quality—and subtle details—that drew her in, so near she practically stood beside him. The tree branched into a Y, and within its trunk...a human form, a figure divided, with two torsos but only one set of legs. It reminded her of conjoined twins and then—she gasped—of the hybrid animal she'd seen in the snow.

Beside the tree was something much less ghoulish: a cabin. He hadn't gotten to its finer details yet, but she recognized the stone chimney. The picture was from the same angle as the printout on the wall, only instead of painting the young trees that were growing beside the ruin, Shaw had conjured the structure that might once have been there.

"Huh." It struck her how well proportioned it was.

He started, uttering a little noise of surprise. "Hey."

"That really looks…right. Like, it fits with the chimney perfectly."

It was as if he'd come out of a trance and now, awake, he looked back to his canvas. A smile softened his features. "While I'd love to take all the credit, I did a little digging around online. Architectural styles of the region and time—guessing a bit, of course. But it might be pretty close." He rubbed his eye with the back of his hand, leaving gray smudges in his eyebrow. "What time is it?"

"Almost one thirty."

"Geez, sorry."

"No, I didn't mean to interrupt you, but I had an idea."

"For a painting?"

The question confused her for an instant. "No. An explanation for the weird…things."

"Oh." He set his brush down and picked up the old tea towel flung over his thrift-store ladder-back chair, now repurposed to hold his supplies. He scrubbed off his hands.

"So, remember when we tried smoking weed all those years ago, and after a few times I had that scary moment?"

"When you hallucinated?"

"Exactly. That was a chemical disruption in my brain. And upstairs I started thinking…we didn't have the well water checked." It made so much sense to her, but his face remained fixed and confused. "Let me back up. So there's a lot of stuff in the news associated with fracking, but this doesn't have to be that. Well water getting contaminated by drilling and chemicals. And what if that happened to our water? We have no idea what's in it, but maybe there's some kind of pollutant in it and we're…"

"Hallucinating. Interesting theory, Orlie." His head bobbed, and she could almost see him thinking back on things.

"We can call someone to come out and test it, and in the meanwhile we can boil everything or buy bottled water for drinking and see if these weird…visions or whatever stop happening. Maybe we're under the influence of…something…half the time and don't even realize it."

Shaw nodded more enthusiastically. "Yeah…yeah, that's good." He grabbed her upper arms and planted a kiss on her forehead.

That's when Orla realized just how worried he'd been, how he'd hidden his troubled feelings from her. But now she didn't feel the victory of her resolution. He could call it inspiration—he could call it being considerate, staying inside and not leaving them alone—but it was more evident than ever: He was hiding; he wasn't wholly comfortable out here. Maybe he really was the city boy she'd always known. Or maybe he'd been seeing—or hearing—unexplainable things too. She wasn't sure which possibility was worse—that they didn't trust each other with the truth anymore, or that they were both doubting their own sanity.

11

Usually the mail carrier just left the mail in their box, situated next to the road at the end of the winding driveway, not visible from the house. They'd met him only a couple of times, when he'd driven their packages up to the porch. He wore a hat with earflaps and drove a four-wheel-drive postal service jeep, and he'd told them he always delivered to them early, as they were near the beginning of his route. Orla had established a new favorite routine, something she never would have imagined enjoying: strolling the sixty yards down to the mailbox every morning, cup of tea in hand. Now, almost two weeks into their new life, she looked forward to seeing how the routine would change as the seasons turned over—come summer, would she brave the walk in bare feet? Would the path be dotted with wildflowers?

It was another crisp, clear day, but she didn't mind putting on all her winter gear to make her serene walk. Steam rose from her mug, and the warmth of the tea, as she swallowed it, countered the chilly air. They were on their fifth day of using boiled and bottled water, and someone had come out two days before, Tuesday, to test their well water. She and Shaw had started consulting with each other every night before bed, but there'd been nothing new or odd to report. The household had been filled with giggles and music and chatter all week, bolstered by a renewed optimism.

In the city, quiet time had been at a premium. Orla realized now she'd craved it more than she'd been consciously aware. Those Saturday or Sunday mornings when she'd snuck out early on no discernible mission other than to see the streets with no traffic, the sidewalks with no people. Sometimes it was a very narrow window of opportunity, and the cars and people would creep into her solitude. But before they ruined it, Orla marveled at how different it all felt, how peaceful, with the city that never slept subdued in its hour of slumber.

And here, beyond the boundaries of a cluster of small towns, they were, technically, nowhere in particular. While she was no longer lacking in quietude, the morning jaunt to the mailbox was often her only chance to be by herself. Or to walk anywhere. Eventually she'd have to summon more courage and start taking little walks around the property, maybe even venture deeper into the woods. She wouldn't survive long term without being able to stretch her legs—beyond her body's need for it, it was imperative she not feel trapped.

She walked in one of the rutted impressions made by their SUV. It had been a few days since they'd driven anywhere—their last venture out was to the nearest pizza place, thirty minutes away—but it hadn't snowed since then and the tire tracks still looked fresh in the parallel ruts. It was so quiet she could hear wind rustling branches in trees far away and, closer, the muffled splat as snow lost its grip on a limb and tumbled onto a drift below. Orla smiled seeing her cheery friend the resident cardinal looking down on her from a branch above her head. The air smelled only of cold and the foreign aroma of cardamom wafting on the air from her tea.

Part of her morning ritual included being very aware; she made a point of noticing things she hadn't seen before. Shaw had picked up the practice in an acting class he'd taken years earlier, and it was something they both incorporated into their lives—when they remembered. It had been harder to do in the city, where slowing down on a sidewalk was likely to result in impatient pedestrians bristling past. But here...she let her gaze wander, paused whenever she saw something that required more of her attention. Such as...tiny footprints?

At first she thought they were bird tracks in the snow—perhaps left by her feathery red friend? But on closer inspection...she was starting to regret the details she noticed every time she leaned in to get a better look at something.

She recognized the pattern. It couldn't have been more obvious; she had a print of it hanging across from her bed. But it was impossible. *We boiled the water.*

Some contemporary choreographers used a system called Benesh Movement Notation, though most of the ones she'd worked with preferred to use video. The choreography was recorded on what looked like a five-lined music staff, but it documented sections of the body, not musical notes. Early in her career she'd become fascinated by older systems to record chore-ography, and she'd discovered Feuillet and the French dances he'd documented in the 1700s. The notations were drawn with swirling lines, as if you were looking down and seeing the patterns on the floor made as the dancers moved around. Her favorite, the one Shaw had framed as a print for her, was called simply *Balet*. It showed in mirror image two double-lined S-like shapes with matching curls and swoops. On their bedroom wall, it looked graceful, if abstract. On the snow, it looked...

Wrong.

She blinked hard, clearing her vision. Maybe it wasn't really there. Maybe she thought of dance so often, even if subconsciously, that now she saw it materialize in the landscape of her new world.

She peered at the markings again. And laughed at herself. "You're losing it."

She'd been right the first time: little bird footprints etched in the snow.

With a bit more haste, she continued on until she reached the road. The shriek of the mailbox's rusty hinges was a violation; it left a bloody color in her mind.

They paid all of their bills online and never got much mail, but she was never disappointed when the box was empty. In fact, it was something of an accomplishment; they didn't need to waste trees to communicate. But today there was personalized junk mail from their new satellite company and their new bank. She stuffed them in her coat pocket and turned around to follow her footprints back to the house. Although she'd been bothered the day they moved in that the house sat so far from the road, now she liked it. She liked walking a deserted path without having a single structure in sight, at least for a short way. And although once that had made the location seem dangerous, that no one knew they were there, now it felt safer. No one could spot them from the road, unless their chimney was smoking.

Slowly, Orla was acclimating to the new concept of invisibility. She was inconspicuous now, a person without a stage, a platform. After so many years of being a performer, she'd anticipated an itchier adjustment. Maybe Shaw had been right that it would be easier for her away from the city, with fewer distractions. Fewer reminders. (Bird tracks in the snow notwithstanding.) Fewer bright lights to linger beneath.

As she brought the mug to her lips, it suddenly blew out of her hands. A gust of wind that caught her by surprise.

She bent down to pick it up. The splatter of tea on the snow reminded her of dog pee—from a slightly ill dog. That made her chortle until a blast of wind knocked her off her feet. The snow came next, descending on her like a wall of wasps. The frozen particles whipped her cheeks, tiny razors that felt sharp enough to draw blood.

Gale-force gusts assaulted her from every direction, and she struggled to stand. The mug forgotten, buried, she shut her eyes against the frenzied snow, uncertain if she should hunker down and wait it out or plow homeward. Last time, the whiteout had ended before she'd even gotten the children into the house; maybe this one would dissipate just as quickly. She kept her body folded over at the waist and made a battering ram of her head, determined to get to the safety of home.

The wind rushed toward her face, forcing itself down her throat. It stole her breath and she gulped like a fish on land, momentarily panicked by the sensation of suffocation. She tucked her mouth in under her coat and struggled onward, glad the kids weren't with her.

There was an excitement to it, to the danger, the randomness. After they'd spent so many years keeping track of schedules—the never-ending who-where-when, the jigsaw-puzzle picture constantly changing depending on what was going on in the busy family's life—it was oddly fascinating to be kidnapped by the unexpected. Part of her even appreciated the weather's show of power. It reminded her to be more humble, especially after an adulthood spent working for applause. There were things about the world she didn't understand, and this—now, as she struggled to breathe, to stay upright—didn't have to be something adverse. She was open to the possibility of being put in her place, a minuscule creature awakening to the vastness, the unknown, spinning in tandem with the perpetual outward force of the big bang.

She pushed forward, unaware of anything but the wind and snow. Even that struck her as appropriately philosophical; she was wholly in the moment. Her new life, she decided, required mindfulness, appreciation, and, yes, becoming more philosophical. In a place devoid of the endless entertainment she'd once taken for granted, she'd go crazy if she couldn't find meaning and satisfaction in the things around her. She'd replace the fine art of ballet with the fine art of contemplative gratitude.

The ground around her started to brighten, not unlike the first moments on a stage, and she turned toward the light. But she didn't recognize what it was until too late.

12

Parallel beams of light emerged through the swirling snow. She realized they were headlights just as the car was nearly on top of her.

The bumper struck her hip; it was like being smacked with a two-by-four, and down she went again, certain the vehicle was about to run her over.

But it skidded to a stop.

And the wind died.

And the snow.

It settled into stillness as it had before. A shaken snow globe set back on its shelf.

And she saw now: it was their car. Shaw scrambled out of the driver's side.

"Orla!" His voice sounded so loud against the now quiet backdrop, the roar of wind silenced by the shutting of a giant door.

"Did you see it?" Orla asked as she lay in the snow.

"I didn't see you! The snow—"

"You saw it, then?"

"Yes, a total whiteout." He fell to his knees beside her. She rubbed her leg. "Are you all right?"

"I think so. The snow…" She was about to say it had cushioned her fall. But it had also caused the accident, which could have been much more serious. "What are you doing out here?"

She hadn't even noticed the SUV missing from the garage; she'd assumed Shaw was behind the closed door of his studio.

"I ducked out to that little bakery we found. Wanted to get everybody some bagels. Are the kids up?"

"Yes, watching TV. I didn't know you weren't in the house."

"Sorry, I thought it would be a nice surprise. Can you get up?" He helped her to her feet. Helped her limp around to the passenger side of the car. "I didn't see you until the last second, I'm so sorry."

She sank into the seat, wincing a little as a tender bruise pressed against the cushion. Shaw went around and clambered in the driver's side. After he closed the door, they sat there in safety, dazed.

"No matter what the water test reveals—" she said.

"No, these weather bursts are real."

Was he implying that other things might not be?

"I don't get it," he said. For a moment he remained deep in thought, his hands on the wheel, looking around at the peaceful land. "Maybe I should call someone. See if this is some new thing. These wind bursts."

"Who?"

"I don't know. I'm sure there's someone local who reports snowfall and wind and what have you to the weather bureau."

Orla nodded, but her thoughts were jumbled. Only moments earlier she'd been ready to believe in the capricious weather's rightful place in the universe, willing to kneel before its omnipotence. She'd been willing to adapt for the sake of holy and important. But Shaw almost killing her with their car…that wasn't holy. "Maybe you were driving too fast."

"What?" He turned to her.

"Snow on the ground…the potential for more snow any second—isn't that what this region is famous for?"

"Not exactly."

"I just think…you shouldn't make assumptions, because a blizzard could happen at any time—"

"Whoa! Are you kidding me? You think the problem is my *driving*?"

Even though on some level she knew it wasn't *entirely* his fault, some of it was—the fact that they were even there. "Whatever the water test says…look, it's winter, it's going to keep snowing. We should take whatever precautions we can."

Beside her, Shaw clenched his jaw. She could read him well enough to know he was grumbling inside, trying to decide whether to fuel the fire or snuff it out. He sighed and his shoulders drooped. "Maybe you were right, what you said the other night. Global warming is disrupting weather patterns all over the world. Maybe this area has become prone to unusual changes. Gonna Google it; maybe someone's been blogging about it or something."

"Okay." That sounded reasonable. "But…we need to find a way to manage this, and with the kids—"

"I know," Shaw said, sounding irritated as well as impatient.

"It's not your fault. I'm sorry if I implied—"

"I did just almost run you over."

"Maybe I shouldn't have been walking in the middle of the driveway."

He shook his head. "It's not you. Once again, I leave you all and…a snow burst."

"No, Shaw—that's just a coincidence."

"Am I supposed to never leave? Was I supposed to not bring you here?"

So he was doing it too, trying to rationalize whatever was

happening. He was internalizing it differently, almost ego-centrically. Was guilt coloring his perspective? Still, she saw him grasping for reason, if not reassurance.

"We'll figure something out." She squeezed his wrist, clueless as to what they might conjure as a solution, but she tried to sound confident. "We should get back."

He turned the key in the ignition and the car lurched forward, but he drove the last thirty yards to the garage at a snail's pace and Orla knew she'd gotten through to him. It could happen again at any time. And one of the children might be playing in the yard.

They'd agreed not to mention the most recent weather burst to the kids, who were on the sofa when they blustered in, blissfully absorbed by *The Iron Giant*, a movie they'd seen a thousand times, as it was one of the few they could always agree on.

"Who wants a real New York breakfast? Fresh bagels!"

"Me! Me!" the kids replied.

Orla saw it in Shaw's actions and the way he spoke—he was overcompensating. She felt it too, a sense of owing the children something. Something safer—less ominous—than the new life they'd been given, though neither had openly complained. She limped after them into the kitchen. Her injury likely required ice, but she opted to stick her aromatherapy pack in the micro-wave instead. She liked the way it smelled, like chamomile and lavender, and she kept its warm comfort against her hip as they ate.

Shaw smeared thick wedges of cream cheese on the kids' apple-cinnamon bagels, and Orla made them hot chocolate. So far, their Adirondack diet was appalling, but Orla was conscious to never crack jokes about how fat they were all going to get lest Eleanor Queen become another girl-victim of unrealistic body expectations. Orla had never liked it when people—friends, relatives, near strangers—made comments about her thinness (or giraffe limbs or swan neck or turned-out duck feet) in front of Eleanor Queen, fearing the girl would compare herself and make judgments about her own body, how it should or shouldn't be. But at some point, they had to get back to a healthier manner of eating.

After breakfast, Orla and Shaw agreed on a half-baked, better-than-nothing plan to create a guideline that would extend along the edge of the driveway from the far side of the garage out to the road. They went down into the basement and dug around the detritus that the previous owner had left behind, searching for usable supplies. Orla soon got distracted by a box of books and lifted up the flaps to see what treasures lay within. "Hey—maybe we should join an online book club. And find one for Eleanor Queen!"

"We can do that." But Shaw's focus was on the wooden posts and the abandoned tools he'd found.

"History. Nonfiction stuff mostly, it looks like." She blew dust off the edges of a slightly mildewed book, absorbed in her find. "Pretty old, most of it."

"This should work. Orlie? Earth to Orlie? I think we found what we need."

It was Shaw's idea to attach a rope between the posts (if they could get them into the frozen ground) and trees, so Orla could trail her fingers on it as she walked to the mailbox. If another whiteout happened, she could find her way back without being in the middle of the driveway.

"Right." Orla closed her box of books, planning to inventory it later, and hoisted it up.

"You're really gonna lug that upstairs?"

"Yup. We need all the books we can get."

"They stink."

"Old doesn't mean bad. Maybe there's a valuable first edition here worth a zillion dollars."

"I don't think anybody'd keep anything down here they really cared about. Carry a bit more?" When Orla nodded, Shaw laid some rope and bundles of cord on top of her box. He grabbed the posts and tools and they headed upstairs.

"Walker might know of someone local who monitors the weather. That might be pretty big around here, like a Meetup group or something," she said. It seemed that weather was a favorite topic for everyone, everywhere; her father started every phone conversation with Pittsburgh's temperature and precipitation forecast. It made sense to Orla that in a place with dramatic weather, where the temperature and precipitation actually mattered, even more people would be in the know.

"Maybe." Shaw sounded noncommittal. "Could ask around too, when I'm in town. Maybe people rely on a certain forecaster more than others. Maybe we need to use a different app."

Orla suspected there was an underlying pride issue and he didn't want to ask strangers—or his brother—unintentionally naive questions. No man wanted to come off as the stupid city guy, especially one who'd grown up an hour away. And were they certain that anything abnormally weird had even happened that morning? In a short span of years, New York City had become more susceptible to hurricanes—they'd been lucky to live just blocks beyond the evacuation zone when Sandy hit. Orla knew she was out of her element in this part of the state, and new and strange weather patterns were a real possibility. Yup. That, at least, almost made sense.

They were being smart; ignoring the mysterious weather wasn't going to make it go away. Better to be prepared, if they could. And making the guideline kept them all busy. Shaw used a sledgehammer to drive the posts into the ground, and maybe they were mostly held up by snow, but at least they were standing. Orla knotted the cord around the posts; they needed only a few, as most of the driveway was lined with trees. She wrapped the rope around the thinnest available trunks, hoping to make the bits and pieces last to the end of the drive. Tycho followed along, jumping in his father's boot prints as he sang a little song about blowy-glowy snow. And Eleanor Queen held on to the bundles of cord, unspooling it as they moved ahead, and explained how people made similar guidelines around the buildings at the science stations in Antarctica—more information she'd gleaned from Derek's book. "Just like this, so the scientists won't get lost if a blizzard strikes. You could freeze to death really fast."

"We're a long, long way from Antarctica," Shaw said.

"And good thing," said Orla. "I don't want any polar bears in our backyard."

"Polar bears!" shouted Tycho, more excited than afraid.

"Did you know that *arctic* means 'bear'?" Eleanor Queen asked.

They all admitted to not knowing that.

"So polar bears live in the Arctic, and *Antarctica* means 'no bears,' so that's how you can remember that there are no bears at the South Pole."

"That is a fantastic explanation," Orla said.

Eleanor Queen looked quite pleased with herself.

"Well, we don't have to worry on either account," said Shaw. "As this is neither the North or South Pole, we're just being cautious, since there are no sidewalks around here."

"That's right," Orla agreed. Though, since the subject of bears had arisen, she couldn't help but glance behind her, unable to shake the feeling of being watched. (Or hunted.) She didn't care how unlikely it was; if Mother Nature could summon the aurora borealis (*We all saw it*) and freak blizzards, why couldn't she summon a polar bear? A lost and hungry polar bear.

In spite of her sore leg, the moment the guideline was finished—tied off around the thick post that supported the mailbox—Orla challenged the kids to race her back to the house. The morning's near disaster and talk of bears had unnerved her. Tycho and Eleanor Queen took it as a game, but Orla was encouraged to see how fast they could run.

13

O kay, that's good…" Orla shouldered the kitchen phone and wrote down everything on a notepad while resisting the urge to ask for correct spelling. "Is that bad?…Should we do more testing?…Okay."

Shortly after the phone rang, Eleanor Queen had left the table, where she'd been doing schoolwork, and wandered to the back door. She lingered there, gazing out, her breath fogging up the glass window.

"You're sure? You'd feel safe having your own kids drink it?…Okay, thank you…We will, thanks again, bye." She hung up. "Shaw?" she called out toward his studio. He didn't respond, but Tycho bounded in carrying a coloring book. He joined his sister at the back door, standing on tiptoes to see out the window.

"Shaw?" Orla called again, though her attention had been diverted from delivering a message to her husband to investigating the object of her children's interest. "What are you guys doing?"

"Looking, Mama," said Tycho.

"What are you looking at?" She peered through the window

over their heads. Tycho, apparently unsure of the answer, turned to his sister. "Eleanor Queen, did you finish your chapter?" Orla asked.

"Can we go out there?" her daughter said, pointing.

Orla had yet to venture into the thick woods behind the house; after Shaw's misadventure their first day, she'd been trying to pretend it didn't exist. Barely twenty-four hours ago Shaw had almost run her over. She wasn't keen on visiting new terrain. "I don't know…"

"We won't get lost," said Eleanor Queen, reading a portion of her mind. "We'll just go visit the tree, it's lonely. It's right there."

"We'll visit the tree, Mama."

"What's out there?" Shaw asked, bustling into the kitchen, seeing his family huddled at the door. His fingers were speckled with orange and red paint. He elbowed the refrigerator door open and grabbed a fresh bottle of water.

"Hey." Orla stepped over and leaned her hip against the fridge. "Just talked to the water guy. He reports…" She consulted her notepad. "No coliform bacteria—that's the main thing they look for, he said. They did find trace amounts of arsenic but he wasn't concerned, said it—"

"Yeah, there are trace amounts in a lot of water. So that's all good?"

"That's what he said."

"Okay." He seemed neither pleased nor relieved. Orla, uncharitably, would have described him as impatient and a little distant, the same mood he'd woken up in. She'd heard him get up and go downstairs in the middle of the night. "Just checking on something," he'd said upon returning to bed. All morning he'd had the lack-of-sleep grumps.

"We're going out to the big tree," said Tycho. "Right, Ele-Queen?"

"Okay, well, have fun." Shaw started to head back to his studio.

"Wait." Orla was growing weary of Shaw's disciplined-artist routine; it seemed more like self-consumed avoidance. "Did you want to come with us? The kids want to check out—"

"I'm working."

"Okay, so." She was certain that if he needed anything, it was a nap, not more time holed up in his studio. "Do you think it's safe?"

"We're not going to get lost, Mama, I already told you." Eleanor Queen sounded peevish.

"Thank you, Bean, I appreciate your confidence, but we don't know everything about..." Orla didn't finish. Did they— she—know *anything* about what was out there? She wasn't a thousand percent sure that trace amounts of arsenic couldn't cause some sort of problem, but Shaw wasn't bothered by it, and the water guy wasn't bothered. And the more days they were there, the more the idea settled in her bones: this place existed outside the realm of other places she had been, and there were gaping holes in her understanding of *natural phenomena*. The logic she'd previously applied to living in a city couldn't be relied on here.

"You're probably better off if I'm not there," Shaw said. "I'll stay inside." He strode out of the kitchen with his precious bottle of water and his wounded ego. Orla didn't have the patience to deal with his self-pity, even if he was, on some level, acknowledging both the potential for future strangeness and a concern for their safety. Between her husband's distraction and her daughter's annoyance, Orla wished she could retreat to her room, where she could shut the door and scream for a moment.

"The water's safe!" Orla announced to one and all. "No more boiling."

"Yay!" Tycho cheered.

"Well, I'm glad someone's happy about that." She poked her head into the living room and shouted louder than was necessary at Shaw's back. "So we don't need to be wasteful with the bottled—"

He shut his door, ignoring her.

She should've knocked, on principle. But instead, she stormed after him and entered his studio. "Doors are not for shutting in people's faces."

"Get out!" He reeled, startled, trying to block his second easel with his body.

"Why are you so crabby?"

"It's not finished, I don't like people to see—it's not right yet."

Since when had he cared about her seeing his unfinished work? But she wasn't interested in that painting. It was the one on the other easel that made her grimace. It depicted a stand of trees, shorn in half by what could have been a tornado— or a giant with a machete who'd whacked his way through the forest. But instead of woody pulp where the branches had been cleaved, the limbs bled. Bones poked through. They looked like sharp, severed *human* limbs.

"That's—"

Shaw moved to stand in front of the painting. "It's just an experiment."

"It's disgusting—no offense. No wonder you're in such a bad mood."

He softened. "It's not part of…it just came to me."

"I'm thirsty!" Tycho galloped into the room.

Orla immediately hoisted him up and spun him around so he faced the door. Shaw, displaying good sense, picked up the offending painting and turned it toward the wall. Orla snagged Shaw's bottle of water from his chair, handed it to her son, gave him a gentle push out of the room.

"You're going to scare the kids," she hissed under her breath.

"See? Good reason to keep the door shut." He gestured toward it, inviting her to leave.

"Nap. You need a nap, not more hours sniffing turpentine." She marched out, and the door clicked shut behind her.

Hands on her hips, Orla considered her options. At the end of her rope and in need of fresh air—some space, some movement—she marched back into the kitchen. "Okay. Boots, snow pants, the works. Let's go visit our friend the giant tree."

"Yay!" both children cheered.

Eleanor Queen's eruption of glee soothed some of Orla's disgruntled edges, though a part of her was still tempted to call through Shaw's door and tell him to send a search party if they didn't return in T minus sixty minutes. She was being overly dramatic. And vindictive? And she was determined to be the less disturbed parent. *Bleeding trees?* They were only going in a straight line—there and back—not trying to survey the property with a map and a malfunctioning compass. Nothing to be afraid of.

14

It was easy. Eleanor Queen led the way confidently, though they were trampling across unblemished snow. Still, Orla kept glancing around, on the lookout for…

They were making enough noise to keep the bears at bay. How she loved her little boy who liked to sing. And she made sure they didn't wander from their chosen path, their chosen mission, lest the weather surprise them with another squall. Her vigilance paid off when she spotted something, not dangerous, but startlingly beautiful—an albino deer stepped lightly between two trees. The delicate placement of its hooves made Orla think of pointe shoes, but the children tromped ahead with such purpose that before she could urge them to slow down and appreciate the scenery, the deer had leapt away.

"Mama, look!" Eleanor Queen gasped a moment later, pointing upward.

"What is it?" Tycho hopped in place beside her, eager to see.

"A snowy owl! With big golden eyes!"

Eleanor Queen sounded so pleased. But when the other two followed the direction of her finger, they saw only dark and empty tree limbs.

"It flew away," she said, hurdling over a small branch in their path.

They'd taken only a few more steps when Tycho inhaled sharply, his face alight as his mittened hand directed them to look at a spot between two drooping trees.

Again, they stopped, but Orla couldn't make out anything but snow-covered brush.

"There's nothing there." Eleanor Queen ran on ahead.

"It was there—I saw a wolf!"

"A wolf?" Orla gripped Tycho's hood to keep him from moving even an inch away from her. The cry of *wolf* made Eleanor Queen halt her steady advance and turn around, her wide eyes uncertain and glued to her mother.

"It was all white, with eyes like little suns—very friendly, Mama."

Orla refused to let her mouth twist into a smile, but she winked at her daughter. Tycho, as younger siblings often did, liked to mimic his sister. "Well, your friendly wolf must have scampered on home."

"Yup!" He galloped after Eleanor Queen as she darted off again toward the towering pine, content to follow her lead.

Orla wished Shaw were there—he was putting too much pressure on himself and could've used a moment of unexpected wonder. Maybe this was what he'd sought all along, a place that ignited his imagination. And she felt some remorse for getting so frustrated with him. He bore a burden she didn't share— his idea, his *turn*—and who was she to judge the content of his work? She didn't like the roller coaster of emotions that had come between them since the move.

Eleanor Queen was already slowly circumnavigating the tree when Orla reached it, holding Tycho's hand. It was as impressive as she remembered. As wide as a person was tall at the base of its trunk, it rose so high she had to tip her head all the way back to see its top. The gray bark looked ancient—deeply ridged and furrowed. Like the surface of a withering planet. Most of the enormous branches radiating from the trunk far above them were gnarled and bare. Only its crown, in the stratosphere above their heads, remained evergreen.

"What a big pretty tree!" said Tycho, skipping around its base in his sister's boot prints.

"It is magnificent." Orla used her cheeriest voice. "And very, very old—five hundred years!"

Tycho beamed up at the giant, full of awe.

Eleanor Queen maintained her pensive stroll around the pine. She'd taken off one mitten, and trailed her fingers along the bark as she walked. Orla was afraid her perceptive daughter had noticed what she'd noticed—the abundance of dead branches, the scattered bits of green, mostly visible near its tippy-top. Death was spreading upward from its roots. Orla thought that probably meant it was already dead, except the upper branches were so high, they hadn't gotten the message yet. Even though it was far enough from the house, it would suck if such a massive tree gave up its hold and toppled over. It would cause so much damage to the surrounding trees and make the back part of their acreage almost impassable. She made a mental note to bring it up with Shaw; come spring, they might need to have a tree person come out and give them advice.

Already losing interest, Tycho wandered over to much smaller evergreens to knock snow from their sweeping lower boughs. Orla tried to keep him within reach while also not losing sight of Eleanor Queen in her meditative march, but a queasy nervousness grew as she juggled the needs of both children. By necessity, she stuck closer to her rambunctious son, but she worried that another squall would strike and swallow Eleanor Queen from her view.

"I think we should go back now." She could have sworn the

temperature was dropping. Maybe this was an early warning sign; maybe she was acclimating to her new environment better than she'd thought. "A storm's coming, we don't want to get caught in—"

"There's no storm," said Eleanor Queen. She dropped to her snow-pant-padded knees at the base of the tree. Like a supplicant, praying.

"Come on." Orla gestured to Tycho. He bumbled over and grabbed her hand.

"Is it time for hot cocolate?" he asked. That had always been their treat in the city when there was a big snow.

"I don't think we can have hot chocolate *every* time it snows here; that would be a *lot* of hot chocolate. Bean, come on, we're going home."

"I'll come home in a bit." She showed no intention of getting up and falling in line.

Excuse me? This was exactly the sort of independence they'd hoped Eleanor Queen would develop, but Orla doubted that even Shaw would think it was a good idea to leave her outside now—especially given the capricious nature of the things they'd experienced.

"I can't leave you out here on your own, and it's time to head back."

"Why not? I led the way here—I know how to get back."

"I appreciate that. I know someday soon you'll be a master explorer and be able to show us all around the land—"

"It's not about that."

"Eleanor Queen." Orla was losing her patience. It was definitely getting colder. She felt it—something was coming.

"Something's coming, Mama."

A chill razored down Orla's spine. "I know, that's why we have to go." She reached for her daughter, tugged on her arm.

"That's why we have to *stay!*" She yanked her arm back.

Tycho started pulling on Orla's hand, ready to go. Orla was caught in the middle as her two children insisted on heading in separate directions. Eleanor Queen squirmed away, forcing Orla to drag Tycho with her as she reclaimed her grasp on her daughter's puffy jacket.

"Now, Eleanor Queen Bennett, I won't tell you again!"

Orla rarely had to use the I-mean-business voice, but her daughter accepted defeat. Tears sprang to her eyes, but she allowed herself to be towed back toward the house.

"You don't understand," the girl whined.

"So explain it to me." But Orla wasn't really in the mood to listen; she kept a wary eye on their surroundings and tried to determine if the air temperature rose as they neared the house.

"I can hear it better out here and it's really, really, really trying to tell me something and I don't know why I can't just come in when I'm ready and there's nothing else to do here so why won't you let me stay outside!"

Orla's breath came out in a great plume of relief when they reached the edge of the forest and the house came into view. She'd caught only pieces of her daughter's disgruntled rant.

"Did you hear me, Mama?" This time it was Eleanor Queen doing the tugging, trying to get her mother's attention.

"We're almost home."

"So no, you weren't listening! That's why you can't hear it! That's why I have to do everything myself!" Eleanor Queen broke away and marched ahead toward the house.

Her daughter seldom spoke with such ferocity, and Orla felt a twinge of guilt. But only a twinge; Eleanor Queen didn't understand what was out there. Orla didn't understand it any better, but she felt the imperative to keep her children safe.

"Don't worry, Mama." Happy little Tycho grinned up at her. "Ele-Queen's just mad 'cause the trees use a lot of big words that she doesn't know."

"Oh, is that it?"

"Yup, she told me."

"Well, thank you, I feel a little better now." She didn't feel better. At all. Were her children whispering in the dark too, like their parents? Comparing oddities that amused—or frightened—them? Her family's once-easy equilibrium was all out of whack and she didn't know how to right it.

They followed Eleanor Queen's boot prints straight through the back door, left ajar. A nagging thing dragged its claws across Orla's thoughts, snagging on a piece of fabric that wouldn't, even with repeated efforts, disclose its big reveal. She'd missed something. In the woods. With her children. And the nagging thing—the sharpness of its claws—warned her that it was very important.

15

Orla lay in bed beneath the cozy spotlight of her bedside lamp, flipping through one of the musty books she'd found in the basement. A few others rested beside her on the comforter, faded, clothbound history books, some with glossy pages of black-and-white photos. On the wall across from the bed, the framed Feuillet *Balet* print winked, drawing her attention. Ever since that day when she'd spied the choreography markings in the snow, the actual step notations looked only like bird tracks. When her friend the cardinal wasn't keeping her company, he was conducting rehearsals with a mismatched corps de ballet of reluctant birds. She pressed her lips together to keep from laughing.

Shaw stood at the window, his back to her, scribbling something in a sketchbook. The blind was halfway up and he peered into the dark night, sometimes almost pressing his nose to the window.

"What are you looking at?" The book was failing to keep her interest.

"Trying to figure something out," he mumbled.

He slept in a T-shirt and boxers, she in well-worn sweatpants and a tank top. It struck her how unattractive they were. Shaw, who'd never been the fittest guy, was growing mushy around the middle. Maybe more physical labor—chopping wood? shoveling snow?—would add some muscle tone to his otherwise shapeless arms, fish-belly white and dotted with moles. And if Orla didn't make an effort to preserve her own muscle tone, she'd end up even more sticklike. Her shirt had a hole in it two inches above her belly button—big enough to poke a finger in—and what looked like spaghetti-sauce splatter below that.

Their sex life had diminished after they'd started procreating, but in addition to both of them being tired and busy, the foldout sleeper in the living room had lacked the intimacy of their former bedroom turned nursery. Once they'd been quite adventurous, making up elaborate stories in which they were different characters. It had started as an extension of Shaw's acting class, but then they'd embellished their scenarios with a sexual element. After meeting on a park bench or at a café—"strangers" making a discovery, surprised by the compatibility of their conversation—they'd end up back at the apartment, erotically charged by their new personas. Their role-playing games had a therapeutic element as well; "Dorothy" and "Dashiell" might admit things that Orla and Shaw couldn't.

They had their own bedroom walls now, their own door— their own single-purpose sleeping apparatus. Perhaps it was time to revisit some of the old characters, or invent new ones.

"What are you sketching?" She gave up on the book and set it aside.

Shaw remained engrossed. They were only feet apart, but her husband felt a galaxy away. Sometimes at night he filled her in on the progress he was making with his series, translating the symbolism of his imagery or explaining the evolution of his ideas. But this was the first time he'd brought actual work to bed.

"You know what we haven't done in a long time?"

His head jerked up, but not in reaction to her question. He scurried backward, as if retreating from something, until he collided with the bed. The mattress bounced a little as he plopped down, his attention fully diverted as he listened to something that most definitely wasn't Orla. Whatever sound he was tracking, it was apparently just beyond his range of hearing; he kept turning his head, squinting, like he'd become a human satellite dish, seeking a signal. It made her skin prickle.

She'd seen him do this before. And, with more subtlety, their daughter had done it too.

Back in the apartment, sometimes her husband or daughter would report hearing a high buzz of electricity that she couldn't detect. And once, long after the rotten-potato incident, Shaw sniffed all around the living room, certain he smelled something burning; concerned, he tracked it to a neighbor's candle, two doors down the hallway. What was he hearing *here*? In the middle of nowhere, where even she swore she could hear the snow fall?

"Babe? What are you doing?" She squirmed over and peered at the sketchbook on his lap, which was illuminated by his own bedside lamp. But he hadn't been drawing. In a messy scrawl she saw isolated words:

IN!
You
me???
together together

MUST!
in???

She caressed his back, her brain a-jumble with unwanted thoughts. He leapt up as if she'd poked him with an icicle.

"Sorry—"

"No, it's fine." He shoved the sketchbook into his nightstand drawer. "I don't wanna do this anymore."

"Shaw?" The inky ghoul that had followed them on the road touched her with its sharp talon. *What's wrong with him?*

He paced, hands over his ears. "I can't do this anymore, don't make me do this, I don't understand what I'm—"

"Shaw—hey!" He'd never sleepwalked, but it seemed like her husband was trapped in a nightmare. On her knees atop the bed, Orla reached out and grabbed his wrist. She was probably gripping too tightly—he might see the bruises of her fingers later—but she reeled him in. "You're okay. I'm not making you do anything. What's wrong?"

He dropped onto the bed beside her, clutching her in his arms. "Oh Orla."

"Please talk to me."

"It's nothing, I'm sorry." He turned away, a little embarrassed. "I've been working too hard—probably never thought you'd hear me say that!" He tried to laugh.

It was some relief that he'd returned from the stratosphere and sounded more like himself. "You've always worked hard, your energies every which way. But now you're so focused— maybe too focused? You can't work every minute of every day. It's not a race."

He nodded. "I feel like…sometimes…I'm going a little crazy. And sometimes I really like it, because it feels so productive, I have so much energy. And other times…"

She rubbed his back. "You don't have to push yourself so hard. This is—"

"I feel like I have to, that I'm being pulled…sometimes I really want to resist, you know? Like, we're here in this beautiful place and I feel like I hardly get to see you, or the kids…but I have to be productive, that's what

I promised. But I didn't realize...this isn't exactly how I envisioned it."

"We're all still finding our way. Just breathe. Don't be so hard on yourself. Breathe."

He exhaled a huge sigh and flopped back onto the bed. As she knelt beside him he concentrated on his breath—in, out, in, out—a technique he'd learned to calm his nerves. The rhythmic sound soothed her too.

She stayed on her knees and breathed with him for a while, her uncombed hair like shutters around her face. Her tank top billowed out, and she scraped at the orangey stain.

"Would it help? If I tried a bit harder? We, maybe. Should we try a bit harder now that we have our own room? Maybe that's what we're missing—remember Dorothy? And Dashiell? We were so creative; it was so erotic. We haven't even tried in a long time." Maybe it wasn't the only source of his anxiety, his stress, but it could be something—something tangible to grab hold of, to work on.

Shaw blinked, calmer than he'd been. He turned onto his side, let his eyes wander over her familiar form; it returned him to the moment. He played with a piece of her hair. "What haven't we tried?"

"To really be...I don't want to say 'how we *were*' because I don't want to live in the past. But maybe you need me to be something else. And this is the perfect opportunity. Out here, we could come up with completely new characters, different than how we played in the city." Orla tugged at her shirt. "I wear the most disgusting clothes I own to bed."

"Comfortable. You mean the most comfortable clothes."

She launched off the bed, whipping her top off over her head. Shaw followed her every movement. His eyes settled on her erect nipples as she stood there facing him.

"We're not...comfort is one thing. I could clean the bathroom floor with this raggedy piece of shit." The stained tank top dangled from her hand.

"You're welcome to sleep in the nude—maybe the door even locks." He fingered one of the old books she'd left on the bed.

"There's a thought." Topless, Orla went to the door and jiggled the mechanism beneath the knob. "Don't think it works."

"Well. We could fix it. Or get one of those little hook things; they're easy to install. Or you could just put on a comfy shirt and come back to bed." She paced in a circle. "Orlie, what's the matter?"

"Nothing." She dug through the dresser and pulled out an old—but not completely mangled—shirt from the Mermaid Parade.

"I'm sorry. I feel like I'm...contagious," he said.

As she slipped the shirt over her head, she slowly blew air through her puffed-out cheeks. Was this a bad time? She wanted the intimacy of a real conversation, especially since Shaw's behavior had become so erratic. But she hesitated to stoke flames that she didn't need to—for the same reason.

"It's not you, or your work. Or here, this place. Behind it all, there's still us. *Us.* You know...it's just easy to imagine blue jeans and moth-eaten wool sweaters, and both kids spending years in hand-me-down boys' clothes from their cousins. And we stop bothering to get haircuts, and we don't care what's in style anymore—and maybe that's a good thing. But if we're going to become so...'just the necessities'...I don't want us to lose, like, who we were. We had our own kind of coolness, didn't we?"

"I think so."

"And it's hard for me to imagine...myself really becoming Mountain Woman."

Shaw laughed. "We're not on a mountain."

"Woody Hill Woman."

"With brambles in your hair, brewing dandelion tea. No deodorant, no brushing your teeth. Stinky Nature Woman. That could be a fun character to explore, half wild—"

"I'm glad you think this is funny." She didn't sound glad, but she crawled onto the bed, consoled more than she could say by his levity, the return of his humor. Half leaning against his knees, she took his hand in hers. "It's more than that, though—"

"I know."

"Us. That's something we can focus on. I don't want us to…"

"Become total slobs?"

"That's just the easy thing. There's a balance. And sometimes, with each other…a mermaid T-shirt? And this is a step up? You might, as a husband, deserve a little more effort on my part "

"I like mermaids."

"But still."

"And maybe you'd like a little more effort from *me*?"

"We just need to be in sync—and not in the way of becoming indifferent together."

"No, I know. You're right. I think about it sometimes. I had all my snazzy clothes, and I liked getting dressed for special outings or special—"

"You looked good in your snazzy clothes—"

"And I don't know what our outings are going to be like here. Different." He rubbed the knuckle on her thumb.

"I mean, I get that we're doing something different," she said. "But while we're changing, there's still a part of us that might not, you know? So, we might miss things about our old life and we have to be prepared for that and not let them be setbacks. But there may be other parts that *should* change but won't if we don't make a little effort. We've settled into a certain way of being together. And often it's so—to use your word—

comfortable. And it's good, but I don't want it to feel like giving up. We might need to do a little more, to at least talk about what we want. From our sex life—whether it's new fantasies, or not. What we need. Because it's different here. We can make this an opportunity to change up old patterns—and that could be really good."

She loved when he made such strong eye contact with her; she knew then he was really hearing her.

"No, you're right." He scooched down so they were curled up face to face. Laid a delicate kiss on her lips. "We should definitely. Be conscious about things. Take this opportunity to keep growing together."

"That's what I want."

"Me too." He smiled at her, dreamy. "You're beautiful, even in a mermaid shirt. Thanks for looking out for me—for us."

"Always." She turned off her lamp and snuggled in beside him, tucking the blankets up under her armpits.

After several long moments with her thoughts, Orla knew she wasn't quite ready for sleep. Beside her, Shaw thumbed through one of the history books, but she had another issue weighing on her mind. "Do you think Eleanor Queen's okay?"

One side of Shaw's mouth quirked into a grin. "She definitely wasn't happy that you made her come home."

"She was so quiet at dinner. And when I kissed her good night, she was just holding her book, staring into space." *Like you.*

"She'll get over it."

"It felt weird, Shaw, out there—the way some things around here sometimes seem—"

"Did something happen?" A quick edge came to his voice and he shut the book.

"Nothing specific. Just something I felt—I'm hyperaware now, on guard all the time. And the way Eleanor Queen...I know you don't want me—us—to be afraid, but I really don't know what to think, and sometimes…it scares me."

If she'd been hoping he'd coo away her worries, tell her some all-explaining thing that he'd found on a more up-to-date weather app, that didn't happen. Instead, she felt him holding his breath. She curled in tighter, closer to him, as she waited for him to speak.

"My dreams have changed," he whispered. "They were so good before; I felt such…warmth. Before we came here. And now…"

"Nightmares?" He nodded. "Is that what happened last night? Is that why you went downstairs?"

"It was one of those dreams where what you're seeing doesn't seem like anything overtly frightening. But—like you said—the way it *feels*. I keep feeling—last night, but also at random times—a heart, stopping. A cold seeping in The very opposite of the warmth I used to experience when I dreamed about this."

"The dreams are still about here?"

"I think so. I got so chilled last night, and I felt like maybe the dream was trying to tell me something, that the pilot light had gone out in the furnace or something. But when I went down to the basement, it was fine. But I feel it all the time. This sense that I'm supposed to *do* something. And so I keep painting and working because that feels purposeful, that's doing something…but the feeling never goes away."

Orla didn't know what to think. There was the obvious interpretation: he was having doubts about moving. Was it too soon to suggest they leave? It wasn't like she hadn't started thinking about it, financial consequences and all. People made mistakes; it happened. They could regroup, take the hits, try again. But the stubborn part of her didn't want to be run out of her new home simply because they couldn't handle being in such a foreign environment. Suck it up—they could get used to it, right? If only it weren't for the different ways in which they—and even their daughter—were hinting at things that defied explanation.

"Will it go away?" Orla asked, because she didn't know how to verbalize her thoughts. "Maybe we'll get used to it and…"

"I didn't expect this to feel like such an out-of-body experience. But sometimes…please don't take this the wrong way—"

"I won't." But everything inside her paused, afraid of what he would say.

"Sometimes I think…maybe the sense of craziness would go away if I could just see, do, feel something from our old life, something familiar. I could get grounded again."

Finally a solid truth, more tangible than anything else they'd talked about. "I feel like that too."

"You do?" He sounded so surprised.

"Exactly—that loss of being grounded. It's more than not having a routine; it's feeling…the absence of everything that was part of our daily lives. But maybe I'd feel like this wherever we were. The only pattern I have so far is walking down every day to get the mail." It was a relief that, in spite of how much had changed, they were still in sync—feeling the same losses, needing the same comforts.

He wrapped his arm around her and pulled her in even closer. "Everything will settle down. This will become the new normal, in time, and then nothing will feel weird anymore." She heard him trying to convince himself, but something hopeful, optimistic, had taken root.

She kissed the tip of his nose, his lips. "We'll develop new routines that don't involve you painting twenty-four hours a day. And we—at least I—have to stop comparing here to—"

"We both do. Ouch." He shifted a little; between them lay Orla's rescued books. With one hand he scooped them up, then turned over and dropped them beside the bed.

They made a clattering noise and Orla winced, concerned for the fragile spines and yellowing pages. She anticipated him turning back to her, kissing her, embarking on the much-needed foreplay that they'd seen so little of in recent months. Already, she felt a tingle between her legs. But the tingle changed to a prickle of fear when, beside her, Shaw suddenly froze, then gasped and tumbled out of bed.

16

Orla's first thought was that it was happening again, the thing that seemed to suck him away from reality right in the middle of an ordinary moment. *Not ordinary, but whenever we have a heart-to-heart.* Could that be it? Some bizarre reaction to their intimacy? It had happened in the living room the night he'd gotten lost, and again tonight. A nightmarish spell where, for a moment, he was far away, afraid of something that didn't exist in her own conscious domain. She scurried over to his side of the bed, half expecting to find him on the floor and convulsing.

But no.

Squatting there, book in hand, he looked deliriously happy.

"I got it right!" He sprang up and bounded back onto the bed. "Holy shit! I got it spot-on perfect!"

"What are you—"

He flashed her a page from the book, a black-and-white photo. "This is the chimney—look! And the cabin I painted—it looks exactly the same!"

"Are you serious?" Shaw didn't want to give up the book, but she tugged it her way long enough to see the page. He'd painted a nearly identical version of the cabin in this…what was this book? Orla squinted at the washed-out title on the spine: *The Settling of Saranac Lake Village.*

"This is the chimney I found."

"It's gotta be a coincidence. I mean, you did the research about what it might look like, but that can't be the literal building that was on our land."

Shaw mumble-read, "'The 1880s…before the establishment of the sanitarium…'" And then, loudly and triumphantly, "'Called *cure cottages* in the surrounding'—that's it, Orlie, that's what I found. That's what I painted. I'm dead serious—that is *our land*!"

Finally, he turned the book all the way around, jabbing a finger on the picture. Now she saw it: the towering tree—healthier then than now, even in black-and-white, but by all appearances the tree behind their house. In the foreground, much closer to the camera, half a dozen wan, grim women stood in a line beside a mustachioed middle-aged man. A couple of the women looked quite young, teenagers perhaps, and they all wore simple, but corseted, Victorian garb. Behind them was a log cabin–like structure with a stone chimney—and it did look like Shaw's painting.

"This is real?" In spite of her shock, something was starting to align, and it felt right.

"It was a tuberculosis-cure cottage—they had these cottages around the area, I guess, before they built the big sanitarium."

"What else does it say?" They were both on their knees now, excited.

He quickly scanned the page with the photo and the next page of text. "Not much…I guess people came from New York City. Other than the caption, it doesn't say much about the cottages themselves." He got lost for a moment, reading.

It was a remarkable bit of incredibly local history, and Orla was starting to fit jigsaw pieces together, but was she crazy for what she was thinking? "Can I see it again?"

He handed her the book. The caption identified only the man, a doctor, and didn't state a specific location. But with the tree...

"This could be it, Shaw."

"I know!"

"No, I mean the reason for everything."

"That's what I mean too. People came here and died of tuberculosis. In our backyard."

She might not have ever believed such a thing before, but it seemed possible now: "Maybe our land is *haunted* by people who died here?"

They sat with that for a moment. Orla wasn't sure how she felt about it. Of all the things she'd considered, a haunting hadn't been one of them. Although maybe that was because of the variety and magnitude; *a haunting* translated as *one* entity, in her limited experience, not many.

"Maybe, somehow, they're showing us...some part of them, their souls or who they were," she said, thinking on the odd and beautiful things she'd seen.

"They showed me *this*." He pointed to the picture again. "I understand it better now, this *wanting* I've felt—they wanted us to know, somehow, that they were here. They wanted me to be aware, to *see*."

"It almost seems plausible," she said, not fully sure what she was talking about. "And they don't seem like...bad spirits. They're not poltergeists, rattling around the house. But it's still kind of horrible."

Shaw laid the book, more gently this time, on the floor and flopped back against the bed with the relief of a man who'd successfully purged a demon. "It's not the house, that's the thing, it's the land. And when they sent people here for the

good-weather cure—how hilarious is that, clean air, I guess—
they had nothing else to offer, medically. It's so sad. And I know
that part is horrible, but…ever since we got here there's been
this weird—"

"I know."

"*Feeling*. This energy in the air. And this, we can work
with this. Maybe they're lonely, or…if their souls are unsettled,
maybe they're looking for some sort of resolution."

Orla saw where he was going, but she wasn't quite as ready to
contemplate the next step, the how-tos of soothing the spirits in
their woods. But it felt like progress. With this new possibility,
she wanted to think back on everything that had happened,
whatever its category—scary, awesome, confusing, maybe even
coincidental—and examine it through this new lens. "I need to
think about this more, look at every—"

"Tomorrow I'll get online and see what else I can—"

Eleanor Queen's wail interrupted him. "Mama!"

Orla scooted on her knees to the edge of the bed, facing the
hallway from where the cry had emanated. "In here, love!"

"Papa." Eleanor Queen slipped in, wearing a tortured frown
and fuzzy fleece pajamas covered in rabbits.

"What's wrong?" Orla lay back and lifted the covers so her
daughter could crawl in beside her.

"Bad dream, Bean?" Shaw asked.

"Uh-huh." Orla held her tight against her body, and Shaw
leaned up on his elbow and rubbed his daughter's back. "It was
very, very, very scary."

"Shhh." Orla rocked Eleanor Queen as she cried.

There'd been a time when she was prone to nightmares,
frighteningly real scenarios that often involved getting run over
by a taxi. Eleanor Queen would claim she felt it crushing her
bones. She'd scream out for help. It had been hard for Orla
and Shaw to promise her such a thing would never happen

in real life, especially when they'd had several close calls with aggressive drivers over the years. Even as savvy, fast-walking city folk, they couldn't always defend against a car making a fast turn to beat out the swarm of pedestrians.

"There are no busy streets out here, so you're safe," Orla said.

"It wasn't about New York, it was about here." She snuffled a bit, and her tears subsided.

Orla and Shaw exchanged glances. "What happened, Bean?" he asked.

"The house…" Her eyes went wide as she looked at them, and then her face crumpled again.

"You're safe in the house," Shaw said. He sounded confident, reassured now that their troubles were "only" the unfortunate result of their home being too near a cure cottage that had offered no cures.

Eleanor Queen shook her head. "There was ice, like a river, surrounding the house. And the house was breaking apart, falling into the water. And we were inside, all crammed together, and we were gonna…the ice was gonna crush us, or we'd fall in the cold water and freeze to death. Tycho was crying. And then Papa fell through the floor!"

She couldn't speak anymore and Orla held her tight.

The fine hairs on Orla's arms and neck flagged their alarm. Eleanor Queen had always had such realistic nightmares for a child, but what was this about their house? And ice?

"It's okay," Shaw said in a soothing voice. "It was just a dream."

"It was real," Eleanor Queen wailed.

"It just felt real—that's the way dreams are." But Orla wasn't feeling as convinced as before. Maybe their daughter was tapping into the lingering energies of people from long ago, but if they could still give her nightmares, that was a very real and immediate problem.

"You know what? I had a dream kinda like that a couple of nights ago." *Was that true?* "But in my version a big boat appeared, and I helped you all climb in—"

"I don't want us to die." Though Eleanor Queen's voice was muffled by blankets, the plaintive desperation was clear.

"We're fine, you're—"

"There's a British saying," Shaw said, overlapping Orla. "'Safe as houses.'"

Orla was pretty sure the expression had something to do with financial investments, not the physical safety of actual houses. But this was even worse than when they'd try to reassure their daughter about the taxis, because her words were so chilling. The taxi threat forced them to be extra-vigilant, and they always made Eleanor Queen aware of their extra caution. "See? I'm looking Mr. Taxi Driver in the eye and he's letting us cross." What could they possibly tell her to dispel her fear of being crushed to death in their new house? She wasn't sure if Shaw was telling the truth about his own dream or simply trying to do right in the moment and comfort his daughter. But she preferred his version, which at least included the possibility of rescue, of them all making it out alive.

Finally Eleanor Queen drifted toward sleep.

"She's sensitive to it too," Orla whispered. "How do we explain this? It isn't fair—"

"I know, but we can figure this out now, now that we have a better understanding. I'm really feeling more hopeful. Tomorrow, first thing, I'll get online. We'll figure this out, Orlie." He kissed her cheek and then Eleanor Queen's before inching up to switch off his lamp.

It was too much to say she felt heartened, but having Shaw back in true partner mode would surely help. She shut her eyes when he spooned beside her, solid and warm in the dark. Until his warmth made her think of his nightmare, a seeping chill, a heart stopping—and Eleanor Queen's fear of them all dying in this place. She lay awake for a long time holding her child, counting Eleanor Queen's breaths. It worried her more than she'd ever allow herself to say.

What if they couldn't figure it out?

What if they couldn't keep her safe?

17

At first she thought it was a teakettle. Still asleep, her mind registered only a shrill and persistent yowl. But as she returned to consciousness, Orla became aware of the empty space beside her where Eleanor Queen had spent the night. And Shaw was still on her other side, a warm lump. No one was making tea; it was her daughter, screaming an alarm.

She and Shaw both tumbled out of bed. Halfway down the stairs, heading toward the scream, they heard Tycho shouting from his room, "We got ten feet of snow!" Just like last time, he saw it as a cause for excitement. And he came galloping after them.

They found Eleanor Queen in the darkened living room. The girl faced the front of the house. Shaw fell to his knees beside her and made a quick check of her physical well-being. Orla couldn't fathom the room's darkness. There'd been daylight in their bedroom, sneaking through the blinds. They rarely remembered to close the curtains they'd put up downstairs, so why was it like night in here? And it was just as dark in the kitchen. The strangeness of it was oppressive and made the shadowy room scary enough that Orla wanted to scream too.

Tycho jumped up and down, pointing at the front window. "Ten feet of snow!"

And then Orla understood. The downstairs was so dark because..."He's right. Oh my God, we can't get out of the house!"

As Orla started to panic, Eleanor Queen let out a final squeak, falling silent as she leaned against her father. Orla opened the front door—to a wall of white.

"Close it!" Shaw called.

She closed it without understanding his urgency. The wrongness of everything—her daughter's premonition, the snow, being trapped—made her skin ripple and she wanted to step out of it, set it aside like a damp leotard and wake up to a different reality.

"Are we asleep?" The words slipped from her mouth, but Orla was relieved that no one seemed to have heard. If only it were that simple.

Eleanor Queen plastered herself to her mother as Shaw abandoned her. He went from one window to the next. In the unlit room, each looked like it had been sprayed over from the outside with grayish concrete.

"They should hold. They'll be fine. We'll spend the day upstairs. And no one open the doors!"

"Why, Papa?" Tycho asked.

"Because if the snow starts to spill in, we might not be able to get them closed again. Come on, go upstairs—go on up to our room."

"We'll bring you some breakfast," Orla said, trying to regain her parental composure. "It's okay." She rubbed Eleanor Queen's back with one hand while trying to peel her away with the other.

"My dream's coming true," she said, clutching her mother's shirt.

"No it isn't. It's just snow. But we have everything we need inside." Even their new shovel was in the basement, thank God. Orla didn't like the way Shaw was pacing around the room like a crazed animal. It gave her further urgency to get the children upstairs, lest Shaw's unease contaminate their efforts to calm them. "And the house is strong and we'll all have a slumber party in our room—"

"Can we play outside?" Tycho asked, jumping in place.

"Not today, Tigger." Orla guided him and half dragged his sister toward the stairs. "Go, we'll be up in a minute. Please, Eleanor Queen, it's okay. Keep an eye on your brother?"

"Come see from my room!" Tycho said, grabbing his sister's hand. Eleanor Queen allowed him to pull her, though the look she gave her parents was one of pure misery.

"We'll be right up, I promise," said Orla.

She and Shaw glanced at the ceiling as little footsteps trundled across the floor above, and a moment later Tycho began cataloging for his sister everything he could—and couldn't—see from his window.

"What's happening?" Orla no longer tried to keep the composure in her voice. "Were we supposed to get this much snow? Is it even possible to get this much snow?"

Shaw flipped on a lamp and collapsed onto the couch. He kept widening his eyes like he wanted to stretch them into focus or wakefulness. "It wasn't in the forecast—I don't know what's up with these shitty forecasts. But it's possible. Oswego got ten feet back in 2007, though that storm lasted several days. Some town there got almost twelve feet. And look, they were fine. They dug out—"

"Is someone going to dig us out?"

Shaw rubbed one eye with the heel of his hand. He nodded as if he were trying to convince himself of some internal argument. "I can get out. Through one of the upstairs windows. Make sure the roof is okay, and start shoveling—"

"Can't we call someone to come help us?" Orla didn't wait for him to answer. She charged into the kitchen and picked up the phone receiver. She punched buttons. No dial tone. No comforting beeps. "It's not working."

"The snow probably buried the dish. Or knocked it off-kilter. We'll try our cell phones from upstairs—"

"This isn't normal." She marched back into the room to confront him. There was an emptiness inside her like she was starving, but the thing that was missing wasn't food. Nothing felt real. It made her a little light-headed, and the room started to spin and wobble and suddenly it was too easy to imagine Eleanor Queen's dream coming true, the walls tumbling in. "Can ghosts make—"

She held out her arms as she swayed, trying to save her balance. Shaw jumped up and grabbed her.

"Definitely not normal, but it *can* happen here. It doesn't happen often, but Buffalo got four feet in a single afternoon a few years back. Though that was western New York." He was so certain there was a logical, real-world explanation, but Orla was spiraling in another direction. "They've got trucks and plows and snow removal—"

"So we just sit here? And wait?" she asked, gripping his elbow, still a bit unsteady on her feet.

"For now."

She saw him battling his fear of something very, very real. This amount of snow was catastrophic. Life-threatening. He started pacing again.

The dark shape that had been lurking at the edge of her vision stepped forward into a spotlight—maybe the things that were happening weren't completely random. Fear shot out from her heart, spreading ice through her limbs. Last night's theory seemed ridiculous now, child's play, because what was happening felt ever so much more empowered, more…intentional.

"You wanted to get online today." She was thinking aloud.

"That's obviously not happening."

"It stopped you. And Tycho—how many times since we've been here has he asked about getting ten feet of snow?" Suddenly it seemed possible—as possible as anything else—that last night, they'd found the cover picture for the wrong box of puzzle pieces. Maybe it was something else entirely, but she couldn't quite—

"What are you on about? Surely you don't think this is Tycho's fault?"

"No of course not, I'm just…things keep happening!" She knew she wasn't as affected by their surroundings as her husband and daughter, but she had sensed something too—something *larger*—and had tried, in her own way, to find reasons. The presence of a tuberculosis-cure cottage in their backyard was certainly interesting, but what if…

She'd expected a winter wonderland with the fantastic sort of imagery she'd seen in films, and she—they—carried a fear of missing their old lives, of struggling in their new ones. And here they were, surrounded by winter and fear.

"Maybe we…asked for this. Somehow. By mistake."

"What are you talking about? You sound insane. We promised the kids breakfast." He strode into the kitchen and turned on the overhead light.

Maybe she did sound insane; she felt it too. But this was a whole new level of crisis. She followed him into the kitchen, where he was already putting bread in the toaster.

"Remember that book we read? *The Secret*? Back when everyone was reading it? About how your thoughts, if you focused on the right things, could conjure your deepest desires?" People got on their knees every day and prayed to a God whom they believed could hear them and satisfy their desires. Maybe she hadn't prayed on purpose—quite the opposite—but maybe it, the unknown godly forces she'd never seriously contemplated (not while her life and ambitions had gone more or less according to plan), worked regardless. "What if praying isn't any different than thinking about things too hard? I've been afraid, and thinking about snow—"

"That book was ridiculous—didn't you dismiss it as an offense to all hardworking people?"

Because she knew you couldn't summon a ballet career with focused imagery, not without endless hours of practice and other fortuitous prerequisites. For better or worse, the natural world clung less rigidly to once-acceptable rules. "I'm just trying to explore all possibilities. Even stupid ones," she muttered.

"There isn't an explanation for everything. It's *snow*. We'll find out how widespread it is. They'll clear the roads. We'll shovel out." He grabbed the coffee beans and slammed the cabinet door. "If I'd known you were going to go full *X Files*, I'd never have seriously talked to you about…" He swallowed the rest of his sentence.

"About our land being haunted? I think you could be *right*! And wrong—this is bigger."

"What does that even mean? We have a serious problem called a shit-ton of snow, and you're just scaring the kids and acting like a lunatic."

The kids hadn't heard her; it was her husband she was scaring. His haunting theory had been a source of comfort because it was familiar, something to grab onto that existed in lore across millennia and, given the local history, a plausible explanation (with a leap of faith). Even without the precise words, she was suggesting something even more inexplicable. Was it the unknown aspect that scared him most?

As if in response, he put the beans in the grinder and jackhammered their peace with the sharp blast of fresh coffee.

"But it is bigger—even if the problem is weather! Hurricanes, tornadoes, earthquakes!" She spoke into the whirring cacophony and he either didn't hear her or neglected to answer. "Fine. You pretend we wouldn't have prepared better if we'd moved somewhere with hurricanes."

She strode to the front window, turning her back on him in every way as she contemplated the snow. Maybe it would disappear as quickly as it had come. That would be an appropriate thing to get on her knees and pray for. "Oh God!" She gasped and clapped a hand over her mouth.

This place was making them all crazy.

Shaw was right; she'd scoffed at *The Secret* and the inanity of praying for *stuff*. And if he hadn't been so distracted by his "muse," he might have thought to put a snowblower on their list of necessities. Would they have shown up in hurricane country with nothing but a flimsy umbrella? And their precious daughter was trying to understand the language of trees because her careless father had made up a story. Now that Orla needed to identify the moment when they'd started losing their grasp on reality, she couldn't. Had the idea of moving been reckless from the get-go?

Or maybe she was just angry. At him. For this. The snow wasn't his fault, but wasn't the rest of it?

Orla huddled in a corner where Shaw, in the kitchen, wasn't likely to see her. She pulled at her hair, swallowed down a scream. These were not helpful thoughts; she was losing her mind. He'd warned them not to open the doors. But the need to, now that she couldn't, ticked in her like a bomb. She'd explode if she couldn't get out. She raced upstairs to the bathroom and heaved open the window. Sucked in air. Didn't come out until the fresh air defused her heart and chilled her tripping brain.

18

The views from the upstairs windows were shocking—and amazing. Only the pointed roof of the garage was visible, the rest lay hidden beneath a deep and endless swath of snow. It buried tree trunks, leaving dark, surrendering branches that looked too immobilized even to wave for help. But it was better than being downstairs. From the second-floor vantage point, and able to breathe again, Orla could appreciate its beauty—and the possibility that it was simply snow. The sky was the same, and that helped alleviate the claustrophobic panic of the living room; the more Orla thought about it, the more reasonable that explanation became. Who wouldn't start to lose it if she felt like she'd been buried alive?

Eleanor Queen believed as Orla did, that if they tried to walk in the snow, they'd sink to the bottom. But Shaw insisted it would hold them, that it would settle some, as snow does, but they wouldn't drown in it.

"So if we lose electricity or anything else happens, we can strap on our snowshoes and hike to town." He chewed his sticky peanut butter toast as he sat on their bed with the kids.

Orla supposed Shaw meant that as a reassuring backup plan.

But she hadn't thought about the electricity that came to their home on fragile cables—fragile cables that kept the furnace running, and the lights on, and the water pumping, and the refrigerator and stove in working order. Surely such a tenuous lifeline would succumb to the oppressive snow…though the few lines she could see from her bedroom window appeared all right, not slackened or weighted down.

"That's a pretty long hike. We have the generator, and the woodstove," she offered—the only practical thing she'd been able to utter since they'd awakened. She didn't know if the generator would work while buried in that much snow, but they could always use the woodstove for warmth and melting water, and to provide a flicker of light.

"True. Right. Can probably hold out, then." He sounded disappointed. Orla wondered if a part of him wanted a reason to leave, to abandon ship. Was he hoping she would suggest it? Did it have to come from her, since the North Country had been his idea? Maybe she'd propose to Shaw later that they keep the house for a summer place so the mistake they'd made wouldn't feel like total failure. But for now, she'd wait; it would be cruel to tease any of them with the possibility of leaving when they couldn't even walk out the front door.

She tried her cell phone again, just in case. But there was no signal. Their bed was going to be a mess if they kept using it as a picnic spot; it was already splattered with crumbs and dribbles from Tycho's milk.

"We should move the table up if we're going to keep eating here," she said.

"You know, I've been thinking about it…it should be totally safe to be downstairs."

"Totally?" Orla raised her eyebrow at him as she tore off a little piece of her toast.

"It's not like the snow is applying force from different angles, you know? It's not *pushing* against the house, it's just straight down, so…it should be fine."

"Should?"

"Are you just going to keep singling out individual words from everything I say?"

The kids, from their perches at the end of the bed, watched them bicker back and forth. Orla couldn't shake the sensation that their bed was a rickety raft about to split apart and plunge them all into a frozen sea. She wasn't trying to antagonize her husband, but everything he'd said and done since they'd discovered their predicament was testing her restraint. Somehow she'd become an octopus, and Shaw couldn't stop trampling on her tentacles. She didn't have enough patience—or arms—to console/care for/entertain her children and demand better survival skills/solutions/apologies from her husband.

"Do you *know* it's safe?" How could he have forgotten Eleanor Queen's dream? She hoped the unspoken question was graffitied across her annoyed features.

"I have every reason to believe…I mean, I understand if you don't want—if the view out the downstairs windows freaks you out. But it could be like this for days, and we shouldn't just stop living. After I work on the roof, I'd like to get some painting—"

"You're going on the roof?" Tycho asked, bouncing a little. "Can I come?"

"The kitchen roof," Shaw clarified. "That's our one vulnerable spot, because of the way it was built. They couldn't put a steep pitched roof on the extension"—he put his hands together so the middle fingers touched, showing the children the shape of the house's roof—"without blocking some of the second-floor windows. So the kitchen roof just slopes down a few feet, and the snow stacks up there—it doesn't slide off like on the upper part of the house and the garage. I'm sure I won't be the first person who's shoveled snow off that roof."

He sounded cheery enough, like such tasks were common-place, and Eleanor Queen nodded at his logical explanation. She didn't seem alarmed, but Orla recognized what a catastrophe it would be if the kitchen roof caved in—the freezing temperatures and loss of food aside, they'd lose access to the basement, where a lot of their important gear and tools were stored.

Orla let out the breath she'd been holding, not quite sure when she'd stopped breathing. Finally something sounded reasonable, a plan of action. "I'll do it. The shoveling."

"Mama's going on the roof?" Tycho asked, just as bouncy. "Can I come?"

"Shut up," Eleanor Queen told him. "You'll die out there."

"No I won't."

"Eleanor Queen, that's not how we speak to each other." Orla's tone was stern, but it was a relief to say something so ordinary.

"No one's dying, and neither of you are going out on the roof," said Shaw.

"He's being stupid. This isn't *fun*," Eleanor Queen spat before slurping down the rest of her milk.

"He's not being stupid; he's feeling more adventurous than you are." Before anyone could say another word, Orla turned to Shaw. "I'm serious, I'll shovel the—"

"It's a lot of work, snow can be heavy—"

"I know, but I need to. Please? I almost had a panic attack—I'm sorry, for downstairs. I didn't know what I was saying. Getting out might help."

His off-kilter grin was forgiving, and unless she was misinterpreting, he looked a little relieved. When was the last time he'd gone outside? Gone were his declarations about needing to walk among the trees. Shaw took her hand, rubbed her thumb knuckle.

"You really want to?" he asked. "I'll do it if you don't..." He sounded like Eleanor Queen steeling herself to sleep without the night-light.

"I really, really, really think shoveling the kitchen roof sounds like a spectacular option."

"Well, you did say please, and who am I to deprive you of a spectacular option?" He winked at Tycho. "Mama's gonna shovel the roof—that was my diabolical plan all along."

Tycho and Shaw shared a conspiratorial giggle. Eleanor Queen gave her father an assessing look, suspicious, and reached a conclusion that Orla couldn't read.

Eleanor Queen might have decided staying indoors—even after her nightmare—was a better alternative to venturing outside. But Orla had never felt so hemmed in in her life. Having nowhere to go had already been a struggle; having no way to get out felt like a coffin lid slamming shut in her face. Surely that was the origin of her shallow breathing, the sensation that she was running out of air and had to conserve it. And hard physical work, even in the surreal, half-buried landscape, would alleviate the sinking feeling of her—their—helplessness.

"And we should get the snowshoes and stuff out of the basement," she said. "And move some of the food into the living room, just—"

"In case," said Shaw, finishing her sentence. "I'll pile up some essentials by the front door, just in case."

"In case of what, Papa?" But they avoided answering Tycho's question.

"In case the house collapses." Eleanor Queen, doomed, didn't say the words to anyone in particular. Shaw and Orla exchanged glances, but before they could contradict or reassure her, the girl slid off the bed. "Can I do my schoolwork?"

"Sorry, Bean—the satellite dish is buried, we can't get online." Shaw gathered up all of their dirty plates.

"You can work on your math pages, that'll keep you busy."

Orla stacked up their cups with one hand, swept crumbs from the bed with the other.

"What about me?" asked Tycho.

They streamed out of the bedroom single file, but Eleanor Queen slipped into her room as the rest headed downstairs.

"We can watch Mama from inside, as she shovels," Shaw said. "Or you can play in my studio while I work?"

Orla couldn't help but remember the guns. They were locked up now, stored out of sight in the studio's closet. But still. She didn't like the image of Tycho playing on the floor with the guns at his back. There was too much danger. Indoors. Outdoors. She longed for the freedom, now gone, to walk—run—through the front door, go anywhere. She needed to get outside, shake off the crushing walls and the fear that moving to the Adirondacks had been a terrible miscalculation. Hopefully that would help. It *had* to help.

But the ghoul from the shadows reached for her, gesticulating, desperate to make itself understood.

What was she still not seeing? Had Orla missed something by not paying enough attention? To Eleanor Queen? To Shaw? Now, everything inside her, from her churning intestines to her frantic heartbeat, was urging her on. Find the pieces. Solve the puzzle.

Before it was too late.

19

Eleanor Queen huddled with her knees to her chin, comforter to her ears, and glared at them.

"Sorry, Bean. It's just the easiest window for Mama to use."

Shaw held the shovel as Orla sat on the windowsill with her legs out, trying to strap on the snowshoes without bonking her head on the window sash.

"You're making it freezing in here!" Eleanor Queen pouted.

"Out of your way in a minute." Orla slipped off the ledge and onto the snow. For a moment she stood out there, expectant, still believing that she might sink into the depths and suffocate. She sank a bit, but it was inches not feet. Shaw handed her the shovel.

"Remind me to thank Julie again next time we talk." She'd found gaiters among the donated winter stuff, and though her boots were tall, the waterproof gaiters Velcroed over her pants all the way up to her knees. And she was prepared for the brightness this time, though banks of clouds were encroaching on the sun; with her sunglasses on, she wasn't blinded as she stepped out into the white world.

The window closed behind her with the hydraulic *swoosh* of

new, smoothly fitted frames. It shut out Eleanor Queen's final complaint, and Orla was on her own.

It was strange to see the tree canopies from this vantage, almost eye to eye and so close, like they were giant dead bushes, not the treetops beyond her daughter's side window. For a moment she had the sensation of levitating and feared, again, a swift plunge through the deep snow. But as she hooked a right toward the back of the house and the kitchen, walking with cautious, exaggerated steps as she acclimated to the snowshoes, she felt a release from the claustrophobia. Breathing came more easily and the frozen gusts that bloomed from her mouth reminded her of childhood, when seeing her own breath had been a source of wonder and joy. Ahead of her, the forest of trees lay buried, with only the great pine's trunk visible above the deep snow.

The plan she'd formed with Shaw was to start on one side of the kitchen roof, at the lowest part of the slope (which was almost at her ground level) and see how much snow she could move by shoveling or swiping, depending on what she could reach. The goal wasn't to clear the roof down to its shingles but to lessen the weight as much as she could. It was more difficult than she'd anticipated, as the snow she needed to remove towered above her. She had to extend her arms fully over her head to even start, but she was relieved to discover it was a feathery snow, light and airy. If it had been dense and wet, it could have been a double disaster of being too heavy to move and too heavy a load for the sloped first-floor extension.

So, without grace, she whacked snow aside. She had no choice at first but to attack lower sections, inevitably causing the collapse of the snow above; snow powdered her face as it was shaken loose. But when one corner was more manageable, she clambered onto the roof itself and did the rest of the work from there, where, using her full height and stretched arms, she could work from the top down.

It felt weird to be standing atop their kitchen. She wondered if Shaw, gathering supplies beneath, could hear her as she shuffled around. As the glare diminished a bit, she perched her sunglasses on her woolly hat, fearing the darkening sky intended to unleash more snow. Gray folds had settled in, hiding most of the sun and confusing the horizon line; all she saw were endless swaths of silvery white. For a moment she reconsidered what had happened; maybe it hadn't snowed at all, but the clouds had found purchase on the land around their mysterious house.

The trees in the distance, far up on a rolling hill above the road, looked more naked—less consumed by meringue—than the ones in closer proximity. How widespread, or narrow, had the overnight storm been? What if, like the aurora borealis, it was only *here*?

Think, think, think…as much as anything, she'd come out here to sort out her thoughts. As if to accommodate her, the land was utterly still. Nothing moved. Nothing emitted a sound.

She listened harder.

Not a bird. Not a distant car. Not the wind.

"Hello?" she said into the silence, half expecting to not hear her own voice. Perhaps it was a trick of the deep snow obliterating the nuances in the terrain, but the audience of trees looked as if they stood nearer together than they had before, and slightly closer to the house.

A part of her felt like a warrior, weapon in hand, battling an enemy force. After a short time, her muscles surpassed their achy point, heated by constant motion and abundant with energy; her body became a well-oiled machine. It was a comfortable— familiar—place for her, reminiscent of the rehearsal process, when she and her partners would practice the same movements over and over, on a mission of perfection. Eventually the choreography became so ingrained it ceased to require conscious thought and became…something else. A reaction, an impulse, a necessity created by the music. And forever after, if she heard a certain piece of music, her muscles were prepared. They'd twitch in anticipation of each crescendo and her hand would lead her arm to its designated position; she'd lift to relevé, movement coiled inside her, even as she stood in the checkout line at TJ Maxx.

Music controlled motion.

Other people might find that a strange concept; for her it was the natural order of things. Maybe she needed to turn other concepts on their head to heed the specter's demand and find the keystone that would give her an answer. Weary but absorbed in a rhythm, Orla pondered the unexplained things that had occurred since their arrival. She'd done her best to find logical explanations—global warming or other meteorological changes; general fear, or discomfort, or a sense of displacement; a shared delusion brought on by toxic elements in their environment. But logic didn't hold. And though the cure cottage was an enticing detail, it was getting harder to believe that it could be the source of their mystery. People died everywhere; was there any reason this place should be more haunted than any other? New York City should be teeming with ghosts if all that was required was a mortal population.

Her meditative work allowed her mind to wander away from reason and toward the unreasonable, where she felt more free to question the absolutes she'd always accepted. That was where the inky ghoul wanted her to go.

With a rigidity that now struck her as closed-minded, she'd been dismissive of astrology and feng shui, life after death and superstitions. (Though, like many dancers, she had a routine on performance days that was sacrosanct—the food she ate, the time she arrived at the theater, her preparations in the dressing room.) Her inner fuel, turning emotions into movement, would strike a lot of people as indulgent; many nonartists considered artists' work to be pretentious, even a complete waste of time. But she'd always felt the inherent—even spiritual—worth of it. And she knew, through observation and experience, how agonizingly receptive a person could be—in tune with, and affected by, their surroundings. Her husband and daughter were living examples of people who absorbed the world in a deep, visceral way, as did many of their creative friends. She'd never disbelieved the complex reality of the highly sensitive people in her circle, or doubted the profound personal and interpersonal worth of an artist's work. She wondered now if she should always have been more open to the other possibilities that human consciousness might tap into.

What else was out there?

Or maybe she was thinking of cause and effect all wrong. In a hysterical moment that morning, she'd tiptoed toward an idea very different from a ghost, something bigger that was responding to their thoughts, desires, fears. Something interactive was going on, action and reaction, but what was its genesis? Were they the music, or the dancers?

Are we doing this together? Are we dance partners?

Orla knew from experience that not all partnerships worked. Sometimes in a pas de deux, movements never became harmonious; the connection was off. That could be happening now. They didn't know this dance, and maybe the choreographer should have chosen different dancers.

Or, playing devil's advocate with herself, maybe the message wasn't written in code; maybe her family was feeling too much and she was thinking too much, and all this time, the damn specter had been holding a billboard.

Wrong choice. Try again.

Shaw could be a painter elsewhere. He could have *his turn* in another house, with different trees. It was the talk they should have had a long time ago, but it wasn't too late.

Orla knocked on the now-accessible landing window near the top of the stairs. Knocked and knocked until someone heard her. Unfortunately, it was Eleanor Queen who came to her rescue, glaring as she opened the window.

"Sorry, didn't want to disturb you. Ask Papa to open our bedroom window? I'll go around and come in that way."

"I'll get it." Eleanor Queen shut the landing window and trudged off to her parents' room.

As Orla clomped around to the front of the house, she said a quiet prayer. "Thank you. This has been very magnificent—something I never thought I'd see—but we're ready to go back to normal now."

She gave one last look across the tree-filled horizon. It was quiet beyond comparison, as if the rest of the world and every sound it made no longer existed. She wouldn't allow herself to dwell on the beauty of it, the little overhangs that crested the drifts, like a landscape that had eroded and evolved over millions of years, not mere particles created in hours as they slept. To be in too much awe of it—too appreciative—might invite more wondrous and horrifying events.

Eleanor Queen opened her parents' window as wide as it would go. Orla wriggled in backward, sat on the windowsill, and removed her snowshoes.

"Much safer now," she told her daughter. She spun around and ducked in, sweaty beneath her layers but rejuvenated by the time she'd spent outdoors, engaged in difficult work. "Safe as houses."

Eleanor Queen didn't look relieved. She didn't soften or grin. After one final glare, she turned and fled back to her room.

20

C an we play outside tomorrow?" Tycho asked, bouncing his floppy-legged moose on his belly as he lay tucked in bed.

Orla sighed as she knelt on the floor beside him. She didn't know how to answer his question. How long would it take for so much snow to melt? Would they run out of provisions? She didn't want to infect the children with her fear any more than she already had; she bore some responsibility for making their situation worse, for the subtle ways she'd affected the household's overall mood, if not for the snow itself. What if she just answered, "Yes"? As an experiment in optimism if nothing else. Or what if—if they might really be dance partners—she took a stab at choreographing? It couldn't hurt to express gratitude, appreciation...or even a desire to play outside.

As a young child, just a year or two older than Tycho, she'd kept a secret from her parents: sometimes she prayed. It was something she overheard relatives whispering about when her little brother got sick. But young Orla had prayed for silly things—to do well on a test; to ride her bike so fast she'd leave the ground and fly. Later, she understood the latter had been impossible while the former hadn't required a deity but a bit more of her own effort. She'd learned a lot since then, much of it quite recently, at least where sending thoughts outward into a nether space might be concerned.

"Do you want to play a little game with me? Before you go to sleep?" she asked her son.

"Okay!" He started to sit up, but Orla stopped him with a gentle pressing of her hand.

"We can play it right here. All we have to do is shut our eyes." She shut hers by way of example, then peeked to make sure Tycho had shut his too. She couldn't help but smile at the expectant look on his face, his tightly clenched eyes and hopeful grin. "Sometimes it's good to acknowledge what you have—the people you love, your home, the important things. Maybe we need to do that a little more often."

Focusing on the positive might also be a balm against her very real worries.

"I'm so grateful we're all safe and snug in our warm house. You're safe, and so is your sister, and Papa, and me. We have electricity and food and everything we need. I'm thankful...we've seen so many beautiful things—"

"Like the snow!"

Her boy's muscles, beneath the hand she'd kept on his chest, telegraphed his readiness to spring into action. And Orla saw she was right when she opened her eyes; his eyes were already wide open.

"Like the snow! Is playing better than praying?" she asked. He nodded with great enthusiasm and she laughed. "Well, maybe we need to add a little something to our prayer, a wish that we can go outside and play tomorrow."

"That's what I wish for! And ice cream!"

"It's a good hope. But I can't promise anything, love." Orla smoothed his hair, tucked the moose under his arm, tugged up the comforter.

"Are we praying to God?"

Orla considered his question. They hadn't talked much about religion as a family. She and Shaw had kept things vague—people had different beliefs, and maybe there was a higher power, but the most important thing was how people treated one another. Neither of them had wanted the children to believe there was a humanoid—a, God forbid, white man—hanging out in a fictitious wonderland waiting for them to die. A humanoid invested in—and responsive to—everything from their daily routine to catastrophic disasters to personal and global suffering.

"I'm not sure what God is," Orla said, truthfully. "But I think the universe contains powerful and mysterious things. And I think it doesn't hurt to say thank you, and think positively."

"Thank you!"

She gave him kisses on his cheek until he giggled and held out his moose. "Thank you for praying with me," she said after giving the moose a kiss. In fact, she did feel somewhat better. Looking at things objectively, she realized they *were* okay. So far. "I love you. Good night."

"Good night, snow!"

Eleanor Queen, book propped on her chest, scrutinized her mother. Orla stayed on her knees beside her daughter's bed.

"What are we praying to?" the girl asked, her intense gaze unwavering.

Orla held up her hands and gestured to a whimsical universe, the everything, the unknown. "To…whatever's out there. People find it comforting—"

"Can you hear it?"

"Hear it?"

"The thing that's out there? On the land?" Her chin quivered as her eyelashes beat away the tears. The girl looked hopeful and expectant. And terrified.

"You hear something…" It wasn't a question but the faint vocalization of Orla's worst fear. The hairs on her shoulders tingled. It hadn't been her imagination, her daughter's behavior. Her husband's. She didn't know what it meant, except that her daughter needed her. More than ever. "I've been…suspicious, but I don't know what it is that you, Papa—"

"Something is out there, Mama."

Her daughter's whispered words sent a piercing pain through Orla's brain, the pounding of a spike. She hadn't wanted to take her imaginative child too literally before, but she couldn't keep denying that Eleanor Queen had been trying to make her understand something. Orla wanted to dismiss it as a game or a hallucination, auditory or otherwise, but that wouldn't erase what she saw on her daughter's drained face. And Shaw *was writing down words!* Perhaps her child was ill? Her husband too? The fox-hare delirium knocked on its door, wanting back into Orla's consciousness. Maybe they were all crazy.

Or maybe they weren't.

Orla treaded carefully, not sure of the territory they were entering. "I know the weather's been a little scary, but—"

"It's more than that."

Yes, Orla believed that, if she was being completely honest. She studied her daughter, small and frightened in her first solitary bed, her first room. Orla couldn't brush it away anymore, chalk it up to Eleanor Queen being afraid to sleep by herself (even with the safe glow of the recovered night-light), or her own trepidations about such an unfamiliar place.

The words were sludge in her mouth, but she had to make them sound normal. "What do you think it is?"

Eleanor Queen turned her head toward her window and narrowed her eyes in concentration. "I'm not sure. Sometimes I think I hear it, something calling. Sometimes it's just a feeling, but it's…many things at once. Excited. Scared. Needy. I thought for a while that Papa heard it, I was sure he did. But Papa doesn't want to hear it. I thought you were refusing to too. I'm glad you know…something's here."

Orla's back tightened and a shiver came on so hard that it filled her mouth with bile. All she heard her daughter saying was *You're failing me*. Orla vowed to stop fighting herself, to stop talking herself out of things no matter how impossible they seemed. One way or another, she needed to protect her daughter. Would Eleanor Queen find relief or terror in the history they'd discovered? Could that be the source of her voices? But she wasn't quite ready to have a conversation about ghosts, not before she and Shaw decided on a resolution. *We'll leave, that will fix it.*

"It's scary, because we don't understand this place yet," said Orla. "But that doesn't mean it's bad."

Eleanor Queen drew a long breath in through her nose. She turned onto her side and scrunched down so her face was closer to Orla's, and they studied each other. Maybe they looked the same, with a squint of worry as they tried to read each other's mind.

"I know you haven't always been comfortable here, and I'm sorry I wasn't…I thought you, all of us, needed time," Orla said. "But now…I've been a little afraid too, and I think I haven't been a very good role model. I'm not gonna let myself be afraid of the weather anymore, not when what really scares me is that *you're* scared and I don't know how to help. Bean, I'm here—I'm always here for you, you can talk to me." That would always be true, even as she grappled to make sense of everything else.

A tiny grin brightened her daughter's face.

Orla clutched herself tighter as she knelt beside the bed. Anxiety was getting the better of them, but that didn't mean her daughter—her husband—couldn't persevere. She still wasn't sure what to prescribe or where to look for answers, but she needed Eleanor Queen to understand she wasn't alone and that her mother was trying to—*would*—help.

"How would you like things to be different? Let's think about what would be good, what would make you happier." Orla pushed apart two storm fronts as they threatened to crush her— one an optimistic possibility where they could still find their equilibrium in this new place, the other the louder, more worrying likelihood that they'd made a terrible, unfathomable error.

Eleanor Queen flipped onto her back and a more relaxed, dreamy expression brought a glow to her cheeks. "I guess I'd like...it's weird being in the house all the time, all of us. I thought I'd like it, but...I guess you're right, if the weather wasn't so bad and we could get out. Do you think there's someplace nearby where I could take violin lessons?"

Orla sat back a little, fighting to keep the surprise from registering on her face. Where had *that* desire come from? In the city, they'd offered her every variety of lesson: dance, art, music. Eleanor Queen had never been interested. She'd enjoyed those classes at school, but refused their offers to expand her abilities with more focused studies. What unbelievably horrible timing.

"Bean..."

"I know, I know what you're thinking." Eleanor Queen shoved her arms under the covers, and yanked the blankets all the way up to her chin, frustrated. "I didn't need more things to do in the city. But I need more things to do *here*. I don't miss school but I miss...I always thought maybe someday I'd want to try an instrument, but there wasn't room at home. I didn't want everyone hearing me practice if I was really bad at it. But I could close my door here. I'd really like to play a quiet instrument, something no one else could hear, but I don't know what that is."

"Oh love." Eleanor Queen was thinking in the right direction, toward making the most of their new situation, doing here what she hadn't needed or felt comfortable doing in their Chelsea apartment. But Orla felt the thin membranes of her shame stretching and threatening to tear; she should've known how self-conscious her daughter was and how she might need some personal space to explore her private dreams. "I'm sure we can find someone local. Papa knows of a school that teaches different kinds of art classes; we can start there. And we'll find something. And you don't ever have to worry about us judging you—it takes time for anyone to learn a new skill. Okay?"

"You're not mad?"

"Why would I be mad?"

Eleanor Queen shrugged. "I feel like…maybe I'm not exactly the same person here as I was in the city."

"There's no reason why I'd ever love you any less."

"I wasn't sure, because…never mind."

Orla leaned over and kissed her forehead and cheek. "It was part of the idea for coming here, that we'd all be a little different—and maybe love each other even *more*. We go somewhere new and learn new things about ourselves. No one's exactly who they were. Every day we're slightly different, right? We learn something new and we're not entirely the same anymore. Papa and I want that too, for you, for us. That we all keep growing and making discoveries. So if you want to try music lessons now, we'll make that happen. Papa and I will make it happen."

"I like it here, some parts of it. But I wish…" She silenced her wish and chewed her lip.

"Tell me what you wish."

"I wish…we had a house with neighbors. In town. And a street, like what you see on TV. With kids riding bikes and going to each other's houses to play."

The tears rose quickly in Orla's throat. Her daughter could have been describing Squirrel Hill, the neighborhood she'd grown up in in Pittsburgh. It was clearer than ever they'd made a mistake in staying in Manhattan for so long. Other families made it work, but Eleanor Queen needed—longed for—something else. Something she'd never felt confident to voice. Maybe that first day when they moved in, the thing Eleanor Queen had been looking at in the yard hadn't been something that frightened her, but something that broke her heart: No neighbors. No people. From one extreme to another.

A tear slipped from Orla's eye; she couldn't promise her daughter the neighborhood she wanted. Maybe she and Shaw had only pretended to include their children in their decision-making. When they'd asked, "Do you want to move to our own house, with a big yard and lots of trees?" how many answers would they actually have heard?

"I'm sorry. I know it's not exactly what you wanted, but when the weather's better we'll make sure we find the lessons you want to take, and we'll find some places where you can make friends. It always takes a little while to adjust after a move." *Maybe we'll move again.*

"I know."

Orla gave her fierce kisses. "I love you so much."

"I know. I love you too."

Orla flicked on the night-light on her way out.

"It's okay, I don't need it anymore," said Eleanor Queen.

"Are you sure?"

"Yes. The darkness helps me think."

Orla switched off the light and blew her a kiss. Unwilling to leave her daughter in complete darkness, she left the door open a crack, overwhelmed by a burden of new worries. They were not, as parents, the good listeners they'd imagined themselves to be. She committed to correcting that. She'd study her daughter more closely and ask more questions. But in the meantime, it troubled her what Eleanor Queen had heard—out there, "on the land." If they were going to stay even a day longer, they needed to figure out what to tell her. Would the specificity of dead tuberculosis patients seem less frightening than the vague "many things" she was sensing? It was almost laughable that Orla was considering easing her daughter's fears with the "It's just ghosts" explanation. And she couldn't shake the apprehension that her daughter's higher power was more present than hers. What if the girl whispered her prayers to something utterly different than the faceless goddesses Orla only pretended to know?

And how would that something interpret a girl's longing for more neighbors, more houses, more kids?

With the curtains drawn, they could pretend it was an ordinary night. Hidden from view were the ominous panes of dense snow beyond each window, as if the world had been erased. That's what Orla kept thinking as she paced the living room. Things had changed too much; they needed to force a reversal to reclaim some amount of normalcy.

"We don't have to abandon it completely, we could keep it for a summer place—"

"Are you listening to yourself?"

The chill in his voice was like a roadblock in her path, forcing her to stop and look at him. He'd planted himself in the open doorway of his studio during her entire rant, clearly illustrating his unwillingness to budge on anything. She'd been sure he would at least see the merits of thinking more positively and understand her desire to be more considerate of their children's needs. But Shaw looked hardened, his face as unyielding as a mask. Orla cowered a little, shrank from him, and started to doubt herself.

"What?"

"You sound insane. This morning you were gung ho to shovel out—now you're talking about our daughter hearing things, but somehow it's *my* fault for not listening?"

"That's not what I said! Your cure-cottage theory doesn't excuse how she's being affected—"

"We spent tens of thousands—"

"I know what we spent!"

"Then you can't seriously think of quitting the life we just started here. Even if we could sell the house eventually, we'd take a loss for the improvements we—"

"So we'll take the loss."

Shaw shook his ragged head at her, his face contorted into a grimace that bordered on revulsion. "You just don't want me to succeed."

"What are you even talking—"

"This is *my turn,* and if it bankrupts us you'll blame *me!*"

"Look!" She pulled back one of the living-room curtains. The lamplight played on the glass, making a yellowish spotlight on the white wall of snow. "We can't live like this."

"It's a freak snowfall. It's not going to happen every day, or even every year. It's nothing—it's nothing!" She gaped at his manic denial. He shut his eyes, breathing deeply.

"We can't pretend it isn't happening," she said gently, sensing her husband's urgent need for stability, for success, in spite of their complicated predicament. "Everything. Since we got here. And now we're trapped, we can't even contact anyone—"

"I'll walk to town tomorrow, I already told you. It's not as bad as you're making it seem. We can handle—I can handle it. I'll fix it."

Pain radiated from him, reaching her like waves sent out from a tsunami. Fear, passion, shame. The burden of everything he'd wanted. Guilt, hope, desperation. Looking at him, she almost expected his fragile skin to crack; there was too much going on inside him.

She'd become all turned around, blindfolded while someone spun her. Where was forward? What was onward? It wasn't enough that Shaw wanted to shoulder the responsibility, to make things better and prove it wasn't all a terrible blunder; his ego couldn't be her primary concern. Eleanor Queen's needs felt more urgent—even if Orla was using those needs to support getting her own way.

"I know you didn't know it was going to be like this," she said, forcing herself to appear calm in an effort to placate him. "Maybe we…go to my parents' for a few months and come back in the spring. We can try again. When the weather's better, we won't feel so isolated."

Shaw's head made small back-and-forth movements as he pleaded with his eyes for her to please, please understand. "I can't. I can't go…"

His voice broke and he stepped backward into the boundaries of his personal sanctuary and shut the door. Orla gripped her head in her hands and paced, this time extending her path between the front door and the back door. Maybe it was all the snow making her batty. Making her lose her sense of self and doubt everything they had agreed to as a couple—had they ever put the children first? Ever, really? Had they always expected Eleanor Queen and Tycho to simply blossom in the shadows of their parents' artistic entitlement? But why was Shaw— previously a loving and attentive father—acting like that wasn't his main priority? Had he heard *anything* she'd said about Eleanor Queen? The place was consuming him, and perhaps, in a different way, it had infected their daughter. Orla didn't care if it was crazy and impossible; something was happening, and she couldn't just sit back and let it play out.

The floors talked beneath her feet, groaning in commiseration, crackling with their own weary doubt. Orla muttered as she treaded from one blocked exit to the other.

"Please. Please, god or goddess of whatever you are, keep my children safe. Be kind to us; we're not ready for this. We need to be free to leave—and maybe we'll stay. I don't know what's best for us anymore. Please be kind to us."

And so she prayed. And went up to bed alone.

She dreamed a jumbled montage of Tycho's wish for ice cream, Eleanor Queen's longing for friends and neighbors, and her own desire not to feel trapped. Sometimes the dream-children were made of ice cream and melted as her daughter tried to befriend them. Sometimes the house appeared as a jail cell with snow blowing through the open bars. She quashed a nightmare in which her children were locked in the house and she, outside, couldn't get the doors to open or the windows to break by forcing herself to see the imagery in a more positive light: The house was strong; no harm befell Tycho or Eleanor Queen. In the dream, she told them to turn away from the windows so they couldn't watch her skeletonize with cold.

It was a bleak compromise, and even her sleeping-self doubted that such a sacrificial maternal instinct would serve its purpose. And where was Shaw in her nightmares of survival? Locked in his studio, painting? If something happened to her, who would protect Tycho and Eleanor Queen? And if they physically survived, some part of their gentle souls would always suffer from the loss.

She didn't understand what her subconscious was asking her to contemplate. Were they heading toward a scenario where she would need to lay down her life? She would do it, if the situation required it. But shouldn't she, as a responsible adult, not let things run so amok? Orla squirmed in her sleep, bumped into something she mistook for an iceberg. It was only Shaw. But something in her mind split and the cold water rushed in.

They were sinking.

21

When she glanced at the clock it was almost three thirty in the morning. Something had awakened her, a sound she couldn't locate. After her fitful sleep, she decided to check on the children, concerned about how they might be processing the snow outside and the tension inside. Shaw wasn't in bed beside her, so that must have been what she heard; he'd probably had nightmares of his own and was wandering around downstairs, maybe checking on the furnace again. She shuffled into her slippers and threw a sweatshirt over her head.

In Tycho's room, she found him curled on his side, all snuggled up, nothing amiss except for his moose, which had fallen onto the floor. Orla tucked it in next to him, on the wall side, so it wouldn't fall out again.

In Eleanor Queen's room, she found less evidence of restful sleep. Her rumpled comforter had half slipped onto the floor, and her sheet was so twisted it covered only her belly and one leg. Careful not to wake her, Orla rearranged her sheet and laid the comforter atop her as delicately as she could.

"Oh, Bean," she whispered. Orla wished Eleanor Queen had

called out or come to her parents' room for consoling, but maybe she hadn't been able to wake herself up. That her daughter might have been as trapped in a bad dream as they were in the house made it even more unbearable.

She went to find Shaw. They needed to agree on a plan.

"Shaw?" It was dark in the living room, but a strip of light glowed beneath his studio door. The curtained windows hid the white evidence of their impending suffocation. She switched on a lamp on her way—no point in stumbling around in the dark, especially since they were both awake. What a sense of purpose he'd developed, at least where his art was concerned. Orla didn't mean to be uncharitable, but she didn't like it. Obsession was not the same thing as discipline, and if he was serious about following through with his plan to walk somewhere in the morning and make sure someone was aware of their situation, it would be better if he was well rested.

She rapped with her knuckle and turned the knob. In recent days she'd stayed clear of his studio and its closed door, hoping his work would evolve past its dark phase. A scream escaped, even as her body froze in the open doorway, one hand still on the knob. Her heart hammered every dissonant chord, its natural rhythm obliterated by the tableau. Her brain couldn't process what she was seeing well enough to help her decide: run to him, or approach with caution.

In her peripheral vision she saw red. Was she too late? But it was only paint. Smeared on a canvas.

Shaw sat on the floor, leaning against the wall beside the closet. The shotgun to his mouth.

"Shaw? Baby?" Her voice trembled. She tiptoed toward him, as hesitant and uncertain as if she were walking across shattered glass.

He didn't look at her, but tears streamed from his eyes. As she came closer, he held out one hand—stop—but kept the other firmly on the barrel.

"I'm sorry—I'm so sorry—I've been trying to understand… everything. And I'm sorry if I didn't. Please, we need you, I need you, I love you." She fell to her knees, weeping, afraid to go closer, her hands in fists as she fought the urge to reach for the gun, snatch it from his hands.

He shook his head, his lips still on the metal.

"We'll fix this—I'll help you fix this," Orla begged, inching toward him on her knees. "It's not your fault, none of this. I know how hard you tried, but this, what's happening, you couldn't have known—"

Finally Shaw crumbled. As he burst out sobbing, he lowered the gun, and Orla lurched forward and took it away from him. She kept her body between him and the weapon as she took him in her arms and let him wail.

"It's not your fault," she said again and again. "We all love you so much—we'll figure this out, you and me, we're a team, we've always been a team…"

She felt the weight of his defeat as he let her hold him.

"Make it go away," he whimpered, turning his face from her.

Orla, thinking he meant the gun and happy to oblige, got to her feet and, with the barrel pointed down and away, struggled to crack it open as she'd watched him do at Walker's house. Tears impeded her vision when she dislodged the unused cartridges. She'd hoped that maybe in his despair he'd forgotten to load it and couldn't possibly have succeeded in ending his life. But no.

If she hadn't awakened. If she hadn't come downstairs.

Her hands shook so badly she fumbled securing the gun in its locker. She shut the closet door and pressed her back to it, not sure which was more likely—that her husband would change his mind and push past her to finish what he'd started, or that the gun possessed some unnatural ability to crawl back out and destroy their lives.

"There." The matter wasn't finished, couldn't possibly be finished until she got her family away from this place. But they were all alive. He'd survived his worst moment. That's where they were now, one moment—one second—at a time.

Still slumped on the floor, Shaw wiped his face on the sleeve of his shirt and looked at her as if he hadn't been fully present before. "What are you doing?"

"I put it away."

"Oh Orlie, it's not that simple." His head dropped back against the wall with a thud. "You don't understand."

"I don't. I don't understand." She sat on the floor in front of him, legs crossed beneath her, and squeezed one of his hands. "Please help me understand."

It gushed out of him, all that he'd been bottling up since they'd arrived. "I thought, at first...I thought it was helping me paint—I know it sounds stupid, but I thought I'd found my muse. But it—they, someone—kept creeping into my head at all hours, when I was awake, when I was asleep. This thing— I don't know what this fucking thing is, Orlie, but it started to really scare me." As his words were scaring her. Steely spiders tickled her skin. "It wanted something. I know I wasn't wrong—it's about this place. The people who died. But I didn't want to understand anymore, I just wanted it to stop. I needed a door to close, a way to shut it out."

"That's what you were trying to do? Shut it out?" she asked cautiously. Maybe he hadn't actually wanted to kill himself but to silence the things he'd been hearing.

"No, it was more than that," he protested. "Someone, something...needed me. I couldn't let it in. It wanted to be inside me. It kept pushing on my consciousness—*In, in, in,* it said. How could I let it in? It scared me, Orlie, scared me so bad. What if I couldn't stop it? I didn't know who I'd be—what I'd be—if it got inside me. I kept telling it in my head, *No, go away, leave me alone!* It's bigger than me, stronger. What does it want with me? And if I lost, if it got me—I think that's what it wanted, with the snow. So I'm here, trapped. And it gets me. And I'm not *me* anymore…and what if I hurt you or the kids? I couldn't take the risk that I'd lose myself, and do something to you, or Tigger, or Bean…"

Orla sat there, stunned. They were simple enough words, but she couldn't fathom what she was hearing. Her husband thought something was trying to possess him? Something that might hurt one of them? In his mind, this attempted suicide was a sacrifice to save them from what he feared he'd become? *This fucking place.*

"We're gonna get out of here." She snuggled beside him, her arm gripping his shoulders. "In the morning, We'll all put on snowshoes. We'll get down to the road, at least, see if it's been cleared."

Shaw nodded. "I didn't want to fail you—"

"You haven't. Don't even think that way. Look what you were willing to do to save…" It didn't matter if she couldn't fully grasp it, the dire voices ricocheting in his head. More important, she believed him: Something was happening here. Sparking madness in their minds. And in the only way he knew how, he'd been trying to keep them all safe.

"Come on." She got up and tugged him to his feet.

"I'm so sorry. For upending our lives. I just wanted an adventure, a chance to do something of my own. I really thought—"

"I wanted that too. And you'll still get it, an adventure, and all the things you want to do." She supported him around his waist as he trudged beside her, stiff and heavy, as if his body had fossilized and he wasn't quite sure how to make it move.

She didn't bother to turn the lights off before they went upstairs; what did it matter? The electric bill would be nothing compared to the loss they were going to take on the house. They'd head to Pittsburgh the moment they could. There was more space in her parents' house than they'd had at Walker and Julie's. The kids could have her old room, and she and Shaw would take the guest room. It had been so long since she'd lived under her parents' roof, but it was the refuge they needed.

Holding Shaw's hand, she led him up the stairs. The wood creaked beneath their feet, and when they reached the top, Eleanor Queen was standing just outside her door.

"What's going on?" she whispered.

"Papa's not feeling well." Her daughter's face was in shadow, but Orla saw her turn her head, studying her father as he shuffled past. "It's nothing to worry about. Go back to bed— we're going to trek out in the morning."

"Trek out? Where?"

"Away." She doubled back and kissed Eleanor Queen's forehead before gently pushing her toward her bed. But when Orla got to her own doorway, her daughter was leaning into the hallway, watching her. "Go to sleep," Orla told her again.

"It's not that simple," said Eleanor Queen.

"Just close your eyes. Imagine yourself writing the alphabet, one slow letter at a time."

"No. You don't understand. It wanted us here. And we're not done." The girl retreated into her room and shut the door.

Orla's mouth tingled with nausea. Everything was slipping away. Only Tycho hadn't shown signs of delirium yet. Once she'd felt a great sense of purpose as a dancer, as the family's breadwinner. Now they needed her to do something else.

Save them.

22

It was becoming an all-too-familiar pattern. The awakening. The shock of something outside, new and strange. The summoning of the rest of the household.

Orla and Shaw stood in their slippers side by side on the front porch, matching portraits of what-the-bloody-hell. Maybe they'd grown accustomed to the temperatures, or maybe…it was warmer, above freezing. Water dribbled from the eaves, plunked down and splashed on the porch's saggy railing. But *one* warmer night couldn't explain the melt-off. And the yard— had anything actually *melted*? Orla would have used the word *restored*. Restored to how it had been before the ten feet appeared. Minus the remains of the snow dragon. It was a miracle, and now she understood how Shaw had felt as he'd witnessed the aurora borealis. It was all so terribly wrong. So terribly impossible.

"See?" she whispered to her husband. "It's gonna be okay."

At least they could safely leave.

He was in a daze as they studied it: the perfect foot and a half of snow that remained in the yard, the water dripping from the gutters. Tycho, per usual, remained unaware of the improbability of what they were seeing. But not Eleanor Queen, who slipped her hand into Orla's.

"Nothing flooded."

"Hmm?" Orla glanced down at her apprehensive daughter.

"If it had melted so fast, there'd be flooding. That's what happens."

"Yes, usually—"

"We *prayed* it away!" said Tycho. "It worked, Mama—now we can play outside!" He bounded around the porch, indifferent to the puddles that soaked his sock-covered feet.

The temptation to revert to denial was strong. But she'd promised herself—and her family—to face reality, such as it had become. She'd *asked* for this. And here it was. Had something heard her? The same thing that was trying...she didn't want to think about the night before, or the voice demanding entrance into Shaw's head—not until they were far away. Orla wasn't as hopeful as she'd been at first, even with their escape route unblocked. Something—in the air? In her gut?—didn't feel right. Poison came to mind. A silent and deadly weapon descending around them in an invisible mist. What if they were all breathing it in?

But to Eleanor Queen, still clutching her hand, she tried to sound cheery. "Nothing to be afraid of now, we can come and go as we please."

"No, Mama—you don't...you're being so blind. This isn't so you'll leave, it's so you'll be happy."

Eleanor Queen didn't sound very happy. The deepening connection between her daughter and what was happening around them turned her bones to ice and she shivered despite the balmy temperatures.

"Okay, it's time to go, let's go." Orla ushered her family indoors just as Shaw had during the glorious night of dancing lights. She was certain she and her husband were of one mind now, with a definitive, if unspoken plan, even if he was over-whelmed and confused.

Inside, she helped Tycho strip off his sopping socks. "Hurry up to your rooms. Pack your favorite things; it's time to go. Papa and I will come back later for the rest." Or maybe not.

Shaw stumbled in from the porch, a thousand times more alive than he'd been a moment before. Something had jolted him back to life. "No, wait. We can't. Not just yet."

His words stopped the children. They looked from one parent to the next, in search of clear direction.

"We need. To go." Orla carefully measured her words so as not to alarm the children with the volcanic emotions that rumbled within her or the scalding reminder she wanted to spew at her husband: *Have you forgotten last night?* "We'll work out the details later, with the house—"

Shaw's look cut her off. He wasn't disagreeing with her; something else was wrong. And he widened his eyes, desperate to say or not say something. He cocked his head toward the kids.

Orla wanted to cry. Massive snowfalls were within the realm of possibility; it happened sometimes in nearby Oswego County, that's what Shaw had said. But could so much snow just...vanish? Momentum surged within her, an urgent and primal desire to flee. Now, while they could. Why couldn't they? She beseeched her husband without words.

"Why don't you guys go up and get dressed," he said to the kids in his composed-father voice. Thankfully he could still appear normal, not like the broken man who'd sat with his back to the wall, a shotgun...

Tycho dashed off, but Eleanor Queen assessed them one final time before following him up the stairs.

"What's wrong—why can't we go?" Orla whisper-barked to Shaw.

He guided her back toward the door and spoke just as softly. "Did you notice the garage?"

Orla shook her head. Willed him not to say what he was about to say…

"It looks like one side collapsed, part of the roof and wall."

"I didn't see it."

"The far side. And from where we were standing, the car looks to be buried in debris and—"

She threw open the front door and flew back out, even stepped into the snowy yard in her slippers. She'd been so distracted before, she hadn't thought to look at the garage, but Shaw was right. And there was something else she hadn't noticed. A little splotch of crimson off to the side, just a few feet away, soggy, atop the snow. The lifeless body of her little friend the cardinal. Had he been buried when the snow came down? Trapped, asphyxiated by the sudden, supernatural descent? Another day Orla might have cried over the loss, sentimental or symbolic, but now she was too agitated. Shaw joined her in the yard but didn't notice the feathery red corpse. Instead, he looked behind them, up toward the roof. She followed his gaze.

Their satellite dish dangled askew.

"Shit. *Fuck*," she muttered. "This fucking place. Did you check your cell?"

"First thing. I check it fifty times a day. Don't panic."

"I'm not—"

"I'm really sorry about last night."

"I know."

"Thank you—for everything, for understanding. I only want us all to be okay."

"I know that. We'll get everything sorted out. For now, let's stay focused—we can still follow through with our original plan." At least outside they could safely raise their voices without alarming the kids. And she didn't care about her feet turning to ice or the snow seeping through the worn fabric of her sweatpants. Focus. "We'll get into town, walk the whole way if we need to. And call Walker—wait. Are they traveling?" The other Bennett clan spent alternate Christmases with Julie's family in North Carolina.

"It's fine, they haven't left yet."

She plotted it all out. "We'd probably only have to stay a night. My parents will come and get us—"

"Maybe we won't need to do that." He must have read the lava surfacing on her face, readying as she opened her mouth to protest. "Have them drive here, I mean. Maybe…" He looked back to the car. "I can try digging it out. It doesn't look too damaged, a few dings. If I can get some of the snow that's blocking it out of the way, maybe I could just back it up under the wreckage. It doesn't matter at this point if the rest of the garage collapses."

Orla nodded. Smart plan. Whatever had infected Shaw hadn't stolen all of his rational thinking. It would have been a long walk for the kids, and she'd never liked the idea of them being on the snowed-over road, without sidewalks and with the berms buried. And they had choices about where to head next, though driving straight on to Pittsburgh seemed by far their best option. She wouldn't let her family make the same mistake again; wherever they ended up living, they needed to be around people. They could worry about the financial loss of all they'd invested later. Or maybe they could sell the house—and maybe it wouldn't be so inhospitable to the next owner. The place was going to be their undoing, and Orla didn't care about the why or how of it. Sixteen days had been long enough. It was time to go.

23

While Shaw was outside trying to free the car, Orla stayed upstairs with the children, going from bedroom to bedroom to assist with the packing.

"Are we gonna see Derek and Jamie?" Tycho asked, piling toys into a box. He sounded eager enough, but Orla sensed a hint of confusion. A few weeks there, a couple of weeks here; did he think this was how it would be from now on, his new peripatetic life?

"Maybe. Or maybe Lola and Lolo—would you like that?" She kept her voice light but didn't otherwise interact with him. In her career, she'd been required to act, to perform roles, but now she didn't trust herself to convincingly portray the Calm Mother. She tied her everything's-fine mask in place and put her thundering heart on mute. Told herself to keep things as normal as possible. It was part of a parent's duty to make sure her children understood the difference between reality and fantasy, but she was hard-pressed at the moment to keep the two straight herself.

Orla stacked Tycho's neatly folded clothes into a reusable bag. Her plan was to squash as much stuff into the back of the

SUV as possible. After getting dressed, she'd gone downstairs and retrieved all of their boots—not to pack, but to wear. She didn't trust that something unexpected wouldn't happen again, and she insisted the children put on layers, in addition to their boots, in case they needed to flee on foot. She hadn't phrased it quite that way, but the wariness on Eleanor Queen's face told her that she understood nonetheless.

Orla heard a clamor behind her and turned around to see her daughter pushing a box of books into the hallway. She heaved a black garbage bag, presumably filled with her clothes, on top of it.

"What about my new bed? And the rest of my stuff?" Eleanor Queen asked.

"We'll try to pack up the house later, but I can't guarantee when. We'll get you a new bed if nothing else. Okay?"

She couldn't bear to see the disappointment, the frustration, on her daughter's face, so Orla busied herself with other tasks. She endeavored to move about methodically and appear composed so as not to give away that inside her was a crazed cuckoo clock, ticking down toward a collapse of mechanics. Nothing made sense and there was no time to analyze it. All she could do was try to keep everything—everyone—calm and hope to avoid, at least for now, the difficult questions that were coming. How would they explain what had happened to their family? The real part, with Shaw and the shotgun, as well as the stuff that would make them all sound delusional? And eventually they'd have to find something to tell the children; at present she was far from having any comforting answers.

"Bean? Are you set?"

"I guess."

"Can you help me? Just finish up with Tycho while I pack your papa's stuff?"

Eleanor Queen plodded down the hallway, eyes on the floor.

She couldn't have looked more somber if she were attending a funeral for all her favorite books. Orla recognized the importance of not leaving them behind; they were her friends. But her daughter also looked smaller somehow. Had she lost weight? Orla expected she'd be glad to leave, glad to be free of this thing that hovered too close to her awareness. *What the fuck is this place doing to my child?* She didn't believe her daughter was mentally ill any more than she believed her husband was; it was this place. They were fine before, and after they left, Eleanor Queen and Shaw would return to normal. In spite of everything, Orla wondered if her daughter was reluctant to lose another home, and she hated that she couldn't give her children the sense of security they needed.

When Eleanor Queen was within reach, Orla caressed her back. "You don't have to worry. It's all just a bit more than we expected, but I'm sure your grandparents will be so happy to see you."

Eleanor Queen lifted her eyes and Orla saw fear. No—terror. They were the eyes of someone too wise, too helpless, who knew she couldn't escape a terrible end.

"Can't you feel it?" Eleanor Queen whispered.

Orla didn't want her to frighten Tycho, so she inched Eleanor Queen around the corner and into the master bedroom. She hadn't had time to do anything more than lay out her own clothes in piles on the bed.

She was usually careful not to baby Eleanor Queen because her daughter didn't like it, but now Orla dropped to one knee. Below her daughter's eye level, Orla could see her face better. The girl appeared paler than usual, and she had faint purple smudges of exhaustion beneath her eyes. Something about her daughter seemed so very old, so very beyond the realm of her limited childhood.

"You all right? It'll be okay soon. Papa's digging out the car—"

"It's very heavy; can't you feel it?"

"Feel what, love?"

Eleanor Queen raised her eyes as if looking for something or following something. A moth, flying in herky-jerky bursts. Or maybe it was a sound she heard, a faint voice, words she couldn't quite translate.

"It's heavier than it's ever been," she said.

"I don't know what that means." Orla sounded more hysterical than she'd intended. But she knew what it meant: They had to leave. Go now. Even the packing was taking too long, the shoveling. She saw herself marching her children through the snow, holding their hands, dragging them if necessary to get them past an invisible boundary to where they'd be safe. "Please—can you tell me? What's out there?"

Eleanor Queen's head bobbled on her delicate neck. Her eyes watered but she wore the empty gaze of a person slipping into catatonia. "Papa's in trouble."

"What? How do you—"

"Big trouble." She said it in a raspy whisper, sounding nothing like herself.

Orla started as Tycho popped into the doorway, his innocent face full of bewilderment. Everyone needed her—her anguished daughter, her frightened little boy, and now...what was wrong with Shaw? Her hands shook and she knew the everything's-fine mask had tumbled off, revealing her slipshod insanity. It was all falling apart. Again. She raced around the bed and looked out the window, scanning toward her left where she expected Shaw to be shoveling behind the car.

What she saw shouldn't have been possible. But *of course* it was, in this place that refused to obey the ordinary laws of space, or time.

* * *

"Take your brother to your room and don't come out! And shut the door!"

Her urgency summoned Eleanor Queen from her trance, and she grabbed Tycho's hand and ran. Orla didn't want them to go back to his room, look out his window and get an even more direct view of what she'd seen by the garage. Could it get in the house? Climb the stairs?

She called to Eleanor Queen's closed door as she raced past, "Don't open it! Stay until I come to get you!"

Tycho whimpered, but Orla didn't have time to soothe him. She almost stumbled on her way down the stairs but corrected her balance by reaching out to the wall on either side of the staircase. She flew into Shaw's studio, flung open his closet door. The fucking gun locker; she'd hoped to never see it again. The combination took no effort to recall; it was her own birthday, backward. She'd insisted when Shaw set it that she'd never need to open it, but even then the words had sounded empty, uttered by her city-self, who no longer counted. Now she wished with her entire gun-hating heart that Shaw had given her more than the most basic verbal instructions; they'd yet to have the actual lesson she'd asked for.

The rifle, she remembered, was for shooting larger game, especially from a distance. The shotgun was for birds and (*suicides*) smaller things that might scamper away. But Orla didn't trust her ability to aim, to hold the gun steady if the creature turned on her. She grabbed the double-barreled shotgun, cracked it open—more confidently than she had the night before—and shoved in two shells. Shaw had warned her about the kickback; she'd have to cram it tight against her shoulder, but at least a shaky aim wouldn't matter so much. The thing outside was huge.

She bolted out the front door, leaving it shuddering in her wake as it crashed against the wall. Her strong legs helped her leap off the porch and land effortlessly in the snow. Boots. Sweaters. A part of her had known, and she was ready. She slowed down only when she was halfway between the house and the garage, then brought the shotgun to her shoulder.

The polar bear, which had been sniffing around the footprints Shaw had left in the snow behind the trapped car, reared up on its hind legs as it caught her approach. It opened its ferociously fanged mouth and made an angry sound, a roar of surprise and warning. The beast looked scraggly, not like the polar bears she'd seen in photographs, plump in their luminescent fur. She could see the bear's ribs through its too-thin chest. In another circumstance—had it been a photo in *National Geographic* revealing the impact of global warming on starving predators— she might have pitied it.

"Shaw!" Orla tried to peer around the bear. Oh God, was she too late? The shovel was still there, abandoned in the snow. She feared Shaw was lying somewhere out of sight in a pool of blood, his innards exposed and half eaten. But maybe he was hiding on the other side of the garage. He didn't reply, but she didn't give up hope; maybe she could still save him.

Papa's in trouble.

The bear dropped onto all fours and wagged its head back and forth with its lip curled up in a snarl. Orla, in spite of her ignorance of the outdoors, sensed what it was doing: gauging her, intimidating her, preparing to attack.

She took a cautious step back. In spite of how she'd charged out of the house, ready to kill, the reality of it was quite different. Uneasy, niggling thoughts came to her; a warning sign flashed somewhere in her mind. She'd worried about bears since they'd first moved in, had even mentioned polar bears out loud, after which Eleanor Queen had explained the meaning of *Antarctica*. It should have been enough that they were nowhere near the North or South Pole, but this place conjured impossible things.

The bear didn't *look* like a mirage, and Shaw—wherever he was, hiding or unconscious—needed her help. Hungry bears would eat humans; she remembered watching a documentary with Shaw, grisly but compelling, about a man who misjudged his expertise in the wild. And once a bear had a taste of human flesh, it wouldn't stop. In the film, the expert was eaten alive as audio rolled, as his unlucky girlfriend tried to beat off his attacker with a frying pan. The bear ate her too.

And after all the other weird shit that had happened, why couldn't a starving bear from the Arctic break into their house? Clamber up the stairs and devour her children? Nothing was impossible anymore.

Orla rocked from side to side on her feet, inching backward as the polar bear started to advance. It roared at her. Reared again. An abominable snow monster towering above her head.

Her finger on the trigger. The gun's butt wedged against her shoulder. Orla fired.

The explosive noise, the force, made her wince and take a stumbling step. But she hit her target. A spray of blood stained the bear's exposed chest and stomach. It staggered. Dropped. Lay in a sprawl, its chin on the snow, and emitted a *whoof* of foggy breath.

"No!" The scream came from behind her. From the porch. Eleanor Queen.

Orla turned to her, wary that the beast, though down, might yet return to its feet. "Go back inside!"

"Mama, no!" Eleanor Queen ran down the porch steps and stumbled toward the bear.

Orla swiftly intercepted her and caught her in one arm.

"Mama!" Eleanor Queen fought against her grip.

Orla couldn't understand her daughter's desperation; even a tenderhearted child knew better than to try and nurse a slaughtered bear back to life. But Eleanor Queen never took her eyes away from the beast, and she struggled to push past her mother to get to it.

"Eleanor Queen, you can't. Stop, it's—"

"Papa!"

Had he emerged from behind the garage? Orla, still clutching her daughter's coat, spun around so fast she accidentally flung Eleanor Queen into the snow. "No…no." It came out so softly, a misted prayer.

But once she saw it… "Eleanor Queen, get back in the house!"

"But Mama—"

"This instant! Get inside and shut the door!" She used a furious voice Orla barely knew she possessed. She didn't turn to make sure Eleanor Queen obeyed her. With her mother's vision, the eyes that really could see behind her, she saw everything: Eleanor Queen tripped her way toward the house, still mesmerized by the bleeding animal and her mother, its murderer. Orla gazed at what she had done—at what Eleanor Queen had seen from the start.

"Oh God." Orla collapsed onto her knees beside the body.

It wasn't a bear.

It was Shaw. Facedown. His innards ripped apart by the shotgun blast.

The snow beneath him turned red as it absorbed his blood.

24

It couldn't be real. Couldn't be real. She'd become a contortionist who couldn't unknot herself. Her strongest impulse was to go back in time one minute, just one minute back in time to undo what she had done—couldn't have done. "No, no no no no...oh Shaw. Oh God, I'm so sorry..."

The warmth she'd felt in the air earlier in the day was gone. Her tears turned icy before they slid past her cheeks.

"I'm so sorry!" She grabbed him, turned him over, clutched him in her arms. Rocked him, though she was the one who needed comfort. How could she have saved her husband from killing himself only to finish the job for him hours later? There came a sharp new aroma in the frosty emptiness, something rancid with life but unpleasant. Blood. And beneath it a heavier level of stink, the smells emerging from her husband's punctured organs.

A faint cloud of breath emerged from his mouth. A sound like wind, accompanied by a bubble of bright blood.

Orla startled, shifted to see his face better when she realized he wasn't dead. "Shaw, baby—I love you, I'm so sorry, I'll get help!"

"Leave," he whispered.

"I'll get help!"

His chin bobbed a little as he tried to shake his head, and his eyes drooped, unfocused. "No…can leave…now. Go."

"We're not leaving you behind!"

"Sorry. Here…all my fault." More blood gurgled from his mouth. "You…go…now. Love…"

He fell silent.

"Shaw?"

She absorbed the full collapse of his muscles as he passed. His head sagged to the side, and his mouth hung open like he still wanted to speak.

"Oh, my love, Shaw…oh my God, what have we done. What have I done…" Her sobs became too heavy for words.

As she held him, her sweater sleeves soaked up his blood. She rocked him, wailing. Couldn't think about leaving, or seeing to the children, or moving from the spot where she had killed her husband. Maybe she'd never be able to think or reason again, not with confidence. She'd blasted a thousand pellets through her own sanity. The pressure of his loss crushed her chest. What had he said to reassure her? That no buildings would collapse on them; it was safer here. But she felt the bricks, the walls, the suffocating debris of her mistakes. She should have known—the two-headed hybrid, the talking snow dragon, the menagerie of white animals that disappeared when someone else turned to see them. Not everything was what it seemed. Salty tears and cold air stung her eyes. This couldn't all be in her head—Eleanor Queen had *warned* her…

What had her daughter known?

Papa's in trouble.

It was too much to make sense of. For a while she was unaware of the cold. But Shaw's body heat dissipated quickly. Time passed. She found herself holding a heavy, frigid mass.

Her arms ached. Her knees, crumpled beneath his dead weight, begged for her to move. But she stayed there, back hunched, blind and deaf, too distraught to cry or protest. If she moved it would all be over. She'd never be able to go back. He would always be gone.

She prayed for time to reverse itself. Why couldn't it? When so many other fucked-up things had happened.

It started snowing. The wind picked up. How long had she been sitting there? She needed a coat, gloves, a hat. The snow covered some of the blood. Maybe if she stayed out there long enough, she and Shaw would disappear beneath the fresh white. The tragedy would be erased.

"Mama?"

Eleanor Queen. Not screaming. Not at a distance. Beside her.

Orla didn't want to look at her. What if she saw a rabid dog and her instinct was to grab its throat and squeeze until it went limp in her hands?

But she turned her creaky, half-frozen neck. Her daughter had bundled up in snow pants, coat, mittens, hood. She draped the throw blanket that lived in a crumpled ball in a corner of the couch over her mother's shoulders. Orla wondered if she meant to sit vigil beside her. Why wasn't the child angry with her? Where were her tears? Maybe they should get Tycho, make it a family affair. Maybe they could all disappear together.

Eleanor Queen, on her knees, squeezed in close to her, hugging her with one arm. "You're going to freeze, Mama."

Her daughter—*Shaw's* daughter—brought warmth with her. A living heart still full of blood. The lingering heat from Shaw's blasted furnace. What had Shaw said? It was so important now that she remember every incredible thing that her husband had uttered. *A heart stopping. A cold seeping in.* Had he been dreaming of his own death? Had Orla played some predetermined role in fulfilling his prophecy? Orla couldn't meet the girl's eyes, not after she'd killed her father.

"I'm so sorry." Her chapped skin, stiffened by frozen tears and the merciless wind, stretched painfully as she moved her jaw.

Eleanor Queen wrapped both thin arms around her, squeezed her, pressed their cheeks together. Her voice broke as she cried, "Oh Mama, it wasn't your fault."

"I thought he was...I saw a..."

"It was my fault, it was all my fault."

Her tearful confession brought Orla out of her gloom. For a time, she'd almost forgotten her children, in the house alone and scared. And Tycho, now abandoned. Where was he? Had he seen? But Eleanor Queen...she knew something. And though Orla would never hold her responsible for what this place could do, she needed to know.

"Eleanor Queen, love." With Shaw's head still in the crook of her left elbow, she embraced Eleanor Queen with her right arm. "You warned me, before—"

"Nooooo!" the child wailed. Her voice grew shrill with emotion. "No, I was all wrong!"

"But you knew Papa was in—"

"Nooooo! Mama, listen to me! It was telling me that Papa was in *trouble*! That he'd *done something wrong*! It was *angry* with him! And if I'd understood what was gonna—"

"No no no no no." Orla pushed herself away from Shaw's body, laid him as gently as she could on the frozen ground. It pained her to move, but she gave herself to her daughter, took her in her arms. Finally, maybe her rocking would soothe someone. "This wasn't your fault. I saw...I know it sounds ridiculous, but I thought I saw a bear. That wasn't you. You can't—this had nothing to do with—"

"I didn't think it was *that* mad—I just knew it didn't want

Papa to leave! Don't you see, Mama? If I'd just told you what I felt, that we couldn't leave. Papa—"

"No! No, Eleanor Queen, look at me." She took her daughter's face in her hands. Eleanor Queen looked stricken, on the verge of breaking, and it gave Orla the resolve she needed. "I don't know what *it* is, and I don't know what it's saying to you. I don't know why these things are happening, but I *know* you aren't to blame. You are *not* to blame. Do you hear me?"

Eleanor Queen gave the tiniest of nods.

"The truth is…" No point in denying it. "We wouldn't have listened. If you'd told us not to go. So this was on us—me and Papa. And Papa…we were trying to keep you safe." By getting them all away from this place, and the thing that haunted it. Their instincts had been right.

Orla didn't want to contemplate what was happening or why, but she had to. Whatever they were dealing with wasn't a mindless partner, as she'd hypothesized before, a cycle of action/reaction, music/dance. That had felt comfortable because it was a reactive process that she fully understood. But the circumstances had become too…personal.

As if something really was *listening*.

She'd toyed with the idea, but hadn't really believed it. It was a mental exercise, an exploration of completely impossible alternatives. How could she be dealing with a conscious entity?

An inventory of events scrolled through her mind. She'd always wanted to see the aurora borealis. Tycho had mistaken ten inches of snow for ten feet, then after the real ten feet arrived, he wished it away. Eleanor Queen had spoken of polar bears. And she and her father both—what had they *heard*? Whispering among the branches? *Was* something trying to communicate with them?

And then there was the day when she'd almost grabbed the gun, stupidly afraid an animal was breaking into the house.

She'd *thought* it, how she'd never be able to forgive herself if she accidentally shot her husband.

What kind of wish fulfillment was this? Certainly not granted by any power she'd ever heard of. More devil than god.

Yet they'd had a theory, and not a completely ridiculous one. Had no one ever experienced the collective power of angry, frustrated ghosts? Had the hapless souls who'd died here been trying to warn them that this place was not a cure? That death awaited, and they hadn't listened?

If Eleanor Queen was interpreting things correctly, it was— *they* were?—angry with Shaw. Was it mad at him the day he got lost? Was he wandering too close to the edge of the homestead, so it issued a warning? But since then, they'd been off the property—even together, as a family, to get groceries or pizza. Did the rules change, or was she still getting it wrong? That first full day, Shaw had followed a plume of smoke and found the cure-cottage chimney. She'd smelled that woody, burning fragrance when they arrived, coming from the same direction. Maybe what Shaw had experienced that day on his walk wasn't a warning but a *greeting*. An acknowledgment of some kind, of his presence?

It had summoned Shaw—she was starting to understand that in an entirely new way. Maybe, after that initial visit, the choice to move hadn't been fully his. Could this thing have wanted him, and then grown vexed that he couldn't understand or wouldn't obey? Shaw had been destroyed by the very muse who'd summoned him. It wasn't fair, but maybe, if It had wanted Shaw to fulfill some transcendental task, maybe the rest of them were irrelevant. Collateral damage. And maybe it was over now.

Is that what he'd been trying to say as he died? Had It possessed him, as he'd feared, and that's why he'd appeared to her as a polar bear?

And if the thing had been inside him when she pulled the trigger…

That's what he was saying! They could leave now—it was over!

Orla launched to her feet, hauling her daughter up with her even as her aching bones protested. "Go back to the house, help your brother into his snow pants—I'll be *right* in. Right in, and then we'll get away from this place, okay? I think it's safe now."

Eleanor Queen looked toward the trees, listening. "I don't hear it."

"Go—it's time to leave!"

A flash of relief bloomed on her daughter's face—and in Orla's heart. This time, she watched as Eleanor Queen trudged through the snow back toward the house, the nylon of her pants *squeal-swish*ing as she hurried. When she opened the door, Tycho was there, sobbing, and held out his arms for his sister.

"I'll be right there, Tycho!" She hoped he could hear her over the wind and distance.

As soon as Eleanor Queen shut the door, Orla draped the flimsy throw blanket around her neck so it wouldn't slip off and straightened Shaw where he lay on his back. Bile and heartache poisoned her throat, threatened to make her vomit, but she grabbed her beloved by the ankles and dragged him through the snow toward the far side of the garage so Tycho wouldn't see. They'd come back for him, the emergency personnel, after she got the kids away and could call for help. She glanced up at the satellite dish, now believing in the intentionality of its destruction—something wanted to keep them isolated.

How would she ever make anyone understand? Maybe they'd send her to prison. At best, they'd declare her insane. *I thought he was a bear.* She wasn't dead, but her children might yet end up alone. Worries for another day.

Fighting another wave of sickness, she dug through Shaw's coat pockets and found the car keys. Maybe he'd cleared enough that she could back the car out, drive away. She tossed aside the split logs that secured the tarp over their wood supply. After folding it in half, she used the waterproof blue material to cover his body, weighting it at the corners and edges with the displaced logs. As if it would protect him; as if the worst hadn't already happened.

This was all too savage. She hurled the half-buried shovel out of the way and almost tossed the shotgun after it. But she couldn't for fear that someone would find it. What if it brought misery to someone else's life? For now, she propped the gun against the woodpile, determined to secure it back in the locker before they left. At least no one could accuse her of *that* particular carelessness, even if she had accidentally—no. She put the words, the images, the reality of what she'd done in a mental box. Wrapped a chain around it. It would undo her, and she had to get her children back to civilization. She stuffed the word *mourn* away too. If she stayed focused, she might not fall apart.

It took only moments of trying to step through the deep snow wedged against their SUV for her to realize she couldn't escape that way. Shaw hadn't gotten that far; she'd need to shovel for hours just to get to the car, and she couldn't waste so much precious time in this bedeviled place. She might have killed It, but there was nothing left here she wanted. Before heading back into the house, she retrieved the shotgun, cracked it open, and dislodged the unused shell into the snow. If one of the children turned into a monster, she'd be in no danger of destroying another irreplaceable life.

25

No one spoke when Orla got back inside. She didn't know how Eleanor Queen might have explained the situation to Tycho, but his slightly dazed look of trauma matched theirs. Orla was glad they didn't ask questions. Small blessings. She changed into dry clothes—clothes not stained with blood—and got the kids ready as best she could. Finally, they gathered at the front door and took a silent moment with their mittens, surgeons all, pulling on gloves for the most difficult operation of their lives.

They left everything behind. Orla didn't even bother to lock the door. She brought a small backpack with their money, official papers, IDs, charged but nonfunctioning cell phones, and a bottle of water, which would probably solidify into ice before they reached St. Armand.

Tycho followed behind Eleanor Queen and Orla brought up the rear so she could keep an eye on both children. The sky was leaden and the snow whipped at their faces. They each kept a hand on the rope guideline, and Orla was grateful they'd constructed it. She didn't trust herself anymore to even walk in a straight line. The fresh snow was deep enough to make walking difficult, especially for Tycho, but it had buried the blood by the time they left the house. His youthful energy kept him going forward, stretching his legs to plant his feet in his sister's footsteps. And stalwart Eleanor Queen never faltered even as Orla wondered if they should have put on the snowshoes. Her daughter understood the seriousness of the mission—and hadn't contradicted her plan—and Orla was counting on easier walking once they got to the more compressed road. Everything, she told herself, would be easier when they crossed the property line, away from this awful place.

The wind teased them and she sensed it wanting to play a cruel game—knock them, spin them, turn them around so they couldn't leave. *It's just weather.* Onward they traipsed. Tycho never asked, *Where's Papa?* His silence bruised her heart.

The visibility worsened, and for a time Orla feared another whiteout would block their way. But while the whiteouts had come on suddenly, the current air grew denser by degrees as the sky seemed to gradually lower itself. She glanced upward from time to time, claustrophobia setting in as the heavy clouds sank. Would the clouds snuff them out? Murder them like a giant pillow held against their faces? She wanted to urge Eleanor Queen to go faster, impatient to reach the end of the winding driveway, but her daughter and son were already huffing out noisy gusts of exertion. Driven by their own anguish, they didn't need to be urged on.

It seemed as if the driveway had stretched and twisted and would never end. "Almost there," Orla called out, hoping it was true, desperate to give them something positive, a reward for the misery of their day—their mother would yet get them to safety. Even if they never forgave her for what she'd done to their father.

They rounded the last bend and Orla expected to see a rising hillside covered with austere sugar maples and beech trees, black trunks and a webbed canopy of bare limbs decorated with garlands of snow. The road that led to their house cut through a swath of forest, but that was not what she saw ahead of them. Instead, there lay a soupy fog. And an expanse of lumpy terrain that looked almost extraterrestrial.

Eleanor Queen abruptly stopped and Orla had to grab the back of Tycho's jacket to keep him from plowing into his sister. He'd kept his eyes downward the entire time, fixed on his sister's guiding footprints.

"No. No, no, this isn't possible."

"Mama?" Eleanor Queen's quavering voice hid a terrible, unspoken question. She'd reached the end of their roped rail: the mailbox. But the world they'd once known beyond it had been smudged out, replaced by a plateau of fissured ice. It ran opposite of how the road should have been, the floor of ice rising on their right where it had once sloped downhill toward a larger thoroughfare. The plateau was too broad to see across, as if it lay between the peaks of a towering, clouded mountain range.

"Don't let go of the rope. Step back and take Tycho's hand."

Eleanor Queen took Tycho's left hand and Orla took his right as she let the guide rope go and walked forward to the boundary. They stood in a line, looking out at what should have been their road. The way out.

But I killed It.

"What is it, Mama?" Tycho asked in the same tone he'd once used when gazing at the northern lights, neither afraid nor awed. Simply confused.

Orla thought of Mount Everest first—she and Shaw had shared a love for edge-of-your-seat rock-climbing films. Some-times the climbers had to cross vast fields of ice slit by perilous crevasses. They'd lay ladders over the fissures and step across the flimsy, bowing bridges like strange, bent-over animals with viciously spiked crampons instead of rear claws. The snow couldn't always be trusted; sometimes, where it looked solid, it was only a thin veneer and walking on it meant falling into an abyss. A plunge into a deep crevasse meant almost certain death.

"Mama?" Eleanor Queen asked again.

"It's a glacier," Orla told them. An almost laughably matter-of-fact explanation for the impossible.

She wanted to collapse. Weep. Shaw had died for nothing. Whatever was happening in this place was far from over. All the more reason to get the children away. Maybe they'd gone back in time—as she'd prayed, but too far back—to when much of North America had been covered in glaciers. Shaw had mentioned in bed one night, while talking about his paintings, an interest in seeing a glacier before global warming made all the retreating ribbons of ice fully disappear. But they'd spent so much on the move; it was a fantasy. Something for his bucket list.

"Wonder what Papa would've thought," Orla whispered without thinking. And immediately regretted it.

Tycho burst into tears. "We can't leave! The monster's gonna get us."

When had he begun to believe there was a monster? Is that what he understood had happened to his father? How quickly Orla's own fear had metastasized, infecting even her little boy: *Something was out to get them.*

Orla was tempted to barrel on past the end of the drive-way into what should have been the road. Maybe the lane was really there and this was all a mirage. *The bear wasn't real.* It was a bleak yet decidedly awesome possibility if the power at hand had no prescribed boundaries. No limitations. Were they dealing with an omnipotent force that she had tried, too late, to fathom? Or were Its powers limited to florid illusions? *I'm the deadly one.*

The part of her that wanted to show the children there was nothing out there to fear stepped onto the glacier.

"Mama, no!" Eleanor Queen lunged forward and tugged her back to the relative safety of the snow-covered driveway.

"It might not be real," Orla said. Her voice sounded hollow, swallowed by the field of fissures. Nothing moved—no birds in the sky, no wind to scatter snow across the ice.

"I don't think you can trust that," Eleanor Queen whispered.

Tycho hung his head, whimpering.

Orla hesitated; she didn't want to give up. She couldn't relinquish the hope that if they just walked onward, turning right onto what should have been the road, it would lead them to safety. The monster would see they couldn't be intimidated by displays of winter wonder. Maybe, if they all kept walking, the glacier would dissipate beneath their feet and they'd find themselves in familiar territory, between the tree-flanked hills of their road.

"Are you sure, Eleanor Queen? It might only look this way for a short distance." Orla hated the desperation that engulfed her voice. And hated that, by questioning her, Eleanor Queen might think her mother still didn't believe her. Orla was all too aware that she needed to heed *more* of her daughter's cryptic words and advice. If Orla pursued what *she* wanted to be true, simply because she wanted it, they could become stranded on the glacier. Or worse. But she couldn't turn back without Eleanor Queen's acknowledgment.

"We *have* to go home," she confirmed, almost as if she'd read her mother's mind.

"I wanna go home," Tycho cried, raising his arms for Orla to carry him. She knew he didn't mean the place that awaited behind them, but there was nowhere else she could take him.

Resigned to defeat, Orla picked up Tycho, slippery in his winter gear. The weather improved as they walked back.

The clouds lifted, revealing a strip of pale sky. *That's what It wanted.* She hated even the perception that she was following commands, but if It heard them—tapped into their thoughts— could she find a way to outthink It?

She'd been right, in a sense, about everything, but they weren't spiritual musings anymore; something was out there, more powerful than she could comprehend. And It had betrayed her. She'd wanted to believe in beauty, in nature, in the promise of the unknown. But it was a ruse, and a trap.

They walked on the trampled path, and the driveway de- livered them to their house more quickly than expected. Could they try again tomorrow, maybe only with the intention of going as far as the mailbox to leave a note for the postman? Would It let them do that, or would It recognize the attempt to communicate with the outside world? Though the pool of blood lay buried, Orla switched Tycho to her right hip so he was facing away from the garage—away from the garish tarp, still bright blue beneath its dusting of snow, that hid Shaw.

One word pounded through her head.

Why.

Why.

Why.

Why did It want them all to stay? Did It plan to pick them off one by one?

It angered her, the pettiness of this force she didn't under- stand. It teased, flaunted, threatened, made them unwelcome, then wouldn't let them leave. Why? Had only Shaw pissed It off? Or had she angered It too? Was there something she could do, something to set things right? Or would It remain volatile and vengeful?

She opened the front door and the children slogged in, sullen, defeated. Exhausted. Orla locked the door behind them. Yanked the curtains across the windows. Ready to try a new plan, silly though it sounded: pretend they were somewhere else. As Eleanor Queen and Tycho stripped out of their coats and boots, Orla headed straight upstairs, indifferent to the melting snow puddling in her wake. She closed every blind, triumphant in her foresight to install coverings on every window.

Block it out.

Make it all disappear.

Convince the children the outside didn't matter anymore, didn't exist. She'd lead Eleanor Queen and Tycho—her imaginative, artistic children—on a game of creating a new reality. Maybe they could confuse the thing that was lurking at their door, eavesdropping on their thoughts. Let the thing read their minds and find no trace of the world It knew, or wanted. If they could forget about It, maybe their tormentor would forget about them.

How long might that take?

And did they have enough food and resources to outlast It?

26

Orla put on one of their favorite Putumayo Playground CDs. It filled the living room with the buoyant rhythms of steel drums and cowbells.

"Each rug can be an island, and—"

"The chair can be Australia!" shouted Tycho.

Orla, unaware of her little boy's retained knowledge of Australia, nodded at him, suitably impressed. "Good thinking."

"The bookcase can be a mountain—"

"That no one can *climb*." Though she'd interrupted her daughter, Orla directed the words toward her son. "But you can make up new animals for the oceans and friendly creatures you might meet on the land."

Once she had them settled in their game of reimagining the living room, Orla planned to carry through with some necessary tasks, alone. She needed to inventory the food. Check the cell phone reception. It felt later in the day than it should have. Time was passing in wonky ways. Orla wouldn't have been surprised to crack the curtain and find the sun was setting. Maybe grief had ruptured something inside her, an intrinsic mechanism that kept her rooted to the real world, the Earth's rotation, the rising moon. She'd become a broken toy, a spinning top launched into crooked motion. It didn't help that the house seemed empty without Shaw. They'd grown accustomed to him being behind his closed door, working, a call or knock away. His absence was everywhere. The children felt it too.

"What about Papa?" Tycho asked as he leapt from one island to another, following his sister.

Eleanor Queen squatted and pulled Tycho down beside her, gazing at her mother in an intense, unnerving way. Orla sensed it was a test—how much did she know of the wrongness, and what would she admit to? She would never lie to her son, but he was still young enough that she wanted to protect him from the gorier aspects of the truth.

Orla knelt in front of them. "Your papa…" She pressed her lips together to stop the quivering. "There was a terrible accident .."

"I know," Tycho drawled impatiently. "But he's going to freeze out there, he should come in."

Orla pressed her cheeks between her hands. Maybe she'd awaken in a hospital and a concerned nurse would say, *You had a massive head injury, we almost lost you.* And Shaw would be there, smiling. And the kids, holding up homemade cards. And she would tell them, *What a horrible dream I had. I thought I'd never wake up.*

She'd had nightmares like that before. Once, she thought she was awake, but as she threw off the sheet to get up and go to the bathroom, she saw a human figure hovering on the ceiling above her. A man in a fetal position, like he was sleeping. A scream ricocheted inside her and she tried to clutch Shaw to wake him, warn him. But when she couldn't move, couldn't vocalize her terror, she realized she was asleep and had never flung back the sheet to rise from the bed. At that point she awakened a second time and shuffled into the bathroom rubbing her eyes, trying to dispel the image of the man on the ceiling. But in the dark bathroom, she almost leapt off the toilet when she sensed in her peripheral vision a form curled up in the bathtub.

It could be like that, a nightmare within a nightmare. And maybe somewhere she lay paralyzed, perhaps in a coma, and no one was really waiting for her to explain to her children the practicality of leaving their father's body outside in the cold.

She tried to take Tycho's hand, but he clutched his sister's instead. They sat there with expectant faces, a united front. Orla still couldn't read Eleanor Queen's focused look and was afraid that Tycho didn't even have a basic understanding of death. She didn't want to explain it—not here, not now, not without Shaw. And not with an enemy hovering outside their door.

"You understand your father died?" she asked, nearly pleading. "There was an accident with…the shotgun."

"It made a big boom."

"It wasn't your fault, Mama," Eleanor Queen said, eyes still riveted on her.

"So Papa's…he's with the universe now, swirling with the stars."

In spite of her misguided spiritual efforts, she could still believe that—and believe that Shaw wouldn't object to such an explanation. For the sake of the happier you-will-not-get-us mood she hoped to create, Orla wouldn't let herself cry. For Eleanor Queen's stoic forgiveness. For Tycho's tender confusion. She'd do it later, and praise a thousand nameless goddesses for her daughter's understanding and her son's innocence. But the tears flooded the hollow places in her face, pressing, pressing, threatening to shatter her delicate bones.

"So, since Papa…his spirit is free, and if we leave him—his body—the cold will preserve him. So that's why we can't bring him in." She had no expectation that Tycho would fully grasp this. But he needed answers, so she gave him spare but honest words. "Do you understand?" she asked Eleanor Queen.

"Nothing else can happen to him. The real Papa isn't here anymore." She elbowed her brother. "That's what I told you before."

"Later, we'll be able to…" Have a funeral? Her hands sought her son and daughter, the reassurance of their solidity. Her children weren't illusions, and this wasn't a dream. Her fingertips touched their warmth, and she hoped she'd explained enough. It was an unbearable thought, that she'd abruptly become a single parent and bore full responsibility for whatever befell them, now and forever. It would have been hard enough in the city. But here? She needed survival skills more practical than determination or instincts.

The music bopped and swayed, *tippa-tippa-tippa* and cooing harmonies, as Orla headed upstairs. She raised her cell phone high in the air, looking for a signal, and went from room to room. The beats from below made her shoulders bounce; her head kept time, her free hand floated with a swell of instruments. Tycho and Eleanor Queen sounded normal as they chattered, describing the magical winged animals in their new world. Was it working? With the outside view forgotten, the inside mood shifted to something more upbeat.

Back downstairs, she held the phone out to the windows. Still nothing. She slipped into the kitchen to make a quick mental inventory. Boxes of cereal. Canned stuff—soup, tuna, fruit. One and a half jars of pasta sauce. A loaf of bread in the freezer with a few bags of veggies. Dry goods—rice, capellini, lentils. A few potatoes, onions, carrots, apples. How many meals would it all make? If they lost electricity and the generator, she could cook on the wood-burning stove. Endless snow to melt for fresh water if the pipes froze or the well stopped pumping. They'd eat well for a week, maybe more. After that they'd start to get hungry. Then what?

It was December. When would Julie and Walker start to worry? Would they try to call when they got back from their vacation? Had other people been e-mailing, texting, calling, wondering why they got no response? Maybe her own parents would miss having them all in Pittsburgh for the holidays and drive north for a surprise visit. It would be the best Christmas present ever. She prayed on it without realizing she was doing it: *Come see us, come see us, please help us.*

Fucking Christmas. Shaw had hidden presents in the basement in what looked like unpacked moving boxes. They had planned to let the children pick a small live tree, which they'd attempt to unearth and bring into the house. She couldn't imagine celebrating the upcoming holiday (or any other) without Shaw. But maybe it was good timing; would her friends think it weird when they didn't get their usual holiday card from the Moreau-Bennetts? Would it be enough to make them worry? And worry enough to act? Or would they shrug it all off—*The Moreau-Bennetts have gone off the grid.*

At some point, she'd have to try escaping again. Maybe she'd go alone and leave the children within the safety of the house. Could that be what It wanted? Their company? Had Orla been looking at it all wrong; was It just lonely? But what if something happened to her out there and she couldn't come back? She couldn't leave the children to starve alone.

She made supper out of the ingredients that would go bad first—the things in the refrigerator. She heated up the leftover chicken in a skillet filled with the half jar of pasta sauce and served it on a spare bed of capellini. It was a small meal, but the children didn't complain. The necessity of rationing food reminded Orla of her early days in New York City, when she had barely enough money to live on and was taking classes and auditioning and trying to figure out where she fit in. But back then, she'd been able to call her parents in an emergency, financial or emotional. And she could always pop out for some cheap ramen.

We'll pretend it's all normal. They'd go about their days as carefree as possible. Orla would have to be deliberate about what she did and didn't say (did and didn't think) and not fret about the weather. *We can outlast It.* It was an optimistic plan, even if it didn't feel…she muffled the doubt. It *had* to work. Her left fist tightened, crushing an invisible stone. She watched her children quietly eat the last forkfuls of their dinner.

Tycho wanted to sleep in her bed, so she read him a story as he bounced Moose on the nubby blanket. She and Eleanor Queen would join him later and it would almost be like home— their real home, without all the rooms and doors—though Orla doubted she'd be able to sleep. How could she, with Shaw weighing on her chest—a tomb of guilt—and the fear of what another morning might bring?

Eleanor Queen hovered in the doorway. Since they'd come back to the house, she appeared to be in a constant state of alertness, always listening for something, her attention elsewhere. Orla's heart skipped a beat, then sped up as Tycho's story ended happily-ever-after; it was almost time to sit down and talk with Eleanor Queen, ask her directly if she knew more than she'd yet revealed. She dreaded what her daughter might say, but she had to ask.

"We'll be up again soon. Sleep tight." She kissed Tycho and shut off the lamp, but left the door wide open and the hallway light on. Both hands clutched imaginary stones, worrying, as she trailed her daughter down the stairs. At least when she'd had to do this with Shaw, there'd been the American Honey to help with the rough spots. It was wrong in so many ways to want alcohol to make it easier to talk with a nine-year-old. But there'd already been too many harrowing conversations in this house, and Orla feared the worst was yet to come.

27

When Orla reached the living room, Eleanor Queen was standing in the open doorway of Shaw's studio, one hand on the knob. Orla scurried past her, plucked the red-slathered canvas from the easel, and put it on the floor facing the wall. Reassured that the other exposed paintings weren't too disturbing, she stood behind her daughter, hands on her narrow shoulders, and waited as Eleanor Queen glanced around the room.

"Looking for something? I'm sure Papa wouldn't mind—maybe you want to try his guitars? When they're not plugged in, they're very quiet." She tried to be as soothing as she could; Eleanor Queen knew too much, a burden no child should bear. A few days ago, a quiet instrument might have appealed to her, but she shook her head. "Then what?"

"I'm trying to figure something out."

Hadn't Shaw said something similar? In the days before his fear overtook him?

Orla decided then: she couldn't let her daughter do it alone. It was time to get real, stop pretending the rules that had once governed their reality still existed. "Can we figure it out together? Can we talk about it?"

Eleanor Queen took a backward half step out of the room, then hesitated. Finally, she looked up at her mother and nodded. They settled in on the sofa, facing each other with their feet curled beneath them, bookends of mismatched size. Orla's heart twisted and pain radiated throughout her torso; this was how she and Shaw had always sat for intimate conversations and apologies. Her eyes stung and she quickly swiped at them so no tears would fall. Eleanor Queen watched her, her mood somber and studious. She'd always been a contemplative child, but she'd changed in ways Orla still struggled to understand. Part of it might have been a cloak of sorrow at the loss of her father—but the changes preceded his death. Orla wasn't sure how to ask the questions, how to even line up words that made sense. But she had to try; fear clung to her daughter like a second skin.

"Eleanor Queen...Bean..." She took the girl's limp fingers and rubbed them with her thumb. "I know it's been so hard, and I've made some mistakes—with your papa, and you. I didn't understand what you were both...please know I'm trying to figure this out."

"I believe you."

"I thought at first...everything was just so foreign to me, and maybe I didn't understand how this sort of land, climate...I thought it was me, unprepared—"

Eleanor Queen shook her head. "It's not you. There's some-thing here."

"You're right. I know that now." Orla held her breath. She curled her fingers around her daughter's, and Eleanor Queen responded. They hung on like that, like something might pull them apart and they were ready to resist. Maybe everything about her daughter's behavior should have worried her sooner; the girl had never had the excuse of a muse or work to do when she was distracted or distant. But Orla had been preoccupied in a silent tug-of-war with her thoughts too, inching toward the

muddy impossible, falling back on reason, desperate to understand why nothing felt quite right.

A shiver crept across Orla's shoulder blades. "Do you know
what It is? What It wants?"

Eleanor Queen's face went blank again. She turned her head,
looking, listening. She sighed with the same frustration Orla
saw in her when she couldn't figure out a math problem.

"It's something...I don't know, I keep trying...it's here, but
I can't...it's trying, and I feel it—just sometimes, at first. But
now more and more and I don't know what it is."

Orla hadn't wanted to influence Eleanor Queen's impressions,
but maybe it would help her if she knew about the local history
and its intersection with their land. "Do you sense...there were
people here. Women, near here, a long time ago. And they came
to get better from a disease that didn't have a cure then. Tuberculosis. It affected the lungs. Your papa found...we considered
that it might be part of what's happening now. The restless souls
who died here. Do you sense anything like that?"

Eleanor Queen took her words very seriously and concentrated even harder, squinting her eyes, even closing them. But
she shook her head. "I try to ask it questions. I try so hard!"

Orla scooted closer to her, but Eleanor Queen didn't want
to be held.

"Mama, you don't understand!" She got to her feet and
angrily pulled back the curtains, made all the living-room
windows squares of glass that looked out to the foreboding
night, the foreboding land Orla had been desperate to make
disappear. "It's out there."

"What is—"

"I don't know what it is! It's not...it's not weather. It's not
snow, it's not...it's more than that. But it shows us what we
know, or what it knows, or...but it's not shaped like a person
or a thing." She nearly screamed in frustration. "It's trying to

understand us, me, so we can…" She stood at the window nearest the wood-burning stove, lingered there, her eyes fixed on something beyond the pane.

"Is it something bad? Eleanor Queen, does it want to hurt us?" Orla again took up a position behind her daughter, but this time didn't try to distract her with physical affection. She tried to see what her daughter felt out there in the antipodal world of white snow, black trees.

"I don't think it's…it doesn't think about bad, good. It thinks about…living."

Orla could relate to that. Though maybe, until recently, she hadn't thought about it in stark or practical terms, the imperative of staying alive when doing so felt more and more perilous.

"Are we just in the way, then? Of…something? Would it happen anyway, even if we weren't here?" *But Shaw was summoned.* She was thinking aloud, still in search of a solid thing that made sense, a rock climber looking for a handhold or a place to set her foot that wouldn't crumble.

The nonreligious part of her still struggled with the concept of an *aware* greater force, an intentional greater force. A god that demanded weekly attendance or daily utterance of its name seemed like a trickster to her. Surely something of infinite power possessed a consciousness bigger than one moment in one mortal creature's life. She didn't, in any way, want what was happening to be personal, a thing being done to them. Because that might mean It had wanted Shaw dead—and wanted Orla to kill him—and she'd never come to terms with being a pawn on some omniscient monster's board game.

"We're…we're part of why it's happening," said Eleanor Queen. "It wanted us here; I feel something *wanting* us. But I don't understand…"

It was not what Orla wanted to hear.

"Does It…" She turned Eleanor Queen away from the

window but resisted the impulse to restore the curtain. "It had a connection with Papa, and you—"

"It likes that we were aware, could sense it. But…I felt it growing unhappy with Papa." Eleanor Queen held her hand out toward the stove, but nothing was burning within. She trailed a finger along the cast-iron surface. Orla saw it in her face, her daughter's search for the right words, her desire to find the explanation. "I think, Mama…I feel a sense of *wanting*…of *hoping* that I'll understand it. Better than Papa did. And I'm trying, I'm trying so hard. But then I messed up with what it was saying about Papa—" She burst into tears and clutched her mother around the waist.

"No, no love, remember what I told you? You are innocent in this. None of this is your fault."

"But I feel it *trying* and *wanting*, and if I'd understood—"

"No." She held her daughter's head against her chest, kissing her hair. "It was my fault, for getting out the gun. And Papa's fault, for having the gun. And no one's fault because none of us knew…we didn't know this would happen."

But.

It would never be Eleanor Queen's fault, but maybe she was the key to understanding. As much as Orla would prefer to protect her from the mess they were in, maybe she needed Eleanor Queen's insight to get them all out. "I'm going to help you, okay?" She pulled away from the tight embrace and dried her daughter's tears.

"How?"

"When you sense something, don't be scared—tell me. Tell me, and try to describe it, so I can help you figure it out. It's like it's a language, but you don't speak the same way. But we need to learn. You're not alone. I'm here, and I believe you. And we'll figure this out. It doesn't want us to leave, right?" Eleanor Queen nodded. "So we'll figure it out together. Okay?"

Hope blossomed on the girl's face for the first time all day. She tightened her arms around Orla again.

"I love you, Mama."

"I love you more than anything. And we're gonna be okay now."

Later, as her sleeping children lay beside her, warm bundles and throaty, open-mouthed breaths, Orla whispered aloud to the only spirit she could name.

"Shaw?" It didn't matter what other people called their God. Jesus or Buddha or Allah. Gaia or Mary or Isis. There was only one spirit out there in the universe who really mattered to her. "Look after us? If you can?"

It was a comfort to think of him here, everywhere, watching them. And for a moment she understood faith in a way she never had. Hope lived on an invisible plane that radiated outward from the person who needed it. Maybe, after all, it wasn't so very strange to give it a name.

Weariness dragged her down into a darkness that flickered with stars.

28

Orla lay in bed, half asleep. The half-aware part of her was attuned to a peaceful vibe she hadn't felt in a long time. The house was quiet. Dreamlike. A few bird trills and crow caws outside the window. She flexed her feet, then slowly pointed them. She inhaled through her nose and let her breath spread throughout her body. She focused on the breath, followed its journey down her limbs. Let her mind go blank. When she exhaled, her muscles melted into the sheets. Sun played at the edges of her closed eyes, the edges of the closed blinds. The urge to dance made her lie perfectly still, her mind at work. Dance had been a meditation, a full body-mind transformation to another way of being. A symphony played in her head and she saw herself moving, telling the story of her adult life.

It was buoyant at first, the excitement of a new arrival. Petite jumps, a youthful animal investigating an unknown place. Exaggerated head movements as she looked outward, onward, searching for a familiar horizon, finding only a strange and wild landscape. And then the music grew more chaotic. Other dancers took the stage. She reached out for them but they spun away as if they were attached to ropes that reeled them in, tugged them off their feet. Orla was supposed to take their hands, form a connected chain, and after much lurching and chasing, they were finally able to dance in a line, in unison. But soon they began separating, drifting into the dark wings, and a new creature stood in a spotlight.

Softer moments followed, a pas de deux of two lovers nuzzling. A pair of wobbly-legged fawns ventured in, darting everywhere, exploring everything. The family's play was ruptured by a bolt of frenzied music—the dancers leapt and fell to the ground, rose and beseeched and raced. Reached and collapsed and extended one leg, then the other. And finally the music became elegiac as the remaining dancers, one by one, were absorbed by the spreading shadows, leaving Orla alone in a harsh pool of light. She beat her breast with choreographed grace.

Orla shifted in the bed, a jerked reaction as her body tried to fix the dream, summon the dancers who'd vanished in the dark. Suddenly conscious, she winced. Her muscles ached; it all came back. The nightmare of her existence. Too long in the snow the previous day, on her knees with Shaw's head on her lap. She opened her eyes.

In real life, the Empire City Contemporary Ballet would never have given her the principal role of Survivor. But here she was, and it was worse than when her little brother had died; then she'd been confused in a different way, but her parents were there. Now she was utterly without a partner, tasked with saving her children and ignorant of every move that would lead their dance to a triumphant conclusion.

The children weren't in bed beside her. Where were they? She tossed back the covers and angled her sore self upward. Groaned as she swung her legs over the edge of the mattress. If Shaw were there, she could ask him to rub her lower back. If Shaw were there, she'd take a hot bath in the claw-foot tub and let him fix breakfast for the kids. If Shaw were there…

But he wasn't. The house felt empty. Where were the kids? She bolted from the bed, still in yesterday's clothes, and shuffled into her slippers.

"Bean? Tigger?" They weren't in their rooms. A moment later, she confirmed they weren't in the living room. Her body felt hungover, abused. They weren't in the kitchen. She poked her head into Shaw's studio, hoping to see Eleanor Queen with a guitar on her knee and Tycho on the floor with paper and crayons. "Eleanor Queen?"

A match whisked to life in her gut, set her insides alight. She'd hoped they were playing in their new fantasy world. But they weren't there. Or here.

"Tycho? Eleanor Queen?" She called loudly enough for her voice to carry throughout the house. When they didn't answer, she had one more idea; she sprinted into the kitchen and whipped open the basement door. They might have guessed where their Christmas presents were hidden. "Are you down there?"

The silence mocked her. If she tumbled down the stairs, she'd land in its mouth and it would swallow her.

It had taken the children. It came for her children in the night and now she was alone and would be alone forever. Was it a punishment? What had she done?

She spotted the boot tray by the front door. Some old shoes and one pair of boots. Hers. That meant—

"Shit!" She kicked off her slippers and stuffed her feet into her boots. Shaw had died wearing his. But the children's should have been there. She couldn't imagine why Eleanor Queen would have allowed her brother to go outside, not after they'd discussed lying low, keeping indoors to see if It tired of them or made Its intentions more clear.

Orla pulled on her coat and hurried outside, her soul ill equipped for another horrible, panic-filled morning. "Eleanor Queen! Tycho!"

Fresh snow crunched beneath her feet as she stepped off the porch and followed two pairs of small prints. There must have been a brief spell of freezing rain; the new snow was coated with a thin layer of glittery ice. It was beautiful with the sun splashing across the expanse, reminding her of the rainbow prisms she'd seen reflected through the bathroom window. She forged her own path, oddly satisfied by each step of her boot cracking through the shimmering shell. If only she could crush everything with her feet so easily, just as she'd once demolished the two-headed mutant in the snow. Crush a trail back to the Chelsea co-op, ambush the new owners—"Surprise!"—and then chuck them out on their asses. How she longed to see her children race to the safety of their cramped old room.

Her mood eclipsed further as she neared the garage; it was all too obvious where the small footprints led. She feared what she would see when she reached the far side: her wise daughter and her fragile boy, mouths smeared with blood as they devoured their father's remains.

When she came upon them, they looked only startled and guilty. They knelt beside Shaw in the snow, pajamas beneath their coats, one corner of the tarp pulled back. Orla fought down a horrible fit of laughter. He looked like a flag—red, white, and blue. White skin tinged blue. Even from afar, his flesh looked unyielding, solid as ice. Ghastly. And the red blood had frozen, like spiked icing on a messed-up, gory cake.

Eleanor Queen had the wounded eyes of a child expecting punishment. But Orla couldn't possibly yell at her. Instead, her own culpability was a stinging gash, made worse by the cold— her children were gazing at what she'd done, and what if they deemed her unforgivable?

"What are you doing here?" Orla went around them and dropped to her knees to secure the tarp.

"He wanted to know. He kept asking, *Where's Papa?*"

"You shouldn't have shown him this." She tucked Shaw in and tried to hide her face behind her own shoulder so the children couldn't see it. She felt their eyes on her, watching her. *Murderer. Monster.* "It was a terrible accident."

"I told him that, Mama."

Tycho pushed himself out of the snow and onto his feet. He held out his arms for Orla to carry him. "We said a little prayer so Papa knows we love him and maybe he'll still play with us sometimes."

Orla rose to her feet and hoisted him onto her hip. As much as she didn't want her children to condemn her for what she'd done to their father, Tycho's easy acceptance made her throat tighten. Someday she'd have to give a more formal explanation to a less loving authority. The thought of losing her children, by any means, made her hug him tightly. "I'm glad. I'm glad you said goodbye. But I don't want you to remember him like this. Remember him full of life, okay? Come on."

A tear trickled down Eleanor Queen's cheek as she got up, taking her mother's outstretched hand. "You aren't mad?"

"I was worried. I thought we'd decided to stay inside for a few days."

"It was so nice out," said Eleanor Queen.

They headed back to the house. Orla flashed furtive glances at the blue sky, the sparkling, untrampled snow, the pair of crows alighting like talkative old friends on an overhanging branch. She didn't trust any of it. And...were the trees even closer than they'd been before? Their branches outstretched like gnarled goblin arms, lunging for the sturdy walls of her home? She ushered the children indoors and glared at the beauty one last time before retreating inside.

"You will not get us."

29

Within two days, Orla had to concede she was losing the battle. Boredom, when fueled by whining children, became a stronger force than fear.

They spent the first day in Shaw's studio, in lieu of a memorial service. Both Eleanor Queen and Tycho tried playing the guitars. With their tentative strumming, the strings sounded muted, ghostly. Orla looked through Shaw's finished paintings and the sketches he'd made for future work. She saw it all with new eyes: a human element had manifested in his flora and fauna because of his awareness of *something* out there, trying in its foreign way to connect with him. But Shaw's essence, his skill, was just as present. Perhaps his effort to silence what he was hearing forced him to concentrate even more on his own ideas. There were so many layers, details found in surprising places—a single leaf that, upon closer inspection, looked like a sea creature; a tangle of bushes that hid a nest of children.

It had scared her before, but now she read her husband's secrets. His heart spoke to compassion, to nurturing, to finding a safe place for every lost and frightened soul. Orla wished, how she wished, that she'd seen it before—not only the thing that was encroaching on him, but the brilliance of his work. In hindsight, her praise had been hollow. He'd deserved more. She longed to lavish him with…everything. How was it possible that she would never again cook him a special meal, or scrub paint from his chin as they showered, or make love to him— the love he deserved, where she gave herself over to the power of their union. They'd been working toward that, regaining the unfettered thing they'd had before time marched away with the special colors of their early days. Now she understood—that's how a marriage became beige, gray.

Shaw had come here to reclaim all the colors they'd lost. And no matter what else he'd sensed in this place, he'd found his talent.

He'd found himself. And lost everything.

She turned her back as their children strummed his guitars, and wept silently.

They spent some time looking through Shaw's old poetry journals. Tycho, especially, liked the silly scribblings that went nowhere or made funny rhymes. By the way her daughter touched the pages, Orla saw she was reading more than the lines; she was taking in her father's handwriting. Sometimes Shaw had left little notes for her in her lunchbox. Before the mood could grow morbid, Orla suggested a snack, and they fled to the kitchen.

Cleaning became a fun activity…for a few minutes. They grew bored of hide-and-seek. Orla taught them some dance moves, and that was fun…for an hour.

Desperate for something new to do, Orla concocted a treasure hunt. She'd started to wonder more about the old man who'd lived—and died—there. Had he sensed anything? When the real estate agent told them he'd died in the house, they'd assumed it was of old age, but what if he, as they were doing now, had locked himself in out of fear? Could he have starved to death? She hoped he had left a clue behind.

Along with the tools and books they'd found in the basement were a couple of tightly sealed boxes. She carried them up, cut the tape, and set the kids the task of looking for treasures among his papers. While they busied themselves with that, Orla brought the old books down from her room, including the local history book with its ever so compelling but not informative enough photograph, and looked through everything again. Perhaps the old man had collected these particular books because each held a piece of the puzzle?

Eleanor Queen made neat piles of the photographs she unearthed, but Tycho whined about the boring boxes full of nothing. Orla didn't find anything in the books; some were in terrible condition, pages clumped together with mildew, and others were exasperatingly off topic. From what Orla could tell, the man had been either an actuary or a lawyer with a passion for mushrooms and birds. Later, after the kids were asleep, she planned to investigate the upstairs closets and bathroom; maybe she'd find a hidden compartment, a place where someone who was losing his mind would stash his most troublesome secrets.

For a few minutes they huddled together examining Eleanor Queen's pile of old photos. Orla couldn't spot any clues, though there were a number of faded color pictures and black-and-whites that showed portions of the giant evergreen that towered over the property.

"Look how fluffy the branches were," Eleanor Queen said.

Indeed, the tree had been a lot healthier once, with numerous, thick boughs. Judging by the cars on the lawn, Orla guessed the photos dated from the eighties and nineties. She stuffed everything back in the boxes and set them aside. Another thing she'd scrutinize later in case she'd missed anything, but the kids were too impatient to dwell on any one activity for long.

Full-on grumbling set in at suppertime; no one liked Orla's bland, carefully rationed meal. Without new entertainment to stream, the children argued over which of their DVDs to watch. They were tired of their games. Eleanor Queen found no comfort in her books. By the next morning, the kids were a unified front, begging to play outside. The weather made Orla's life all the more difficult by being well behaved: moderate temperatures, clear skies, a fresh layer of powdered snow; a tempting landscape like a baker's display of beautifully frosted delights. But she knew It was still dangerous and only pretending to be good. "No" became her answer to every question.

Still itching for more information, Orla planted herself in the ugly but comfy chair, which she dragged in front of the door to keep the kids from escaping, and reread the entire chapter in the Saranac Lake Village history book where they'd found the cure-cottage picture, hoping to find a detail she'd missed. The book was vexing, so tantalizing with its initial clue, yet it revealed nothing else specific to their area or anything that might explain what was happening. If only Shaw had been able to get online to do more research.

She ignored the kids as they squabbled and didn't object when they decided to hold a race back and forth across the upstairs hallway. As their feet thundered above her, Orla turned back to the photo of the cure cottage and the women who had once stayed there. She scrutinized every inch of it and felt very much the detective scouring a crime scene photo. Could these women, or others like them, be part of what was troubling their land? (Ruining their lives?)

They looked so mortal, so fragile, that it was hard to transpose them into a future where they terrorized a family. She didn't know what sort of evidence she was looking for, and nothing jumped out beyond the sadness of the wan faces. Had they believed this place would cure them? Or did they know they'd been sent here to die? One, especially—the youngest of the group—appeared too emaciated for her clothing. As Orla looked closer, she realized that the arm around the girl's tapered waist might not be a gesture of friendliness but a necessity of the girl's weakened condition.

Inspired by the impressions that began to emerge, Orla burst up and darted into Shaw's studio. She found his magnifying glass in the top drawer of his desk and returned to the chair and the book. The tree, even without magnification, was certainly the one behind their house.

"Mama, can we slide down the stairs?"

"No."

"Can we make cookies?"

"No."

From upstairs she heard the children harrumph, and within seconds they were back to racing. Orla let them, in spite of how the noise grated on her nerves; maybe it would tire them out and they'd all get a better night's sleep.

She passed the magnifying glass over the people, taking in the details of their clothing. The smug look on the man's face. The smoke coming from the stacked-rock chimney. She hadn't noticed it before, but the branches of the deciduous trees were bare; it was later in the season than she'd previously thought. When imagining a healing climate for tuberculous patients, Orla automatically pictured spring or summer—sunshine and warmer weather. But maybe the patients stayed year-round. Or maybe they came after the first frost, when there were fewer allergens in the air?

All of a sudden the picture was full of minutiae she hadn't noticed. There was a wreath on the front door. The people posing for the photo weren't wearing coats, but could it have been as late as December? A few of the women were wearing necklaces with small pendants that under the magnifying glass became crosses. The skinny girl—the sickest—was holding something in her hand, a chain, but the thing that dangled from it was the wrong shape to be a cross. The image only blurred as Orla brought the magnifying glass closer.

Using her finger as a bookmark, she clutched the book and sprinted up to the second floor.

"I win!" Tycho shouted, out of breath, as Orla reached the hallway.

"Can I borrow your microscope?" she asked her daughter.

Excited to have something new to do, Eleanor Queen charged into her room, her little brother at her heels. They all sat on the floor in front of the bed as Eleanor Queen set up her junior microscope.

"What are we looking at?" she asked.

"I need to see this picture. Here." Orla opened the book and pointed at the item in the girl's hand. "Can you focus on that?"

"Sure."

"Can I look?" Tycho asked.

"After Mama," said Orla, holding the book flat as her daughter focused on the image. Suddenly certain that this was of great importance, she grew antsy as Eleanor Queen fiddled with the knobs. "Can you see it?"

"It's a necklace. I think."

"Do you feel…this was taken near here. I was telling you about this—your papa found a chimney, and we found this book. There was a cure cottage on our land, a place where they sent people, women, who had tuberculosis."

"What's tooberk?" Tycho asked.

"It's a lung disease—it makes it hard to breathe." She watched Eleanor Queen, curious to see if, beyond the image, anything else came to her.

Eleanor Queen slid the book out from under her microscope and brought the picture very close to her face.

"I wanna see!" Tycho shrieked.

"In a minute; this is important." Orla turned back to her daughter. "Anything? A sense of something being familiar?"

"Maybe…only in the faintest…I'm not sure, Mama. Maybe."

"Can you tell what's on the chain?"

Eleanor Queen slipped the book back under the lens. "I can't…"

"Let me. Please." Responding to the urgency in her mother's voice, Eleanor Queen inched over and let Orla peer through the eyepiece. She tightened the focus until the image was clear.

She gasped. She was right—it wasn't a cross like the other women were wearing.

"What is it, Mama?" her daughter asked, her curiosity piqued.

"A star. In a circle. It's called a pentagram."

"Does that mean something?"

"Maybe."

Something ancient and invisible touched her between the shoulders and she shivered.

Orla's prayers that the children would sleep easy went unanswered. Tycho lay on the couch kicking and screaming instead of brushing his teeth. And though he then insisted on sleeping in his own bed, he ran out every fifteen minutes to demand something: A drink of water. The retrieval of a missing toy. Another trip to the potty. A story. Another prayer for Papa. Finally he fell asleep, with tears on his cheeks.

Eleanor Queen didn't throw a tantrum, but she also didn't want to go to bed. Instead she stayed up past her bedtime and watched a movie. Orla sat with her on the sofa, still clutching the history book. Sometimes she thumbed through it, but she was too distracted to read, and though she'd meant to make some notes—her spare remembrances of paganism or druidism or Wicca—the only word she wrote down was *nature*. She was almost certain that nature applied to all three, as perhaps the pentagram did. She drew a star in a circle. Over and over. Ever since identifying the object in the dead girl's hand—and she was certainly long dead—Orla felt a new unease. A wraith of paranoia floated around the room, a chill that defied the temperature on the thermostat, and she almost believed she saw the wispy apparition of the girl from the photo.

From upstairs, Tycho coughed. They'd been fortunate, so far, that the children had remained healthy through all this. But judging by the phlegmy nature of the cough, that luck might be changing. As the fit subsided, Orla couldn't help but think of the girl who might have coughed literally to death.

Everything she learned only brought more questions, and she had no resources for answers other than her own befuddled brain. The pentagram was an old symbol, that much she knew. It had been used across multiple religions, but were any of them routinely practiced in the late nineteenth century? Had the girl worn it as a decoration, or had it meant more? The way it dangled from her hand, more like a rosary than a piece of jewelry, made Orla think it was important to her. It was *active,* the opposite of the passive crosses that the other women wore, as if it were used with a purpose.

Or maybe it meant nothing.

Until they could flee, escape this place forever, Orla needed to keep working on the puzzle. Perhaps it was little more than a mental pastime, not so different than her children's made-up games; they all needed to *do* something. She'd wanted to engage with Eleanor Queen all night, but her daughter grumped every time Orla interrupted her movie. Finally the music rose and the image faded and Eleanor Queen clicked Stop.

"Can we talk now?" Orla asked, wishing she weren't so desperate for the girl's help.

"About what." Maybe Eleanor Queen was simply overtired, but she sounded crabby. It probably wasn't the best time to talk, but Orla couldn't wait any longer.

"We've been inside for a while now. Do you sense It moving away?"

"No. It's just waiting. This is stupid." Eleanor Queen huffed off the couch, ready to head upstairs.

"What do you mean, *waiting*? Eleanor Queen?" Orla untangled herself and sprang forward to stop her daughter's exodus.

"I don't know. But we can't just sit inside forever. What are we doing?"

"I thought we'd agreed—"

"I think it's clear it didn't want us to leave. You were the one who said we shouldn't go outside."

"It was for your safety—"

"How long? There's nothing to do."

Orla sighed. Eleanor Queen tapped at the bottom step with her foot, in limbo between fleeing and staying.

"I'm just afraid we…we might do something wrong outside, something It doesn't like. It's safer inside, don't you think?"

Eleanor Queen shrugged. "I guess. But I don't think it's going to forget we're here."

"Then what? What do you think we should do?"

The revenge for asking a nine-year-old's advice was seeing what she'd be like as a teenager: The exaggerated eye-rolls. The slumped you're-hopeless shoulders. The you're-too-annoying-to-talk-to tone of voice. "I don't kno-wuh."

"We agreed to figure this out together. I know we can't stay inside. I don't want to stay here forever, but I need you to tell me when it's safe to—"

"It's waiting. That's what I know. It…learns by seeing what we do, and we're not doing anything."

"I wanted It to lose interest in us—you." But Orla felt it and knew her daughter was right: it was time for a better plan. The image of the old man too weak to get out of his bed spurred her on. "Tomorrow morning we'll go outside. Cautiously. We won't try to leave, we'll just…see what you sense—are you up for that?"

Orla saw the rebelliousness deflate. Eleanor Queen just seemed tired then. Small and uncertain.

"Yes. Maybe we can try to talk to it," she suggested.

"That's a good idea," Orla said. "Ask some direct questions?" Eleanor Queen nodded. "Maybe about this girl in the book?"

Eleanor Queen shrugged, then nodded. Her head sank to her chest and she trudged up the stairs.

It wasn't fair, Orla thought, for her daughter to bear this burden. And it was crazy that they were having such conversations. While she hadn't anticipated such a quick onset to her children's cabin fever, the time indoors hadn't been a total loss; her achy muscles felt better. She was strong enough to do whatever came next. Explore new tactics. Orla had to find them all a better way out of their predicament, and if leaving remained a fraught and uncertain possibility, maybe stepping outside and listening was a fair compromise.

Ask the thing—the ghost—what It wants.

30

She put a little splash of milk in the children's oatmeal—the last of the milk. Another beautiful day, and she'd already promised them they'd go outside after breakfast. Eleanor Queen wouldn't make eye contact with her over her bowl of hot cereal and Orla wondered if she was worried about the mission they'd agreed on the night before. She'd never asked her daughter how it felt to be aware of this thing that was haunting them, imperiling their lives. It had to be terrifying; maybe Eleanor Queen pushed it to the farthest reaches of her consciousness. Maybe her sensitivity would undo her, draw her to the brink of madness (*like Shaw*), if It couldn't make her understand.

Tycho warbled a song as he ate. *"Papa, Papa, sleeping in the snow. Papa, Papa, nowhere to go."*

Her children were going mad. This place was going to continue unraveling them. At some point Orla would have to weigh the merits of keeping them physically safe against the likelihood that they would become batty fragments of their former selves. Lost in the mind. Lost on a glacier. She considered talking to him—both of them—about Otto and how her family had survived that devastating loss. But what could she say, what had she learned? *You wake up and keep going.* They were already doing that.

"You feeling okay?" she asked him. "I heard you coughing last night."

Instead of answering, he hummed as he chewed. Orla put the back of her hand against his forehead; she'd have to reconsider their plan if he was coming down with something. "You don't seem like you have a fever."

"Nope!"

"Just choking on some water last night?"

"Nope. Not coughing, Mama."

Maybe he didn't remember it. Or maybe…she shook her head; if only it were so simple to make improbable things go away. Was she hearing things now too? That's what she got for obsessing over the girl in the book.

She left the dishes in the sink to soak as Eleanor Queen challenged Tycho to a race to see who could put on all their snow gear first. Orla let them charge out of the house ahead of her while she zipped her coat, adjusted her scarf.

Tycho stomped through the snow like Godzilla, annihilating one building, then another, and another, and a bridge for good measure. Orla, hands in her pockets, stood sentinel, her eyes on Eleanor Queen, who did her looking thing, her listening thing, but didn't seem to find anything to concentrate on. She leapt farther into the yard and made a snowball. Threw it at Godzilla.

"You're wrecking all the snow!" Eleanor Queen told him.

Godzilla roared and stomped around.

"I think there's plenty of snow for everyone." Orla kicked at the top layer as she meandered a few feet away from the children. She felt like a prison guard, watchful that the cooped-up inmates might make a sudden run for freedom. She wished she could take them somewhere, hop in the car—even if she only had a learner's permit—and drive them all away. How had she ever wasted any energy being afraid of driving? How easy it sounded compared to this. She wanted to hug her parents and cry. Be a child instead of the sole adult trapped with her children in a nightmare.

Eleanor Queen traipsed off toward the undisturbed snow near the back of the house.

"Not too far, love." Her daughter either didn't hear or didn't care that she'd spoken. Orla stepped closer to the garage, where she could keep an eye on both of them. She looked upward, but couldn't figure out what to focus on. The sky? The heavens beyond? The woods? "If You're listening...we're not going anywhere. Just outside, getting some fresh air."

"Who are you talking to, Mama?" Tycho asked.

"I'm not sure. Sometimes what happens here is confusing to us. And maybe we're confusing to...whatever's here."

"Can I try?"

Orla wanted to say no, afraid of what Tycho might blurt out. He plowed through the snow to stand beside her, all smiles and swinging arms. "Yes, but be very nice."

"Hi, world!" Tycho yelled to the sky. "Hi, snow!"

"Thank You for giving us another lovely day." Though she didn't yell as loudly as Tycho, she projected her voice outward. "We're not going anywhere. See? We're just stretching our legs, enjoying the day. We don't always know what You want...we don't understand. I'm just trying to keep my children safe."

"We don't have any more milk," Tycho bellowed. "Can you rain us some milk?"

"That's a great idea, but I don't know if It can—"

"Mama?" Eleanor Queen had her back to them.

Orla hadn't meant to stop observing her. "Eleanor Queen?"

Her daughter pointed at something. Orla tramped over, and Tycho bounded behind in her footsteps.

"What is it?" But it was easy to follow the precise trajectory of her daughter's outstretched hand. The towering tree. The ancient pine.

"It's listening, Mama." Her fear was tinged with awe. "It's listening to you."

"The…the tree. It's the tree?" She buzzed with excitement; a puzzle piece shifted, locked into place.

Eleanor Queen had a glazed look, part concentration, part…absence. "It's here."

"Are you sure?" But even to Orla, it made sense. After their first visit to the land, it wasn't the surrounding hills or the house that started appearing in Shaw's paintings; it was the tree.

"I think so. Yes. Nearby." She took off running through the deep snow toward the forest and the giant pine.

"Eleanor Queen, wait!" Orla grabbed Tycho's hand and chased after her. "You can't just run into the woods—you could get lost!"

The trees were so dense. Orla couldn't forget how Shaw had expected to follow the trail of his own boot prints, but they had disappeared that day. And so had the towering tree. Eleanor Queen wasn't slowing down. The bright sky faded under the canopy of tight, bare branches and evergreens. The temperature dropped. The birdsong stopped.

Or maybe it was all her imagination. Neither of the kids seemed frightened.

Tycho sang little rhymes even as Orla half dragged him forward, not wanting to let the red of Eleanor Queen's snow pants slip from her sight.

Her eyes were so fixed on her daughter, ten paces ahead of her, Orla didn't notice at first when she reached the great pine. It was Eleanor Queen's absorption, her stillness and slack-jawed wonder, that made Orla stop and really look.

It didn't appear exactly as it had the first time they'd come to see it. The graying bark was even more fissured…like the glacier. Though, perhaps because it had been made of ice, living water, the glacier had looked more alive, its fissures like vents—gills—breathing. The tree, however, wasn't faring well. Glancing around, Orla saw debris from the upper branches—twigs and woody bits of its skin—scattered atop the snow across a wide perimeter. She tried to shutter the word *dying* from her conscious mind. Yet a part of her was sure: It knew. It was aware of Its own impending death.

Could this be the source of all their problems?

Tycho pulled away from her to slap his mittened hand against the bark. "Nice tree!"

"Don't touch it!" Orla said, tugging him back.

"Why?"

"Eleanor Queen, is it safe to touch? Is this…is this It?"

The girl only gazed upward.

"I *love* this biggest tree!" said Tycho. "It's a million years old, right, Ele-Queen?"

"It's dying," the girl said softly, full of regret.

"I think you're right," Orla whispered to her daughter, hoping to avoid upsetting her son. Not that he loved the tree as much as he'd loved his father, but still.

With Tycho's hand in hers, Orla eased him along so they could stay close to his sister as she moved around the tree, gazing up, listening. A soft breeze stirred, and swirling patterns danced on the surface of the snow. Orla thought of the choreography notation, of bird tracks, of ghost writing—of a hundred invisible hands trying to spell out their desire. The more she watched the pictographs appear, fine lines etching across a thin layer of snow, the more she wondered…

"Bean?" The deeper question in her voice brought her

daughter back around to investigate. "Do you think that means anything? Could it be…"

Ghosts? As Eleanor Queen knelt to study the emerging patterns, Orla went quiet. Finally, the girl shook her head. "I don't…it doesn't feel like anything. Unlike—"

She stood up, reaching out to touch the tree, and Orla instinctively grabbed her coat and pulled her back. "I don't think you should—"

"I have to. It's here—in here somewhere."

Orla didn't want to let her get so close. But this was what they'd come out for. Answers. And the sooner they knew what they were dealing with, the sooner they could leave. Like a blind person reading a message in braille, Eleanor Queen let her hand roam over the tree's trunk. Curious to know how it felt, Orla imitated her. But all she felt was rugged bark. Brittle. Primeval.

At her feet, already bored, Tycho used a stick to scribble alongside the mysterious etchings. Maybe it was just the wind blowing around small clusters of snow and chaff, leaving markings in its wake.

"Oh." Eleanor Queen, startled, abruptly lifted her hand from the bark.

"What is it? Did It…"

Her daughter turned to look at her, wide-eyed with wonder. "It—the thing—isn't the tree. It's the thing *inside* it."

"What does that mean?" Dread made her squirm. Orla hated that she believed in any part of what was happening. And that she'd allowed—no, encouraged—her daughter to participate in it. The urge to flee surged through her again. Maybe if she took them straight through the trees, they'd reach the road. Bypass the house and the driveway and plunge cross-country toward the nearest exit off their property. But instead she asked, "What's the thing inside it?"

"I think it lives here, with the tree. It's not the tree, it's something *else*."

"The thing lives in the tree?" Like the human figures in Shaw's paintings, embedded within his trees. What had he sensed, known, seen? Had he mistaken the imagery that came to him as subject matter for his artwork when he was supposed to have gleaned something else?

Her twenty-first-century self fought the urge to reach for her dead phone. She wanted to Google *tree spirits. Entities that live in old trees. Malicious forest demons.* Something. Anything that might get them an answer. She was ready to accept any super-natural possibility if it would help her keep the children safe. Help them get away.

"What does It want from us? Will It tell you?" She turned away from her daughter and looked upward. The branches towering above her looked so skeletal, so doomed. Her small breakfast somersaulted, rotten with jitters. Unnerved, she was tempted to laugh, knock a *yoo-hoo* on the thick wood: *Anybody home?* She was aware of her children watching her. How had this become their lives? "Why don't You want us to leave?" she asked.

If she understood what It wanted, she could find a solution. Or strike a bargain, perhaps? Reason with It?

Maybe they were close.

A poisonous thought blackened her momentary optimism: Had Shaw accepted what It wanted, if he'd remained open to whatever It needed him to do, probably none of this would be happening. He'd mistakenly believed that killing himself would spare his family, not understanding that the only way to spare his family was to surrender himself. And maybe, after his freak-out, the thing had found him unworthy and switched all Its attention to Eleanor Queen. Shaw had resisted and denied. And that's what killed him; to blame his denial was better than blaming herself. Orla hated him for a moment. Everything was his fault—the move, the snare from which they couldn't escape. What sort of father let his little girl take on the battles he couldn't handle?

The ferocity of her thoughts startled her. Of course she didn't hate him, and he couldn't have known how their lives would unravel. It was grief and hysteria talking. Hunger. But she couldn't take the time to further examine such resentments, not when she believed they were on the right track. They needed to understand what this tree was trying to tell them. And she'd promised Eleanor Queen her help.

"You're doing really well, Bean. It isn't too scary, is it?"

"A little." She extended her hand back toward the trunk. "I can hear it better. It's starting to get clearer…"

The part of Orla that had seen too many horror films expected her daughter to go wide-eyed and rigid as a diabolic force poured its energy into her; the part of her that couldn't get away from this place fast enough hoped it would open a channel of clear and intelligible communication—*Follow steps A and B and I will set you free.*

But with her hand back on the tree, Eleanor Queen only looked more perplexed.

"What is it?" Orla asked.

"Around and around. Patterns, spirals. I don't know what it means."

Orla, again, looked at the markings on the snow, now half obliterated by Tycho's doodles. Is that what Eleanor Queen was seeing inside her head? Feathery writing? Is that what the tree—the thing that lived there with the tree—was trying to explain in whatever way It could, hoping they could decipher the message? "Are they like these marks? Is that what you see in your mind?"

As if answering her, a gust came and erased the swirls. Tycho yelped, surprised, as his writing stick blew from his hand.

"No. Stop being so distracted." How annoyed the girl sounded. And for a flash Orla wondered if she was only getting in the way of her daughter's efforts. But then Eleanor Queen's little shoulders slumped, and a weariness settled in; it was taking a toll on her.

"I'm sorry, I'm just trying to find…clues. Signs. We can try again another time." Orla gently pulled Eleanor Queen away and refused to be disappointed. "You made progress, don't you think?"

She huddled next to her mother. Nodded. Orla held her tight. Her daughter's skin looked so papery, so pale, so unequipped to protect her against something so formidable.

"You okay? Should we not have tried?" Orla asked, willing herself to be a better shield, a protector. What sort of mother, aware of her daughter's mission, didn't provide her with the defenses she needed?

"No…we have to try."

"I'm sorry." Orla kissed her head. "I wish I could sense It the way you do so you wouldn't have to do this at all."

"I know, Mama."

Orla clung to Eleanor Queen as they made their way back through the woods—their boot prints an easy path to follow. The girl drooped at her side, dragging her feet. Tycho tried to bounce away, to talk to other trees, but Orla kept a hand on his coat so he couldn't stray more than a step or two.

"You can run around in the yard when we get back, okay? Not here." She turned to her daughter. "Are you all right?"

"Yeah, just…thinking."

"You're still trying to hear It, aren't you?"

"It's important."

"I don't want you to tire yourself, or—don't obsess on—"

"It's not just important to us. It's important to *it*."

Orla had believed she was onto something with the dying

girl and her pentagram. But a thing that lived in a tree? And Eleanor Queen still referred to *it*—she clearly didn't sense anything the least bit *girl*-like. "All the more reason not to obsess. Eleanor Queen, we don't know what we're dealing with—"

"But the sooner I understand—I want to go home!"

"Are we going home?" Tycho asked, full of pep.

"We're going back to our house, not the apartment. Remember, we can't go back there. But while you're playing outside I'll see what I can do about the garage. We can't leave it like that, it's a hazard." She tried to make her thoughts like a deck of cards, flipping them facedown so only the innocuous design repeated on the back was visible. She hid the image of herself shoveling out the car. She hid the image of driving her children to Pittsburgh, to their Lola and Lolo. If only they could get there by Christmas. Her parents would be so surprised, but they'd shower their grandchildren with love, help to soften the trauma of all they'd experienced. But she didn't voice it, for fear of disappointing them.

"Look!" Tycho gasped as they emerged from the woods into the clearing around their house.

Orla shielded her eyes when they left the shade of the trees. A cluster of snow rollers had formed in the yard. Some were small, only a foot high. But the larger ones were the size of the hay bales they so resembled. Tycho pulled from her grasp and ran ahead to explore, more interested than he'd been the first time.

"So many, Mama!"

Indeed. This time the phenomenon struck her as unnatural. They'd formed by rolling in the same direction. Away from the house. Toward the path they'd used to enter the forest. An unsettling welcome party.

The wind gusted and all of the snow rollers crawled toward them.

Tycho screamed and galloped back to his mother.

They stood where they were for a moment and watched. Along came another exhalation of wind, and the rolls inched toward them again.

"They're gonna get us!" He clambered up her side.

Orla lifted a hysterical Tycho into her arms. The aurora borealis hadn't frightened him. Nor the much more perilous glacier. But every time the wind made one of the rolls move, he screamed.

"Tycho, love, it's okay—it's just the wind."

Just the wind and a little help from the weather-loving thing that lived in their giant tree.

"I think,,," Eleanor Queen strode out among the snowy field of rollers. "It's not trying to scare you, it…I think it thinks it's playing. It just wants to play—"

The wind gusts turned hard and frequent, increasing the movement of the rolled snow.

"Mama, help!"

Orla had no choice but to flee toward the house with her frightened son rigid in her arms, skirting the snow mounds in her way. Behind her, Eleanor Queen shrieked an alarm.

"Eleanor Queen?"

Orla stopped on the porch, Tycho still on her hip. Behind her, Eleanor Queen barreled through the obstacle course and chaotic wind. The snow rollers spun around, picking up speed as they chased her. Orla set Tycho down, ready to plunge into the minefield to help her daughter. But Eleanor Queen was quick. She leapt onto the porch, reaching for her mother's hand. Orla opened the door and the children scrambled into the house.

Beyond the steps, the bundles of snow lay in wait. A trick of the icy particles misting off their arched shapes gave the illusion they were breathing. Panting. A pack of wild dogs, different sizes, alert and hungry.

They wouldn't let her leave.

She wished she understood how It did these things, and she still wasn't certain if It was transforming the land—the snow, the sky—or their minds. It felt real. Looked real—real enough that she'd mistaken her husband for a polar bear. But how was it possible? No mere ghost would have so much power over terrain or people, right? And what was It trying to say, or do? Its desperation seemed obvious now, and lacking other evidence, she assumed there was a connection between Its dramatic behavior and the quickening decline of the great white pine where It "lived."

The pack of snow rollers tracked her every movement as she lingered on the steps. They didn't have eyes, but she felt them observing her. Judging her. Waiting to pounce if she did the wrong thing. Orla wanted to swear at them—at the fucking being. It wasn't fair that she couldn't understand It but It could read her. So much for her plan to finish shoveling out the car. Speed away. It was too easy to imagine the horde rolling up on her, smothering her. Making orphans of her children.

No, she knew better.

"Okay. We're trying." She held out her hands: *Stop*. Raised them: *Innocent*. "We're trying."

The snow rolls waited, an impassive audience. For the next act—

Orla exited the stage and disappeared into the house.

31

Before she left the city, Orla read a book by a Korean-American who'd gone to Pyongyang to teach at what was considered an elite school. North Korea was a fascination she and Shaw had shared; they watched every documentary they could find about the secretive, authoritarian nation. The young people were so sheltered, forced like meat scraps through a grinder into a homogenous consistency. Even their ideas of friendship haunted Orla; "buddies" were *assigned* and they looked out for each other, but what of free will? What of love? It was all so very Orwellian—eliminate language to eliminate thoughts, except nothing can permanently suppress human emotion. That would require some science fiction tinkering, the surgical removal of an essential part of the soul.

That book led to another, a collection of short stories that was smuggled out of the country. It was in one of the stories that Orla learned there was a punishment for openly crying in public. Such displays of angst were considered proof of someone's antiestablishment tendencies; no North Korean who truly loved their country would ever have any reason to cry.

Any reason, ever. Losing control of one's emotions could mean banishment. Or execution.

As Orla spent the entire next week inside with her children, she learned how much harder it was to suppress emotions than physical pain—every day, all day, not just for a performance of an hour or two. Especially challenging were the emotions that might make a person cry or scream or rant or hyperventilate. For her, she feared the unknown consequences if the being caught her thinking the wrong things. *Banishment, execution.* She forced herself to maintain an optimistic front for Eleanor Queen and Tycho while her insides roiled; she worried that expressing her emotions would finally unravel her, over and beyond the being's retaliatory punishment. The yarn would pull away, tangle on things, and in the center would be nothing.

The nothing scared her. The nothing would be her rocking in the corner, eyes unfocused, while Eleanor Queen set her shirt on fire in an attempt to light the woodstove, while Tycho bloodied his hand trying to open the last can of SpaghettiOs.

To keep the nothing away, she locked up the terror, the sorrow, the anxiety, the regret. She praised her children every day for keeping busy, for not complaining. Tycho was finally too scared to even suggest playing outside, and Orla pretended this was a victory—no more cooped-up tantrums, like he was a big boy, growing up under normal conditions. They made up a lot of games, often involving hitting various targets with a rolled-up pair of socks. Orla dragged a couple of empty boxes up from the basement and they made a cardboard canoe. Pretending to row the canoe across a mysterious ocean full of friendly aquatic life made them all forget about their confinement. The living room—now the size of their three conjoined imaginations—no longer felt small. They could go anywhere, as long as it didn't actually exist.

The peanut butter was gone and so was the bread. Honey

on crackers was the newest treat. They'd acclimated to having water on their cereal, though there was only half a box left. Orla could ration out a bag of frozen vegetables so it lasted three days. She'd serve it alongside a heated-up can of chicken noodle soup divided into three bowls. Tycho didn't complain about the lima beans, which had once been a food he preferred to play with rather than eat. Orla didn't even think to strip the bedding and haul everything downstairs to the washer. Water wasn't a pressing concern and the electricity was on, but such was their mentality that the essentials of their former life felt luxurious and unnecessary. Though Orla continued to check both cell phones for a signal many times a day.

They all but abandoned the second floor. The bathroom was an imperative, but none of them wanted to be alone in a room with its prison-cell door. Orla lugged her mattress down the stairs. During the day, it leaned against the front door—it wasn't as if they were going anywhere. And then at night she dragged it to the middle of the room and dropped it. Tycho and Eleanor Queen carried over armfuls of blankets and pillows, and they slept like puppies, nuzzled against whatever body part was closest.

Often, after Tycho fell asleep, Orla and Eleanor Queen retreated quietly to the kitchen to discuss whatever Eleanor Queen might have sensed during the day. Orla made herself the official interpreter when her daughter had only colors or a perception of movement or a feeling to report. Over the days, they'd assembled a working theory. And on the solstice—the longest night of the year, and one of the most ancient holy days—they planned to have a ceremony during which they hoped to put the restless spirit at ease once and for all.

Eleanor Queen continued to describe a palpable cloud of fear. Orla still didn't fully understand the nature of the entity—was It one with the tree? The ancient pine and some manifestation of Its spirit? Or were they separate creatures? She'd kept her eye on Iceland over the years, an interest that began in the nineties with her discovery of the Sugarcubes (and her love of Björk had only increased since then), and she followed a couple of Icelandic bloggers. She recalled that people there—and in Ireland too—used to believe (and maybe a few still did) that certain rocks on their land were homes to spirits. Children weren't allowed to clamber on such rocks, and no one sought to remove the boulders from their yards. They respected the sprites who dwelled alongside them and tried not to disrupt them.

One blogger had posted a piece that read like fiction about a construction foreman who dreamed about a spirit on the grounds where a new airport was being built. In the dream, the land wight asked for a delay on the construction so the family of wights could find a new home. It was a crazy thing to happen in the modern world, but construction did not resume until after the foreman dreamed that the land wights had safely moved on. And weren't there people in Ireland who still left little offerings of food for the pixies? Such stories sounded cute and harmless, but maybe something similar was happening on their land with an especially disgruntled and needy spirit.

The longer Orla thought about it, the more plausible it became, if for no other reason than she possessed the knowledge that other people out there believed in such things. And if the winter solstice held great significance for pagans and Wiccans—in spite of the Romans taking over the festival to make it about Christ's birthday—all the better. Orla wasn't certain of a pagan connection, but once a sick girl had come here with a pentagram for solace. It couldn't hurt to use every tool in their arsenal.

They agreed the tree was dying, so did that mean the entity was too? Was that what It wanted from the family, someone to bear witness? It was easy to anthropomorphize the fear of dying alone, so that became the cause and effect of their predicament, and the solution. Orla envisioned their ceremony as a hand-holding of sorts, a sitting by the bedside of a dying loved one. Eleanor Queen didn't disagree with her interpretation, so on the solstice eve they finalized their plans. They couldn't actually sit with the tree throughout the entire long night—they were in the midst of a cold spell, and hypothermia or frostbite would become a real risk after too long a period of exposure. Still, the symbolism was important, and Orla felt they were being sufficiently understanding and generous even to venture out in the dark, given how much It had terrorized them. Taken from them. Was It lashing out because of a fear of the unknown, eternal sleep? Could they soothe a powerful, sentient being into Its final slumber?

Orla planned a vigil of an hour or so; she'd wake the kids at eleven and be in the tree's company during the crucial midnight hour, the bridge between the conclusion of the year's longest night and the gradual reemergence of the life-bearing sun. Eleanor Queen itemized everything they would bring in her spiral notebook.

"Sound good?" Orla asked.

Her daughter nodded. They smiled at each other, sharing the same thought. The victory of a plan. It was almost finished. They'd pay their respects and then...Orla winked at her, knowing Eleanor Queen was smart enough to hide the rest of her thoughts: *Then we'll flee.* There were things they had agreed not to talk about, not to think about, so the tree wouldn't feel betrayed. Truly, they had no desire to betray It or deceive It or harm It in any way. They simply wanted—*needed*—to get away.

She sent Eleanor Queen to bed to get a couple hours of sleep. Orla sat in the ugly plaid chair, sipping watery tea made with tea bags she'd used multiple times, watching over her babies on the mattress at her feet. During the day, which she hadn't allowed herself to think of as their last day (lest the plan be ruined), she'd helped her children make paper crowns large enough to wear over their hats. After they finished decorating them, she'd cut strips of different-colored construction paper and Tycho and Eleanor Queen glued them into a long chain.

"It has to be really, really, really long," Eleanor Queen had said, "or it won't fit all the way around."

"Is it our Christmas tree?" Tycho asked.

"Sort of," said Orla. "The tradition of having a tree at Christmas, an evergreen, symbolizes the eternity of life. Especially during winter, when things aren't growing."

A historian or theologian might take issue with the accuracy of her explanation, but it fit the ceremony they were planning. If It was listening, she wanted It to find comfort in a theory of everlasting life. She heard Shaw's voice in her head throughout the day and night, amused that she was now the one anthropomorphizing the forest.

"We can't put a star on top," Tycho said.

Orla and Eleanor Queen laughed.

"Unless we learn to fly," Orla said.

"There will be stars in the sky. The whole universe can help decorate the tree," said Eleanor Queen. "Even Papa."

Tycho beamed above his gluey fingers. "It'll like that."

It better like that. Orla still struggled to understand why Shaw had had to die when the being had so many other tricks at Its disposal. Was it the unfortunate confluence of the It and their fucking firearms? Maybe It had not known they possessed such weapons. Or, if the thing had understood Shaw's darkest impulse, his desire to end his life, it might have been wish fulfillment. Or, for all she knew, the being had intended something entirely different and harmless—the meeting of two bears, where they would wrestle in the snow and argue and reach some sort of conclusion. But what conclusion would that have been? Leave? Stay? Fear me? Love me?

Her tea had gone lukewarm. But she stayed in the chair and kept the images in her head of Tycho and Eleanor Queen preparing for a party, a celebration. *My children love you. We're coming to help.* She hoped It appreciated her earnest, generous children and all they'd sacrificed.

Eleanor Queen awakened with the gentlest prodding, as if she'd never reached a deep slumber. Orla roused Tycho next, and he whined a bit in protest. His hair stuck up every which way and she realized it had been a few days since she'd given him a bath, washed his hair. He sat slouched on the mattress, rubbing his eyes, while Orla dressed him in all his warm gear. The cold air would wake him soon enough. Before leaving the house, she placed their crowns atop their hats.

"Are we going to the party?" Tycho asked, finally coming to life.

"Yes, it's time—our very special party. For a very special tree. And we have all of our special things." She looked to Eleanor Queen, who half turned to show her she was ready, backpack on.

Tycho whimpered as they stepped outside into the frigid air. He pressed his face into his mother's coat. Orla turned on the flashlight, then scooped him onto her hip. They set out toward the tree.

Orla had never been outside in the snow so late at night in such a remote place. The moon helped light their way, burnishing the landscape—silvered snow, tree trunks like carved shafts of lead. During the day, sometimes a plane crossed the sky high above them, or they might hear a rumble from a truck on a distant road. But now the world slumbered as they walked into the pillowed dark. Even the birds were sleeping, silent save for the occasional call of a cautious owl. The air carried a faint perfume of burning wood; somewhere out there was a neighbor with logs on the fire. Her heart beat faster as they neared the tree line. She dreaded going into the wooded shroud and stood for a moment with her face upturned.

"Look," she said. Such a clear night. This was the sky Shaw had wanted her—all of them—to marvel over. In the city, lit windows replaced the stars. They'd sought bridges and sky-scrapers from which to view the city from afar and above, its unnatural constellations a wonder of human occupation. Look-ing upward was to witness the depths of infinity, impossible distances where galaxy upon galaxy spun out their mysteries. Their planet was a speck among many, their sun a pinprick of light.

"We look this small to someone else," she said. And maybe there was someone far away with a similar view and similar longings, someone with an aching heart in need of a way out.

"Are there people up there, Mama?" Tycho asked. "On other planets?"

"Maybe. Maybe so far away we haven't found them yet."

"Can we go visit them?"

"Not right now."

"Oh, what's that?" Eleanor Queen asked, pointing skyward, more excited than she'd sounded in a very long time. "Look, it's moving!"

Orla found the traveling mote of light. "It must be a satellite."

"A satellite!" Tycho was wide awake now.

"There are lots of satellites up there, for communication, and weather." Orla took a moment to absorb her children's faces, full of wonder.

A cry fractured their tranquillity. An almost-human-sounding wail of pain.

Tycho stiffened in her arms and clutched her neck. Eleanor Queen huddled against her side.

"Mama?" she asked.

The creature bayed again, and this time Orla was certain it was an animal, not a person. She'd watched videos on YouTube with Shaw to familiarize herself with the local fauna. Animals, she'd learned, could make very unexpected vocalizations. Deer barked. Even squirrels could sound vicious.

"A fox, maybe?" she said aloud. Though in the video, when the cute rambunctious ball of fur filled the screen, its cry had sounded adorable, not tortured. The snowy fox-hare hybrid wanted her to retrieve it from her hiding place, hold it up for further inspection, but she kicked more snow in front of its door, burying it a bit deeper. It didn't matter what was out there. They had to go.

She took Eleanor Queen's hand and hurried them into the dark forest, lest one or more of them should voice a preference to run back home.

32

Tycho held one end of the long paper chain as Eleanor Queen walked the rest of it around the tree. Orla kept the flashlight angled toward the snow at the base of the giant pine. She held her breath when the trunk's girth made a disappearing act of her daughter; it was frighteningly easy to imagine her being swallowed up in the dark: Tycho would stand there waiting for his sister to come around to attach her end to his, and grow impatient when she didn't appear. And Orla, desperate, would follow her tracks behind the tree and find they stopped midway. The construction-paper chain would be a pool of ringlets left in the snow.

But Eleanor Queen came around and solemnly took the end her brother had squashed in his mitten. Orla took off her gloves to squeeze out a half-frozen glob of glue onto a final strip of paper, and Eleanor Queen made the final loop and joined the ends of the chain together.

"Perfect fit," she said and looked up at the tree with a pleased expression. "Like we made it just for you."

Orla let Tycho hold the flashlight while she and Eleanor Queen tamped down the snow with their boots, making a flat area at the base of the tree. He shone the light up the endless trunk and across the endless woods and in her face and any-where that wasn't helpful to the task at hand. But they didn't complain. She and Eleanor Queen didn't need much light to dig the thick candles out of the pack. They pressed them into the altar of flattened snow.

Eleanor Queen handed her mother the big box of wooden matches. As Orla struck one into life, the flare momentarily consumed her vision. The candlewicks caught easily and she imagined the tree as an eager child watching the bloom of light on a birthday cake. She registered a warmth, a do-gooder's sense of accomplishment, certain the tree was happy for their com-pany, happy for the effort they were making. She could almost feel its faraway branches bending over to get a closer look.

"Is It aware of us?" she asked her daughter.

"Yes, it's listening, it's...curious."

The piece of plastic sheeting—something she'd found in the basement—wasn't very wide, but Orla laid it on the snow so it faced the candles. As planned, Eleanor Queen unfolded a bath towel and placed it on top.

"I think we're all set," Orla said to Tycho, ready to take the flashlight from him. "Oh. Maybe one last..."

She outlined a circle in the snow with a gloved finger. And inside it she drew a star. A dying girl had found comfort in this symbol; maybe a dying entity within a tree would too. *Nature.* It was a symbol for nature, and as unnatural as everything felt, somehow it was still rooted in the living world around them.

"A pentagram?" Eleanor Queen asked.

"Might help. Can't hurt." Orla sat cross-legged on one side of the towel, and Eleanor Queen sat on the other. Tycho sat in his mother's lap.

With the flashlight off, they sat there for a moment, gazing at the half a dozen flaming wicks. They each danced to their own music, and their movement, their teasing warmth, lulled them into an easy peace.

In unison, they took a sharp intake of breath as above them something like fireflies appeared, dancing in the frigid night air. Between the branches, gleaming droplets of fire flitted to and fro, on and off.

"Lighting bugs!" said Tycho.

Orla reached up. When a speck of light touched her glove, the glow extinguished.

"Magic." Eleanor Queen was full of awe.

Orla thought she knew what was happening: The being recognized them and had finally communicated something she understood. Gratitude. They had brought light—love—and It thanked them, mirroring their display of candlelight with Its own form of enchantment. She sensed a surge of confidence within her daughter as she sat up a little straighter; they were doing it right this time. They'd learned enough to converse.

Eleanor Queen's soprano voice rose like a wisp of smoke, sweet and organic. *"Si-i-lent night. Ho-o-ly night…"*

Orla held Tycho more tightly and began to sway slowly as she joined her daughter in song. *"All is calm. All is bright…"*

The brilliance of the candlelight narrowed her field of vision to only the broad base of the tree and the specks in the boughs above them. In her shadowy imagination, animal ears twitched and gleaming eyes popped out of the darkness.

"Slee-ee-p in heavenly peace."

They fell into a natural cradle of silence after several repetitions of their song. Eleanor Queen got on her knees and retrieved their offering, safely stashed in a sandwich bag, from the outside pocket of her backpack. In the space between the candles and the pentagram, she laid out three of their precious crackers and three slightly stale dried apricots.

"We share what we have with You," Orla said to the great

tree. "It isn't much, but it's heartfelt. Maybe You know—we don't have much left."

Eleanor Queen snuggled up next to Orla, focused—in her listening way—on the ancient tree in front of her, and something more nebulous in the beyond.

"My daughter tells me You're dying. We wanted to be here with You on this longest night, so You would know it isn't the end. There is no true end—Your spirit will become part of the universe, where You were born."

"It likes that, Mama," Eleanor Queen whispered.

"Don't be afraid. We're honored we could be here with You in the final days of Your long life. We're sorry there have been misunderstandings. We hope You're sorry too…" Her voice cracked and she took a moment to recover.

"I feel something, Mama." Eleanor Queen gripped Orla's upper arm in both hands. Orla felt the tension in her muscles, her daughter ready to leap up.

"What?" Orla said. The girl started weeping. "Oh, love."

Eleanor Queen shook her head. "It isn't me, it's the…not the tree…it's crying."

Orla wanted to know more but was afraid to push her. Was the thing within the tree crying for Itself? Or did It regret the suffering It had caused? She still wanted to understand Its intentions, and the breadth or limits of Its power. Had It made mistakes? There was little comfort in that, but it remained better than the other possibilities.

"I don't think it's trying to hurt us," Eleanor Queen said. And Orla wondered, not for the first time, if her daughter had some perception of her thoughts and feelings as well. "Or…no…"

"Is it too much? Being so close to It?"

Eleanor Queen nodded, burying her crumpled face into Orla's scarf. "It's very, very needy, Mama."

"Okay, shh." She held her children, one in each arm, and

cleared her mind to be the warrior-mother ready for spiritual battle.

"Ancient one…" She had no idea what to call It, how to picture It, but they'd come for this; she pocketed her misgivings, wanting to sound earnest. "We have tried for You—we are trying. But You're causing my daughter pain, and my son. They didn't deserve to lose their father, and he didn't want to leave them. But we want to reach an understanding, and ease You through this time—Your transition to the next life…"

Though she'd called It ancient, It had become, in her mind, an out-of-control toddler. It threw tantrums and acted on whims. She remembered Mamère—that's what her father always called his mother, in the French he'd learned from his father, so Orla did too—so frail in her final years after her stroke, the opposite of a toddler. Her skin became translucent, revealing the tributaries of veins throughout her arms and hands. Had she looked at her grandmother's abdomen, she might have seen all of her inner workings, like one of those plastic anatomy models: The liver tucked under a rib cage. The gray and wormy expanse of intestines. Her ninety-two-year-old grandmother, with skeletal arms more delicate than a baby's, fingers stiffened by arthritis, could never have summoned the strength for a final fight, or even a display of frustration, or anger, or fear of death. She'd slipped silently into her eternal sleep, mute for the last months of her life.

No, Orla expected wisdom and acceptance from old age, not dangerous fits that threatened to starve her children. She pushed the thoughts away, afraid It would hear her. The thing within the tree needed to be soothed into slumber, placated into accepting Its inevitable end.

"Is this what It wanted?" she whispered to Eleanor Queen. "Our company? Does It feel less afraid?"

The girl concentrated, her eyes traveling up the wizened

trunk. "Yes…" But she sounded hesitant. "But…I think there's more."

Orla thought of ghosts who needed to have their spirits avenged before they could rest. What could this spirit possibly need? "Do You need us to do something?" she asked the tree.

"We can't help if we don't understand," Eleanor Queen implored. "We want to help; you have to believe us!"

As Orla watched, her daughter concentrated as if tuning into something fuzzy. "Is It talking to you?"

"Yes…I only understand…I just hear one word. *Home. Home. Home*."

Something soured inside Orla. Her sympathy. In a matter of seconds it shriveled and turned to rot, and the thing it left behind was rage. She scooped Tycho off her lap and on to the towel and stood up to confront the tree. *Home*. What a thing to throw in their faces. Did It want them to go back to the house, hunker down there forever? She didn't think It wanted them to leave, go back from whence they'd come.

"Old things *die,* it's the cycle of life!" She kicked at the bark. "You can't keep us prisoners here, destroy my family, and then tease us—"

"It's listening, Mama—you don't have to yell."

"I have to yell because I'm angry—tell It to *speak clearly*. We can't do this forever!"

Eleanor Queen squeezed her eyes shut. Orla's anger evaporated and she almost begged her to stop. She hated the role her daughter was playing, of interpreter—no, worse. Conduit. And hated that she took it so deadly seriously. Their survival— and the thing's survival—shouldn't be the responsibility of a young girl.

"It's not used to this either," Eleanor Queen said, her eyes clenched tight. "Being…outside of itself. It had never been so far outside of itself before we came. It felt something, something it recognized, in Papa. And then me. But it had never needed to…communicate. It tried…first showing us its power. But we were scared."

The specks of flame swooped out of the branches and swarmed toward the ground. They hovered over the indented pentagram Orla had drawn in the snow, then settled in the shape of the circle, the star, leaving them aglow.

Orla knelt near the children, unsure what it meant and ready to protect them, but Eleanor Queen laughed, unafraid.

"See how it's trying? It keeps trying to figure out a way to make us see and understand. It wants to know us, but…it doesn't understand everything yet—"

Eleanor Queen suddenly gasped for air and slumped. Tycho looked to his mother with frightened eyes. Orla extended a comforting hand toward each of them.

"Oh, Bean!" It was the most her daughter had gleaned from It, but the information had come at a cost. Eleanor Queen huddled beside her brother, looking as small and frightened as he did. "You did an amazing job—you did so well!" And Orla wouldn't let her do more. "Why don't I take a turn now? See if I can explain to It what—and who—we are. Is It still listening?"

Her daughter gave a weak nod and wrapped her arms around Tycho.

33

Orla stood. Left the candlelight and meandered around the tree, trying to find the words to explain.

"One day I went to the Brooklyn Museum. Shaw and I had been married for a while, but we hadn't started a family yet. He was... I don't know, maybe doing that play? I don't remember, but I had the day to myself and there was an exhibit I wanted to see." Orla laughed. "That wasn't what left the impression on me. Instead, I found *The Dinner Party*. I'd never heard of it before. I had an epiphany—that's why I'm telling you this."

She looked from the tree to her children before continuing. It seemed as if it had been months, decades, since she'd had a real conversation, said anything of value. How good it felt to reminisce, to talk. "I would've called myself a feminist if anyone asked. But I saw this display, this homage to women. And it was the names on the floor, even more than the fancy place settings. All of those names. A thousand women, and I hadn't heard of most of them. And I thought, *Why don't I know who these women are?* And if I was someone who genuinely wanted to know and didn't, what did that say about how many people were actually familiar with those names, those women?

"I bought the coffee-table book—fifty bucks, which was a lot of money to us. But I needed to know who all the women were. And it was reading the introduction to the book—that's when I really had my revelation."

She slipped off her glove and placed her hand on the nubbly bark. For a second, something flashed inside her, a quick spark of electricity, and then it was gone. She wasn't sure if it was her own memory, the emotion that still ignited whenever she thought of the abrupt opening of her mind, a flower exploding into existence. Or the spark might have been some sort of response from the being she was trying to communicate with. Is that what Eleanor Queen had to decipher? Morse code responses doled out in beeps and flashes?

"I had always viewed history…I thought the world had been a place that for centuries denied women access to the full breadth of possibilities of what they could do. And I thought that was why you didn't hear of many historical women who were scientists, or artists, or philosophers. And I knew—I knew as a woman—there was no reason why women *wouldn't* always have been interested in these things, in everything. But society didn't accept women as intellectual equals, creative equals. They didn't have the same *access;* they were told they didn't have the right temperament, the right abilities.

"But after seeing *The Dinner Party,* and in the very beginning of the book…I realized women had *always* been doing *everything.* They'd never *not* been participating. Maybe they were behind the scenes or not given credit—a husband given credit for his wife's work, or a brother for his sister's. But it made me realize we've been involved in every aspect of human endeavor forever, and it's *history* that has erased us. It was clear then. I couldn't believe I'd never seen it: history had systematically *erased* women from the collective consciousness of human civilization."

Just as it had the first time the epiphany struck her, tears tangled her throat. The injustice. But equally as powerful, the possibility of a great reckoning. A correction. The reinstatement of women's contributions. She kept her hand on the tree, hoping it would help bridge the gap between them. This thing—this formidable force—didn't want to be erased or forgotten either. And with absolute certainty, Orla understood it now as female.

"I looked at everything differently after that. And I couldn't forgive myself on some level for not seeing it before. It was like...when you see the hidden picture in an optical illusion. And it's so clear after that you wonder how you hadn't seen it. I seriously questioned if I could stay with Shaw if he couldn't see what I saw—sometimes you *can't* compromise. And he started reading the book too. And together, we went back to the museum. And he *got* it. He got why it meant so much to me. Even in ballet—I was lucky at ECCB, because Galina would never put up with stereotypical interpretations, or power structures that didn't elevate women. She wouldn't stand for a patriarchal company."

Orla hadn't thought about Galina since they left the city. Her old boss was embedded in ECCB, as intrinsic as the worn floors, the scuffed mirrors, the odor of sweat that lingered in every studio. One thing Orla knew: If her fiery mentor ever found herself in such a predicament—pleading with a *tree,* trying to save her children's lives—she'd utilize every bit of her steel. Galina might not even need an ax; her bare hands and Russian-inflected commands might have bent the enemy to her will. Orla hadn't fully considered when retiring, when moving, that a key part of her community had been fierce women. Their presence had allowed her to feel even more powerful, and she longed for them as the cold worked its way up her fingers, the warriors she'd left behind. Just thinking of them renewed a bit of her own strength.

"And then, when we were ready to have a family, we talked about how we needed to make our children understand how society had worked in the past, and why it wasn't good enough, so they could grow up as fully dimensional as they desired—whoever they wanted to be."

The dry air was making her throat hurt. She hadn't spoken so much in weeks. Before leaving the house she'd tucked a bottle of water into the inner pocket of her coat, to keep it from freezing. She took a few gulps and offered it to her daughter, who shook her head, and then to Tycho, who took it from her outstretched hand.

"I don't think it understands, Mama," said Eleanor Queen. "I only feel…confusion."

"I know, I'm rambling." Worse than rambling, she'd wandered into a gray area that much of society still debated. She needed to focus, to simplify, to create mental pictures that illustrated her words. When Tycho finished gulping from the bottle, she set it beside their other offerings. "Life. Don't you see?"

She tucked her other glove into her pocket and placed both bare palms—strengthening the connection—against the tree's rough skin. "This is the first thing I want you to see. *The Dinner Party*. A table like a triangle—" She glanced at the flaming star, its five perfect triangles. "Thirteen place settings on a side. One of the thirty-nine was for Eleanor of Aquitaine. She was married to two different kings, so in her life she was the queen of two different countries. And when her son was too young to rule, she ruled in his name. Like any powerful woman of her time there were plots against her, and she used everything she had to maintain her influence."

She concentrated on images, uncertain of how the being absorbed information: a crowned woman standing in golden light, with smaller figures kneeling before her. She didn't know how to summarize all the books and movies about royal intrigue and the battles for dominance. But on some level Orla believed the being would understand. It, too, was attempting to maintain Its power, and long past a mortal life span.

"I named my daughter after her—Eleanor. Queen. Because my daughter will not be forgotten. Her contributions to the world will not be erased. She is not less than the men who have claimed the great moments of history."

And she is not going to die here.

She couldn't say the words aloud lest she frighten the children more. But that was her greatest fear. That Its—Her—energy would consume her daughter, and leave her son behind to starve.

Orla exhaled a great plume of breath and eased onto the towel beside Eleanor Queen. She took Tycho back onto her lap. She'd meant to keep going, to tell Her about her little singing bundle of joy. And Shaw. All the important moments of their lives. So She would know what She had destroyed—first mentally, then physically. Her creative man and his capacity to love—people, ideas, nature. But it was wearying being in direct contact. The spirit pulled the words from her fingertips; her monologue, her breath, traveled in veins of wood, spiraling upward, spreading an understanding to the last green boughs hidden in shadows above her.

Eleanor Queen clutched her arm, pressed her cheek against her shoulder. "Mama, it's alight inside!"

"What does that mean?"

"I can *feel* it! It understands! You're my *mother,* a great...force? And you created me, and love me. And I'm a force too. And something else—I think it loves me too," Eleanor Queen gushed. "It's been alone for a long time. But it feels how we're connected. Your *love,* Mama. It understands love."

Orla squeezed her tight. It was enough, for the moment, that

She grasped mother-and-child. The older generation and the young; love. Would She respect how that love needed to protect her progeny? She sent out her gratitude through her heart, through her thoughts—and the wicks of joyous light flew back up into the boughs to dance above them.

She sat there clutching her children with the last of her strength. Orla was exhausted enough to lie down in the snow and sleep. She shut her eyes, but only for a moment.

Tycho's breathing slowed and the fullness of his weight settled in her arms. *Like his dead father.* No, like a sleepy boy. The wax sputtered down the sides of the candles. Orla could almost believe the tree was going to sleep too, settling in for an everlasting slumber—surely that explained the gradual extinguishing of its firefly flames, popping out of existence one by one. Had she eased the spirit on through Its darkest night? *She's been alone for a long time.*

"Are we safe now?" The words barely a whisper.

Eleanor Queen arched her back. Yawned. Stretched a little. She leaned in close to her mother. "We helped it sleep."

Her daughter's breath felt deliciously warm against her ear. "*Her.* She's a her, I know it now. Let's go home."

They left the candles to snuff themselves out when they reached the snow. They left their small offering and the paper decoration that belted the tree. Eleanor Queen shouldered her backpack and led them with the flashlight. Orla carried Tycho, who barely stirred, and walked back slowly.

"She liked hearing us talk," said Eleanor Queen. "I think it…she was matching words, with how we felt when we said them. She's learning."

"I think I felt Her, when I had my hands against the tree. A sense of something in there. Is She getting…stronger?"

"Not stronger. More…confident? About communicating with us. Remember when you talked about magic? After we first moved here? And I said we'd find real things? Well, this is both. It's real, and it's magic. No one might ever believe us, Mama, but it's real!" Eleanor Queen did a little skip.

Under other circumstances, Orla would have seen Eleanor Queen's newfound bravery as heartening—the very thing Orla and Shaw had wanted for her. But Orla couldn't fully shake that they were both beyond the tipping point, making bargains in the darkness in a desperate effort to get away. And…what if they'd been mad for weeks? There'd be no victory if, in the end, they were suffering under a persistent delusion. She kicked the thought into the little mental room with the things she couldn't look at. Too much had happened; it had to be real. How else could she save her children?

They stepped out into the shrunken clearing that surrounded their house. Orla had hoped that, in recognition of their progress, the trees would have retreated a bit. At least they hadn't moved in closer. But then the sky burst into color to welcome them. Even more than the first time, the appearance of the aurora borealis felt like a reward—a celebration. Something inside that magnificent tree had more than just the instinct to live. She had desire.

"I think She likes to feel understood," Orla said, never fully comfortable with their path, or the creature they shared it with.

"Me too!" Eleanor Queen beamed at the glorious display of lights.

They gazed upward as the colors shimmered and rolled. An invisible artist splashed her paints across the sky, dabbed at them with her brush, swirled them together into new combinations of color.

As she'd done before, Eleanor Queen lifted her finger—and once again, the colors contracted to a point above it. But it was much more obvious this time, the way the swaths of light obeyed the direction of her hand. She painted an infinity symbol. The arch of a rainbow. A smiley face.

"Oh, love." Orla wavered between awe and terror. Tycho, still asleep, groaned in protest as Orla shifted him, freeing up a hand. She gripped Eleanor Queen's shoulder, wanting to pull her away, return her to an ordinary girl who couldn't manipulate the sky.

The colors abruptly altered their behavior, bursting forth in starbursts of color—tie-dyed flowers in teal and turquoise.

Eleanor Queen squealed and clapped her mittened hands. "It worked!"

Orla didn't have to ask. She recognized her daughter's favorite colors and the puffy chrysanthemums she liked to draw. The heavens were fully under her control; the connection between Eleanor Queen and the being was growing stronger. She tugged at Eleanor Queen's coat, urging her toward the house.

"She likes me, Mama!" She stomped the snow off her boots before heading in.

Spiders crawled inside Orla's skin. If they found an opening, they'd spill out and form themselves into words. A message. A warning. Orla thought she understood: She had to get Eleanor Queen away. And soon. Before she lost her forever.

34

Late-morning sun speared the living room in window-size shafts. Orla awakened with her head and left leg off the mattress. She rubbed her stiff neck and sat up, alert. And optimistic. Eleanor Queen was already up, off in the kitchen, softly clattering about. Tycho, exhausted from their midnight outing, was still asleep, sprawled out on a disproportionate amount of the bed considering his small size. Orla chuckled. For the first time in a long while, it felt okay—to be awake, to be alive.

For breakfast they ate the last can of food—tuna—and shared a single-portion cup of applesauce. It was to be the last morning—*Sshhh*—so Orla wasn't overly concerned about finishing off precious staples; they needed protein to complete their mission. *Sshhh*.

"Are we going to play outside?" Tycho asked as Orla helped him get dressed.

"Yup, that's exactly what we're gonna do." It wasn't at all what they were going to do, but she wouldn't allow herself to think the truth, let alone speak it. Eleanor Queen knew, but Tycho was too young to block his thoughts, and so much the better if She heard only his excitement, saw the images in his mind of playing in the snow.

The night had healed them all in some tangible way. Tycho wasn't afraid to go outside anymore. Eleanor Queen's movements were no longer interrupted by periods of lost focus; whatever was out there had stopped demanding her attention. The curtain of fright had lifted from her eyes. Orla hoped—prayed—the entity had died during the night, but she couldn't risk their escape on some lingering tendril of Her consciousness.

It had snowed a little, a fresh dusting that softened old footprints. Tycho bumbled ahead of her down the stairs in his layers of more or less clean clothes—they still used the upstairs to store their things—but Orla stopped in Eleanor Queen's room when she saw her daughter sitting on her bed. She was holding one of her favorite books, and Orla was afraid she'd changed her mind. They'd agreed not to bring anything with them so it wouldn't look as if they were fleeing. *In case She's only sleeping.*

"We'll be back. Again and again and again," Orla whispered. *Don't let Her know the truth.*

"It's not that. I feel like...last night, I should have given her more. A better offering. Something I love, like this."

"You don't owe Her anything. Remember what we said?" She did little more than mouth the words; it barely counted as a whisper. At full volume, she said: "Today we're full of smiles and love."

That's all they would think as they tiptoed away. Happy thoughts. *We love you.* And she'd get Tycho to sing about the wheels on the bus, a song they'd discouraged him from singing for its annoying repetition. But it would distract him, and maybe, as they mumbled along with him, the soundtrack would provide a more solid barrier against their thoughts—and against the excitement welling up within her.

Orla had already tucked her wallet, phone, and important papers into her coat's inner pocket. They weren't carrying anything else. History joggled like an old film across her mind, poorly lit families with the outward appearance of a convivial excursion. Golden Stars of David walked without eye contact past the swastika-clad occupiers. No luggage. The parents afraid their thundering hearts would trip the alarm. Someone somewhere was always trying to slip away unnoticed: To reunite with long-lost family in South Korea, a gun pointed at their back. To cross invisible borders to a less perilous life. *Sneak away.* She shuttered the words like a guillotine.

Maybe She would let them. Maybe She was traveling at the speed of light toward Her next destiny. Maybe the good morning feelings would last. But Orla wouldn't tempt fate. Wouldn't flaunt their escape.

"Are we going home soon, Mama?" Tycho asked as they stepped outside. He asked every couple of days but never did more than grump and slouch when she said no.

"This is home," Orla said. *See, we're not going anywhere.* How soon would she start to see his little ribs protruding through his sweater? Never. Because she was going to get them food. Soon.

"Should we check the mail?" Eleanor Queen asked, just as they'd planned, before Tycho got too involved in renovating his abandoned snow fort.

"Want to take a little walk down to the mailbox?" Orla asked her son. She'd given up her morning walk to collect the mail a while ago, hoping the mail carrier would have some reason to come up to the house or would simply grow concerned if the family's mail went uncollected.

"Okay!" said Tycho.

It lifted Orla's heart to see her children return to more

normal behavior, even if they were reluctant to tell her how often they were hungry. She let him bound ahead down the driveway, releasing some of his pent-up energy. He walked in the old ruts, though even then, the snow came almost to his thighs, but he pushed on, like he was trudging through deep water.

"The wheels on the bus go round and round," she sang.

Tycho picked right up where she'd left off and continued through the verses as they strolled down the winding path. Orla didn't even try to stick to the side with the guideline lest she appear too cautious. The car was buried, its driver dead.

Orla's heart trilled in quick succession when the mailbox came into view sooner than expected. She distracted herself—and the spirit—by showing a renewed exuberance in her singing. Eleanor Queen must have held similar fears of celebrating too soon and losing control of the words in her mind, the emotions in her body. She hated the song even more than Orla did and had left her mother to accompany her brother, but she jumped in and sang along, loud.

"The doors on the bus go…"

There was the road. Twenty paces ahead. Snow lay piled on the far side, and it looked like it had recently been plowed. As they got closer, the road was even more remarkable for being so utterly just as it had always been. The snow, flattened and gray, was imprinted with tire tracks; ordinary lives had continued on while they were in isolation. To their right, the road descended down a gentle slope, and to their left it continued curving upward, disappearing between two walls of trees. Somewhere off to their left would be a neighbor and perhaps a pull-off where summer tourists parked to hike the designated trails. But if they made a right, their small road would meet a larger one, a more traveled one. They could walk it into town. Maybe cars would even pass them along the way and Orla could flag them down, beg for help, get her children somewhere safe with ample amounts of food. And as they got closer to civilization she could call 911. Report what had happened. Give her husband the proper memorial he deserved.

"*The mommies on the bus say, 'Shush, shush, shush,'*" she practically shouted, drowning out her eager thoughts.

"Can I get the mail?" Tycho got to the box first. Orla half expected him to vanish in a whirling dervish of snow. But he didn't. He grinned, one mittened hand ready to find a prize, and waited for his mother to give him permission to lower the little curved door.

Orla and Eleanor Queen exchanged glances. "I love you and it's a lovely day."

Eleanor Queen just nodded in reply, her face expectant. With her cheeks so rosy with cold, she looked happier—and healthier—than she had for weeks.

"Go ahead," Orla called over to Tycho.

He grinned. Had there been less snow, he might not have been able to so easily reach what was within. He scrabbled with both hands to hold on to everything. Orla and Eleanor Queen hesitated at the boundary where the driveway met the road. Tycho handed off the mail.

"Thank you, what a good mail gatherer you are."

Ever so casually, Orla meandered onto the road, sorting through the mail, which looked to be mostly holiday cards. Behind her, Eleanor Queen tugged on her brother's coat so he would follow them.

"Looks like we got…a Christmas card from Lola and Lolo. And another one from Uncle Walker and Aunt Julie. And…" She stopped narrating for a moment when she read the return address on another card—from Lawrence, Shaw's best friend in the city. But then she continued on. "Pilar and Gwen, Xin and Deshi."

Looking at her friends' handwriting threatened to make her wistful, wreck her façade. She flipped through and found the junk mail, such as it was. A local company offering to plow their driveway (if only they'd come up to the house and inquired!). A flyer from the nearest grocery store. No wonder the mail carrier hadn't been concerned; a handful of cards and a few ads. He probably hadn't even needed to stop at their box on most days. Orla kept on with her nonchalant stroll, her nose buried in the mail. She bit down on the tips of her glove to free her hand and started tearing open an envelope.

"Let's see what Lola and Lolo have to say." She craved her parents in a way she never had. "They're having a warm December," she said in a cheery voice, reading the card.

Eight feet down the road. Eleanor Queen and Tycho a step behind her. Ten feet. Twelve.

A shattering sound, like something tearing beneath the earth. Grinding tectonic plates.

A sharp crack louder than lightning striking at close range.

Tycho shrieked, wide-eyed, and Orla reached back to grab him. Eleanor Queen whimpered, her face stricken as if blood rained in her eyes.

"No, Mama, no no no no!"

Orla clutched her too. She yanked them around and darted back up the road. "We're going back, see? We didn't mean—"

The ground rumbled. She stumbled past the edge of the road and collapsed in a heap beside the mailbox. But whatever was happening had only just begun. Orla huddled over her children as everything around them quaked, afraid the trees would shake loose from the earth and bury them beneath the clawing, pointing hands of angry branches.

"I'm sorry! I'm sorry!" Orla screamed into the cacophony. "We're not leaving! We're right here!"

The entity either didn't hear them or didn't care.

"Tell Her, Eleanor Queen—ask Her to stop!"

The trees shook off their snow and the wind blew it in their faces. Everything around them turned white, and still the ground beneath them rocked.

"I can't!" Eleanor Queen wailed. "She's angry, Mama! We were her friends! She thought we were friends!"

A ferocious gust of wind roared over them and Orla lay atop her children, hoping her weight was enough to keep them from being lifted and swept away. The children might have screamed beneath her, but she couldn't hear them. She shut her eyes and prayed the spirit would let them live. If the gale-force blast kept up, it would strip them of their clothing or hurl them against the solid trunks of surrounding trees. Or maybe She planned to bury them, like the ash at Pompeii, and some future day someone would dig them out. Frozen sculptures, just as they'd been in the moment of their deaths, Eleanor Queen's face scrunched in pain, Tycho's hands grasping for his mother.

More cracking and rumbling. The ground beneath them shifted, dropped. Rocked.

It started to grow quiet again, a decrescendo of destructive noises. But even in the numbed silence, the blizzard raged on. Orla didn't like the unabated sense of movement, like they were on the deck of a small ship. Was she just dizzy? If she stood, what would happen? Would she lose her footing and go tumbling into…what? An abyss? She eased off the children a bit, afraid her efforts to protect them would end up smothering them. "Are you all right? Are you okay?"

She could see well enough through the white, snow-infused air to distinguish their nodding heads. She risked the wobbling ground enough to get to her knees. It was no longer snow beneath her, but ice.

"Oh no."

The slosh of water.

They weren't on a boat, and they were no longer on land.

The blizzard abruptly lifted like a curtain at the start of a show and confirmed what Orla had only just begun to fear.

The world around them was nothing like it had been. No trees. No mailbox or road. Instead, they were adrift in a sea of ice floes.

"No, no…"

Tycho tried to stand up but Orla grabbed him, dragged him onto her lap. She reached for Eleanor Queen's snow pants and, with little effort on the icy surface, towed her in closer. The kids gawked at the new world.

"Wow!" Tycho took in the landscape, dazzled. Confused.

"It's like my dream." Eleanor Queen wore the hurt face of ruin, of personal failure, of doom. "It didn't work, Mama."

Orla held her close. "We made Her happy. We did."

"But she still didn't want us to leave—I should've known, I messed up everything!" She crumpled into tears.

"It's not your—"

"We'll never get home now. Look! It's not even there anymore!"

She was right, of course. For as far as they could see in all directions, there was nothing but a frozen expanse, the gentle bobbing of a polar ocean. In the distance Orla saw a continent of ice, its edges ragged and vivid green-blue. They were stranded in the middle of it all on a floating chunk of ice. Sometimes it collided with another, and they bobbled in the half-frozen sea. It was an astonishing sight; carved green archways and pillars stood like ice islands in the water. But there was nowhere for them to go. No way to even return to the precarious existence of their humble house. Orla didn't want her daughter to panic, or blame herself.

"Maybe it's…" The more she considered what to say, the more

reasonable it seemed. "It's like the aurora borealis—She wanted to show us something amazing, not frighten us. She's trying to make us understand something about Her power—"

"Yes—her power to stop us from leaving!" Eleanor Queen wailed.

"But that doesn't mean…this might just be a display, we're not hurt—"

"But we'll never get away!" She sprang to her feet, angry. "I don't understand what she wants, and everything that's happening is my—"

Orla reached for her, alarmed, as the ice rocked like an unstable canoe. "Be careful!"

Eleanor Queen squirmed away from her reach. "We're going to die here—"

Orla couldn't stop it from happening. Eleanor Queen's feet scrabbled for purchase on the ice; her arms flailed. But she was too unbalanced to right herself. She fell backward with a yelp that was quickly smothered by the water.

It was a matter of seconds. Seconds before her daughter would slip forever beneath the icy surface, in shock from the cold. Seconds before another chunk of ice would strike her, crush her in the congested waterway bobbing with floes.

She lifted Tycho from her lap—"Don't move!"—and stretched out on her belly to grab at Eleanor Queen's desperate hand.

The girl's lips were already turning gray, and her wide eyes blasted panic. She gabbled for breath, half sputtering, half gasping. Orla grabbed the sleeve of her coat, tried to pull her up, but the water weighed it down, made anchors of her snow pants, her boots. The frigid water sought to claim her daughter, drag her into its deadly frozen depths.

"This isn't what You want!" Orla yelled. Because she knew that whatever the entity wanted, Eleanor Queen's death wouldn't help.

She slithered toward the edge of the ice floe, grasping, yanking at her daughter's sodden sleeve. "I've got you! I've got you!"

Though her mouth was open, the girl was too terrorized, too cold, to scream or respond. Orla played a tug-of-war with the icy water. But for every inch she gained with Eleanor Queen, Orla slipped farther along the top of the ice. Until—

"Mama!" Tycho called from his perch on the floe.

Orla tumbled into the sea.

She saw Tycho on his knees above her, his tearful face poking over the edge of the ice. His image wavered above the water and he mouthed *Mama!* over and over, but she couldn't hear him. The cold deafened her. It struck her with the force of a speeding truck. She expected to surface, to choke back a gulp of desperate, lifesaving air. But Eleanor Queen's coat was still bunched in her left hand. Though the weight of her dying daughter dragged her downward, Orla couldn't let go.

35

Her mind cycled through its archive of especially photo-graphic life moments, zeroing in on one of many filing cabinets, and then one of its many drawers. Next, her subconscious chose a file, revealing…

She'd felt as delicate as a moth in her lace wedding dress. With her father beside her, she walked down the aisle toward Shaw in his purple paisley bow tie, beaming his crazy, toothy, overly exuberant grin.

And a day with sunbeams, rainbows. Her dad, a big man, tiptoed like a goofball fairy through her mother's garden— her mother mock angry—as Orla laughed, in love with his silliness. He retrieved her Frisbee and put it on his head like a hat.

The day she won the only trophy of her life, a gold star set atop a fake marble column—green! It was her prize for winning the fourth-grade spelling bee. In spite of her prodigious abilities at dance, she'd been a terrible athlete at school, lanky and unaggressive. Wretched at sports. A loser. And her first few academic years had been a struggle too. *Retarded giraffe*. That was the name that had bothered her most. After she won the spelling bee, she finally believed her parents when they insisted she was smart. The trophy was a magic wand; school got better.

A view of the darkened audience beyond the lights—her first time onstage with the corps at the Empire City Contemporary Ballet, a professional dancer who'd barely started to grow breasts. But even then, she appreciated having achieved what 99 percent of most dreamers never did. She'd been so nervous in the wings before she took flight onstage.

Maybe the images went on for hours. Or maybe it was moments. Or maybe she saw nothing. She didn't have a clear memory afterward, just the sense that things had occurred beyond what she could recall, not unlike waking up after a night of tumultuous dreams. Though the feeling of drowning lingered. Concrete in her lungs.

She wasn't sure if her eyes were open or closed. There was darkness. And the momentary sensation of slipping into nothingness, like falling into anesthesia. A few seconds of feeling altered before oblivion took over.

When she returned to herself, she was on her mattress on the living-room floor. Cold. Stunned. *I'm getting our bed all wet.* She sat up, and a puddle squished beneath her. Water dripped from her soaked knit hat, ran in rivulets down her heavy sleeves. She kicked her stiff legs, her boots, over the edge of the mattress. Fumbled with the zipper on her coat. Her gloves. Fingers of bony ice. Half conscious.

With her outerwear in a sodden pile, she kept going. Stripped off her socks. Her sweater. A part of her knew she couldn't get warm until she was dry. Instinct. The rest of her awareness tottered like an old incandescent bulb at the end of its life. On/off. Blink. See. Dark. Blind.

Her hand—a mother's hand, before the mother was even fully awake—felt along the mattress for a small arm, a small foot, the reviving limbs of her children. It grew more frantic, reaching, fumbling. And finally the mother broke through her daze.

Where am I?

Home. The living room. Her bed.

Where are the children?

Not beside her. Not in the room.

"Eleanor Queen? Tycho?" Her wet pants felt too constrictive against her skin. She peeled them off so she could run faster. Where?

Even in just her underwear, she wasn't as cold. The wet clothes had been a body bag; now she was free. The air in the room was warm. The house normal, just as they'd left it.

"Eleanor Queen? Tycho?" She spun. Stepped a few feet toward Shaw's studio. And a few feet toward the kitchen. No children. Where were they?

She remembered being on the ice floe. Magnificence in the background, sculptural wonders in all the rich ocean colors—turquoise, indigo, cerulean—and chaos in the foreground. Eleanor Queen flailing in the water. And when Orla slipped in just after her, they started to sink.

And she'd awakened here. Home. In her bed.

Orla charged up the stairs. "Eleanor Queen!"

She reached her daughter's room first, and through the open door she saw her, rising to a sitting position, wobbly like a drunk. The girl started coughing.

"Love—are you okay?" Orla didn't wait for her to answer. She started stripping off her wet coat, boots, snow pants.

"I'm okay," Eleanor Queen said, sounding sleepy. Dazed. Her waterlogged hair dripped in her face.

"Get out of these things, I'll check on your brother."

Orla reached the end of the hallway in two long strides. "Tycho?"

His door was closed. She flung it open, expecting to see her weepy boy shivering on his bed.

There was just the mattress and its fitted sheet. The rest of his bedding had migrated to the living room the previous week. Still, Orla came in with her eyes glued to the bed. Did she expect to witness him rematerializing? She got on her hands and knees and looked beneath the bunk bed. Dust bunnies. A sock. A few Lego pieces. For good measure, she ran her hands over his mattress. Crazy. Of course he wasn't there, so tiny she couldn't find him, or an invisible lump that waited for her touch to turn him visible.

She checked the upper bunk. Threw off his stash of toys. It was easy to picture his face emerging beneath the stuffed elephant and the golden-maned lion. But no. "Tycho?"

Her frantic hands wouldn't stop, even as her mind voiced the possibility—the fear—that he truly wasn't there.

"Mama?" Eleanor Queen stood in the doorway, wrapped in a blanket.

But Orla didn't look at her daughter—couldn't look, not until she found her son. "Where is he?"

"Mama, he's not here."

"Tycho?" Orla ran next door to the room she'd once shared with Shaw. A naked bed frame. Box springs. Some dirty clothes scattered on the floor. She tugged on a pair of old sweatpants and a crumpled shirt. Opened her closet in case her son had been transported incorrectly. That's what must have happened.

"He's not here," Eleanor Queen said again, shocked but emphatic.

"I'll find him."

Something jittered in her head, her heart, a thing that wanted to slice her apart—but she was determined not to let it. She'd prove it wrong; she'd find him. She jogged down the stairs, barefoot, a moldy body aroma rising from the unwashed clothes. Shaw's studio seemed like a possibility—it had been a bedroom once. She went straight for the closet. The gun locker taunted her and she slammed the door. Eleanor Queen chased after her, but Orla barreled past, heading for the kitchen.

"He's not here!" her daughter yelled as Orla stupidly checked the cabinet beneath the sink. Eleanor Queen beat her to the basement door and used her body to block it. "Mama! He didn't fall in the water! He's not here!"

Orla froze for a moment, trying to make sense of her daughter's words. "What? What are you saying?"

"I don't know! I just know he's not here, I don't feel him, and he needed to come through. With us. But he didn't."

"He needs to come through the water?"

"I think so."

Orla raced for the front door. If the spirit—fucking monster—sent them home through the water, then Tycho needed to *jump* in. But he'd never go into the water without her encouragement.

She didn't even have socks on but she hurtled out the door, expecting, hoping…

Why couldn't their house have been an island in a sea of glaciers? Water lapping up the porch steps? Tycho clinging to a patch of floating ice? She'd scramble across the floes as they drifted close to each other until she reached Tycho's. And she'd carry him home the same way, leaping from each small berg to the next.

Except the yard was normal—land, snow, wrecked garage. Tycho's abandoned snow fort. Even their footprints in the path they'd taken to the mailbox. But the trees. The branches swayed in unison like black veils—mourning her loss? Or had they gathered to berate her? She couldn't pretend anymore that it was a trick of the weather or her confusion: the tree line was even closer. The yard was half the area it had once been and populated by twice as many trees—all stark and leafless, not an evergreen in sight.

Eventually they would form a fence around the house, a wall, solid and menacing. Charcoal trunks packed too tightly to allow their escape. Ready to crush them, if they proved too obstinate.

"No…no. Tycho!" She paced the porch like an animal in a shrinking cage.

Eleanor Queen held the door open, shifting from one cold foot to the other. "Maybe it starts at the end of the driveway—"

"Yes!" Orla leapt off the porch. That's where the troubles had started; she'd find him bobbing on an ice floe at the foot of the drive.

"Mama, wait!" Eleanor Queen ducked inside, popped back out, and tossed her mother the sturdiest shoes from their boot tray, an old pair of Shaw's slip-on Merrells. They were a little short for her, but Orla shoved her feet into them. Eleanor Queen held out her blanket, beneath which she wore only pajamas. "Here!"

Orla grabbed the blanket from her daughter's outstretched hand. "Get back inside in case he comes home!"

Eleanor Queen nodded and started shutting the door, but kept her face in the crack, watching her mother.

Orla's toes rubbed up against the end of the shoes, and the snow came well past her bare ankles. But she didn't care. She pulled the blanket tight over her head and shoulders, clutched it beneath her chin, and ran as fast as she could. Tycho didn't like to be alone, not even if someone else was in the next room. She prayed he would grow impatient, hysterical even, and try to find his own way home. Under normal circumstances she'd never beg for her young son to fall into frigid water, but it was the only conduit she knew to get him back.

The driveway had grown longer again. She ran and panted, afraid she was on a treadmill. Finally the mailbox came into view and the thing that had been threatening to gut her made a move, a sawing motion. Searing pain wailed up from her severing insides.

"No...please!"

There lay the road. Ordinary and deserted. Not an other-worldly landscape of water and ice.

She stumbled past the driveway and onto the road. Did a crazy dance in a circle, spinning, looking for an opponent. Arms toward the heavens, body beyond the homestead boundary, she implored the entity to punish her again as She had before.

"Come on! I'm back! What are You waiting for?"

She pranced and hopped her way farther down the road. "See! I'm going! Come on!"

But nothing happened. No rumbling ground. Not even the slightest bit of blowing snow.

Orla fell to her knees, breathless. "Please! Give me my son back! Please!"

She rocked forward, her energy spent, and laid her forehead on the gray, rutted snow. "Please give me my boy back," she wailed. "Please give me my boy."

Frightened Tycho. Alone. Freezing. Gone from her forever. Choking as he sobbed and called for her, heartsick when she didn't come. There was nothing else to imagine. The fucking monster had killed her husband, and now She had taken her precious little son.

"He's just a baby! Please give him back!"

She was willing to pray there all day, maybe forever, even if her forehead stuck to the snow and turned black with frostbite.

"Take me instead...please! You can have me."

A part of her didn't want to keep living. A more distant part of her rumbled from beneath its hiding place. Pushing toward the surface.

Her parents, her brother. She had had a little brother, and her parents hadn't forsaken her after Otto died. A part of them might have died with him, but they came back—for her. Their love for their surviving daughter had only grown bigger. They hadn't given up. And Orla couldn't forget she had one child left. A little girl who needed her. Even a shattered, brokenhearted mother was better than none at all.

Orla wept as she dragged herself home. Maybe she should have made a run for freedom, for help, while the road appeared normal. But she couldn't let the thing win, swallow her entire family, and she was certain that's what would happen if she left her daughter alone: Eleanor Queen would be gobbled up, erased from the earth like her son. And Orla would have no more reasons to live.

"What have I done to You that You should take everything from me?" She stumbled. Wanted to lie down in the white grave and die. But she kept going.

Why was the fucking spirit—what *was* She?—trying to destroy her family? Had Orla been such a terrible person? Made so many horrible or selfish mistakes? Had she done something so awful to the world that she deserved such vengeance?

"I'll do better." She limped up the stairs to the porch. Everything hurt. Her flesh and blood no longer existed; she'd been flash-frozen, dipped in liquid nitrogen. If her heart screamed its distress, her entire body would shatter. If she so much as wiggled her toes, her bones would splinter into fragments.

She was barely aware of what she was putting on—Shaw's sweater, a second pair of pants, layers of dirty socks; she had to be prepared to stay outside for a long time. There was only one thing to do: scour the haunted land until she found her son. But Eleanor Queen seemed determined to block her way. The girl chased her down the stairs, grabbing onto the hem of her too-large sweater. "Mama!"

"I don't have time, Bean—he's going to freeze to death!" He might still be out there, somewhere.

Orla rammed her arms into her coat sleeves. Eleanor Queen snatched her mother's wet boots from the floor and hugged them to her chest as she backed away.

"You're not listening!" the girl screamed. "I thought you were going to *listen*!"

The frenzy subsided. Orla turned her shaken attention to her daughter. Eleanor Queen spoke with the solid, even cadences of an adult—an adult who couldn't afford to lose the fleeting attention of her wounded audience lest something worse happen.

"Mama, Tycho isn't *here*. He isn't inside. He isn't outside. He is *not here*." Orla felt herself start to melt, the cold collapse of an ice sculpture slipping from its base. "I'm sorry. It won't help to look. He's..." Eleanor Queen shook her head. "Gone."

Her voice broke and she wept, clutching her mother's boots like a life preserver. Orla slipped off her gloves, let them fall to the ground. She took Eleanor Queen in her arms, startled by her warmth—this one creature in all the world was still alive.

"We can look...we can try..." Orla's voice fractured too. It felt too much like giving up.

"Please, Mama. I don't want anything else to happen."

Orla held her tighter. It wasn't fair. They'd tried so hard to do right by the spirit—and she'd thought She understood about a mother's love for her child. She should've gone on, pushed past her exhaustion the previous night to tell Her about Tycho, the sweetest little boy. She screamed in her mind so She would know: *You're not getting anything else!*

Orla had to find a way to resurrect herself from her grief, as her parents had done. They'd shown her the way; one child was reason enough to keep on living.

The entity wasn't going to let them leave. She still wanted something from them—from Eleanor Queen. Orla had to make herself a fortress, a barrier no monster could break through, and protect the last of her family.

36

She remembered there being a little white coffin. It was a false memory. Her little brother, Otto, had been cremated. Her parents were practical people—her mother, Aoife, a pharmacist; her father, Thomas, a veterinarian. They'd known Otto might die since he was one and a half years old. It started with what Aoife had thought was a stomach bug; the doctor hadn't initially been concerned. When the vomiting persisted, they rushed him back for more tests. His digestive system, it turned out, was fine; he was diagnosed with medulloblastoma, a type of brain tumor.

The seizures started in the hours before his first surgery. Orla, then almost six, remembered being scared and confused, but mostly because her regular life was upended when her parents took turns staying with Otto at the hospital. It was as if they'd gone from a family of four to a family of two, in rotating pairs. But eventually things settled into a new routine in which they all treated baby brother like a featherless bird who'd fallen from a nest.

Young Orla didn't think it was weird that her baby brother always seemed like a baby. He crawled instead of walked, babbled instead of talked, even when he was three, then four. Her parents said it was because he was sick, and the chemotherapy was Very Serious Medicine. Otto was like a living doll, and Orla had loved him way more than either of their two cats. They'd all thought the Very Serious Medicine would fix him, but later her parents sat down and told her baby brother's Very Bad Cells couldn't be fixed.

She was eight when he died. Everyone wept quietly at the funeral, like they were afraid of making too much noise. People spoke with lowered voices; they even moved slowly. Judging by the adults around her, young Orla thought death must be a most precarious situation, one in which the newly dead could easily become unsettled. His little urn was surrounded by massive bunches of flowers, every color of the rainbow. Still, Orla always recollected seeing a white coffin. He couldn't fit in the urn, even all curled up, even though he'd always been such a small and delicate boy. In her mind, she gave him a coffin with squishy toys and soft blankets. She even left lots of extra room, in case he grew.

People said things to her like "He just wasn't meant to be here very long"—which made Orla wonder *where* he was meant to be, and if he would grow up there with new parents and someone else as his sister. She thought about that a lot when she was still little, in elementary school, and sometimes it made her sad that Otto had left them for another family, and sometimes it made her happy that maybe he wasn't as dead as everyone seemed to think.

For months after he died, relatives and random old people would tell her, "He's watching you from heaven now." If her mother was present, she'd purse her lips and narrow her dark eyes and say, "I know you mean well, but please don't confuse her." If her father was present, he'd look at his shoes and not say anything. They couldn't, at that point, find a way to explain to one child why another had died. As Orla grew a little older she figured it out for herself—there was no rational reason for his death; it was no one's fault, and no one could have prevented it, neither doctors nor priests. She couldn't voice it to her parents, ever, but she'd understood then, on some level, that Otto had had a defect—something wasn't right in his head. His cells grew altogether wrong and pushed on his brain and that's why he could only act like a baby. And never grow up. A *fatal defect*.

It was only after Eleanor Queen was born that Orla came to fully appreciate what her parents had endured. She'd doubted then her own ability to carry on if anything happened to her heart—and that's what her daughter became the moment she was born, Orla's heart, on the outside of her body. As Orla grew up, she and her family never forgot about Otto, but he became less a part of their everyday lives. When she was ten, they stripped the carpeting out of his old room and put up a mirror and a barre so she could practice dancing whenever she wanted. By the time she turned thirteen, they didn't talk about him much anymore; he was pictures on a wall, a birthday, a death-day.

She was so busy with dance, and her parents were so supportive. Only later did she wonder if they threw themselves so fully into her interests as a distraction from their pain. But they arranged their schedules to pick her up from school early every day and drive her to her preprofessional dance classes. One or both of them went with her when she auditioned for competitive summer programs. And her parents saved up their vacation weeks, and they all traveled as a family to San Francisco, Toronto, and, finally, New York City when she was accepted into each of those competitive summer programs.

It hadn't struck her as odd or exceptional that they never complained about the cost of her training or the money spent on airfare, hotel rooms, and new leotards and shoes. On her own in New York City, she came to understand how financially blessed her upbringing had been and how advantageous it was to have endlessly supportive parents. When she had roommates, before she lived with Shaw, she'd tried to keep the refrigerator and cupboards stocked with food and never asked her roomies to pitch in. Some of them kept crazy hours—taking extra dance classes, working extra jobs—trying to make their way in the city. She'd held more than one hand at Penn Station or Port Authority, kissed more than one wet cheek, as a friend or soon-to-be-former roommate packed it in and went home. The city was merciless in its mangling and disposal of dreams.

Orla never forgot that her talent might not have been enough, nor her hard work; her parents—and their support—had been the magical element of the equation that made her life, her dreams, possible. Her parents came to see her in every new role, a weekend here, a weekend there, every season, until she retired. How many costumes had they seen her wear for different roles in ECCB's jazzy *Nutcracker*? Her whole life, they made her feel like she was everything they'd ever wanted—and never *the only child they had left*.

Orla thought about these things as hours passed into days. They were wretched days. She heard the hacking cough again—and knew it wasn't Tycho. It wasn't Eleanor Queen either, as she was always nearby and the coughing came from the second floor. The house had started to smell bad too, but in her morose state, Orla couldn't tell if it was them—their unwashed bodies and clothes—or...something else.

They couldn't risk trying to flee again, and a part of her didn't want to leave Tycho behind. He would haunt this place, and it might be the only bit of him she'd ever have. The powerlessness of their situation weighed on her, but every time she caught Eleanor Queen concentrating, trying to communicate with the spirit, Orla severed her connection. She'd shake her or clap angry hands in the girl's face. Eleanor Queen insisted that they needed answers, that it was the only way, but Orla couldn't let her channel such a dangerous entity anymore. She told her daughter she'd think of something. She told her the tree would die soon and they would be released.

What was she still missing? This was tormenting her too. The imagery in Shaw's paintings. The pentagram in the hand of a dying girl. And the more visceral things. The coughing. The sickly stench. When she got too bored, Eleanor Queen would sniff along the walls, searching for a dead rodent. She never found one. But the puzzle pieces were everywhere, as fragile as cherry blossoms in a strong wind. None of Orla's theories stuck together, and Eleanor Queen maintained she had no sense of a *girl*. The thing that was tormenting them might be female, but She wasn't human.

In her worst moments, Orla wondered if Eleanor Queen had told the spirit—on purpose or accidentally—that they were running away. Maybe some part of Eleanor Queen hadn't wanted to leave, the part that still had compassion for the thing and Her plight. Or maybe She had sensed them leaving the land when they passed the invisible threshold at the mailbox.

They subsisted in the living room like two forgotten prisoners; their supplies dwindled, but no one came with the key to set them free. They were often sleepy, weakened from lack of food. Eleanor Queen made the couch her territory; from there she read her books and kept a watchful eye on her mother. Sometimes Orla sat in the ugly plaid chair. Sometimes she lay sprawled on the mattress. She'd scold herself in her mind— *Figure something out!*—but then succumb to absent staring and thinking about the past. Too many times, Tycho became Otto, and she saw herself as a little girl playing with a baby brother who talked and walked and looked like her son. But he still ended up insectival, curled up in an urn with his Tinker-toys spine.

Inevitably, it also made her think of Shaw. And Ziploc bags full of freezer-scorched meat. Is that what he would look like if she went out and lifted the tarp? And what of Tycho? The best she could hope for was that he'd fallen asleep, slipping into death while his fingers and toes burned with the false heat of hypothermia.

She shut her eyes and clenched her fists, the invisible once-smooth worry stones now jagged; her palms bore the bloody half-moons of her fingernails digging too often and too hard. But it was the only coping method she had to keep from continually bursting into tears in front of Eleanor Queen—though her daughter was too aware not to know what was going on.

She felt it as Eleanor Queen perched beside her on the ugly plaid chair's arm. "Mama."

Orla peeked at her. Then she squeezed her nose, as if her emotions were just looking to drip from somewhere. Eleanor Queen pulled her mother's hand away, glanced at the red hieroglyphs etched on her palm.

"We can't hide forever."

She nodded, because her daughter sounded so reasonable. She wanted to scream, not at Eleanor Queen, but at the cruel hopelessness of their situation. The thing out there was unreasonable; It had proven that (and maybe It didn't deserve a gendered pronoun). Sometimes Orla wished she could let herself drift into an endless sleep. Who had she been to assume for so many years that heaven was a fantasy, a fiction? Why couldn't there be a marshmallow wonderland where a billion souls reunited? She wanted to try it, dying. Would Tycho be there? Shaw? Otto? Could she be one of those mothers who sacrificed their children first and then committed suicide?

The thought punched her in the throat. No. There were more

things they could try. And this wasn't how her company of graceful warriors would behave, nor the women who'd earned spots at the table—or on the floor—of *The Dinner Party*.

Orla swept Eleanor Queen onto her lap, enveloped her in her arms. She felt ribs, bones, through her daughter's dirty pajamas. They'd been surviving on disgusting things. Brothy soups made with water, dried oregano, and garlic powder. Salad dressing swirled on a few mouthfuls of rice. Orla felt it in her own body, the eating away of her muscles. She'd been strong, but eventually her energy-consuming organs would run out of things to siphon calories from. They were running out of time. She chastised herself for taking those two days to mourn Tycho— or had it been three? And could she really call it mourning? It wasn't like she'd been sitting shiva as her Jewish friends did or doing anything practical to honor the dead.

No. She'd let herself fall into a quicksand of slimy, sticky self-pity and inactivity. Her eyelids drooped; she wasn't sure she had the strength to climb away from her misery. Maybe it was the lack of nutrients. Everything was so cloudy, so nebulous and hard to follow—time, her thoughts, her movements.

Wake up!

"Is it Christmas Eve?" she asked her daughter.

"I think so."

"Okay. Okay." She wasn't certain what she was going to do, but she was going to do something to salvage Christmas, and her daughter's future. "You should go to bed early, so Santa will come."

Skepticism made an aged and doubtful mask of Eleanor Queen's increasingly narrow face. But she kissed her mother's cheek and acquiesced.

37

Orla didn't stop Eleanor Queen as she bypassed the mattress and went upstairs, listless and subdued. Sometimes the girl liked to nap in her bedroom, but they still spent their nights camped on the living-room floor. Tonight Orla wanted to lay out a surprise; the least she could do was bring up the Christmas gifts. Maybe she'd call Eleanor Queen back down later. The thing knocked on her child's mind at random times, and Orla couldn't miss an opportunity to put a stop to it.

Die already. That would be the best Christmas gift of all, if Eleanor Queen awoke in the morning, eyes wide and gleeful, the entity severed from her consciousness.

She glanced around the basement as she went down the stairs; maybe there was something yet to find. The old man's belongings hadn't yielded any definitive clues, and if he had a special hiding place, it remained hidden. If only he had been receptive, aware of the thing on his land, maybe none of this would have happened. (If he were still alive, she would've killed him.) Everything in the cold cellar looked familiar; it had no more secrets to give up. Her husband's heart—the furnace he'd loved—was still keeping them alive; its reassuring presence burned off some of her bitterness.

The Christmas gifts were concealed in a big box marked LAMP/FRAGILE. There weren't a lot; they hadn't finished Christmas shopping, and Shaw and Orla had decided not to exchange presents since they'd purchased so much for the house. The children's gifts were already wrapped, one special thing for each of them and a few smaller ones. They'd learned long ago to wrap everything the moment it was brought into the house. In the apartment, sometimes they'd had nowhere better to hide things but atop the kitchen cupboards or in their one bulging closet. The sight of Tycho's presents made her breath hitch for a moment, but she carried his things upstairs with Eleanor Queen's, and switched off the basement light.

It hadn't occurred to her to decorate, to hang any of the Christmas lights or the festive drawings and ornaments that the children had made. And the last thing she wanted to think about was a tree. But now, looking around the living room, arms full of presents, she saw a squatter's mess; her daughter deserved more than that.

She plopped the gifts onto the couch and quickly tidied the room. Even though the mattress would soon be back in use, she straightened all the bedding, fluffed the pillows. Maybe she'd let Eleanor Queen open her presents at midnight. That might be a nice surprise, and different from what they'd always done together as a family.

There's only two of us now.

Tycho's presents, again, threatened to undo her. Would they have the same effect on Eleanor Queen? She couldn't stop seeing herself slipping beneath the water, her baby boy trapped on the ice, calling, "Mama." What if she had let go of Eleanor Queen? Her efforts to clamber back onto the floe might have sent Tycho tumbling into the water, and they all might have come home together. She couldn't forgive herself; it was almost as bad as the mistake she'd made with her husband. If only she'd known the water was a conduit, she could have grabbed them both and jumped. But she hadn't known. And at that moment, only Eleanor Queen had seemed in imminent danger.

Around and around the anguish spun.

Orla pinched Tycho's lumpiest, softest present. A monkey with long arms and legs and Velcro on the hands and feet. Eleanor Queen had had a similar one that she used to attach around her neck and waist and wear like an appendage. He loved his stuffed animals. Orla knew what all of the rein-deer wrapping paper hid and imagined her son giggling as he tore open his treasures. The special Lego kit he'd been want-ing. Supersoft fleece pajamas covered with…polar bears. (She winced.) And a rocket-ship backpack on which she'd sewn an authentic NASA patch.

Could they hold a memorial of some sort for him? Make these gifts an offering to him, wherever he was? Would Eleanor Queen like that, a sense of closure, or would it break something inside her? Children's souls, like their bones, were more pliable than adults' and could bend a fair ways before breaking. But that didn't mean they weren't deeply affected. Trauma swam inside them, left bundles of eggs on swampy leaves; sometimes too many hatched. They could grow and gather and turn a person into someone else. Orla hoped that wasn't happening to her brilliant girl.

Afraid of making things worse, she arranged only Eleanor Queen's gifts around the wood-burning stove. It was the best centerpiece they had, and in its own way, it symbolized life. The rest she carried into Shaw's studio to hide in his closet.

She lingered in his room. It smelled of him; he was everywhere. She'd kept his door closed, afraid of the reminders. But now she realized she needed the reminders, just as she needed not to forget the fierce women who had made her stronger. His paintings were like kisses, freely given, so much a part of him. Here he was on display, on his two easels and on the floor leaning against the walls.

Maybe there was something of Shaw's that she could give to Eleanor Queen as an extra-special gift. She squatted down and examined the paintings, turning each over to see if Shaw had scribbled a title anywhere. Some, she knew, had names, and maybe there was one in particular that spoke of daughters or of love.

The paintings were beautiful, but the prominence of trees…even if the thing wasn't a tree but some essence that lived inside it, it still didn't seem like an appropriate gift. She considered finding the paintings he'd done in the city before they left; maybe one of those would work. But she couldn't quite sever herself from the mysterious woodland images and the cabin that Shaw had…channeled? He'd mistaken It for his muse; Orla understood why, based on the depth and detail of his work. Once again, the camouflaged forms captured her.

"What were you trying to say?" she asked aloud, spotting an assemblage of leaves that, viewed sideways, revealed the contemplative look of a human face. "Did you sense something out there? A consciousness? Did you know it was in the tree?" She sighed, letting herself fall into a sitting position on the floor. "Do you have the answers—are they here somewhere? I need to know what It wants. Why It won't let us go."

"I've been trying to tell you."

The voice startled her so much that she scampered backward, knocking into one of Shaw's easels. The painting toppled onto her head, and only after she tossed it aside—as if a rattlesnake had fallen on her—did she get an unobstructed view of the speaker.

Orla opened her mouth to scream, but the scream wouldn't come.

She whimpered, pushing herself along the floor to get away from the figure who stood in the doorway.

He stepped toward her to close the distance, but recognizing her fear, he held out his hands and made the same two gestures she'd once made to the snow rollers: *Stop. Innocent.*

Her features aghast, her heart a revving semi on a collision course, Orla shook her head and gaped at her husband.

Shaw took another step forward. "I can't stay for long—"

"How are you doing this? How can you do any of this?" She wasn't fooled. This was an illusion or a trick. Or maybe the final avalanche of her sanity making its riotous descent toward the void.

He knelt down a few feet in front of her, so similar in mannerisms to her husband that Orla felt herself inching forward, wanting to embrace him. To apologize. To hold him and never let go. But she kept her distance even as her eyes scrutinized him, expecting to find a flaw, a glitch in his appearance that would expose the sham of his identity. But he looked in every way, from his crooked teeth to his messy hair, like the husband she needed—

"I can't stay like this for long," he said again. His voice had a robotic quality, as if he were trying too hard to make each word clear, and the tempo and pitch were a bit askew. "It's the most difficult thing, more taxing than conjuring beauty in nature, to communicate like you do. But you need answers—"

"Yes. *Please!*" She rose to her knees.

"You shouldn't have stopped the young one when we were making so much progress."

He—It—was talking about Eleanor Queen. A moment ago

Orla had wanted to touch him to verify his solidity—was he warm with life?—but now she wanted to slap his face, knock the mention of her child from his traitorous mouth.

"I didn't do this to hurt any of you, and I'm sorry for what's happened. I know I've made mistakes. I thought the little boy would follow you into the water. I had to make a quick choice—channel the two of you to safety, or try to maintain the ice where he floated. I needed a lot of power to do either; I couldn't do both."

Orla wept. Hearing the acknowledgment of Tycho's death from her husband (even if he wasn't)...raucous sobs threatened to crack her open. Shaw slipped forward and embraced her, which only made her cry harder. It felt like the man she knew. She clung to him. He didn't stroke her hair or whisper in her ear the way a lover would, but just to have him for a moment...she wanted more, but he pulled back.

"Listen," he said. Orla obeyed the command. She smeared away her tears and snot with the back of her hand and gave the thing her rapt attention. "I need you to understand—"

"Why are you doing this to me?"

He looked uncertain. "I lived for a long time, in my home...my time is different from yours. I had forgotten who I was. How to speak. Where I came from. And when I started to realize my home was dying...I found myself able to do things I hadn't...I hadn't even tried before. I realized, after all my years of becoming one with the life force around me, I had become *more*. Maybe it was triggered by the memory of death. So I started...reaching out. Exploring. Drawing from the planes of my world, trying to understand more urgently who I was, what I should do." He took in a deep breath, but instead of releasing it, he began coughing—a terrible, body-shaking hack that spewed droplets of blood.

Horrified as the blood splattered her, Orla inched back farther. "Who are you? What are you?"

"This man, who I appear as, sensed me. And through him I tried…I wanted him to understand, and be my new…I didn't realize then how frightening it would be for him. I've tried to adjust, for the young one, so she won't be afraid." He coughed again, spraying a mist of blood.

"Please leave her alone. Tell me what you want. We don't want to all die here—that can't be what you want!"

"It isn't! I was dying before, long ago. I found the memory. And now, as then, I want my life to continue on and…I thought I would be alone forever. Now that I understand—I know what I did, all those years ago. I can do it again. Move into a new home."

"So move! There are trees all around—" Her exasperation rose in tandem with her anger.

"I don't want another tree. I wanted this." He gestured to his physical body. "And when he made it clear he wouldn't offer it, I panicked. I didn't understand his…his choice. I…lashed out, I felt betrayed. I remembered a night…a solstice night—"

"That was us! We were trying to help!"

"No, longer ago. I was dying. I looked"—he reached a ghostly finger toward her, and his arm extended, growing like a tree limb—"like you. Like the young girl queen. I needed something that would outlive me. I said…I don't know, I don't remember words as they are to you. But I believed in something, believed in what was bigger than who I was, the glorious roots and leaves that connect the world. I said…a prayer—you call it a prayer. And then I moved—the tree accepted me, and I moved so I wouldn't die."

Tectonic plates shifted again, but this time they were in Orla's mind. Her skin tingled, tightened as its glacial surfaces crashed together. "Were you the girl? Who died here? You *were* the girl with the penta—"

"Was I a *girl*? I think I was. I was dying." He coughed again, and Orla, instinctively afraid of the deadly contagion that was tuberculosis, covered her face with her arm so it wouldn't infect her. "When I asked the man—I can't just…take. Steal. There has to be an agreement. If I'd been able to explain it to him better…he didn't have to be afraid. I am more than I was—not a girl, much…bigger. More layers. I grew powerful…but he and I could have lived together."

Orla shook her head, appalled as crimson phlegm dribbled from the edges of his mouth, down his chin. The words he spoke were commonplace, but the meaning was more foreign than anything she'd ever heard—as was the strange, off-kilter way he spoke. Shaw had been right about the cure cottage, the photo, the tubercular women. No, not all the women. One particular dying girl. But they hadn't had enough dots to connect. And none of it made sense; she felt skeletal with fear, about to collapse into a useless puzzle of bones.

He stood, towering over her, elongating like the tree in which he—She—lived, and Orla gazed up at him in horror.

"I hope you understand now. My efforts—to show you things of wonder, and explore my own untapped powers—they diminish the time I have left. I didn't know you would see the beautiful world and react with such fear, when all I meant was for you to stop and listen. Please listen; we're running out of time. It is the young one now—how I love her! You, the mother, made me see and remember! And she is open to me, more open than the man, than you. She is not afraid of new possibilities. If she offers herself to me, we will be together and she will be like herself still, but also like me, the immense presence I have become—"

Orla shook her head, an emphatic refusal. "No!"

"—and when she lets me in, I think there's one last thing I can try…"

He succumbed to coughing, and faded into nothing. It

reminded her of the transporter from an old *Star Trek* episode, dissolving a traveler into specks of light.

She jumped to her feet, panting as if she'd been exerting herself. She wanted to run from the room but hesitated to pass through the spot where her husband had appeared. The spatters of blood remained. Clutching her head, she made quick strides back and forth, then finally leapt around the space *She* had occupied and fled the room, shutting the door behind her.

Orla, too, had been right; she would never disregard her intuition again. There was no way in hell she'd let her daughter do what the entity wanted, even if Orla felt sorry for that long-ago lonely girl. But now she knew.

Exactly what she needed to do.

After cleaning herself off in the bathroom, scrubbing away the blood that couldn't possibly be there, she went into her daughter's room and snuggled in next to her on the twin bed.

On Christmas morning she'd give Eleanor Queen the gift she most deserved: the rest of her life.

38

For a moment, it was like an ordinary Christmas morning. Eleanor Queen's face lit up the instant she reached the bottom of the steps and saw the long, flat package leaning against the squat stove.

Now she sat cross-legged in front of her mother, seemingly unaware of Orla braiding her hair, enthralled by the coveted gift. Orla and Shaw had paid a lot for it, certain that Eleanor Queen wouldn't mind getting fewer presents than her brother. Had things turned out differently, Shaw would've retrieved the last secret gifts (which they'd never gotten around to buying): a pair of plastic sleds, one for each child. They hadn't quite figured out where they'd go sledding; Shaw suggested the road, but that sounded dangerous to Orla (long before she'd experienced anything truly life-threatening). While Eleanor Queen tried out her special present, Orla had planned to pull Tycho around on his sled.

"It's beautiful." Eleanor Queen looked truly happy for the first time in recent memory. Her hand followed the bow's curve, stopped at the wooden grip. As Orla finished the first braid and wrapped the tail in a band, Eleanor Queen held the bow up, testing the elasticity of the string. While her mother worked on the second braid, the girl fit all the fiberglass arrows into her new hip quiver.

"I'm sure you'll be just as good as Katniss," Orla said in her ear. Eleanor Queen flashed her a grin. "You're a warrior now. With a special mission."

"I am?"

"You are." Orla hadn't realized at first how violent a story *The Hunger Games* was, and after she read it herself, she hadn't let Eleanor Queen get the sequels. But she'd never objected to her daughter's interest in a badass girl who saved her sister and fought against a despotic regime. She wanted her timid daughter to be a rebel of some kind; Katniss wasn't such a bad role model. And for what Orla had in mind, her daughter needed to be brave.

They both got dressed in warm clothes, and Orla laid out a pathetic breakfast of ketchup, mayonnaise, and mustard.

"I was thinking I could give it my *new* book—that's something special to me, so it would make a good offering—and then maybe it could learn to *read*. That would be helpful, if it could write messages!" Eleanor Queen gobbled up her little red and cream mounds. She hated mustard, so Orla ate that, licking it off a spoon.

"That's a good idea," Orla said, withholding what had happened and what she'd learned in Shaw's studio the previous night.

"I'm really, really close now, Mama—I'm going to find out what it wants us to do." She squeezed out another serving of her preferred condiments.

Orla held the knowledge now and she couldn't tell her daughter that she already knew. The spirit had appeared as her beloved husband to comfort her, to make her more trusting. But Orla desired Her diametric opposite; Eleanor Queen's future lay elsewhere, in the human world, where she could grow up and become anything she wanted.

"Bean?" The girl licked ketchup off her finger. "I made a decision last night. I figured out something that will work. And it's going to take both of us—we each need to do something very important."

Eleanor Queen looked at her, and not with the wobbly uncertainty she'd once possessed, but genuine interest. "What?"

"It—She likes you." Her daughter nodded in agreement. "She won't hurt you."

"No...I don't think so." The brightness of her eyes diminished for a moment, and Orla was certain she saw her remembering her papa, her brother. The thing out there had caused pain around her but not *to* her.

"You're going to go to the road," Orla said. Several inches of new snow had fallen overnight, but she'd already set one of the smaller pairs of snowshoes by the front door. Along with Eleanor Queen's bow and quiver. She'd zipped Shaw's driver's license and her state ID into the pocket of Eleanor Queen's coat so she could show someone who her parents were. A bottle only partially filled with water so it wouldn't weigh her down as she walked. Shaw's charged phone (her own was too waterlogged after her fall into the frozen sea to ever work again). The last stale granola bar she'd found in the pocket of a lighter-weight coat—one of the snacks she always had on hand when she went anywhere with the children.

Eleanor Queen gazed at her with round, curious eyes. "I am?"

"Yes. Down the driveway. Make a right onto the road. Then a right onto the bigger road when you get to it. Cars will go by. Don't get in any—wave someone down and ask them to call 911."

The wary girl within Eleanor Queen returned. "What about you?"

"We can't both go. But She won't hurt you. And I'll be at the tree the whole time, talking to Her." Offering up her own life. "She's getting better at understanding me. I'll put my hands on the tree and tell Her more about us, me. I think She'll understand this time, how I'm going to help Her. And She won't mind then if *you* leave—you can find someone…"

Orla stopped speaking as the knot of tears bulged in her throat. She couldn't let her daughter see any sadness. Couldn't tell her—even though she wanted to—that her Lola and Lolo would raise her and be wonderful parents. Orla didn't believe, regardless of how reassuring the entity had tried to be—in the guise of her husband and with the memory of the human girl She had once been—that the offering she was about to make was anything but a death sentence.

She read the hesitation in her daughter's frozen posture, the returning terror in her unblinking eyes. Eleanor Queen had never been left alone or gone anywhere by herself. Unlike her brother, she was happy enough on her own with family in another room. But what Orla was asking—telling—her to do was far beyond her life experience.

"You'll have your bow for protection." Eleanor Queen followed her mother into the living room. "See, everything you need. We'll leave at the same time, and you should get to the end of the driveway about the same time I get to the tree. You won't be alone for long." Though Orla wasn't sure that was true. How busy would a North Country road be on Christmas morning? "I put Papa's phone in your coat, and if that doesn't get a signal or no one comes by, you just keep walking until you reach St. Armand. There will be lots of people there. Okay?"

Orla needed her daughter to have faith in the plan, faith that her mother, without a translator, could help the entity within the tree. She didn't want Eleanor Queen to turn back and witness her mother's last living moments. And Eleanor Queen needed to complete her own task and bear the burden of walking alone on unfamiliar roads. She watched the scenario play out across the girl's face.

Finally, Eleanor Queen nodded. "Okay. But you have to help her—she's counting on us."

"I'm going to."

"And when I find people, we'll come back for you."

"Of course you will." Her child would be brokenhearted, but she would survive. "You're going to get away this time, Eleanor Queen. She won't hurt you, and I'll give Her…what She needs."

"I wish we could go together."

"I know."

They bundled up in their gear and stepped out onto the porch. Eleanor Queen turned her gaze toward the snow-covered driveway.

"You can do this, it's a safe walk," Orla said. "I think everyone around here will be friendly—a girl on her own. Christmas. And you ask them to call 911."

"I have my bow." In the snowshoes, with the bow worn across her body, her daughter looked every part the warrior, the Arctic survivor.

"Just like Katniss. I'll stay with the tree until the police come back for me—you tell them where I am."

Orla wasn't sure if the police would ever find her or if—like her baby boy—something inexplicable would disappear her from the earth. But she didn't care. As long as Eleanor Queen lived, got away. Fulfilled her destiny. She didn't want her daughter to see her cry, didn't want her to think for a second that this was a final goodbye.

It took the bulk of Orla's self-discipline not to turn around and watch her go, recede against the white backdrop. But the girl had her own role to play, and Orla willed herself to walk away. She hoped Eleanor Queen didn't stop and look back, expecting a wave or some last words of encouragement. They needed to go in their opposite directions.

One toward life.

One toward something unfathomable.

39

Orla tramped along the path they'd made through the trees, familiar with the way now, even though the new snow had covered their prints. Her once-muscular legs needed more protein; her body was withering. Her heart throbbed large and crooked. It had been dissected, neat lines drawn down and across, pinned at the corners: one black and sunken quadrant for Tycho, one for Shaw. The lower left quadrant bore an older wound, dry and shriveled, from the loss of Otto. The last quadrant pumped bubbly red while Eleanor Queen still breathed. If Orla lost her daughter, there would be no reason for her heart to continue circulating blood. (How she hoped her parents didn't share similar thoughts, but she couldn't worry on that.)

I will give Her myself.

She prayed that the strange, powerful spirit would accept her final gift, and leave her daughter alone.

It was only a few days ago they'd hung the paper chain around the tree. The sight of it made her wistful. Tycho's fingerprints were preserved in the glue.

"I'm here," she announced. "I'm here, and willing." Her body wasn't as strong as it once was, but she felt real pride for the

306 • Zoje Stage

vessel she could be. She'd worked hard, physically, for most of her life. She barely had the stamina for it, but it was the best way to show the spirit who she was—that she was worthy, tough, a suitable replacement for the magnificent tree: Orla danced.

It was time. The entity knew about her daughter; now She needed to approve of Orla. Toes pointed within her boots, she swept around the tree, a winter waltz in clumsy turns, her arms fluid and exaggerated. Clumps of snow had collected on the paper chain, and she lifted and dropped the chain as part of her dance, releasing the snow.

Sometimes she brushed an ungloved hand along the bark, seeking to strengthen the connection between herself and the strange being within the tree. The word *hybrid* suddenly came to her; like the fused fox-hare she'd seen in the snow, somehow a nineteenth-century girl had fused her soul with an unlikely but sentient ally. Would Orla become all of them when the spirit took her body?

Her thoughts became images. Orla showed Her the most difficult choreography she had ever mastered, and the passion she'd shared with Shaw. She showed Her how they'd made love—tenderly, then ferociously—and how she'd pushed out her daughter, her son. *I created life.* How she fed them at her breast. The unearthly radiance she saw in their questioning infant eyes. How, because of her, they grew and thrived.

Around and around she went. The movements came from within. They sped up and slowed down. And once she leaned forward until her chest was parallel to the ground, raising her right leg behind her—through the arabesque and into a penché until her toe pointed toward the sky. She held it there until her muscles started to shake, wanting to impress with her flexibility, her power. Her life force. All the while she played movies in her mind: Tycho's tottering first steps. The evolution of his musical babbling into actual songs. Orla wished she could show

Her how it felt to snuggle him in her arms while he giggled or drifted toward sleep.

The air around her smelled of Christmas mornings. A Fraser fir in an enclosed space. Freshly brewed coffee. Peppermint candy canes licked by red tongues. Chocolate candies chewed by small teeth. The scent of new items as they were released from their boxes. These imaginary smells hid the truth: a wild wood, relentless snow, their empty house. Distant wood smoke lingered and Orla wished the other remote families a better Christmas than she was having. Maybe one of them would stumble on her daughter, and she'd finally reconnect with the outside world.

She pressed her hands hard into the tree, so hard the edged bark seared her tender palms.

"But even after everything You've taken from me…I'll give You myself. You need a home? You need a volunteer? Well, take my body. Do with it what You need."

She expected a flash, an internal pop of light that indicated the spirit's awareness. Or a vibration. A small earthquake. Or tiny floating flames in the branches above her. There was nothing. And without Eleanor Queen, she had no one to ask if the presence had registered her at all. Her movement, her images— had Orla gotten through on any level?

"I'm here! I want to help You! You can't have…the young one, she's too young to make such a promise of her own free will. But You can have me—I understand the sacrifice I'm making. I accept it. Please."

Not so much as a gust of wind. The tree—and whatever resided within it—appeared dead, or at least unresponsive. Its bark was paler than that of the trees around it. As she looked upward, she worried for the first time that too much wind would send its lifeless branches, each the size of one of the neighboring trees, crashing onto her head.

"Hello? You can't accuse me of not listening and then ignore my offer. This is what You wanted. You need a human. I am the only one who understands and is fully willing."

A whisper of wind moved through the trees. She watched, unsure what to expect, but then everything grew still again. Was it possible…could the evergreen's last living cells have died during the night? Or perhaps She had overextended Herself, coming to her as Shaw. If the tree died before the girl's spirit moved on…could She be entombed now within Her former host? Safe as houses?

Could Orla go find her daughter and take her back to civilization?

She felt no sadness if the entity had died. But the lack of response started to anger her. She kicked at the tree, chipped away at the thick but surprisingly brittle bark.

"Wake up! You can't terrorize my family because You want help and then refuse it when it's offered! Wake the fuck up!"

A noise like a horn startled her, a deep, hollow sound. At first she mistook it for the reply she'd demanded, but then realized it was coming from a distance. It made an insistent lowing, like a Tibetan long horn. But as it moved closer, it sounded more animalistic. Behind it, she heard chuffing and grunts. And as it came nearer still, there was the crunch of trampling snow and breaking branches.

She pressed her back against the tree, eyes wide and alert for the first sign of the creature moving toward her. While she'd been gazing upward through the boughs, a fog had settled in behind her, obscuring the view, heightening her fear as the strange sounds reverberated in the gloom. As the call grew louder, she drew on her gloves, made fists. Ready to fight.

A mass of beasts moved on the horizon. In the murk, she couldn't tell at first what they were, only that they were large, and there were a lot of them, ambling toward her through the trees. The low calling sounded again, this time very close. Louder.

Orla squinted, as if that would clarify their form. She was prepared to meet her end but didn't like the not knowing; was she about to be devoured, or trampled, or killed in some fashion by that sorrowful cry? She saw the antlers first, massive and wide, poking through the fog. The animals moved at a steady, deliberate pace, but once she recognized them—moose, dozens of them, all snowy-white albinos—she didn't doubt their intention to impale her against the tree.

She could've run for it, turned and dashed deeper into the forest than she had ever gone. Maybe they'd follow her, grunting and murderous, or maybe she'd just collapse from exhaustion and die lost in the snow. But she'd told her daughter to tell the police that she'd be at the tree, and that's where Orla intended to stay. Let these beasts take her—she'd offered herself, after all.

Something akin to joy tingled across her skin. In Shaw's form, She'd all but admitted She couldn't do two things at once: if these creatures were here, then Eleanor Queen was elsewhere, heading away.

The moose spread out, surrounded her. She knew now; the white animals weren't fully there but conjured by the spirit's powerful magic. But, as Shaw had, they looked real, sounded real. The long-legged, knobby-kneed herd, heavy-antlered and shaggy-furred, came to a stop a few feet away from Orla. The lowing quieted, though some of the herd still grunted, chuffed.

They exhaled plumes of fog and Orla wondered if that was the source of the mist. Maybe she was inside their lungs. Maybe She had accepted her sacrifice, and Orla's transformation—her journey—had begun. But then a final moose moved through the murk, a mighty beast, and headed toward her.

Orla's joy blistered, burst, rotted into black, and her legs gave way. She sank to the ground, the bark ripping the fabric along the back of her coat, mesmerized by what she saw—what she didn't want to see. From the ground, the animals loomed above her.

"No!"

40

Orla blinked hard once, then again, willing it to be another part of the illusion. If only the king moose had come forward as her executioner, the one summoned to impale her. But there astride its muscled back sat her daughter, bow in her hand, a smile on her face.

"Eleanor Queen…"

Her daughter gripped a tuft of fur behind the moose's head. She looked so small atop the beast, like a character from one of her favorite books who rode a polar bear. The herd appeared quite docile, unlike what Orla had heard about stampeding moose. A single moose could trample a person to death, according to a dancer friend who had grown up in Alaska. But that was in real life, and they weren't in the real world anymore. Little girls rode giant moose—tame and friendly, like the stuffed animal Tycho had cherished.

"She wouldn't let you go…" Snow seeped through her pants, but she couldn't get up.

"It's okay, Mama."

Orla shook her head.

"They're very gentle."

"But they wouldn't let you go."

The king moose bent its knee, lowering itself regally so Eleanor Queen could slip off its back. It stayed down, transforming into a misshapen lump of ice before melting into the ground.

As Eleanor Queen approached her mother, the rest of the herd turned in unison and evaporated into the fog. Orla let out a vicious cackle of laughter. "You should have shot one of them while they still had a shape. If we can't get out of here, we're going to need something to eat." But lost hikers, stranded mountain climbers, died from eating snow; it lowered their body temperature. No, snow animals, even while they looked like real ones, couldn't feed them. This is what hunger—delirium—was doing to her. *I've lost it.*

Eleanor Queen dropped onto her knees beside her mother—her braids, her bow and quiver of arrows, her smile. Orla couldn't help it; she flinched from her reaching hand, just for a second, convinced her daughter had become someone else.

"No, it's good, Mama. I learned something—something so important!"

"Did you?" Orla sounded exhausted, half dead. The failure weighed on her. The spirit didn't want Orla, even to talk with; she was out of options. And she already knew what her daughter was going to say. "She wants *you.*"

Eleanor Queen laughed. "We did it backward!"

Orla burst up from where she'd crumpled to the ground, manic with a new resolve. "No! Absolutely not!"

"Mama—"

"Come on, we're going home." She grabbed Eleanor Queen's coat, and when the girl resisted, Orla hauled her away from the tree.

"Mama, you don't understand!"

"No, *you* don't understand!"

"She doesn't want to hurt me, She feels connected to me—

like I feel connected to Her. I understand now. And that's why She wants us to live together—"

"*Live?* As *what?*" Orla yelled in her face and didn't care when Eleanor Queen shrank from her. "You don't understand what She's asking—"

"I know more than you! She *was* a girl once, but now—"

"Whatever She was once, She's not that girl anymore. Look at Her power. You can't…if She were inside you, where would *you* be?"

"She won't hurt me! And Mama—"

"She will *replace* you!"

Eleanor Queen glowered at her with her too-wise, too-old eyes. The starvation that had settled in her face, forming ridges of her cheekbones, made her look even older. "You're wrong, Mama. She didn't replace the tree. The tree's been alive this whole time, doing fine. Maybe it's the reason the tree lived this long—you're still not *listening*." Scorn and pity oozed from her words.

Orla grabbed her daughter's arm and continued marching back toward the house. Violent thoughts stormed inside her, none of them directed at her daughter. *Get the ax. Chop the tree down.* The thing had lived long enough. She didn't deserve another chance. "Old things die, Eleanor Queen. It's the way things are."

"But then we can leave. I'm trying to save you, Mama!" She shook herself free from her mother's grip. "You and Tycho."

Orla stopped. Gazed at her daughter with a look that blended terror with revulsion. Was it too late? Had the spirit already corrupted her daughter's mind, made a trickster and liar of her to get what She wanted?

"Tycho's dead, you know—"

"No, Tycho's *gone*. But I think we—I—can get him back."

"How?"

"I'm not…not completely sure yet. But it's part of…if She makes me Her new home, then…"

As if She were trying to prove how far removed She was from human—did She really think Orla would bargain one child for another? She rested her hands on her daughter's narrow shoulders, her anger gone. She couldn't fault Eleanor Queen for wanting to save her brother.

"You don't owe Her anything. You don't owe *me* anything, or even Tycho. I knew…I offered Her myself. That was a fair compromise. I'm an adult, I can make that decision. What She's asking of you is not something a nine-year-old can decide. I explained that, and *She* didn't listen. She can't be trusted. When She was a girl she practiced witchcraft, or believed in something…dangerous—that's why this happened. She transferred Her soul into a fucking tree!" Orla took her daughter's hand and resumed the trek home. "We're done now—we'll wait it out. The tree will die, or She can choose another damn tree. Or a fox, or a rabbit—it's not our fucking problem. We shouldn't have come here, but I'm getting *you* out, not the other way around."

"I just wanted to help," her daughter said in a small voice.

"Of course you did, because you're a brave, smart, strong girl. Trust *me,* not *Her*. Whatever She's become, She's not your friend."

Eleanor Queen gazed up at her with keen, evaluating eyes. Slightly distrustful eyes. Orla wished she could read her daughter's mind, desperate for the thoughts she kept to herself.

They strode the rest of the way home in silence. Sometimes Orla shook her head. This could've been finished. The spirit was too stubborn for Her own good. Or maybe…she shuttered the thought. Didn't want to remember the way Eleanor Queen had stood in the yard, receptive since the beginning to something the rest of them couldn't see. Maybe it was Eleanor Queen She had wanted all along. *The familiarity of a girl.* Shaw might have been aware of something he didn't want to understand. But their daughter had always been the more susceptible one. Fireworks of impossibilities, regrets, exploded in her brain. Appearing as Shaw had been the ultimate attempt to influence her. No, well, presenting Herself as Tycho would have been worse. But she wouldn't be fooled; She couldn't be trusted. And yet...

What special connection—what magic—did Eleanor Queen inherently possess?

Maybe that's why everything with the move fell into place; maybe we were fulfilling some preordained destiny and my daughter belongs...

No.

Because she also remembered her daughter's fear. That plaintive question as she'd gazed at the windowless windows: "Are we going to die?"

Eleanor Queen didn't want this. Had never wanted it. She wanted a house on a residential street and children to play with. A normal life. She wanted to practice a musical instrument too quietly for anyone to judge her.

Waiting for a tree to die wasn't the most proactive operation she could undertake, but keeping her daughter alive was her calling above all others. Keep her from starving. Keep her from giving away any more of herself.

Orla wished she *could* flee on her own, run for help. But if she left Eleanor Queen alone—or even turned her back—the girl would run into the woods and offer herself. And then the last quadrant of Orla's heart would wither; the Moreau-Bennetts would be gone.

Shaw's brother's family would be home in a few days. Their inability to reach them might not cause immediate concern, but they would come. One week, two weeks. She just had to keep Eleanor Queen safe—alive—until then.

41

Eleanor Queen stamped into the house without bothering to kick the snow from her boots. She tossed the snowshoes by the door, propped up her bow, and threw herself into the ugly plaid chair. Orla closed the door behind them. And locked it.

"Why are you locking it?" Eleanor Queen demanded.

Orla shrugged. Locking it was a useless defense, but the impulse to keep Her out was strong. "Don't be mad."

"I'm not mad." Eleanor Queen tugged off her sweater and threw it onto the floor. "I could do something and you don't want me to do it."

Orla wished her mattress were in its proper place, on her box springs, upstairs in her room. She wanted to crawl up the stairs, get into bed, pull the covers over her head, and awaken only when she was certain the tree—and the blasted thing within it—was dead. But she couldn't keep an eye on her daughter from there. "What's the saying? 'I'll sleep when I'm dead'?"

"You aren't making any sense." Orla saw the false bravado in her daughter's exasperation; Eleanor Queen was close to tears. She perched on the arm of the plaid chair and pulled the girl in close. "You're smothering me." She pushed away Orla's needy arms.

"I'm trying to keep you safe."

"It's too late, why can't you just let me—"

"It's not too late. She's dying, with the tree. When the tree's dead, the spirit inside it won't be a threat to us anymore. But in the meantime, before we're too weak to do it, we need to try our hand at hunting."

Eleanor Queen shot her a cautious look. "Like...kill an animal?"

"We can't wait until there's literally nothing left to eat. And there's almost nothing."

Something complicated made the muscles in her daughter's face twitch. "We don't all have to die." The wistful words, barely a whisper.

"That's right." The truth was Orla didn't see herself as a hunter, skinning an animal as its warm flesh steamed in the cold air. Nor did she see herself as a survivalist, learning her way around the complicated woodlands that surrounded their house. They had water, electricity, heat. And if she could keep them fed...

"Sometimes..." Orla said. "I read something, a long time ago, about how when you die, your electrical circuits go crazy, and maybe that's why some people who were briefly dead come back and report seeing a tunnel of light, or visions from their life. I know you feel connected to the spirit, the girl, but dying is a natural process." Unless it happened because of a gun. "I think what we're seeing is Her...circuits. Going crazy. We tried to help Her—you know we tried. But I think we need to let Her go. And we need to keep ourselves as healthy as possible, while we wait. Are you okay with that?"

"Mama, I don't want to kill anything. I don't want to shoot an animal, and I don't want the spirit to—it's a life, Mama. I believe Her—we saw Her *picture*. She was a girl who came here from the city, like me. We share a connection, and it's easier for Her with me than with Papa. She wasn't trying to do anything bad—you *told* me there was no cure for tuberculosis. What was She supposed to do?"

Of course Orla couldn't blame a scared young woman for wanting to live, but whatever was happening now wasn't natural. A girl didn't just become a supernatural element that lived in a tree. But she wouldn't admit any sympathy for the course of the girl's life; it might give Eleanor Queen even more reasons to feel sorry for Her.

"She hasn't been a *girl* for more than a hundred years. She knows about…things, far beyond—"

But Eleanor Queen tuned her out, a rapturous look on her face. "It's amazing, when I feel Her inside me, because I understand it all better now. She's not evil. She's like this amazing creature. She's…" She searched for a word, struggling to find it. "Maybe…like when we studied the Greek gods in school."

"She isn't—" But Orla's denial fell flat. Maybe She was. That didn't make any part of what was happening any better. With power came selfishness. "We tried to say goodbye and help Her move on. I offered Her a new home, Bean—She said that's what She wanted."

"I know. And I know you'll never forgive Her because of Tycho and Papa. But…it makes me sad. I can hear Her, I can feel Her. It's like something's dying in me too when She tries to make me understand."

Orla fingered her daughter's hair, the gathered ends below her braids like silken paintbrushes. The caged animal within her wanted to toss her last baby onto her back and run as fast as she could. Eleanor Queen was right; she'd never forgive Her for Tycho and Shaw, but she also held a volatile grudge about being trapped. Sometimes the sensation was so strong, Orla gasped for air. She was trying to make peace with their prison, but it always tugged at her, the urgent desire to get away.

"I know you want to help—She's taking advantage of your goodness. I hate that She's hurting you, but She needs to let you go, and you need to let Her go. You have to try. Build a wall in your mind, your heart, when you feel Her trying to get in. That's how you help Her move on now, you make sure She knows *you* aren't the answer. Can you do that?"

"I don't know." Eleanor Queen slumped against the armrest.

"When She's trying to get in, you tell me. And I'll talk you through it, building a wall, shutting the door. Locking it. The symbolism is important. I think She will understand."

Eleanor Queen nodded but didn't seem very confident. Orla was afraid the girl had already opened herself too much, that some tendril of the spirit's consciousness was already inside her, expanding, tying Herself to her daughter's soul.

"And if that doesn't work, I'll…bang the pots and pans, jump around." Orla did a crazy dance, bounding around, flailing her arms, shouting random whoops and battle cries. Eleanor Queen giggled. "No one could concentrate through that. Right?"

"I guess."

"Let's get ready, before we lose the light."

Orla held out her hand, and Eleanor Queen rolled off the chair.

In their former life, she'd never have suggested dragging either of her sensitive children on a hunt. They—in her heart, she was still the mother of two children—would have buried their horrified faces when the first blood dripped onto the snow. But even if Eleanor Queen hadn't felt connected to the spirit, there was no way Orla would have left her behind, not when Shaw had appeared in animal form. And not when the being was continually improving on Her tricks. The spirit might claim She wouldn't hurt her daughter, but it was too easy for

Orla to imagine shooting a deer, only to have a corpse stare back
at her with Eleanor Queen's brown eyes.

They nibbled on the sweet pickle relish. Lunch. Tycho had
eaten most of it—it had become a favorite side dish during their
lean days—and there wasn't much left. Eleanor Queen agreed
to bring her bow so she could shoot at the occasional target. Orla
had debated between the guns. The rifle remained the more
logical choice for shooting large mammals. But Orla decided
to go for a pheasant or a goose, even a crow. She told herself it wouldn't be so different from preparing a Thanksgiving
turkey, though the turkey came with its innards conveniently
segregated in a plastic bag. The shotgun would work better for
a rabbit or a squirrel too, though she guessed the local squirrels
weren't quite as domesticated as the ones she'd cooed over at
city parks, fearless beggars that had almost taken food from
outstretched hands.

She hated the gun and hated loading it. For her final pre-
cautionary measure, she tied one end of a rope around Eleanor
Queen's waist and the other around her own waist. So they
couldn't get separated. So there'd be no mistakes. *So Eleanor
Queen won't run away.* Her daughter scowled and rolled her
eyes. Orla tried to convince herself it was hunger turning her
sweet child surly, not the influence of a powerful and desperate
entity. Her plan was to walk in a circle or a square—not unlike
what Shaw had intended on his first venture away from the
house—and not double back on her snow prints until it was
time to return home.

While they'd been eating their meager lunch, the tree line
had closed in yet again; it stood only feet away from the house.
They eased through the trunks, turning as they needed so their
coats wouldn't scrape against the bark. Eleanor Queen must
have felt it too, the fear of one coming to life and grabbing

her if she awakened it with a touch. Orla worried that even if she could summon the energy for another round of hunting on another day, the trees might have fully imprisoned them by then. The dying spirit was unhappy; she read Her displeasure in the tight placement of the trees. Once they were past where the tree line had once stood, the land opened up a bit. Orla resumed breathing.

They headed off in a direction between the garage and the giant tree, and Orla planned to circumvent both; Eleanor Queen didn't need to see the blue poking through the snow—the tarp that hid her father's body.

"We're going hunting, not leaving," Orla called toward the giant tree. "Eleanor Queen needs to eat—You don't want her to starve."

In her mind it rained, and then the sun beat down. And the leaves caught the water, the light, and channeled the nutrients downward through the veins in a thick trunk, into a hidden expanse of roots. *That's what Eleanor Queen needs, so she won't die.*

"She understands hunger. She wishes She could help," said Eleanor Queen.

"So She can read me when She wants to. How nice—"

"But you can't understand *Her*."

Well, she could when the entity looked like her husband. Maybe later she'd try summoning Her—is that what had happened the night before? If She couldn't be convinced to take Orla instead, maybe Orla could waste more of Her energy, Her life force. Orla clearly remembered Her saying how taxing it was to speak so directly. What a victory it would be if she could get Her to talk Herself to death.

"She doesn't have long, Mama—"

"Build your wall, Eleanor Queen."

"It's hard to ignore when something's crying—"

Orla turned and sprang at her daughter, mooing like a crazed cow.

The girl shrieked, then got angry. "What are you doing?"

"Breaking your concentration."

Eleanor Queen shot her a glare, and they resumed walking. Orla didn't like the silence that settled between them, or the squint of concentration on the girl's face. Was she listening to Her? Or was Eleanor Queen doing the talking now, ratting Orla out to the spirit, telling Her how her mother didn't want them hanging out together anymore? *Mama said you're a liar.* Orla couldn't afford to lose her influence over her own child.

"Why don't you try out your bow? See if you can hit that fallen tree." Distraction, a mother's handy backup plan whenever reasoning—or pleading—failed.

They stopped on some part of the homestead they'd never been before, and Eleanor Queen nocked an arrow onto her bow. Orla stood silently and watched her focus; she had no advice to offer, knowing nothing about archery, and trusted that Eleanor Queen, an avid reader, had done some research somewhere along the way. Her daughter's patience was impressive. She pushed the bow away from her body and sighted her target— a rotten tree, half of it upright and supported by a living tree. When she was ready, she let the arrow loose.

It connected with a *thwunk* that made them both grin. "Well done—you're a natural at this."

Connected by their rope umbilicus, they trudged through deeper drifts to retrieve Eleanor Queen's arrow. Orla opted to believe that as they moved farther from the great pine, her daughter's connection to the spirit lessened and she became more herself, alternately watchful of the world around them and absorbed in her private thoughts. She huddled a few feet behind her mother whenever Orla aimed the gun, and covered her ears when she fired. Unlike Eleanor Queen, Orla never hit her intended targets, wasting precious shotgun shells. Their dinner flew away squawking. Panicked. Maybe they were treading too heavily, making too much noise. More likely she couldn't shoot for shit. Her only triumph was not getting lost, their footprints a guiding path back to their prison.

What a failure. She needed to put supper on the table but could only hit a stationary target the size of a bear who masked a frightened man.

42

Eleanor Queen picked out a movie to watch, but Orla had a hard time sitting still. She got up often, needing to move, to do something useful. She'd never understood before how some of her slightly anorexic company-mates had the energy to dance; Orla had needed huge meals to counterbalance the calories she lost through constant physical activity. But now that she was wasting away, some internal mechanism had clicked on and she felt like a perpetual motion machine. She tidied the living room and kitchen and washed all of their bedding.

To her surprise, instead of sticking with her movie, Eleanor Queen went wherever she did and helped with every task. She was like a different child, and it unnerved Orla that her daughter was behaving more like her son. Staying close, even to do chores, where once she would have begged off after a while to do her own thing.

"You okay?" Orla asked as they fitted clean sheets on the mattress. She would have understood if her daughter needed her company or reassurance. But Eleanor Queen only smiled, her eyes full of secrets.

Orla had the uncharitable notion that Eleanor Queen wasn't needy or trying to be conciliatory or helpful—she was keeping an eye on her. Keeping her mother within sight, as Orla was doing with her. But why?

After numerous breaks, they finally reached the end of the movie.

"Mama? Just so you know." Eleanor Queen tucked the DVD away on its shelf.

"Hmm?" Hunger was making Orla drowsy.

"She didn't crush the house. With an avalanche or anything."

The words *crush* and *avalanche* startled her. She perked up, alert. "What?"

Eleanor Queen slipped onto the mattress, snuggled under a blanket. "She could have. But She doesn't want to hurt you. See, She's given you this safe house to come to, again and again. And She's giving you as much time as She can to come to your senses."

Within minutes her daughter was sound asleep, breathing evenly. Orla wasn't sure what to make of Eleanor Queen's words, which seemed less a reassurance than a warning. If she'd been hoping the day would wedge some distance between the spirit and her daughter, now it seemed more likely that She—They?—had been letting Orla's productivity lull her into a false sense of security, even as they continued scheming. In spite of everything, Eleanor Queen had taken Her side. How would Orla bring her back around? Would the spirit be yet another soul her daughter would mourn?

Now was Orla's chance. She ducked into Shaw's studio, leaving the door ajar an inch so she could hear if Eleanor Queen got up. As she had the night before, she focused on a painting— one that featured the cure cottage, with the surreal imagery of the great pine behind it. It made more sense now, why a sickly girl would have wanted to go from a bleak temporary home to a more regal and permanent one. Orla let the images, the myth such as she knew it, fill her mind as she spoke aloud, hoping to repeat the actions that had summoned Her in human form.

"Shaw? I think…you knew more than you realized. The more I know, the more I see how you were painting Her legacy, Her desire. How do I make you—Her—understand, and agree, that I am the home She needs? Please, let's keep discussing this."

Wind rattled the windowpane. But Shaw didn't come.

Her attention wandered to another painting, the one where the bones protruded from the trunks as if something had mowed down the forest. Could this be a message directly from Shaw, not from his muse? Is this what he'd really wanted to do to the trees before they'd identified the source of the problem?

What else had he kept from her? Were they things he hesitated to analyze himself, or was he simply too afraid to share, to vocalize, lest she write him off as deranged? In a frenzy, she started going through his stuff. His sketches, his notes, his books. What research had he done, cooped up alone in his room, to try and understand what was happening? She scanned his reference books. He'd collected various types over the years—art history, how to write/draw/knit/sculpt, encyclopedias of his various interests…of course!

She should have thought of it sooner. Shaw hadn't seen the close-up of the pentagram, but this was where Orla should have looked first. She seized his book on signs and symbolism and sat on the floor, flipped to the index at the back: *Pentagram, page 127.* Quickly, she found the section, complete with a bold drawing of a star in a circle.

"The five elements," said a voice.

Orla screamed. Earlier she might have been expecting someone, but not now, and not this one. It was her daughter. In the doorway. A sleepwalker. A ghost.

"What do you know about this?" And how had Eleanor Queen known what she was looking at?

"Earth. Air. Fire. Water. Aether. I looked it up in Papa's book, after we saw the necklace under the microscope." She nodded her head, a response to some faraway communication. "She's remembering things."

"Stop listening!"

"With *one* point up, it means 'spirit ascending above matter.' It's a beautiful thing. And it worked! She ascended above matter!"

She checked the book; Eleanor Queen had quoted it exactly right. Orla scrabbled to her feet, leapt over the blood droplets from the night before, and clutched Eleanor Queen's shoulders. Shook her a little—to wake her, or separate her from the entity, or rattle her back into the shape of her beloved daughter. "Eleanor Queen! Please stop, please."

The girl blinked, as if waking up. "Are you coming to bed, Mama?"

"Yes, yes, right now."

Eleanor Queen, looking a little perplexed by Orla's distress, took her hand and led her back to the living room.

It was God-knows-o'clock before Orla fell asleep. The answers were falling into place, but she still didn't have the Get Out of Jail Free card. *Spirit ascending above matter.* A nameless girl used her arcane beliefs to evade death, to project herself into a sturdier body. Had she mastered the five elements? Was that the source of her power, and of whatever she had since become? Orla kept her arm around her daughter. *Keep her close. Keep her safe.* She would have reattached them both to the rope if they could have slept comfortably that way. The girl squirmed in her sleep and turned over so their spines were pressed together. A good enough connection.

Orla dreamed of ballet. A younger version of herself who

partnered with an older version of her son. He was strong and magnificent. Ten effortless pirouettes. The thin arms of a boy not quite a man. It gladdened her to see him in a future she hadn't ever envisioned. Her growling stomach awakened her early. The wan light of an overcast day filled the windows, but she wished they could sleep, sleep...sleep until the blasted entity died or moved on.

She doesn't have long; that's exactly what Eleanor Queen had said.

But Orla needed to hunt, to keep searching for food. Sitting back and waiting wasn't a viable option—how long was "not long" to a creature who had devised her own immortal evolution? In another few days Orla might be too wasted to traipse through the snow. Or, if the trees lost patience, she might not be able to squeeze her way past the porch. She thought it might be common practice to clean a gun after every use, but Orla didn't intend to try. The likelihood of blowing her own head off seemed too high. Maybe she'd take the clean rifle instead; the trees would probably appreciate not having their limbs splintered and pocked with buckshot every time a bird she was aiming at took flight.

For the millionth time, she tried not to think of how different things would be if she had the internet. Beyond being able to summon help, she'd have so much more info, so many more choices, with the armament of technology. Maybe she could've learned a spell as effective as the TB girl's had been, one that would trap her or silence her or put her to "sleep," as Orla's father had done to so many elderly animals.

When she rolled over, the bed beside her was empty. Eleanor Queen had likely slipped upstairs to use the bathroom, but Orla had had too many frightening mornings to rest easily on that thought.

Upstairs, the bedroom doors were closed; they'd agreed it was too upsetting to see so many reminders of their once-normal life and the people they'd shared it with. The bathroom door stood open, but it was empty. Orla backtracked to her daughter's room.

"Love?"

Maybe the girl had crept up to her room at some point in the night, tired of postapocalyptic indoor camping. (But in her mind she knew.) Orla hoped to see her burrowed under her comforter, angelic in sleep and unaware of their troubles, but when she opened the door, the bed was untouched. She checked Tycho's room—maybe her daughter missed her old bunk. (But in her mind she knew.) The abandoned state of the room was doubly unnerving. She checked her own room, though it was no longer a comfortable place for sleeping.

It was coming. Again. The madness. The terror. She hurried into layers of clothes.

"Eleanor Queen?" Back downstairs, she darted into Shaw's studio, then the kitchen. But in her heart she knew.

Maybe the entity hadn't let Eleanor Queen sleep at all. Maybe they'd made an arrangement that excluded Orla, a secret rendezvous. Her head throbbed against her tight skull at the possibility that her sweet girl had agreed to some plan long before they started watching movies and cleaning. Had her daughter been humoring her? Waiting for her to succumb to exhaustion? Pretending to be helpful and agreeable—and then asleep—only because she'd mastered the entity's silent language and was planning to slip out the door?

Was it too late?

The ax was in Shaw's closet, brought up from the basement when they'd feared the kitchen roof might collapse.

The ax was the weapon she needed, not the rifle.

She grabbed it.

Got into her gear.

Headed out for the final battle.

43

Eleanor Queen was sitting on the ground by the ancient pine, her legs folded beneath her, her eyes closed. She didn't react as Orla strode toward her, and Orla didn't ask what she was doing. She went to the other side of the tree and drew back the ax. Struck it with all her might. Drew back and struck again. The solidity of it reverberated in her hands, up her arms. It was like striking a rock. She might break herself trying to destroy it, but she considered it worth the risk.

Mow it down. Even if it bleeds.

"Stop!" Her daughter's voice, shrill and panicked.

Orla didn't stop. In the outskirts of her vision, Eleanor Queen jumped to her feet, her face a haggard mask of terror. But the girl's despair was fully human, which brought a relief that drove Orla even harder.

Thwack!

Thwack!

Her arms tingled all the way to the shoulders. Chunks of bark crumbled away, but the ax barely made an indentation in the trunk itself.

"Mama!"

Thwack. "Step back, Eleanor Queen."

"Stop it!"

"You let my daughter go now! You've lived Your life, You greedy fucking—" *Thwack.*

Eleanor Queen collapsed to her knees, howling in pain. Her body convulsed, throwing her backward, but she fought to right herself, arms flailing as she grasped for the tree.

Orla had almost expected some physical sign of her severing the entity from her child's mind. But Eleanor Queen's screams were too much to ignore. She dropped the ax and flung herself at Eleanor Queen, afraid her daughter's spasms were going to break her slender bones. A war waged inside the girl and Orla had barely the strength to hold her on her lap.

For a terrible moment she feared she'd succumbed to another illusion—had she taken the ax to her daughter, not the tree? Why was Eleanor Queen writhing in so much pain?

"Eleanor Queen!" Orla ran her hands over her, fumbled open her coat, searching for blood. But whatever the pain's source was, there were no external wounds.

Finally her daughter's body started to relax, and the howls turned to noisy, ragged breaths.

"Oh, Mother. You hurt me."

"I'm sorry, I—"

"Not me, I was talking for the other self." Eleanor Queen went rigid again, her eyes in a frozen gaze. A moment later she gasped and fought to free herself from Orla's arms.

"What is it?"

But Eleanor Queen pushed her away and scrambled on her knees toward the tree. She flung off her mittens and groped the bark, feeling for something with clumsy fingers. Seeing her daughter's wide, unfocused eyes, Orla feared she'd lost her sight; she pawed at the tree like a person suddenly blind.

"What are you looking for? Tell me what's happening!" Orla crawled over on her knees, ready to envelop her daughter.

"He's here," Eleanor Queen whispered.

"Who?"

"He's here—now I know!"

"Who? What's She saying?"

"Tycho. She's saying...he's here." Eleanor Queen's voice pitched high at the end, full of surprise.

A silence descended. A stillness. Orla shut her eyes. A river coursed through her: Blood. Hope. Fear. Longing. It surged in rapids around her heart, dove past her organs, gushed down her legs. The force of it escalated inside her until she half expected her skin to fissure from the pressure.

Orla rose, her focus drawn back to the tree, where Eleanor Queen was still desperately in search of...a way in?

"Tycho?" The question came from Orla's mouth, but she heard it as if from a distance.

Eleanor Queen suddenly became animated. She jumped and sprang back and forth. "He's here, Mama! He's here!"

Orla struggled to make sense of it, of her daughter bounding around the tree, clapping the bark in excitement. Tycho...how could he be...was it true?

Her legs wobbled beneath her but she joined Eleanor Queen and touched her bare, trembling hands to the bark, ready to help her look. "Where is he? Tycho?"

"He's inside, Mama! I understand everything now! He's here, he's okay, I can get him out!"

"How...how, love? Tycho—Mama's here, we're here, baby!"

Eleanor Queen stopped and listened for a moment.

"Can he hear us? Can you hear him?"

"No. He's sort of...sleeping. But Mama—" She gripped Orla's fingers. "She was telling the truth. She wasn't trying to trick you. All I have to do is offer myself to the other self—"

"You can't become Her new…" For a fleeting moment, she'd almost believed she'd get her son back. But she couldn't— wouldn't—if it meant exchanging one child for another.

"I can, Mama!" Her eyes glittered with a strange, foreign excitement. "She can live in me, and teach me about Her power, and the moment She moves—when She leaves the tree and comes to me—this tree, Her old home, will crumble and I can get Tycho out! She's been keeping him safe, until we were connected enough that I could—"

Orla shook her head. "Just tell Her…tell Her to let him go!"

"She can't, Mama—"

"Why?" Orla was aware of her daughter's coat, Eleanor Queen's arms, gripped in her white knuckles. The madness was coming on fast, a herd of murderous circus clowns. Her eyeballs felt like stuffed balloons ready to burst. But Eleanor Queen remained calm. No, she wasn't calm. She was radiant. At what she could be. A supernova suddenly aware of its own dynamic potential. The fucking spirit had given her daughter a way to be a hero—the girl couldn't say no. But was it a trick? Would it cost her both her children?

"I can't live in a lesser creature now. I'm too…conscious. And I know you offered—I wish that could have been a solution. But we aren't…compatible. If I don't move, the boy will die with me. I'm sorry."

It sounded like her daughter, but…not. The words belonged to the motherfucking entity.

"Let her go!"

"I didn't mean for this to happen. Didn't mean to imperil your family. But it's your daughter who can make all the difference now, she is a queen—"

"No! She's a little girl!"

"We'll live here together—"

"No!"

"And you'll be our mother. It's the only way. To give your boy back."

Orla fell to her knees, clinging to the pockets of her daughter's coat.

"Mama!"

At the sound of her daughter's voice—Eleanor Queen's true, bright and childlike voice—Orla locked her in an embrace.

"I forbid you. Make Her leave you, don't let Her—"

"She's not inside me yet, not physically. But it's easier to let the other self speak than to repeat all of Her words."

"Please ask if there's another way." She looked into Eleanor Queen's face, beseeching. Her brittle body wanted to break apart. The world had become glass; she was glass; everything was about to shatter. "She can have me—"

"Mama, there isn't another way."

"I can't give you to Her, I can't give you..." Her words bubbled, turned frothy with tears and snot. "Does Tycho know? He's sleeping, he's peaceful?" Eleanor Queen nodded, and Orla mirrored her. "So he won't know, then. He won't feel any pain?"

"I don't want to leave him, Mama." Now it was Eleanor Queen's turn to succumb to despondency, to beg. "Now that I know he's here, he's okay, I can't leave him."

"Oh, my baby." Orla rocked Eleanor Queen on her lap. As much as she didn't want to leave her son behind, entombed forever in the carcass of a tree, she didn't want to lose her daughter. It was too cruel to force her to choose. "I can't let you die."

Eleanor Queen wriggled out from the vise of her mother's arms. "I won't die. I keep telling you that. I'll be me. Me and the other self. She promised I'll still grow up and be like a person. But I'll have other...different abilities. And I might even be able to leave here someday, when the other self gets used to moving around."

It was like listening to a foreign tongue she didn't understand. "So you wouldn't…you'd have to stay here?"

"Not outside. We'd live in the house, with you and Tycho. A family. And we could move around the land. And…not sure about the next part, how long it might take. The other self is connected here, beyond the tree, to this place. But we think, as our boundaries grow, we could take short trips. Into town. And later, with practice, maybe farther."

Our. We.

Orla shook her head, the disbelief as strong as her refusal. Eleanor Queen already thought of herself as joined with the entity, as if it were her long-lost twin. But at least there was still enough of Eleanor Queen's true self to seek her mother's permission, and to obey. Orla would accept the devil's deal of staying in the place she'd fought so hard to leave if it meant the survival of both her children. But she didn't trust Her. Who—what—would Eleanor Queen truly be if she accepted the union? It would be unbearable if she looked the same but lacked the essential humanity that made Eleanor Queen her wonderful, loving child.

"Can't She…can't She just let us go now? You and me?"

Eleanor Queen frowned. "What about Tycho?"

"I know you love your little brother, but…how can I agree to this?"

"I thought it was the perfect solution." Her sweet daughter's crumpled face looked so wounded. "I want to do it, Mama."

"I know She's very persuasive."

"And She's dying faster because of everything She's trying to do—communicate with us, keep Tycho alive. We're running out of time, we have to—"

"I don't want to lose you! Eleanor Queen, I don't want to give you to some immortal…thing that makes ghost animals and snowstorms and glaciers."

"You're not giving me away—you're letting me be something that no one has ever been. Something only I can do. I'll be special, Mama."

"You're already special."

"You know what I mean." How easy it was to convey annoyance by overemphasizing the right words.

Something shifted inside Orla. A door appeared in the wall of resistance. She dared to crack it open and catch a glimpse of what lay beyond.

"Can you...will you be able to control it? The power?" A temper tantrum would look entirely different if it came with a hailstorm or a blizzard.

"Yes..." She hesitated. "Once we're together, as one, I'll know everything then. I'll be young, but the other self will still be old."

"And the girl? How old was she? Is she still there too?" In truth, Orla feared the human part of the entity almost as much as the supernatural part, perhaps because humanity's dark side was eminently more familiar.

"There's a bit of her, the part that builds the bridge between what she became and me. I think she was...a teenager. You have to believe us, She wasn't trying to scare you." The girl's pupils grew large and black as she spoke for the other self. "I emerged onto a plane of consciousness that was different than where I'd been. I was scared; I knew I was dying. I finally understood the whole of my essence; I'd tapped into something greater than I'd ever expected, and just as quickly I was poised to lose it. I want to live. Please, Mother."

Orla could relate to that. After she'd turned forty, she'd started thinking of dying more and more, and not as an abstract possibility but a very real one. She'd weighed the merits of various types of death—quick versus slow, aware versus unaware, catastrophic injuries versus terminal diseases. She opened the door of possibility a bit wider. "So you couldn't…if you and Tycho got in a fight, you couldn't—" *Blow him away into the sky.* "What are Her limits? Can She do other things, in other types of weather, environments? What is She capable of?"

"She hasn't explored everything—She took Her long life for granted. Now we understand better. Consciousness, the elements. I don't know everything we're capable of—that's the truth. But I'll still be your daughter."

"And so will…?"

"It still scares you, the part of Her that isn't human, and the part that is. The girl missed her mother. Her mother died before she came here, and how it scared her, knowing she shared the same fate. It's a wonderful gift you could give Her—give *us,* the spirit the girl became and me—to have such a mother as you."

Mother of an immortal spirit. Orla felt the tug of an infant working its way into one of the blackened chambers of her heart. Were her maternal instincts so strong that she couldn't deny this orphan?

"Eleanor Queen, promise me," Orla begged, on her knees. "Promise. Promise me you'll always tell me the truth. From now on, no hiding. Tell me…the absolute truth. No more shutting me out."

"I promise. I didn't want to, Mama, but I needed to know. I needed to listen, because what She had to say was bigger than me, or you, or anything I'd ever heard of. But I won't shut you out. Ever again. I can learn from Her, like She learns from me. We'll both…we'll do better with each other. Be the best parts of ourselves."

Orla imagined her family—herself, her parents, Tycho—many years in the future, traveling with an adult Eleanor Queen to restore the polar ice caps. Could she do something like that? The entity might not even know such a need existed, but if She was powerful enough—They—and if They were more mobile, with Eleanor Queen as Her home and Their combined will…would her daughter live longer, be stronger, smarter, healthier? Did She deserve Her second chance because of all the good Eleanor Queen could do?

"Could you quell a hurricane? Summon rains to a parched land?"

"Maybe, Mama. We'd want to try. *I* want to try."

She looked at her daughter in a way she never had. Saw her limitless, awe-inspiring potential.

Maybe she really could have both of her children.

44

What do you have to do?"

"Open myself. Tell Her I'm ready."

"Invite Her in? That's all?" Like a vampire. But Orla kept the shadowy doubt to herself.

"Like She said when She came to you. All this time, Mama, She was never going to take me. She needed me to fully understand, fully agree. Even if I am only nine. She waited."

"Then...I'll be able to leave? Get food for you and Tycho?"

"Yes, of course!"

"It isn't a trick? Offering me my son to get my daughter? What if you say yes—but Tycho might still be gone, and She gets rid of me, and you become—"

"Mama, I'll still be *me*. She wants to *live;* She doesn't want to hurt anyone. Please let me do this. We can't fix what happened with Papa, but the rest of us can live on together."

Do I have a choice? Eleanor Queen would starve soon. They'd be trapped in the house. Her daughter was already half gone, and her son...if this being was telling the truth, her son would go from "gone" to dead if the tree died before She merged with Eleanor Queen. For so long she'd been afraid of losing both of them; resuming her life as a mother to *two* children had been an impossibility.

Orla's resolve—her fight—was waning. She still had so many reasons to say no, but equally as many to say yes. She still questioned Her claim that She regretted what happened to Shaw and hadn't meant to terrorize them. But she had faith that her daughter would maintain her integrity no matter how the spirit might tempt her to change. *If she's strong enough.* It lay unspoken between them that their relationship—their souls—would forever be riven if they walked away without Tycho. Though Orla suspected her daughter would have tried to convince her to allow this even if Tycho's life hadn't been a piece on the board. Eleanor Queen was already so deeply entangled, her understanding so recently refined. Was she already a different girl? Or had she simply taken up her mother's challenge to become fearless, the hero of her own crusade?

At least Eleanor Queen was still waiting to receive her mother's permission. And Orla wanted to believe in the magnitude of her daughter's character—to tell the truth, to remain herself, to use the powers she gained toward the betterment of their world. Eleanor Queen deserved a mother who'd have that much faith in her.

"You're ready, then?" Orla asked her.

"Yes." She bore an aura of confidence, a sense of peace. "Okay?"

Orla gave the smallest of nods. Eleanor Queen replied with a grin, then shut her eyes.

Mere seconds later, the young woman from the photo emerged from the tree—her hair, her dress, the pentagram clutched in her hand, all identical to the photograph. She wasn't a ghost floating through a wall but a girl climbing, pushing, wrenching herself through a surface that appeared solid.

Orla gasped; she'd expected high drama. Tornadoes of snow. Lightning strikes. But not this.

Eleanor Queen opened her eyes and smiled. "Don't be frightened, Mama. I showed Her what She looked like once. We thought it would be easier for you. Just a girl, not the unknown thing you fear."

Orla watched as Eleanor Queen waited patiently, rosy with excitement, while the girl crawled out of the tree, the opening barely big enough to accommodate her. The tree sealed itself behind her once She was free.

It was uncanny to see a photograph come to life; Orla wanted to shut her eyes but couldn't. She needed to bear witness, to know what happened. The young woman and Eleanor Queen locked eyes, their grins sweet mirrors of innocence.

The dying girl turned toward Orla. "Thank you, for trying so hard to understand me. I'm sorry for the sorrow I've caused. Your love is a palpable thing, and I'm honored to join your family." Orla only swallowed, unsure what to say. The girl turned back to Eleanor Queen. "Do you accept me?"

"I accept You."

"We'll be the best of ourselves, together. Just as you promised."

"I know."

And they embraced.

Orla pressed her fingers against her mouth, against the temptation to scream, afraid this would be the last time she ever saw her daughter.

As Eleanor Queen kept her arms around the dying girl in her Victorian dress, the young woman's form dematerialized. She became disintegrating particles that passed through, into, Eleanor Queen. When she'd absorbed the last speck of the other self, Eleanor Queen turned to Orla, a broad smile on her face.

Orla was torn between feeling let down by the anticlimax of it all and the relief that it had been painless, effortless.

"Step back. It's starting." Eleanor Queen gestured for her mother to move out of the way.

A shiver ran up the tree. Orla didn't know how far to go; if the tree collapsed, which way would it fall? How much of the forest would it crush beneath it? Eleanor Queen stayed beside it, focused, unalarmed as bits of dead branches began raining down.

"Bean?"

"It's okay, Mama."

At least she still called her Mama; her daughter wasn't gone.

"Thank you for the years you housed me," Eleanor Queen said to the tree. "Your protection, your vision. The gift of the slow course of your life and your intrinsic knowledge. You are free to resume the course of your evolution." She held out her hand, monitoring something, controlling something in the air.

Would this spirit speak such words to Eleanor Queen someday as she lay on her deathbed, elderly and empty? A hollow shell after her other self moved on?

The sound of splintering wood multiplied, amplified, as it surged upward from belowground. Small branches broke off and fell around them, but that wasn't the worst of it.

Orla tilted her head back to see the very top of the tree. At first she thought it was on fire, engulfed in black smoke. But no; it was crumbling from the top. Soon darkened flakes began plummeting downward. Filling the air. Making it hard to see, hard to breathe.

"Eleanor Queen?" She said her daughter's name, but it was her son she was thinking of. Where was he? They were almost out of time. They needed to retreat before the ashfall buried them. She tugged her scarf up over her nose to keep from inhaling the fine debris.

Eleanor Queen concentrated on a lower part of the massive trunk. She brought her hands together, a silent clap, then flipped them so they were back to back. As she moved them apart, a crack appeared in the trunk. The farther apart her hands moved, the wider the crack became. Her arms trembled with the unnatural effort as more of the upper reaches of the tree cascaded as silt all around them.

Nestled in the dark womb, Tycho lay curled on his side, asleep.

"Tycho!" Orla charged in, scooped him into her arms.

"Run!" called Eleanor Queen.

Above them, the largest boughs cracked, broke away, and started to fall. One of them smashed down on a tree only feet away, exploding into splinters on impact. Orla clutched her unconscious boy to her chest, ducking as she grabbed Eleanor Queen's hand. They fled homeward. Behind them, the tree collapsed in a cloud of dust and shattering limbs.

When they emerged in the clearing behind the house, the tree line had retreated to its original place, no longer a threatening encroachment. Orla dropped to her knees, choking. Particles of blackened tree tickled her throat, her nostrils, but the expanse of snowy yard was a balm, a relief from weeks of pressing claustrophobia. And it filled her with hope that her daughter would be able to keep her—their—word: Orla would finally be able to leave the property and fetch food for her children.

Eleanor Queen stopped beside her, hands on her knees as she too coughed, clearing out her lungs, restoring her breathing—as the nineteenth-century girl within her had never been able to do. The forest behind them lay in a blanket of sooty fog. The ash settled like dark snow.

"Tycho?" Orla laid him gently on the snow, shook him a little, brushed the hair from his dirt-streaked, unresponsive face.

Eleanor Queen huddled beside her. "Is he all right?"

"Tigger?" She kissed his cheeks, rubbed his arms. "Why isn't he waking up?"

"I don't know…Tycho?" Eleanor Queen gripped her brother's fingers, and his eyes sprang open. He blinked, groggy.

"We're right here, baby." And Tycho smiled at her. "Oh, love."

As she held him, rocked him, Eleanor Queen wrapped her arms around both of them.

Her son had come back to life. Her daughter contained a powerful, ageless entity. Christmas miracles. Orla laughed even as her scratched throat protested.

"I'm thirsty, Mama." Tycho pushed himself into a sitting position, rumpled from his long slumber.

Eleanor Queen cupped snow in her hands. "Tilt your head back."

He listened to his big sister. The snow emerged from her hands as a little stream of water, which he caught in his open mouth.

"Me too?" Orla tipped back her head and opened her mouth. Eleanor Queen scooped up more snow; it trickled like a faucet from her hands.

Not quite a human ability, but a practical one. A generous one. The spirit might not have always remembered Her human relationships, or communicated the way they did, but She had Eleanor Queen now—a kind girl who would become kinder, wiser.

The threat, at last, was gone.

As Orla carried Tycho the rest of the way to the house, great flakes of snow began to fall. They stopped to marvel at them, each six-pointed wonder the size of a hand, with intricate dendrites. The delicate sculptures drifted from the sky to be caught on outstretched woolly mittens.

"Oh boy!" said Tycho, finally delighted by the magic he'd never understood.

Eleanor Queen tried to hide her pleased grin. "You're welcome."

45

It wasn't the priority it had once been to find a signal and call for help. When Orla was ready, nothing would stop her, but first she ran a bubble bath for Tycho. Washed him, warmed him. Fed him grape jelly with a spoon. He sang a little song about living in a cave as Orla helped him into clean clothes. He hugged his stuffed moose to his chest, and Eleanor Queen told him about the herd of moose and the one she had ridden.

"I want to ride a moose too!"

"I might be able to arrange that." She stroked his cheek like she'd never felt skin before. "People are so soft," she murmured.

Orla looked at her daughter. It didn't matter anymore what the spirit was, beyond being part of Eleanor Queen. She wouldn't think of them as separate or wonder which aspect of her was doing or saying what. She wasn't sure when she'd decided that, but it felt right; she would treat Eleanor Queen as a human child, even if that meant chastising the transcendental part of her if it grew mischievous. Orla would keep raising her daughter, making sure she remained thoughtful and brave. A girl with integrity and all the potential in the world.

Tycho fell asleep on the couch soon after they came downstairs. Orla retrieved Shaw's phone, and when there was no signal inside, she stepped onto the porch and then into the yard.

"Eleanor Queen? Can you help me?"

The girl shuffled out, wearing boots but no coat. She took the phone from her mother and held it toward the sky. "There."

Forty minutes later a parade of flashing lights filled the driveway: a pair of police cars and an ambulance. The men and women moved about without urgency; greeted one another; asked about their families and holidays. The volunteer firefighters arrived next; they worked on the garage—towed out her trapped car and tore down the rest so the structure wouldn't be a hazard.

A freckled EMT, like a grown-up Pippi Longstocking, showed Tycho around all the emergency vehicles while Orla and Eleanor Queen huddled with the police officers by the blue tarp.

"I couldn't leave the children, after he died, and Tycho was feeling poorly and I didn't want him to walk all that way in the cold until he was better, and I kept trying but the phone wasn't working..." She gestured to the satellite dish dangling from their roof. Orla's excuses sounded suspicious even to her own ears, though her tears came naturally.

One of the officers lifted a corner of the tarp—again—and they peered, again, at the remains of Shaw's body. A second officer stepped carefully around the scene, taking photos of the deceased and the surroundings.

"I don't deny it was my fault, but it was an accident." She trembled and turned away from them to wipe at the snot that dribbled from her nose, stupidly embarrassed by her emotional breakdown.

A part of her wanted to hug the rescuers, tell them how beyond glad she was to see people again. But she knew she'd always have to hide the particulars of what they'd endured. They'd lock her up in a psych ward, at best. If they arrested her, now or later, what would happen if they tried to remove the children? Even if just to take them to the station? As it was, Eleanor Queen preferred to be outside, and she acted restless when she was in the house. It would be a long process that they hadn't yet begun, exploring how far away Eleanor Queen could go, and for how long. Her combined selves couldn't predict the consequences. Could she defend herself if they grabbed her, maybe transform into an owl and fly away? Orla had phoned her parents right after she'd called 911, and Walker after that, but it would be hours before they could come to the children's rescue if the police wanted to haul them all away.

"Mama didn't mean to," said Eleanor Queen. "It was a bear, too close to Papa. He didn't know what to do, run or stay still. So Mama got the gun. But she can't...she doesn't know how to shoot. She missed the bear and hit Papa."

Orla inhaled a short, surprised breath, taken aback by the deftness of her daughter's lie and the perfect tear that rolled down her cheek. So Eleanor Queen *could* still lie. Had she lied—or would she—about anything else?

The cops kept their heads bowed, solemn.

"I know I need to come in, to make a statement, but my parents are on their way from Pittsburgh. And Shaw's family; they're coming back from vacation. It'll be several hours. I just want to get the children some food."

"There's no hurry," the oldest of the cops said. Orla couldn't remember any of their names. He went to his car and brought back a handful of greatly appreciated granola bars. "I'm sorry you've had such a hard time of it out here. It can be a tough place to move if you aren't used to the winters."

Orla smeared away the last of her tears. Eleanor Queen pressed against her, and Orla wrapped an arm around her; she'd thank her later for telling the cops a plausible but inaccurate version of how her father had died. And maybe ask if she'd withheld any secrets that Orla needed to know. A shiver clambered up her spine, a naughty imp with ice for hands, when she thought of the possibility that She may yet have manipulated her. The persuasive teenager who'd devised complex schemes to ensure she got her way.

Her daughter—the precious girl who looked exactly like the Eleanor Queen Orla had always known—unwrapped a granola bar for her little brother and guided him inside. The EMTs bundled Shaw's body into a bag and loaded him into the ambulance. The cops took a few more pictures. Asked a few more questions. The volunteer firefighters got her car started. She kept a smile from tweaking the corners of her lips; hopping in the car and driving to the local market had never sounded more appealing, or easier. Why had driving ever intimidated her? It wasn't like she had to worry about tightly packed streets or changing lanes on the freeway. Deserted roads and a few turns. Load up on supplies and hurry back to the kids.

Orla was afraid someone would ask about the massive tree that no longer towered above their property, but when she looked...a new giant tree, with more evergreen boughs, all dusted in picturesque snow. An illusion, of course. She glanced at the house; Eleanor Queen gave her a little wave from the living-room window. It should have been a relief, how well her daughter could now protect them.

A call came in on the police radios, a road accident, and Orla tried not to look too happy as the first responders headed to their vehicles. She had to go shopping and dismantle the post-apocalyptic camp in her living room before family descended. Maybe Eleanor Queen would help her figure out what to tell them—not the straight-up lies they'd told the police, but maybe something with a few vague nods toward the truth. She could not set an example for Eleanor Queen of constant evasions and falsehoods. Not if integrity was the imperative she demanded.

She stood up straighter, hands clasped under her chin, as the ambulance pulled away, silent but with lights flashing. The police cars and fire truck trailed behind it, everyone ready to get back to work. Their cautious departure down her snowy driveway reminded Orla of a funeral procession, the bumper-to-bumper crawl from the funeral home to the grave. Her husband had loathed the idea of being embalmed. He'd liked some of the more modern options—becoming part of a coral reef or a forest. Cremation wasn't out of the question, but he hadn't wanted to be stuck in an urn like a genie in a lamp waiting for someone to rub it.

They hadn't had a homestead back then, a place where he'd want his ashes to be dispersed. But Orla knew exactly what she would do with them when the weather grew warm and they knew their way around. She and the children would scatter him on their land. Around all of the places where they liked to walk. They'd always be together.

Home.

46

Spring came late to the North Country. After days of forceful sunshine, mud season was almost over, though the green smell of wet earth lingered. Orla still wasn't sure if the summers lasted long enough to grow a proper garden, but she intended to try. She and the kids were planting green beans and tomatoes to start with; she envisioned fresh canned goods on the basement pantry shelves. She'd enrolled in a gun-safety and shooting class in town, and Walker and the boys were mentoring her on hunting and dressing various types of animals. One way or another, they'd never run out of food again.

Tycho, bored now that their little plants were in the ground, ambled off with his stick that had magically become a sword.

"What are you fighting?"

"The dragon and me are just playing," he said. "She's a very friendly dragon."

"Okay." Orla grinned as he swashbuckled around the yard. She turned to Eleanor Queen, who knelt beside her, knees and hands grimy with freshly turned soil. "The one thing I forgot to get? A hose. We've got the bucket, though."

"We could wait for it to rain again." The girl looked up, evaluating the sky. "Probably be a couple days."

There were many moments now when Orla wondered if she was witnessing the knowledge of a tree—attuned to the elements in a way she couldn't yet fathom—or something greater.

"I think it's best for newly planted plants to have at least a little drink of water." Orla pushed herself up and slapped the dirt from her hands. "Back in a minute."

She headed toward the house. It hadn't been so bad, acclimating to their reclusive life. Eleanor Queen hadn't made it all the way to town yet. Partway there she'd inevitably start to feel weak, mumble something about passing out, and they'd turn back. But a violin teacher was coming out once a week to give her lessons. And with the internet, and regular video chats with her parents, and visits from Walker and Julie, Orla didn't feel so isolated anymore. And her family accepted her excuse for why she and the children couldn't travel or visit: they weren't ready to leave Shaw behind, even for a day.

Orla had gotten her driver's license and didn't mind leaving Eleanor Queen alone for short periods when she and Tycho went out to do the shopping; the girl was more than able to look after herself. And when they were all home, with Shaw's paintings on the walls and the music he loved accompanying their lives, he seemed near at hand, part of everything. They'd scattered his ashes in a circle around the house. And Orla saw him in her mind often, wearing his toothy grin. He liked the woman she was becoming, as independent in the country as she'd been in the city. And the children were happy; they played outside every day, regardless of the weather, and Eleanor Queen's new boldness was rubbing off on her brother. He played by himself sometimes, imitating the songbirds, while his sister tested the whats and hows of her power. Tycho called her a magician. Neither Orla nor Eleanor Queen corrected him.

When Orla came out with the heavy bucket of water, she smirked at her wasted effort. She left it on the porch, spilling a bit on her shoe as she set it down, and strolled back to the garden—once the spot where the detached garage had stood. She'd had the generator moved to the other side of the house, and the SUV now had a new graveled slot where the driveway met the yard.

Eleanor Queen had summoned a cloud; a light rain fell on their little patch of earth.

"Make a rainbow!" Tycho skipped in a circle nearby.

With her outstretched hand, Eleanor Queen changed the direction of the falling water. The sun shone through it in such a way that a bright rainbow appeared, a bridge of color that spanned from one side of their garden to the other. Tycho skipped through the bands of color, tried to reach up and grab them as if they were fireflies.

Eleanor Queen manipulated the cloud, made it so the rainbow chased Tycho as he ran around. He squealed and let it chase him, fully accepting of the magic, and of his sister. Of the beauty and simplicity of their new life.

Orla dipped her hands in the gentle rainfall her daughter had created, washed away the dirt, and headed inside.

Before she made it back to the kitchen, the house rumbled from an earsplitting crack of sound—the kind that lights up your bones, makes you duck and wince even though the danger is unknown. Tycho screamed. Orla charged back out, certain the house—or her son—had been struck by a wayward lick of lightning.

She wasn't far off.

"Sorry, Mama." Eleanor Queen was too ashamed to look her mother in the eye.

Tycho ran to the safety of Orla's arms. Relieved that he was okay, she finally saw her daughter's mistake; the SUV still smoked from the strike, one tire flattened, the front hood mangled, the windshield shattered. It wasn't the first thing Eleanor Queen had damaged, but it was the largest.

"Bean, you need to be more careful—"

"I *know*!"

"You can't just experiment all the time."

"Mother, how else am I going to *learn*?"

Annoyance flashed on the girl's face. Orla had come to recognize the discernible presence of the other self. She didn't emerge often, but She was distinctly not her daughter.

"Eleanor Queen Bennett, we've talked about this." About not letting the older, otherworldly parts of herself surface; Orla still worried that She would ultimately overpower Her young host, her real child. But she hoped her maternal love would eventually soften Her rough edges; She wasn't used to being mothered anymore, but She seemed to like it. In her most patient, most of-course-I'm-right tone, Orla added, "We made an agreement."

"I'm sorry." Her daughter drooped with defeat.

"Thank you, love. Well, it's time to come in anyway—you can set the table." A beautiful table. Solid oak. With only one char mark on it from where Eleanor Queen had been lighting candles. Without matches.

Eleanor Queen leapt across the yard and ran up the stairs and through the doorway, clearly relieved to get away from her mother's admonishing eye.

"You go and help." She set Tycho down and he chased after his sister.

"I'm doing the spoons!" he yelled from the living room.

Orla gazed at the car. Had the lightning strike gone all the way through the hood; was the engine ruined? At best, the SUV was currently undrivable, and if she needed to replace it...it was an expense she couldn't afford. A little nest had been growing inside her, hatching tiny termite eggs. Hungry, they took turns on her ribs, gnawing. That Eleanor Queen sometimes misjudged the execution of her new powers didn't surprise her. But this reminded her too much of those early weeks. Trapped. Unable to hop in the car and go.

Was there a chance Eleanor Queen had done it on purpose? Could her other self yet have an agenda of dangerous secrets? *Do I really know my child?*

The trees had unfurled their endless varieties of green; delicate new leaves fluttered like waving hands all around her. Maybe it was an illusion, a trick of how much larger they seemed, blooming with life, but had the trees come a little closer? Curious neighbors desperate for gossip?

Orla had nothing to say to them. She retreated indoors to her children, unwilling to be undone by things yet to come. And she knew. Something was coming. Though she also knew shutting the door wouldn't help.

The problem lived inside her house.

ACKNOWLEDGMENTS

I enjoy a good challenge, and that's the truth. Making a career as a writer is not the easiest thing, and while I like the thrill of the hunt, I'm incredibly grateful when it results in an opportunity to share my work. I hope these opportunities keep coming, but I approach each book as its own moment in time. So much of my debut year as an author felt unreal, so to be more grounded now makes the whole process of this second book even more meaningful.

As ever, I'm indebted to my dad, John Stage, who is always up for brainstorming and beta reading. It's been exciting and gratifying to bring my whole family along on this journey as we gain new experiences in the world of publishing.

I get to bring this book to readers because of Emily Giglierano, and I can't thank her enough for her insightful perspective and passion for this story. Thank you so much to the whole Mulholland Books team: Josh Kendall, Reagan Arthur, Pamela Brown, Alyssa Persons, Laura Mamelok, Pamela Marshall, and Ben Allen. Thank you to copyeditor Tracy Roe for catching all those little things my brain-sieve can't handle. And a special shout-out to Gregg Kulick, who designed an absolutely brilliant jacket that planted itself in my head and never let go.

This book has had a somewhat odd journey and I'm grateful for my writer friends who have provided camaraderie and support along the way, including Mitey de Aguiar, Rea Frey, Jennifer Hillier, Caroline Kepnes, Paul Tremblay, Wendy Walker, and my Women Do Everything Better Salon (Jenny Belardi, Brooke Dorsch, and Jennifer Green). My beta readers are an ever important part of my crew and I appreciate their honest feedback on earlier drafts: Paula D'Alessandris, Jennifer G., Scott Keiner, and Christie LeBlanc. Thank you to Sarah Bedingfield for all of her efforts. And thank you, also, to Stephen Barbara and Claire Friedman.

Last, but certainly not least: I feel blessed to have so many enthusiastic readers—including booksellers, librarians, bookstagrammers, and bookbloggers—whose passion for reading slightly odd stories matches my passion for writing them.

MULHOLLAND BOOKS · READERS' PICK

READING GROUP GUIDE

WONDERLAND

A novel

by

Zoje Stage

A LETTER FROM THE AUTHOR

Dear Readers,

Though I grew up in a city, I was blessed to have many, many outdoor experiences as a child—camping in West Virginia, horseback riding in the Smoky Mountains, backpacking in the Grand Canyon. I've come to understand that for people without these experiences, nature—even on an ordinary day—can seem…uncomfortable, if not foreboding.

I love to drop characters into unexpected and extreme circumstances and see what they do. For Orla, every part of her move to the Adirondacks was going to be a challenge. It was very important to me to have Orla process her experiences as deeply and realistically as possible. In a similar situation, no one would jump to the conclusion that they're in a horror book, or ever think that such things could really happen. I wanted her to reach her understandings—about herself, her environment, her family, her situation—in a way that was true to her grounded upbringing and her creative spirit.

Thank you for reading! (And I hope you gasped a time or two.)

Zoje

QUESTIONS AND TOPICS

FOR DISCUSSION

1. Why does Orla leave behind the city and the career that she loves so much? Do you think she has made peace with this decision?

2. In moving to a bigger house, Orla worries her family will grow apart. Does this worry prove true? Do you think the size of a home affects the relationships inside? What about for your own family?

3. Discuss Orla and Shaw's relationship. Is it different in the Adirondacks than it was in the city? How does Orla feel about Shaw's painting? Does their agreement to focus on Shaw's career change how Orla sees her own art?

4. How does each family member—Orla, Shaw, Eleanor Queen, and Tycho—handle the move from the city to upstate? What do these two distinct settings represent?

5. Discuss the scene in which Orla confronts the bear. Is she right to try to shoot? Is she guilty of a crime? What would you have done?

6. What message is Orla trying to send when she talks about *The Dinner Party* by Judy Chicago?

7. The trauma of losing her younger brother, Otto, hangs around the periphery of Orla's narration. How does this loss inform her perspective as a parent?

8. Is Orla a good mother? Why or why not? Does she think of motherhood differently at the end of the novel than she did when she was living in the city at its start? Do you?

9. Both Orla and Shaw make sacrifices, for different reasons, at different times in their relationship. What does sacrifice mean for each of them and how does it figure into the larger plot?

10. How does the family's relationship with the natural world change or evolve over the course of the book?

11. Do you think there is any hidden meaning or symbolism in the animals that appear in the book?

12. If Orla hadn't been so naïve about—and afraid of—the natural world, do you think the story could be reframed as something magical? Or miraculous, even?

13. Did you consider any correlations between the tree's ability to adjust to a new occupant and the earth's experience as a host to *all* humans? Do you believe in the possibility of a sentient ecosystem?

ABOUT THE AUTHOR

ZOJE STAGE lives in Pittsburgh. Her debut novel, *Baby Teeth,* was a *USA Today* bestseller and a finalist for the Bram Stoker Award and is soon to be a major motion picture.

Keep reading for an excerpt from Zoje's next novel, *Getaway.*

PROLOGUE

It might not have been a beautiful day. In her memory, the golden leaves of a ginkgo tree shimmered in poignant juxtaposition to the harrowing splatters of blood. But in reality, it could have been an ordinary maple tree. And the blood, though it had been shed, pooled indoors, beyond her field of vision.

Within moments of it happening, Imogen lost track of what was real, what was imagined. Had she heard screams? Or were those in her head too? Later, she could only tell the police her name, why she was there, what time she'd arrived, and other unhelpful details. When they asked what she saw, Imogen had shaken her head, distrustful of her awareness.

Unsure of her faith and skeptical of organized religion, she'd been going to the Etz Chayim synagogue for only a month or so. Growing up, her Jewish mother had insisted she was Jewish—it being a religion of maternal lineage—but as a family they hadn't really practiced anything or discussed their beliefs. Imogen was the only one among her old school friends who hadn't gone to Hebrew school or had a bat mitzvah. She'd tried telling people she was half Jewish and half Christian, but even at ten that hadn't made sense. She'd never liked that empty space of not knowing where she belonged.

It wasn't until Kazansky's closed—the deli she'd relied on for matzoh ball soup and Reubens and kosher pickles—that Imogen even started thinking about the culture she didn't know. The matzoh ball soup had satisfied an easy kind of hunger, and without it she wondered what else there was. The first book she read on Judaism made her blink as if she'd just awakened, emerging into sunlight after a long slumber beneath a dusty tarp. She'd never heard of a tree of life that mapped levels of reality, or the possibility that the soul might have five distinct planes. Judaism wasn't opposed to the concept of God as a tree, or the universe; it didn't exclude those who believed one thing in the morning, and another thing in the evening, and nothing the following day. The spirituality of it intrigued her.

Curiosity killed the cat.

Imogen didn't die. But she hadn't been the same since that October morning. She'd gotten in the habit of going early, as that was when a group of the older congregants arrived to socialize: men and women whose parents had gotten them out of Germany before it was too late; Pittsburgh-born seniors who reminded her of her grandparents, dead for over a decade. They were friendly and welcoming, happy that a "young lady" was rediscovering her heritage. Almost thirty-four, Imogen remained petite and youthful, with a smattering of delicate black tattoos (which she kept covered in the synagogue), and had been assumed younger than her actual age for much of her life. She enjoyed their attention and their eagerness to chat with her.

The shooting had started as she'd approached the glass front doors.

That was how she saw herself, in her memory of the morning. Her arm outstretched, her hand never quite making it to the door handle. Frozen.

It was her first time in the vicinity of a human slaughter but she instantly recognized the sound. As loud as a cannon.

(An exaggeration.) Flesh ripped through with bullets meant for a battlefield. (Not an exaggeration.) She couldn't decide if her fragile early-bird friends had looked surprised, mouths agape, dentures exposed in shock. Or had they, in their wisdom, always known it was coming.

A part of her had wanted to rush in, find the gunman, launch herself in front of his weapon or onto his back to tear out his hair, puncture his eyes. The part of her that lived in the real world scampered off to the side of the building to hide behind a bush.

She kept trying to call 911 but her hands were shaking too hard and she couldn't even unlock her phone. It didn't matter. The sirens came anyway. And more sirens. And more. And the SWAT team. And television crews. She was still hiding behind the bush when the news alert first broke on the internet and her neighborhood plunged into mourning.

1

They were too busy to watch the sunset, or the moonrise, beyond the two-story windows of Beck's Flagstaff living room: they would be getting up before dawn, and still had a lot to do. The cathedral ceiling was buttressed with thick timber beams that suited the rustic locale and made the space feel huge in spite of the heavy furniture and clutter. Night now hid the pine trees that made a perimeter around the house, but Imogen swore she could still smell them, even through the glass wall.

It looked like a bomb had exploded. Ziploc bags filled with travel-sized toiletries, first aid gear, fire-lighting stuff. Puffy sleeping bags, backpacks, mattress pads—of both the egg crate and inflatable varieties. Hiking boots, padded socks, hoodies, adjustable nylon straps, compact flashlights, bamboo walking sticks, plastic bowls, protein bars, crushed rolls of toilet paper, fuel canisters, water canteens. Of some items there was only one: the small stove; the pot it fit in; the fluorescent orange plastic trowel for burying poop. Of some items there were many: lumpy freeze-dried food packages that turned into tantalizing dinners with the addition of boiling water.

Imogen's sister, Beck, had lured her out of her hermit's cave with the promise that nature would be healing. The subtext couldn't have been more obvious: *Stop brooding and get out of the damn house.* They'd talked about it on the phone four times in a span of two weeks. When Imogen questioned if she could fly all the way to Arizona by herself, Beck reminded her she'd done it many times before; when Imogen questioned if she was strong enough for such an arduous trip, Beck reassured her that back-packing was in her blood. For every doubt Imogen expressed, her sister was ready with a breezy counter. She'd said "You can do this" so many times that Imogen had started to believe it.

In the months since the shooting, Imogen had cycled through bouts of overwhelming sadness, and fear, and maddening frustration at her own uselessness, all of which had made her reclusive tendencies even worse. She'd started ordering delivery instead of going around the corner to pick up her Vietnamese food. Once a week she headed up Murray to the Giant Eagle for bananas and snacks, and hurried home with her eyes on the sidewalk. The names of her lost friends were still posted in the storefront windows, another tragedy for the Jewish community to *never forget.* Crocheted Stars of David dangled from branches, parking meters, telephone poles, shipped to Squirrel Hill from around the country; a constant reminder that Imogen didn't want to see.

And yet, her hermit's cave was no longer the sanctuary it had always been, where she could shut away the world and make productive use of her imagination. She hadn't believed writer's block was a real thing, but over the past year every story she considered felt empty, unworthy, too trivial to bother with. It was a miracle of good fortune that her second novel, *Esther's Ghost,* had sold just weeks after the shooting; it gave her a slight distraction from the horror and lack of words. While Beck grew ever more cautious about inquiring about the "dry spell" or the "wordless hiccup," Imogen knew it fueled her concern. No doubt that if Beck needed inspiration she'd find it in the Grand Canyon, but would it work for Imogen?

The months of preparation—walking up and down her building's stairs with a daypack full of canned goods—had brought back fond memories of backpacking with her family. (Though she couldn't pretend she'd done nearly enough exercising; every time one of her neighbors exited their apartment she'd scurried back to her cave before anyone could see her.) She'd never had an apartment with so much as a Juliet balcony to stand on to watch a thunderstorm or get a breath of fresh air. But once upon a time, nature had been a balm, an essential thing that satisfied her soul. After Beck had first suggested the trip Imogen realized just how far she'd pushed nature to the back of her thoughts, as something she couldn't have. Her world had been shrinking for many years, even before what happened at the synagogue. She appreciated that her sister wanted to give her a gift and return her to a place where she'd once felt at peace with her surroundings. But it came with its own hiccup, beyond having to leave the safety of her four walls.

Tilda.

Tilda, whose friendship had once filled a critical void and helped Imogen survive high school. No, she'd been more than a friend—the trio had been like sisters, present for each other as their home lives imploded. It was a formative time, their three reckless paths converging as they dog-paddled toward a future they couldn't quite see.

Tilda hadn't called even once to check on her over the past year and it wasn't like she didn't know; the massacre was international news.

Sometimes, when Beck and Tilda were back in Pittsburgh for a holiday, the three of them got together for a museum excursion or high tea at the Frick. Imogen and Tilda could smile at each other and speak in upbeat voices, but they were mere masks of civility. Imogen was better acquainted with Tilda's public persona, which she followed on Instagram. Real-life

Tilda scared her a little; Imogen often couldn't read her. They
hadn't had a serious conversation in four years.

Their relationship had gotten rocky after their first year of
college. Imogen left the University of Pittsburgh during her
sophomore year, a consequence of The Thing (though she
would've denied that was the reason). They never talked about
The Thing, but it left a residue, a rust-colored ring like a half-
healed wound; Imogen understood it slightly better now, but
only because of how society had changed.

As Tilda and Beck surged forward with their busy, ambitious
lives Imogen was alternately proud of their success, and envious
of how easily they moved through the chaos of ordinary life. She
harbored a more recent, more specific jealousy too; Tilda's six-
figure book deal was another thing they hadn't gotten around to
discussing. There were periods over the years when they grew
closer, but it never lasted. Someone would say something that
ruffled the other's feathers, and they'd stop communicating again.

The silences were getting steadily longer. Beck seemed confident she could function well enough as a bridge between them,
and that spending real time together as a trio would bring them
closer. But Imogen was less sure. Backpacking in the Grand
Canyon was difficult enough without the added burden of
personal baggage. Yet, here they all were.

With the grace of a dancer, Tilda's pedicured magenta toes
found floor space amid the detritus as she held her phone over
the scattered piles of gear and snapped photos. Tilda had been
documenting her expedition prep on Instagram and YouTube
for weeks: the purchasing of her pack, boots, clothing; scenic
strolls in the San Gabriel Mountains with her boyfriend, Jalal.
When Beck revealed that she'd planned the trip for the three
of them, Imogen was certain Tilda would bow out, perhaps at
the last minute. Her idea of a vacation was a five-star hotel with

its own private crescent of beach. Could Tilda even survive being dirty and sweaty without the refreshing promise of the false-blue water of her Los Angeles swimming pool?

Beck insisted Tilda had been game from the get-go, ready for an adventure and a chance to discover new things about herself: she'd never been so much as car camping or spent an entire night out of doors. (Rather than an "adventure," Imogen thought it more likely that Tilda needed new material for her motivational speeches and videos—and possibly her book.) Imogen was well aware that Beck had cleverly manipulated them both into coming, suggesting to each of them how a week in the wilderness would benefit their personal situations—and tying it up with a bow at the reminder of the twentieth anniversary of their friendship. Dr. Beck liked to fix people, even when they weren't her patients. Imogen didn't want to invest too much thought in a grand reconciliation; she had no idea where Tilda stood on the matter. Even now, Tilda would barely make eye contact with her.

The connection they'd shared as teen misfits was long gone, but for years it had been effortless. The week before the Blum sisters transferred to Beechwood, a private alternative high school run by hippies, Imogen had turned fourteen; Beck was crashing toward sixteen. They were barely past the threshold when Tilda Jimenez sashayed toward them, beckoning them in with her vintage cigarette holder, everything about her as flamboyant as a drag queen. While she was Beck's age, the three had all bonded over shared feelings of parental abandonment: the Blums were workaholics even before the divorce, Mr. Blum a commercial photographer (who preferred his wife's last name), Ms. Blum a local politician. Mr. Jimenez, an engineer, drowned himself in work too, after Mrs. Jimenez's sudden death. At the time, their parents' failings—avoidable or not—had been unforgivable.

Tilda might've been destined for fame. And Imogen might have encouraged it, writing her a starring role in the school musical that earned them all their first press coverage. There was no question that both Blum sisters were impressed—amazed—by how much mileage Tilda had gotten out of finishing eleventh on her season of *American Idol:* she'd turned her fifteen minutes of fame into a twelve-year career. But the more of a public person she became, the less Imogen could relate to her. Tilda expressed things to strangers that sounded more personal than anything she'd say to Imogen. Now Tilda was the opposite of an outsider or a misfit. She lived for other people's approval and couldn't exist without a constant influx of Likes.

Imogen wasn't sure what to expect from her on this expedition—was Tilda just playing a role? Was this a performance piece for her followers? Would Imogen be expected to applaud? But given that they were going to be together for the next week, Imogen hoped they could avoid any awkwardness by simply being nice—a superficial solution, but potentially effective.

"You look *fit,*" Imogen said, noticing Tilda's muscle definition, even through her leggings.

"Thank you!" Tilda beamed, and stopped taking pictures. "Extra yoga classes. Spinning. Plus my weekly hikes with Jalal. I may not be outdoorsy, but I can handle exercise."

Beck grinned. Imogen had almost forgotten how much game Tilda had when she was embracing a new challenge. She'd always had an enviable, curvy shape, and with the muscles packed on Imogen could admit to being a little jealous. Imogen was like a squished version of her sister: lean and short (bordering on scrawny) instead of lean and long (bordering on majestic). An image came to her of Beck and Tilda dressed as warriors. Beside them, Imogen felt like the hand servant who scurried after them to clean their weapons.

"I like your hair—it changes with the light." Tilda tilted her head, examining Imogen from different angles.

Imogen touched her bobbed hair, which she'd dyed lavender the week before. "I was going for an inspired-by-the-sunset color, but I bet after a week in the sun it's going to look really washed out."

Tilda shrugged. "It's still cool. You were the only one of us to ever make brave hair choices."

That sounded mostly like a compliment, but Imogen wasn't absolutely positive. (Brave, in this instance, could also mean questionable.) Beck had been wearing her sandy-brown hair short for more than twenty years, and for just as long Tilda's nearly black hair could usually be found in a messy knot atop her head.

"Who wants gorp?" Afiya, Beck's wife, floated in from the kitchen, her smile a white gleam against her dark skin. She clutched pint-sized resealable bags in both hands, shaking them like percussive rattles. "I've got the high-protein mix with assorted nuts and seeds, the fruity extravaganza mix with almond pieces, and a big quick-energy batch of M&M's and cashews."

"Ooh, I'll take those." Imogen reached for the baggies with the chocolate candies.

"You can't have all of them," Beck said, irritated.

"I wasn't going to take all of them, but I don't like the others as much."

The three of them descended on Afiya like vultures, stripping her of the proffered food. More calmly, they took a moment to divvy up the varieties of trail mix. Afiya crossed her arms and watched them, an amused smile tugging at her lips.

"Everyone should keep at least one bag in an outer pocket, so when we take breaks it's easy to grab." Beck's intensity softened as she caught Afiya's eye. "Thanks, babe."

"Master Gorp Mixer, at your service." Afiya gave a dramatic bow.

Imogen grinned, relieved by Afiya's presence. But then she started fantasizing about how much better the trip would be with Afiya along rather than Tilda, and her smile faded. Was this a mistake? Afiya wasn't just a better human, Imogen trusted her with her life. The same couldn't be said for Tilda.

2

Tilda and Afiya sat on the sofa performing an elaborate (or so it seemed) tea ceremony with fancy herbal bags that smelled like lemons and fresh-cut hay. Imogen stuck near Beck, sampling the M&M's. She knew she should be doing more, but she wasn't sure what, and she really didn't love her sister's approach to packing.

Imogen had always been well organized when it came to projects, and this was a large project—with no room for error. Had it been up to her she would have made lists (just as she had to get ready to travel from Pittsburgh to Flagstaff), color-coded by pack and person. And if the lists had their own lists, all the merrier. But Beck was the leader of this expedition, the resident Grand Canyon expert, and her system was to inventory everything first, then claim personal items, and then divvy out the rest by weight.

"Need help?" *Cruncha-muncha-crunch.*

"You could stop eating our food." Imogen hated it when her sister chastised her, but Beck shot her a playful smirk—and handed her a fuel canister. "This can go in your side pocket."

Instead of zipping it into one of the long pockets on either side of her forest-green pack—specially designed for the petite wearer—she tucked it under her arm and watched as Beck put the stove and pot in the main compartment of her own rust-colored Kelty pack.

"Don't you want them together?" Imogen asked. "The stove and the fuel?"

"Too much weight."

"Well, we could distribute the other things in your pack differently, so you can keep them together." Beck flashed her a flinty glare, chafed by her attempt to micromanage. But it made so much more sense to keep the items together that Imogen risked a harsher rebuke and kept pressing. "I'm just thinking, what if—"

"I know what you're thinking." Beck cut her off. The cold look in her eye extended to her voice, but she spoke softly. "But we're not going to get separated, so we don't need to worry—"

"Well of course we wouldn't *intend* to get separated, but you know it's theoretically—"

"Imogen." Beck cut a quick glance behind them to Tilda. In spite of the miles and years that moved between them, Imogen understood what her sister was trying to say: don't scare Tilda. The set of Beck's jaw, her unblinking eyes, made a plaintive case for not reminding their already-new-to-all-of-this friend that, if things went awry, even a hot meal might not be an option.

As teenagers they'd shared Canyon stories with Tilda, including the one where their family had gotten separated for nearly twenty-four hours. Had Tilda forgotten those stories, or had she written them off as adolescent hyperbole? Beck was in charge now, as their dad had been then, and part of her responsibility was encouraging everyone to get mentally and physically ready. If she was this concerned about scaring Tilda over how they *packed,* had she kept other, more serious dangers from her too?

Suddenly Imogen was certain Beck had left things out. If Tilda knew the entirety of the hazards that could befall them— and death wasn't *impossible*—she might not have agreed to the trip. Or might have canceled, as Imogen had anticipated. Something electric short-circuited, sending skittering flames of anxiety though Imogen's gut. It wouldn't matter if Tilda was physically strong if she was mentally weak; there wasn't an emergency exit if Tilda decided she wanted out. Had Beck done her due diligence in helping her prepare?

(Or maybe Beck had realized that Tilda was only equipped for physical training and the mental training would be a lost cause.) *Snarky. Be nice.*

If Imogen and Tilda had been on better terms, Imogen might have had a chance to talk to her about the things her sister wouldn't say. But it was too late now and, unlike Imogen, Beck didn't share a philosophy of preparing for the worst.

"Okay, I was just trying to be careful," Imogen conceded, a bit of whine in her voice. Sometimes (often) she hated how easily she played her old familiar role, as if her life were a theatrical production and certain voices prompted preset responses. She wanted to change that, but for now she put the fuel canister in her pack.

"There are many ways to be careful, grasshopper." Beck's eyes sparked mischief, with the undercurrent of a challenge.

Imogen accepted the bait. "If you say so, bull's pizzle."

"'Oh, plague sore! Would thou wouldst burst!'"

Beck's British accent was terrible, but Tilda, overhearing from the couch, erupted with laughter. "Oh my God, you still call each other that?"

"Only on special occasions." Beck gave Imogen a little wink.

"What's that from?" Afiya asked.

"Shakespeare. They started it in high school," Tilda explained.

"Why?" Baffled, and a touch disgusted, Afiya looked from Imogen to Beck.

"Because she was a genius," said Beck, "the next Shakespeare."

"Hardly," Imogen mumbled. (It used to please her that *Imogen* was associated with the play *Cymbeline,* but now such references made her feel like a fraud. She was pretty sure the Bard never suffered from writer's block.)

"She wrote a musical, the whole thing, play and lyrics, when she was only fifteen." Tilda sounded proud, which made Imogen a touch nostalgic. "Our teacher discouraged profanity, so she worked in some Elizabethan insults instead."

"Oh *that*," said Afiya, finally having context.

"I saw you have the article framed, behind your desk." Imogen was staying in Beck's home office, on a foldout sofa, since Tilda was using the guest room. She hadn't expected to see the article in a place of honor on her sister's wall.

"Really, you still have that?" Tilda asked Beck.

Beck shrugged, but Imogen thought it was interesting too: of the three of them, only Beck had preserved—and displayed— the newspaper piece written just before *Eighty-Seven Seconds* had opened for its two-night run. The musical took place on an airplane filled with strangers who formed last-minute connections with the people around them when they realized they were about to crash. They talked (and sang) about the loved ones they were leaving behind, the mistakes they'd made, and the things they'd always hoped to do. While the first act had teetered between not bad and pretentious, the second act turned into a trippy hallucination of the afterlife.

"Beck's always had so much faith in your work." Afiya said this with such earnestness that Imogen sifted through her words for the subtext, but couldn't quite figure it out.

"Did you get all your clothes in?" Beck asked Tilda, forever engrossed in the task at hand. Tilda bounded off the sofa and she and Beck chattered about socks and windbreakers and if they should bring a few tampons "just in case." Seeing them so bubbly together made Imogen feel left out.

* * *

Afiya strolled over and casually rested a lanky elbow on Imogen's shoulder. Towering above her, Afiya had to hunch to whisper in Imogen's ear, bringing with her a scent of soapy apples.

"How're you doing? You ready?"

Those five words registered a kindness utterly different from anything Imogen would ever receive from Tilda, or even Beck. Only Afiya would openly acknowledge her agoraphobic tendencies, which hadn't improved even though the shooting was almost a year behind her. At thirty-four, Afiya and Imogen were the same age, though Imogen always thought of her sister's wife as older, wiser. Maybe it was her drive: Afiya earned a PhD at twenty-three and became the youngest tenure-track professor at Northern Arizona University. It took a few years, but she almost singlehandedly reshaped the cultural studies department, transforming it into the most intersectional program in Arizona. But it was more than that. Afiya carried an understanding of people, a maturity that struck Imogen as motherly.

She saw the concern in Afiya's eyes. "I'm okay."

"It's not too much? All this—out and about?"

Of course Afiya knew that Beck was trying to help her— *fix her*—and for all Imogen knew the whole trip could've been Afiya's idea. But in demeanor, Afiya was by far the most sensitive to Imogen's enduring trauma. She wondered, and not for the first time, if Afiya came by this naturally because of her own difficult start in life. She'd emigrated from Rwanda at three, with her brothers and her mom, and it had taken her mom some time to get the hang of their new country. Afiya's father was never spoken of. The writer in Imogen liked to invent dark secrets for people, but it was also possible that Afiya's goodness came from *not* being burdened with secrets, dark or otherwise.

Imogen didn't feel comfortable answering Afiya's question in front of Beck and Tilda. Too often over the years she'd been at the receiving end of their scorn when they thought she was being ridiculous. They probably wouldn't be so heartless now, given the circumstances, but she remained reluctant to let her guard down. Without being able to fully immerse herself in another world—an ability she'd taken for granted as a lifelong writer—she'd had no extended hours of peace or engagement. The last several weeks had been especially stressful. Even with the airport's security protocol, she'd dreaded wading into the zoo of bustling people. She didn't feel safe in groups; groups were targets.

Afiya seemed in tune with Imogen's thoughts—or perhaps Imogen's face betrayed some semblance of fear. Afiya gave Imogen a quick squeeze, then spoke to her as Imogen imagined a mom might (though her mom lacked such warmth).

"You're going to be in one of the most beautiful places in the world, with your big sister and your oldest friend—"

"I wish you were coming."

"This is for the three of you. You'll challenge yourselves and see how strong you are. The Canyon's going to give you a big hug and welcome you home." That made Imogen smile. She wanted that. She needed that. "Why do you think we live here?"

"Your dream home?" Imogen knew how proud Beck was to have provided her wife with this magnificent house, on its picturesque parcel of land.

"The Grand Canyon's our backyard. A place where we can forget the unimportant things, and remember the things we most need to know. When we start to lose track, we go there and remember."

Imogen nodded. "I'm ready."

"You *are*."

Unlike Tilda, Imogen knew how hard the journey would be. She'd backpacked in the Grand Canyon four times when she was younger, but hadn't done any real hiking in over ten years. Still, Beck was counting on her. Beck needed her to be reasonably competent *and* helpful, and Imogen didn't want to let her down. That was a worry she carried, almost as heavy as her pack promised to be, that some part of her weakness would jeopardize their trip.

During the past year Imogen had been infected with loneliness, a new condition for her. It was far-fetched, but sometimes she fantasized about being an adventurer, someone at home in every corner of the world. She was a long way from being that person, but thankfully nature in general—and the Canyon in particular—had always made her feel more immune to the anxieties she experienced in her everyday life. Mentally, she could do it. Push through if she got tired or sore, but what if she really was too weak?

A minor stumble in the Canyon could end the trip. A major stumble could send her hurtling toward her grave.

MULHOLLAND BOOKS

You won't be able to put down these Mulholland books.

· ·